ADVANCE PRAISE FOR
ONE FOR ALL

"Lainoff's female Musketeers beguile and swashbuckle their way into the ornate citadel of power that was Louis XIV's court with wit, tenacity, and stirring sisterhood. You will cheer for them to carry the day in this sweeping story about becoming your best self in the midst of a society trying to relegate you to a specific category." —JENNIEKE COHEN, AUTHOR OF *DANGEROUS ALLIANCE* AND *MY FINE FELLOW*

"*One for All* is a reimagining that is both poignant and fiery—and like no other Musketeer story you have ever read. Just like the blade her teen protagonist Tania wields, Lainoff's prose is effortlessly precise, fluid, and sharp. What I love about *One for All* is that it's a breathtaking adventure story set in the past that also speaks to our present and future—the best type of historical fiction. Tania's story is for anyone who has wondered how to carve a path through a world that does not accommodate your whole self." —TRACY DEONN, *NEW YORK TIMES*–BESTSELLING AUTHOR OF *LEGENDBORN*

"A captivating, stereotype-shattering fantasy about defying the odds and finding your place in the world. A heartfelt, gender-bending read featuring a disabled heroine whose differences give her the strength and courage to fight for her dreams." —KAMI GARCIA, #1 *NEW YORK TIMES*–BESTSELLING COAUTHOR OF *BEAUTIFUL CREATURES*

"A story brimming with strength. *One for All* will whirl you away to a 17th century France of pulse-pounding duels in beautiful ball gowns, following a sisterhood knitted together by duty and an indomitable heroine to cheer for." —CHLOE GONG, *NEW YORK TIMES*–BESTSELLING AUTHOR OF *THESE VIOLENT DELIGHTS*

"A thrilling, big-hearted novel that is sure to become a classic in the canon of YA historical fiction, *One for All* is everything readers could want in a feminist adventure . . . A stunning debut that hits all the right notes." —CARLY HEATH, AUTHOR OF *THE RECKLESS KIND*

"Fierce, breathtaking, and absolutely unputdownable. *One for All* is an adventure-packed historical retelling that you won't want to miss!" —JUNE HUR, AUTHOR OF *THE FOREST OF STOLEN GIRLS*

"A rousing tale of lady spies and swordplay, with a dash of romance. Tania is a formidable heroine, driven to carve out a place for herself among the Musketeers. Lillie Lainoff has crafted a story as thrilling and compelling as any fencing match." —EMILY LLOYD-JONES, AUTHOR OF *THE BONE HOUSES*

"A thrilling mystery from start to finish. Lainoff has masterfully created a feminist retelling of *The Three Musketeers* with a strong, determined heroine. Chronically ill readers will delight in seeing themselves starring in their own adventure. Lainoff is a fierce new talent to watch out for." —KERRI MANISCALCO, #1 *NEW YORK TIMES*–BESTSELLING AUTHOR OF *KINGDOM OF THE WICKED*

"The fierce, disabled heroine of *One for All* discovers her strengths and defies expectations in this swashbuckling tale of girls who have each other's backs. A delightful, empowering adventure!" —JOY MCCULLOUGH, NATIONAL BOOK AWARD–NOMINATED AUTHOR OF *BLOOD WATER PAINT*

"A dashing tale full of heart, courage, and friendship, with an unforgettable disabled heroine. *One for All* is revolutionary in more ways than one." —MARIEKE NIJKAMP, #1 *NEW YORK TIMES*–BESTSELLING AUTHOR OF *THIS IS WHERE IT ENDS*

"There are no limits to the will—and the strength—of this unique female hero." —TAMORA PIERCE, WRITER OF THE SONG OF THE LIONESS SERIES AND THE PROTECTOR OF THE SMALL QUARTET

LILLIE LAINOFF

ONE FOR ALL

Farrar Straus Giroux
New York

Farrar Straus Giroux Books for Young Readers
An imprint of Macmillan Publishing Group, LLC
120 Broadway, New York, NY 10271 • fiercereads.com

Our books may be purchased in bulk for promotional, educational, or business use.
Please contact your local bookseller or the Macmillan Corporate and Premium Sales
Department at (800) 221-7945 ext. 5442 or by email at
MacmillanSpecialMarkets@macmillan.com.

Library of Congress Cataloging-in-Publication Data

Names: Lainoff, Lillie, author.
Title: One for all / Lillie Lainoff.
Description: First edition. | New York : Farrar Straus Giroux Books for Young Read-
ers, 2022. | Audience: Grades 10-12. | Summary: In 1655 sixteen-year-old Tania
is the daughter of a retired Musketeer, but she is afflicted with extreme vertigo
and subject to frequent falls; when her father is murdered she finds that he has
arranged for her to attend Madame de Treville's newly formed L'Académie des
Mariées in Paris, which, it turns out, is less a school for would-be wives than a
fencing academy for girls—and so Tania begins her training to be a new kind of
Musketeer, and to get revenge for her father.
Identifiers: LCCN 2021025224 | ISBN 978-0-374-31461-3 (hardcover)
Subjects: LCSH: Women fencers—France—Juvenile fiction. | Schools—France—
Juvenile fiction. | Conspiracies—France—17th century—Juvenile fiction. |
Fathers and daughters—Juvenile fiction. | Murder—Investigation—Juvenile
fiction. | Vertigo—Juvenile fiction. | Adventure stories. | France—History—Louis
XIV, 1643-1715—Juvenile fiction. | Paris (France)—History—17th century—
Juvenile fiction. | CYAC: Fencing—Fiction. | Schools—Fiction. | Adventure
and adventurers—Fiction. | Conspiracies—Fiction. | Fathers and daughters—
Fiction. | Murder—Fiction. | Vertigo—Fiction. | Paris (France)—History—17th
century—Fiction. | France—History—Louis XIV, 1643-1715—Fiction. | LCGFT:
Historical fiction. | Action and adventure fiction.
Classification: LCC PZ7.1.L234 On 2022 | DDC [Fic]—dc23
LC record available at https://lccn.loc.gov/2021025224

First edition, 2022
Book design by Angela Jun
Printed in the United States of America

3 5 7 9 10 8 6 4

For Mama:
You told me once that I was your hero.
What I didn't tell you then, but should have,
is that you have been, are, and forever will be mine.

CHAPTER ONE

Lupiac, France, 1655

EVEN IN THE darkness, we could see it: the door half-open. A shadow angled across the threshold, spilled into the falling night, then disappeared.

"Stay here," I said.

"Tania—" my mother whispered, but I was already headed down the twilight-stained cobblestone that led to the front of our house, my fingers clasping onto the fence Papa built me four years ago, right after my twelfth birthday—something to hold on to for balance when the dizziness became too much.

My fingers passed over the smooth, worn stakes. I inched my way along. Soft step after soft step. At the door, dizziness overtook me in an onslaught of gray and black waves. I pressed my face to the cool wood. Once the cloud lifted, I peered around the door.

The kitchen was in disarray. Pots were scattered everywhere; my gut wrenched as I took in the spatter of red along the cabinets—no, not blood. Crushed tomatoes. The table, the countertops, everything was dusted in flour.

Papa hadn't returned from his trip yet. Maman was by the front gate. And here I was, empty-handed.

"Dammit—check again." Voices floated short and sharp from the shadows. There wasn't any time to go to the barn, to draw my sword from the weapons rack. A kitchen knife wouldn't do any good, unless I was in close combat . . . or somehow managed to throw it, but the very thought curled my stomach. I'd probably end up injuring myself. My eyes scanned the room, finally locking on the fireplace. The fire poker was the best option. The only option.

Fingers vise tight on the iron, with my eyes closed . . . with the feel of metal against my palm, I could almost pretend it was my sword.

I followed the voices to Papa's study. Two men, cloaked: one riffling through the desk while the other kept watch by the window. We'd taken a shortcut home from the market. He wouldn't have seen us; his view was of the main road, the one we hadn't taken. *Please, Maman, please stay where I left you. Let me protect you for once.*

"Did you hear that?"

My heart lurched at the unfamiliar voice: raspy, as if it was being used for the first time in weeks.

"Probably nothing." A different voice this time, not as strained, oily and smooth. "It'd be better if the wife and their little invalide show. We could gut them and leave the remains for de Batz to find. Make him think twice about sticking his nose where it doesn't belong."

My focus slipped, foot sliding along the loose floorboard with a creak. And with the movement, a wheeze of breath.

"Now, what do we have here?"

A man loomed in the doorway, so very tall. The second voice. His eyes lighted on the poker. "And what, pray tell, are you planning to do with that?" I brandished it, doing my best to mimic Papa—fierce, strong, unflappable—even as my legs trembled, even as my vision narrowed. He leered at me, at my unsteady legs; my pulse crashed in my throat. "The invalide has a bit of fire in her, non?"

My world blurred. But even my dizziness couldn't mask how his body stiffened at the sound of carriage wheels on stone. Had my mother gone to alert the maréchaussées? This would usually have hurt, frothing behind my chest—why did she never trust me?—but for once, with my screeching heart, with my wobbling legs and the tall man in the black cloak, I didn't care.

The men transformed into a flurry of footsteps and papers. In their haste to escape through the window, one knocked over their lantern. I lunged, but I wasn't fast enough: It slipped and fell to the floor, flames catching the frayed carpet and careening toward the wall. In the glassless, unshuttered window, the hem of a cloak fluttered, then melted into the night.

I stumbled through heat, through ash, until I reached a side table with a water pitcher and used the last of my strength to overturn it on the fire licking at the curtains. The flames cooled with a slow, charred hiss. My throat was tight with smoke and tears.

I'd let them escape.

Papa wouldn't have let it happen. Papa was stronger, and faster, and he didn't have dizziness biting at his corners.

My pulse wouldn't slow, couldn't slow, was throbbing in my teeth. The horrible, unshuttered window doubled, then tripled.

Three gaping black holes sucked me forward, legs buckling, kneecaps snapping to the floorboards with a crunch.

And then, hovering above me: my father's worried gaze. It had to be the dizziness warping my vision. He wasn't here. "Papa," I tried to say. But my tongue was sealed to the floor of my mouth. The next moment, I was swallowed in pitch.

"Slowly, ma fille. You took quite a spill."

I winced at the light and pushed myself up so my back rested against the wall. Papa's desk settled sideways on the ground like a corpse, curtains mauled beyond recognition . . . a trail of ash, fire-eaten wood, and half-charred papers.

And when I turned, there was Papa. I shied away, failure still bitter on my tongue.

"I was so worried," he said, his eyes darting to his pocket watch. "It felt like so much longer than five minutes, waiting for you to wake." Then he studied me with a creased brow. "Tania, what happened?"

"Robbers. I couldn't stop them. I tried, really I did, but there was a fire and I had to—but Papa, how are you *here*?"

"My meeting ended sooner than I expected. I thought I'd come home a day early. A surprise," he laughed, hollow, as he surveyed the overturned room.

Papa traveling to nearby towns was nothing new. Wealthy locals were always looking to start a new fencing academy, and Papa was an ideal candidate for head swordsman. He'd never yet agreed; he'd received plenty of requests since retirement, and would occasionally humor the would-be founders: give a few lessons, pocket their money. But I knew him better than to think coin was the major factor luring him away. The visits provided an excuse to visit friends, his comrades from days in service of la Maison du Roi—the Royal Household of the King of France—who now held influential positions as maréchaussées across France or as military advisers. Papa would never admit to it, he wouldn't, but I knew part of him longed to return. Not to Paris, the dangerous and glittering city with its leaden underbelly and blood-dappled alleys, but to the friends he'd risked life and limb for, day after day. To his family of brothers.

I'd met a few of them, when I was little. Vague childhood memories of large men with booming laughs—but it was like looking through a pool of water at people on the other side: light fractured, features distorted, the final picture not always resembling the original. And with things the way they were now . . . with the dizziness, with Papa's friends spread across la France, busy with work and families and protecting the country, it wasn't likely we'd have a chance to meet again.

Papa ushered me into a chair where he worried over me until I assured him I was fine—well, he knew what I meant. Through the haze, I watched him bend down, trail his finger along the dusty remains of a journal with a cover curled from heat, its leather boiled black. I thought I saw relief on his face. His gold signet ring, stamped with the French fleur-de-lis and intersected with two sabers, sparkled against the ash.

He straightened. "How many were there?"

"Two." Shame leached into my words. I'd done my best. But then, my best was never good enough. "I should have done more."

"My dearest, most foolish daughter . . . how, exactly, would you propose fighting off two intruders while also ensuring our house didn't burn down?"

I didn't respond. Not that it mattered; he was too busy combing through the unscathed papers, the broken desk drawers and their scattered contents.

"What did they take?" I asked.

"Nothing of value."

"Why were they here, then, if not to take anything of value?"

There, there was the tick in his jaw, the way the corners of his eyes narrowed into dagger points—the face I'd tried to mimic earlier to hide my fear. "No doubt they were rummaging for your mother's jewels when you walked in."

"But they knew your name. They said . . . they said they'd kill me and Maman and leave us for you to find."

Anger flickered in his eyes. But then his arms looped around me and pressed my cheek to his shoulder. And I couldn't see his face then, not at all. "I'm proud of you."

"If it wasn't for the fire . . . if I hadn't been so dizzy, I would've caught them. I would've protected us."

He pulled back to look at me. "How could you ever say—no, even *think*—such a thing? You showed courage. A true de Batz."

I wanted to ask where Papa thought they were from. Who else but other villagers knew about us . . . knew about me? But then, the sound of footsteps—and there was Maman in the doorway. Her face wasn't stained with tears; it was hard as rock. Her gaze swept over me and the destroyed furniture, lips locked, before landing on my father. A look passed between them that I didn't understand.

"I wasn't expecting you home for supper. It'll take a while to pull something together. You see, I'll have to find food currently not plastered to the walls."

"Ma chère . . . ," he attempted, but her eyes blistered him on the spot.

"And don't even get me started on you," she said, rounding on me. "Running off in the dark to play hero. You're just a girl, Tania. And you could have fainted! This very minute, I could have been scraping you off the floor." Her mouth trembled. "You *did* faint, didn't you? The bruise is already forming on your forehead."

Yes, I was just a girl. A sick girl. One who, when the time came, was helpless. Because that was what being a sick girl meant.

"I'll see about finding a locksmith in the morning," Papa finally said, hesitant. "I won't let anyone hurt us."

"You can't guarantee that," she shot back.

His hand twitched—the right one, the one not supporting my elbow in case my world started spinning—as if he was reaching for her. But by the time I'd closed my eyes and opened them again, my vision was filled with Papa's frame. Then by my mother bustling around with bowls, the creak of wooden chairs, and Papa's laughter melting together into a song, one that was less of a memory of years past and more of a feeling, one amid the past few months' arguments and icy eyes I was sure I'd forgotten.

What do they call someone like me? Fragile. Sickly. Weak. At least, that's what doctors one, two, and three told my mother when she presented me to them at age twelve, the sky swimming like some inverted lake above me.

Each one looked at me like I was something not of this world. Then again, maybe I wasn't. That was what the priest thought, at least, when my mother took me to the local church in a last-ditch attempt at a cure.

The dizziness hadn't happened suddenly. I didn't wake up one morning and, instead of leaping out of bed bright-eyed and ready to start the day, fall over in a dazed stupor. No, it was slow, careful, pernicious. It crept in, only soft waves at first. A bit of blurred vision while playing in the marketplace, an ache that whined in my head. Then came the weakness in my legs upon standing.

At first, my mother thought it was a trick. I was, after all, a child. That was what children did, wasn't it? Faked being sick to keep from doing chores?

Normal girls didn't have to grasp the sides of their chairs before standing. Normal girls didn't see everything drowning in pools of black ink, didn't feel their hearts screaming against their rib cages, didn't have legs that trembled before collapsing underneath them. Normal girls didn't watch helplessly as men— men who'd threatened to kill their mothers, who'd threatened to kill them—escaped into the night. Normal girls didn't let those men run between the dark spires of trees with swords ready and waiting until the next time, until the next time they came back and slit their throats through—

I woke up gasping so loudly it almost drowned out the whispers carrying through the cracks in the paneling.

The robbers. They were back.

No—my parents; the lilt of their voices. They were talking about what had happened. Which meant they were talking about *me*. And this time was different, somehow, than their past discussions. There'd been something different in how my mother regarded me as I stood up carefully amid the ruined study, the blaze in her eyes the one she always used to conceal hurt and pain. Once, when she'd slipped and hit her knee against the table, turning the skin mottled and blue, she'd had fury in her face for days. She'd never looked at me like that before, though. Like she could no longer only blame my body for all the trouble I caused.

Maybe I didn't know, truly, what normal girls did and did not do. But what I did know? The way how, under my mother's gaze, I shrank to something so small, so insignificant, I wasn't sure I could recognize myself in the mirror. And oh, how I wanted her to see me as someone strong and worthy of her arm always supporting mine. How I wanted to be a reflection of her carefully controlled blaze.

"I don't understand what I did wrong." My mother's voice.

Careful not to overexert myself, I raised myself out of bed, paused until my world had righted itself, then went to press my ear against the far wall. My bedroom used to be Papa's library. But that was before I became sick, before stairs were no longer an option for my dizzy body, my crumbling legs.

"You didn't do anything wrong," Papa soothed. "You and Tania, ma chère, you are all I've ever wanted."

"It's bad enough I couldn't give you a son, but I gave you a daughter who's . . . who's . . . *broken*."

Papa said something I couldn't hear.

"I don't want you training her anymore. No more fencing— promise me. I know you want to impart your talent, but you can't expect to live vicariously through her without consequences. I can't have her wasting every waking moment, all her energy, on something that will never aid her in the future. She doesn't need to know how to protect herself—she needs to learn skills. Women's skills. For when she is . . ." She stopped, but I knew. I knew what she was going to say: when she is *married*.

"We'll figure it out. No, listen to me. We will." A pause; words muffled by the wall. My father's voice again: "Those bastards waited until I was out of town. Well, they've underestimated my willingness to stay home when my family is concerned. They won't dare try anything while I'm here."

"You know there's more to it than that! What will she do when I'm gone? When *you* are gone? You're not infallible, especially now that—"

There was a loud sigh. Some crying and the distinct rustling of fabric. I retreated to clutch the bedposts. My head bowed, my feet purpling gray, as they always were when the waves of dizziness were at their strongest.

No matter what my mother said, no matter how much I wanted her to see me and not just my weaknesses, she wouldn't take fencing from me. I'd heard it all before. How a girl didn't need to learn the proper way to hold the grip of a sword, didn't need to learn the angle at which her arm should tuck into her side as she prepared for the onslaught of her opponent's attack. Girls did not need to know these things—especially not sick girls.

Until tonight, Papa's response had always been a shake of his head. That wasn't who I was, he explained. "She is Tania," he liked to say. It irked my mother to no end. "She is Tania."

Tania, the daughter who should have been a son, the daughter who should have carried on her father's legacy. But no one would want a sick girl for his bride. Even if she was a Musketeer's daughter.

Chapter Two

Six Months Later

"MON DIEU!"

"See her, resting against the wall? Comme une invalide, non?"

I lifted my chin, palm against the stone storefront. The girls had been visible from far away, their dresses blotches of color against the cobbled street. I fought against the heat rising in my cheeks, fought against the anger and ripening embarrassment, and smiled a sickly sweet smile. "Geri! What a pleasant surprise."

Three or four girls I'd known as a child broke off from the group, left Marguerite and the rest behind. I knew their type. Uncomfortable, but only up to a point. Not enough to step in.

Marguerite's eyes flashed briefly, something pained and fragile in the irises. I was the one who'd given her the nickname. Back when we ruled over fields of sunflowers, ran through the outskirts of town, accidentally braided each other's hair into knots so fierce that our mothers had to cut them out . . . But the look was gone with a curl of her lip—she'd learned that from the other villagers. There was a proper way to examine pauvre Tania.

A proper way to tilt your head and let your gaze travel down the bridge of your nose.

"We've been over this. I prefer my true name, Marguerite. Geri is the name of a child." She sniffed, smoothed her skirt's pleats, then, scowling, picked an imaginary piece of dirt off the green fabric. She must have bought the gown on her sixteenth birthday, during her visit to Paris, the trip she'd crowed about in the village square. It was too fine to have come from Lupiac.

We used to celebrate birthdays together. Ours were a mere few days apart. One year our families traveled to a lake and we stood on the freckled sand and felt the cold water nipping at our ankles and looked out at the incredible vastness of it all, this wide world we were growing into. But that ended four years ago when everything changed. At twelve, Marguerite let me go, because someone who was forced to spend all her time in the shade, someone who was forced to shadow her anxious mother . . . well, that someone wasn't much fun at all. Papa had wanted to pay Marguerite's parents a visit, tell them what he thought of their daughter's betrayal. But my mother insisted he'd only make things worse. What could he say, what could he do, that my body wouldn't disavow time and time again?

My thoughts came sharper, harder. I grasped at them like broken threads. Marguerite's figure blurred. I clenched my toes together, a trick I'd learned by chance to help combat the dizziness and clear my vision. "As engaging as this conversation is, I must be going," I said.

She clucked her tongue. "Busy? You?" She glanced at my basket full of purpling wildflowers. "Pretty. Such a shame you have no one to give them to."

"Not like she ever will," another girl added. "She doesn't even *talk* to any boys, let alone know one who'd want to *marry* her."

I sucked in a pained breath, pressed the basket closer to conceal it; the wicker scratched at my dress. I wasn't alone. I had Papa. Maman.

But I had no biting retort. Feelings were difficult to hide, especially when it came to emotions so close to my skin. To my body and how it failed me. To the prospect of life extending after my parents were gone, life without acceptance of who I was, life without anyone who cared for me not despite the dizziness, not because of the dizziness, but just cared, fully. Was it really too much to hope for someone who looked at me and saw me, and me alone?

Marguerite smirked. "I'm off to my fitting. What a scandal it would be to wear gowns from last season's trip to Paris!" There was a hint of something in the last sentence, as if she was aware of the ridiculousness of the words, of the sentiment. Or maybe I imagined it because I so desperately wanted it to be true.

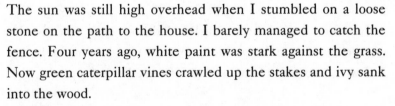

The sun was still high overhead when I stumbled on a loose stone on the path to the house. I barely managed to catch the fence. Four years ago, white paint was stark against the grass. Now green caterpillar vines crawled up the stakes and ivy sank into the wood.

"Maman?"

The door to the parlor was open a hairline crack: back to that night, the poker in my hand slick with sweat, smoke choking my lungs . . . no.

They weren't here. We were safe. They weren't coming back.

I knocked before entering. My mother's head settled against the back of her favorite chair, a note in her lap. I turned to sneak out the way I'd come. But then there was a shifting sound, a cough. "Tania?"

"I brought you these." She looked at my outstretched arms, at the basket filled with flowers, then down at the letter. Was she struggling? Perhaps I could help her, like she helped me, and—"Is the handwriting too difficult to read? Too small? I could read it to you—"

"No. It's fine." Her words were tense and short as she folded the letter into quarters and tucked it into her shawl, away from my prying gaze.

"It's really no trouble," I continued.

"I said it was fine, Tania."

"All right." My hand hovered near a small table in case I needed support.

She rubbed at her brow. "Your uncle sends his love. I'll be fine," she added as I began to protest. "Go work on that new embroidery pattern, the one your aunt sent you." It wasn't a suggestion.

I backed out of the room. But I didn't go to retrieve the untouched pattern design hidden inside a book in my bedroom.

I would never trade my sword for a needle and thread.

Papa practiced an intricate series of footwork in the barn, the movement of his right hand so fluid that his sword appeared to be an extension of his arm. He hadn't been the greatest swordsman in the Musketeers, but he'd certainly been one of the best. Though there was a chance he might've said that only to keep himself from getting too big a head. It was hard to imagine anyone more talented at fencing than he was. And he loved it more than anything . . . until he met my mother. A widowed vicomte's daughter who, after she made it clear that Papa wasn't a courtly fling, was cut off, despite her status as a second child with an older sister married off to a wealthy lord.

The Musketeers might've been heroes. But, unless King Louis XIII, and Louis XIV after him, decided to bestow their goodwill, the few who entered the Musketeers without land, without titles, exited in the same fashion. There weren't many of these men, like Papa; they were vastly outnumbered by the sons of noble families, those who regularly bought their way in. But Papa had his skill with a blade and that couldn't be bought with any amount of money in the world.

Papa gave up his Musketeer duties when I was born to be a constant presence in our family. At least, that was what he told me when I was little and hung on his every word, begging bedtime stories from the man who'd willingly given up glory beyond my comprehension, all for my mother and me. But now I knew better—Papa would never have given up his post voluntarily. Not even his brothers in arms could have protected him, a titleless Musketeer, against a vicomte's influence. No, Papa was forced into retirement. But he had my mother, who refused to obey her father's wishes. And together they had me.

If only they didn't have me to argue over, or to use up all their funds, perhaps it wouldn't have been such a terrible trade. Romantic, even. To love someone so much you were willing to give up everything for them. But then, I'd only ever fenced with

Papa. I didn't know what it was like to be part of a community, dedicated to the study of the sword, only to have it ripped away.

Drawn out of my thoughts by a clap of foot to floor, I watched Papa switch seamlessly from pointe en ligne—arm and blade in one straight line, chest height—to a beautifully executed parry. His blade whistled through the air as he performed the block.

"I'm never going to be able to do that."

My father turned to look over his shoulder and pushed strands of graying hair out of his face with his free hand. "You will."

While the barn did house Papa's aging stallion, trusty Beau, its interior wasn't what one would expect. The walls were lined with practice swords and extra equipment, the center of the floor cleared and swept free of hay. A dummy fashioned from a used sack of flour and leftover straw was mounted in the corner for target practice.

"Not with an opponent running at me with a sword," I grumbled. Papa opened his mouth, but I continued before he could speak. "Not running; you know I didn't mean running. It was a figure of speech. You know I meant advancing."

A smile reached across his whole face, new wrinkles around the corners of his eyes, his mouth. It was times like these when he looked young and old all at once, when I understood how he could have disarmed even my mother, a proper courtier, into considering a man without an impressive title. His stories of wooing her, to my delight and her dismay, were ones filled with intrigue and danger, young lovers destined for one another but hauled apart by rank, by jealousy . . .

As Papa told it, he didn't want to raise a family in Paris. He griped about the city: how dark the narrow streets were, how bright the wide streets were, how the docks stank of sweat, how the social engagements were unavoidable. He listed them off, each reason as flippant in tone as the last—but even he couldn't hide the weight behind the final one, the memory of the people he had lost. My parents never returned to the city: for a time, to keep from accidentally crossing paths with my mother's father. But by the time my grandfather passed away, and Paris was safe for them once more, the dizziness had already started to consume me. A good portion of our family's money was squandered on failed doctors' visits. My father wasn't poor by any means—he had a bit of coin from his late parents, more from his time as a Musketeer—but Paris residences were expensive. Money went much further in Lupiac. A two-story house with an attic wasn't out of reach for one family. Papa valued saving money more than spending it. Traded fencing lessons for anything pricier than the cost of groceries. But even with his savings we'd be lucky to have a roof over our heads in Paris.

"A dizzy spell?" he asked as I pulled myself back into this time, this place.

"No, just thinking."

"Ah, well, then. It's time to get to work, Mademoiselle la Mousquetaire!"

I tucked my skirts into my waistband, the one Papa enlisted the tailor to design, the bottom of the breeches under my dress now visible. Next, I assumed the proper stance: right foot forward, toes pointed straight; left foot back and angled to the side. Knees bent just so, as if I were a coiled spring, ready to shoot forward at any moment. Torso centered and upright.

My father didn't warn me before he struck. It would defeat the purpose—an opponent would never inform you of his planned attack. Papa's blade flashed as my sword moved to meet it.

My shoulders were back, loose. Strong enough to take a solid parry to block his attack, relaxed enough to adapt to the unexpected. His favorite action was to wait until I was close enough to land my lunge before knocking my sword aside with a beat.

Beau let out a disgruntled snort from his stall in the corner. His long tail flicked back and forth to swat away des mouches, those pesky flies, as he chewed at his oats. One was redirected and flew into my face. Dieu, how I hated that horse.

I attempted the newest parry we'd been working on, one that covered my left flank and part of my head. Dust kicked up around my heels as I retreated to block Papa's attack, still keeping him within arm's reach. I thrust my arm immediately forward.

He hadn't expected such a quick riposte. As he leaped back, he tossed his sword from his right hand to his left. Then he performed a block so clean that my sword tumbled to the barn floor.

"That's not fair!" I cried out in indignation.

Seconds later, I was scrambling for my sword, fingers grasping dust as my father triumphantly held my weapon in the air. "Aha! Disarmed!"

"Papa—"

"Don't you *Papa* me. You know the rules, Mademoiselle la Mousquetaire—lose your sword during drills, an extra half hour of embroidery." Of all the ways to assuage his guilt from going against my mother's wishes, it had to be this.

"You cheated," I grumbled as I retrieved my sword.

He snorted along with Beau. "Not everyone has a Musketeer's decency and honor. Few of your opponents will be of that caliber; fewer still will have the training of a Musketeer. Not only brilliant swordsmen, but upstanding individuals." Papa had a distorted view of his brothers in arms. He saw honor in all of them, even the ones who hadn't earned their placement, who were there because of their money or titles or families. They were his friends. At least, the Musketeers of his era. The ones who came later, well . . .

"I wish I could have that. That camaraderie," I murmured, more to myself than to Papa. What a silly wish. What a silly wish for a silly, sick girl. No matter how foolish it was, it unfurled in my mind: the barn transformed into a wide room full of fencers. Yes, the task of protecting the King, protecting France, these brought them together: all this laughter, this clashing of blades. The streak of blue-embroidered cassocks flashing through the air. But together, they were something even greater than their duty. As ridiculous as it was, I imagined them as girls, like me.

Un pour tous, tous pour un. That was how Papa finished all his bedtime stories to me as a child. One for all, all for one.

Papa smiled, a strange expression quickening across his face. "Oh, Tania. How I wish you could have what I had." There was a faraway look in his eyes, strands of hair sticking to his face, sword in hand, ready to answer a call to arms only he could hear.

"Papa," I said. He didn't answer. He was somewhere else. "Papa." He blinked. "Have you ever thought about going back?"

"Back where?"

"To the Musketeers."

"There are no more Musketeers."

Brow wrinkled, I opened my mouth, but he continued: "Oui, the Musketeers of the Guard still exist. They still protect la Maison du Roi. But the true Musketeers, my Musketeers . . . no, they are a thing of the past." A shadow crossed his face. "They are too much glory now, and not enough honor. Boys who can't fill the boots their predecessors left behind and are much too occupied with polishing their swords. But that's what you get when you accept too many full coin purses. Fighting for the King used to be about more than fighting for the monarchy. It was about fighting for la France. Fighting for one another. Keeping your brothers alive, safe. Sometimes," he whispered, soft enough I had to strain to hear him, "I forgot the King even existed."

Beau let out a whinny, stamping his hooves in protest. "Ah, Monsieur Beau! All finished with your oats?" My father moved to his stall, apple in hand. I glared at Beau; he glared right back. "Have you spoken to your mother today?"

The hitch in Papa's voice made me pause. He had his back to me, hand steady as Beau blissfully crunched through the apple core.

"Yes . . . why?"

"We have a guest for supper tonight. *Guests*, really."

"Guests?" Papa turned; his shoulders deflated. My gut sank. "You can't make me. I won't do it. I won't!"

I wasn't built like Marguerite or the other girls in the village, didn't look comfortable in extravagant fabric. I'd never been plump in the right ways. My body wasn't one that blended into space. I was all curves and muscle—perfect for a fencer.

Not, however, for a young lady being assessed like a pig on market day.

My parents and the other couple watched us through the window, all of them still seated at the table with their postdinner glasses of wine. All but Papa, who'd sworn off the deep ruby liquid after he left the Musketeers.

The Chaumonts were friends of my uncle . . . and my mother's main target in her attempt to marry me off. She'd been planning a meeting ever since her brother let slip their son was around my age. That's what my uncle's letter had been about—that the Chaumonts would be arriving soon, how he hoped his note would arrive in time, that he knew it was last minute. An imposition, yes, but my mother would forgive anything for what she saw as a chance to secure my future.

The air was thick and sweet in the garden; I hoped it was enough to cover the smell of anxious sweat that pooled in the unforgiving creases of my dress.

Jacques stalled at the beginning of the flower rows. The boy had cheeks that turned pink whenever his parents worked his excellence into the conversation, a feat they'd seemingly mastered. His mother managed it even when discussing completely unrelated subjects, like the efficacy of ladies-in-waiting: "One of the Dowager's lady's maids is quite unfortunate looking. And at the last party of the season, not a soul asked her to dance! The poor thing—but Jacques, such a gentleman, asked her for the next two dances. Such a kind and thoughtful young man. Even Madame de Treville said so. She came up to me herself, can you imagine? She started a bridal preparatory school a couple of months ago—all the nobles in Paris are trying to get their daughters on the wait list—I suppose you wouldn't know, what with your being so . . . isolated from Paris. She must have her sights set on arranging a match between one of her ladies and our Jacques. But she'd do well to realize how high in demand he is. A first son with such good manners!"

In the slowly dimming light, Jacques turned back to the window; Madame Chaumont gave him a little wave. My mother, on the other hand, caught my eye and then jerked her head toward Jacques.

I shifted uncomfortably, slippered feet unsteady on the uneven grass.

"Do they know?" I'd asked my mother earlier, after I was stuffed into an uncomfortable pale blue gown decorated with swirls of gold embroidery.

Her eyes illuminated in comprehension in the mirror. Her hands froze in the middle of smoothing my sleeve. "They know what your uncle has told them."

"Which is?"

"When he suggested we meet, they inquired as to why they hadn't seen you during the season. He told them we kept you from traveling to Paris because you were too weak. You were sick, but nothing serious."

"You want me to *lie*? Lie about . . . about . . ."

She reached to fix a hairpin, her movements sharp. The pin bit into my scalp. "I've done my part. Now you must do yours." I shook my head. "Tania," she said, gripping my shoulders, "we must find someone. Don't you understand?" Of course I did. Her words looped in my head endlessly. She'd thrust me at the village boys more times than I could count. As the dizziness grew worse and my hopes dimmed, the words morphed, multiplied. Even if she didn't say it, I knew what she truly thought, the reality at the heart of every bodice cinch, of every hairpin stab. It didn't matter that she'd married for love.

Sick girls didn't have suitors. Sick girls had to fight for what they could get. But this kind of fighting was infinitely harder than fighting with a sword.

So I nodded at my mother's gesture and then smiled sweetly

at Jacques, pretending to arrange my skirts while actually fumbling for the railing my father had installed around the edge of the fence, low enough for my grip to go unseen. It was too tall of a fence to use the stakes for balance, like I did with the fence at the front of the house.

If one were to search for the perfect mixture of my parents, one would find it in the garden: The refined, manicured shrubs were my mother's favorites because they looked like the ones at the Palais du Louvre, the main residence of the King. The bursts of color, though, the bright blues and reds. Those were Papa's doing.

I cast around for something to say. "Well, dinner was . . . interesting." Interesting? Had I really said *interesting*?

"Yes. Interesting."

The skirts of my dress whispered across the grass as we passed a shrub cut into the likeness of a flower.

"Do you—" he said.

"I've always thought—" I started.

"Please, go ahead."

"I . . . I thought—that is, I've always thought it strange." I nodded to the shrub.

His brow furrowed. "How so?"

"Don't you think it's odd: the idea that a shrub resembling a flower could ever be considered more beautiful than the original?" Cheeks warm, I glanced at him in the predusk. The waning light cut angles into his face where there were none. "What was it you were going to say?"

"Would you like to sit?" he asked. We'd reached a bench that looked out over the flowers.

Curls of baby hair framed his face, his muted blue eyes. There was nothing passionate lurking in their depths, no fire lying dormant. But there was nothing cruel in them, either. Nothing to make me recoil. And there was kindness in his face, even if I was just determined to see it and painted it there myself. He'd offered to dance with a girl abandoned by everyone. If I couldn't love, I could have kindness. And kindness, in its own way, was a type of love.

"Do I have something on my face?"

"No," I assured him, too loud.

"Good." He cleared his throat. "I'm sure you know why we're here: I'm of age and will be seeking a bride in the near future. My parents were told you're in a similar position."

It was transactional, the language he used. But not everyone could be a poet. Just because he didn't employ the language of love didn't mean the potential for the emotion was absent from his body.

"That's right." I waited, but he didn't continue. "Is there anything else you wanted to talk about?"

"Our parents are discussing matters." He motioned to the house. "There's not much else to say."

"Oh." I swallowed the feverish feeling in my chest that attempted to make its way up, up and out of my throat.

He did not care about knowing me. Did not care about learning my likes, my dislikes, if there was something in me he could grow to love someday.

It was then, in the haze of upset, needing to be anywhere, anywhere but here, that I made the mistake. Not thinking, blinking away tears, I quickly stood up.

CHAPTER THREE

BLACK PETALS BLOSSOMED before my eyes, more recognizable than any flower in the garden and darker than the center of a sunflower.

Jacques's concerned face wavered in front of me, fingers light at the bend of my elbow as I returned to my seat. Still, the world kept spinning, spinning. "Is everything all right? Should I call for—"

"No!" I interjected, then adopted as pleasant an expression as I could manage. "No," I repeated, gentler this time. "There's no need to worry."

"No—no need to worry?" he stammered, glancing from me to the house to me again.

I clenched my toes. It didn't do much to help the dizziness since I was already seated, but the action was natural and familiar and relaxed the frantic terror gripping my chest. Deep breath in, deep breath out.

When my vision focused, I looked at Jacques. I was good at keeping pain off my face. All it took was gritting my teeth. Sinking my nails into my palms.

"I really should fetch our parents," he said.

"Please don't; they can't do anything."

He peered at me through the dimming light. "What do you mean they can't *do* anything?"

The excuse was ready on my lips. But there were his eyes, more well water than clear sky. Eyes that belonged to a boy who once danced with a lonely girl, a boy I might marry. A boy I could try to love someday. "Sometimes I get dizzy. It's not that bad," I added at the alarm on his face.

"So, you're . . . sick?"

"No." I rushed to explain. "I'm fine, really, I—"

"You don't have to explain."

I stopped short. "You . . . you understand?" Relief bloomed from the tips of my toes to the crown of my head.

"Yes, of course. Why don't I help you back inside?"

Reaching out for his proffered arm, tentatively, hesitantly, my fingers connected with his sleeve, dark blue fabric almost black now that the light had started to fade. He didn't flinch.

I tried to find his eyes again. But there were too many shadows, so I had to make do with imagining what I'd find there. Perhaps it was better this way. This way, I could make his eyes say whatever I wanted them to.

"Tania!" When we entered, my mother ushered us into the sitting room. "Did you show Monsieur Jacques the garden?"

"It's charming, Madame." Jacques led me to a rose-printed settee, flowers twisting together in pale blush and sage. "Are you all right now?" he asked. I nodded. "Thank you again pour la visite du jardin." He turned back to my mother. "Madame, would you be so kind as to tell me where my parents are?"

"I had my husband escort them to the parlor. It's at the front of the estate." As if we lived in a spacious mansion rather than a village house. The moment Jacques disappeared she was at my side, adjusting one of the hairpins clustered on my scalp. "What did he mean, are you all right *now*? Did you have a dizzy spell?"

"It's fine."

"Did he notice? Did he say anything?" A frantic edge stained her voice.

I didn't know how to respond, so I repeated, "It's fine," again.

She took a steadying breath. "What happened?" Her expression shifted as I recounted my interaction with Jacques and tried to ease her worry, tried not to look over my shoulder for fear of the Chaumonts walking through the door. "Tell me you didn't tell him you've had this for years," she ground out.

"All he knows is I get dizzy sometimes. He said he understood."

"He said he understood." She punctuated each word as a question.

"Well . . . yes."

My mother let out an angry bark of a laugh. "He . . . said . . . he . . . *understood*? Tania, how could he understand? How could he *possibly* understand?"

Tears burned; I shrank into the settee. "There wasn't anything else I could have said, could have done. Maman, please," I implored, reaching for her. When was the last time we'd touched when she wasn't providing support for my wavering legs? When was the last time she'd reached for me and it wasn't because I needed help?

"Now, what's going on in here?" Papa, who leisurely strolled through the door, halted at the sight of us: my mother, her body an angry, taut string; me, wanting nothing more than to hide in the barn with the swords. A few more tears slipped down my cheeks. He would be so disappointed in me. A coward, afraid of facing disapproval.

"Where are the Chaumonts?" my mother asked.

"The boy requested a word with his parents, so I gave them some privacy. What a stuffy woman his mother is." He threw me a wink. "Rather unpleasant, if you ask me."

"Thomas!"

"Whatever is the matter, ma chère?"

"He knows, Thomas."

"Who knows what . . . ?"

My mother didn't have a chance to answer. As Papa trailed off, the parlor door opened. Jacques.

Hand gripping the settee, I stood, balanced myself against the armrest. I had to show Jacques I was a normal girl. Convince him the flush from earlier tears was a mere healthy glow.

"Madame. Monsieur. Mademoiselle," Jacques intoned.

"Monsieur, we thought you retired to the parlor with your parents?" my mother said.

"My mother wanted a moment to collect her things. She feels we've delayed our journey long enough."

"But it's dangerous to travel at night," my mother reasoned. "And you need rest. We planned on you staying for one, if not two, nights, at least."

"With all due respect, that was before . . ." Jacques paused as his gaze landed on me.

"Be careful how you choose your next words, *Monsieur*." Papa's eyes were sword sharp.

Jacques raised his chin. "Monsieur, I assure you I meant no disrespect."

My mother yanked Papa's arm, muttering about finding Monsieur and Madame Chaumont, and dragged him after her in the direction of the parlor. She was so flustered she didn't consider that she was leaving us without the watchful eye of a chaperone.

The edge of the settee dug painfully into my spine. I didn't move. Not because of dizziness, but because I was frozen there. A block of ice waiting to be sculpted into a swan.

"Mademoiselle, I must bid you adieu." Jacques performed a polite, shallow bow.

Finally, I regained my voice. "How could you pretend that everything was fine? When we were in the garden?"

A mixture of amusement and confusion marred his face. "I did nothing of the sort. You have these, what do you call them . . . dizzy spells? That is what your mother called them, yes? They make you feel sick and make it difficult for you to walk? It's unfortunate. I am sorry that you suffer."

"I don't understand."

He laughed. Not mocking, not harsh, but the words themselves, the way they sounded like a prelude to something awful, felt like a slap. "Au contraire, I'm the one who doesn't understand. Obviously I could never make you an offer of marriage."

"But you—your mother said you were kind. You danced with—"

"Dancing with a homely, partnerless girl at a party is not the same as marrying a girl like you. Even in your condition, you must be able to understand that."

There was still no malice in his eyes. No disgust, no cruelty. He didn't think he was doing anything wrong. He didn't think he had *said* anything wrong.

Madame Chaumont burst through the sitting room doorway.

My mother was close on her heels. "We're leaving." Madame Chaumont threw the words at her son. "Your father has gone with the driver to ready the carriage." Her gaze raked the room, eyes narrowing into stormy shards of glass as she marched over to my corner. "Who do you think you are? Was this part of some plot—to seduce my son and spread your ghastly disease on to his offspring? Are you bent on bringing shame to my family? What a horrendous political trick. I, of course, am well versed in court intrigue and scandal on account of spending so much time in Paris, but you outdo even the most power hungry of the lower noblesse—"

"Step away from my daughter." Papa was in the open doorway, ablaze.

Madame Chaumont spluttered, "I—I must've misheard you. No gentleman would speak to a lady of my rank in such a manner!"

"Would you like me to repeat myself? I'd be happy to do so." Papa took a step into the room.

"Merci, Madame de Batz. Thank you for a wonderful meal," Jacques cut in. "We won't encroach on your hospitality any longer."

"Madame Chaumont." My mother approached her. "There's been a misunderstanding—" The older woman shot her a look that made me want to curl into the wall. It wasn't the anger, although fury did spark at the corners of her eyes. No, it was the intense, palpable disgust. Her gaze ran down the bridge of her nose to fall at my mother's feet. As if she, for the crime of being my mother, was worth less than the dirt beneath the floorboards. I'd thought I felt small in my mother's eyes before. But nothing prepared me for the way my mother turned to me, looked me over, as if she had never truly seen me in her entire life.

CHAPTER FOUR

SLASH. THE CUT of my sword against the target was usually a release. But there was no breath in this, no sigh I could exhale to unclench the knot of my upper arm, the stony expanse of my shoulders.

"This is your fault. You filled her head with those stories. Romance like that can never exist for her."

Slash. Blade against fabric. Blade against wood. If I squinted, the target was Jacques's face, open and closed all at once, thinking he had nothing to hide.

The very next moment I flinched, sword clattering to the ground. It was one thing to use upset and anger to fuel my training, but another to picture the face of a boy on my target, to imagine cutting him until he crumpled. Until he understood what he'd done.

The voices outside the barn paused. My breaths were ragged in the quiet.

"She's still young; she could—"

"She is *your* daughter. If she spent more time learning what it actually means to be a woman, we wouldn't be in this mess!"

"How did you come to that conclusion?"

"Well, for starters, she would've known how to manipulate that simpering little boy."

"My dear, *our* daughter is quite possibly the least likely individual to manipulate another person in all of France. She is far too kindhearted for that. She doesn't use her light, her strength, to hurt others." There was something off in his voice, but my mother pressed on, continuing to argue.

I would've laughed if I didn't feel like sobbing—here I was imagining a boy's face on the opposite end of my sword. I wasn't kind. I was nothing; I was an amalgamation of wrongs.

My father was far too generous with me.

"The invalide has a bit of fire in her, non?" The man advanced through the darkness. But this time my hands were empty: no fire poker, no sword. Nothing to prevent him from stabbing me through the heart.

I was useless. Hopeless.

"Tania."

I shot awake; my room was bathed in early morning sun. Papa idled by the window, shutters opened. Everything was too bright. "Three days. Three days since those wretched people left, and you've barely stepped foot out of your room. You've only been to the barn to practice once. You're not doing yourself any good wallowing."

"I'm not wallowing," I muttered.

"Then get up. It's time for training."

"I can't." I buried my face in my pillow, the fabric damp with tears or sweat or both.

"I don't need to remind you it's going to get worse if you don't practice, especially if you don't leave this bed—you'll throw away all your hard work." I shifted to glare at him. The longer I stayed in bed, the worse the dizziness would be when I eventually stood up: a fact my body never let me forget. A fact that Papa had also learned over the years. "You are too strong for this. Where's my fierce daughter?"

I was not strong; I was weak and tired. But still, I pushed myself up with a wheeze. Swinging my legs over the side, toes all purple and gray, I attempted to stand.

Papa's arm shot out to prevent my fall as I stumbled, my legs shaking as they tried to hold up my body. "You told me so, right? Staying in bed makes it worse. You can say it. Go ahead," I said bitterly as he looped his arm around my waist.

His eyes reflected back mine. He swallowed. "No, Tania. Of course not." A chest pang twisted, deep.

It'd only been a few days since I was in the fencing studio, but it felt like lifetimes: the familiar tickle of hay at the back of my throat, the wonderful creak of floorboards. Beau's dark eyes assessed me as I crossed the room, Papa guiding me to an old chair he'd placed in the barn for times like these.

It was like being at my most sick again. Twelve, thirteen, fourteen, years when all I had the ability to do was sit and watch Papa train. Every so often I'd practice bladework while seated, learning technique without footwork. I hated this—feeling helpless. Feeling like I was twelve all over again.

"Tania." Papa was brushing Beau's mane with a wide-toothed comb, loosening the resistant knots and burrs. "We have to talk about what happened."

"I thought we were training?"

He set the comb on a nearby stool. "You needed to get out of that room."

"You lied to me."

I knew he was going to push the strands of hair out of his face before it happened; the action was that familiar. "Not all lies are bad things, ma fille. With good intentions, they have the potential to help, not harm."

The corners of my mouth pulled down into a scowl, the one my mother hated. She told me I looked exactly like Papa when I frowned. Ladies didn't frown. And they definitely didn't scowl. "You're talking about *him*."

"You knew how important this was," Papa said. I raised a brow. "How important it was to your mother," he corrected. "I know he was not, no, *could* not be your first choice of suitors. How could he be, when the only thing to recommend him was that he danced with someone at a ball? But—"

"That's what you think this is about? Papa . . ." I fought off angry tears. "Papa," I tried again, "please tell me you understand. I couldn't lie to him, not to his face like that. I *couldn't*."

"Your mother would ensure you're provided for. And I know that seems like a very far-off concern, but, Tania, she worries. As much as I want you to find happiness in whatever form that takes, I don't want you shut up in some nunnery. If I thought that life would bring you joy—but that's not what you want, and I won't have you relying on the goodwill of relatives. Most of all, I won't have you alone."

"It's not my fault boys write me off as a sick girl!"

"Tania," he interrupted, "that's enough."

If only I could storm off. But I knew what would happen if I tried: the dizziness, the spots across my vision, the world falling out from under me.

"It's not that I don't want to marry," I said. "Or that I don't want to find someone. But how am I supposed to fall in love if he doesn't even know this part of me? It's not everything, but it's still part of me."

"Marriage isn't always about love. It can start that way, of course. And continue that way, too. But it is more than that. It's partnership. It's someone who can help you become a better version of yourself, both when you're together and when you're apart. It is someone who recognizes your strengths and celebrates them. And as much as I hate to admit to your mother being right on this occasion, marriage does provide a measure of security." He stood up gingerly, as if in pain. "And you need security. Especially now that . . ."

"Now that what?"

He paused, working the words between his teeth. "It's not important."

"Papa . . ."

He sighed; his expression was resigned. "I fear I've let you grow up believing that France is a safe, impenetrable place. All those stories I told you about vanquishing foes, defeating enemies regardless of who they were and where they were from . . . but the heroes do not always win, ma fille. And it is hard, so very hard when both heroes and villains want similar things— think they want similar things. Each and every man is a hero to himself." As he spoke, he fiddled with one of his rings, the metal catching and reflecting shards of light. Curiosity bubbled up in me, but anger still clenched at my fists. "I must leave; my presence has been requested at another prospective academy," he said.

"But, Papa, what about—"

"The robbers won't be back. Hitting the same maison more than once is asking to be caught by the maréchaussées. Besides, I've put off important work. Six months is long enough."

"Work? How is traveling to fencing academies and humoring noblemen *work?* You think they're ridiculous! You just want to see your friends, your brothers. You just miss being a Musketeer." He didn't understand. He hadn't been there that night when all that separated me from a dangerous man was a fire poker. In one last-ditch effort, I crossed my arms. "Maman couldn't have agreed to this."

That made him chuckle. "You are more alike than you realize. I had a similar conversation with her not an hour ago." He went silent for a moment, then bent to press a kiss to my forehead. "I'll be home by sundown tomorrow. You won't even have time to stew about how angry you are." He saddled Beau, but looked back over his shoulder before he mounted. "Keep your sword in your room tonight."

"But Maman—"

"She doesn't need to know. It will bring me comfort knowing you have the means to protect yourself and your mother within arm's reach." He gathered Beau's reins and adjusted the saddle.

"If you're so sure the robbers won't be back, who do we need protection from?"

He reached out to clasp my hand. "I hate to inform you, but your father is becoming a paranoid old man. Humor him, won't you?"

I'd failed to protect us. And yet, there he was, looking at me like he believed in me, in my strength. I didn't have a band of brothers in arms to rely on when everything was bleak. But I had Papa. And no matter how much I wanted to argue with him, wanted to grab Beau's reins and force him to stay, I didn't. Because even though he was no longer in service of la Maison du Roi, we were our own Musketeers, he and I. The two of us. Our house might not be as grand as the palace, but we would protect it all the same. We would protect each other.

CHAPTER FIVE

THE CANDLE ON the dresser burned low, the wick nearly disappearing into a pool of molten wax. After Papa left, I distracted myself with caring for the swords—but it wasn't long until my mother was calling my name. I hurried outside so she couldn't tell I'd been in the barn, but as if she knew what I'd been doing, she forced me into a dismal embroidery session. And then I slept through supper. Rather, I hadn't been woken for supper.

Tania.

Startling from sleep, I sat up in bed.

Tania.

Visions of cloaked intruders and leering grins danced before me. I squeezed out a breath, reached for my sword. Papa was counting on me.

I spied around the door frame before moving into the hallway, making my way along the wall, fingers running over the crack in the wallpaper here, the shelf there.

"Maman?" I hesitated in front of her bedroom.

My mother was asleep, blankets wrapped around her like a shroud. Only a sliver of her face was visible. Stepping back, a sudden twist of my stomach at intruding on this space, I stumbled on the carpet. I nearly dropped my sword, too, but regained my grip at the last second.

"Tania," she mumbled, then shifted. Her dark sheet of hair spilled across her shoulder blades. There was something tender in the way she said my name. She was still asleep.

Tania.

Goose bumps raced along my exposed neck as I twisted to look for the source of the softer, lower voice. It hadn't been my mother, not this time. But the hallway was empty.

I started at a sudden noise: only my mother snoring, her body melting back into deep sleep. Shaking my head, I laughed at myself, at how easily scared I was. How scared I was at the sound of my own name.

Loose grass crinkled under my feet all the way down the main road, dragged along by farmers on their way back from the fields, by wagon wheels and workers' timeworn boots. For the first time in weeks, the sky was blissfully overcast. Retrieving ingredients wasn't something my mother tended to ask of me, but I would've done anything to escape the house. My whispered name drifted along the walls long after I fell asleep. My name and eerie faces and fire pokers that shattered when hit with a sword.

This would show my mother I was competent, that she didn't have to worry about finding me someone, that I could take care of myself. When she mentioned needing ingredients for supper, I jumped at the chance. It was the perfect opportunity to make up for the disaster that was the Chaumonts' visit. And later, I would meet Papa right when he arrived on Beau, like old times, so we could walk home together, the three of us. Angry until I saw his face, his delight in response to mine at his return. And then we would finish our conversation.

I spent hours in the supply store winding through dried thyme and lavender suspended from the ceiling, perusing heavy linen bags of flour, sugar, and salt that required two sets of hands to lift, picking wheels of cheese so creamy that cutting into them was like unleashing a thick stream of wine, and skimming my hands over white and brown eggs with smooth freckled shells. Even when the shopkeeper insisted how it was "so good to see me up and about" and that my mother must be thrilled I was "feeling better," my smile didn't fracture, lips drawn so tight they couldn't move. When I first became sick, my mother sought help from the other villagers. They grew less friendly when they started to understand the extent of my condition. As time passed, my mother stopped. But the damage was done—they knew about the dizziness, about my inability to stand without something nearby to catch me. Now, whenever I had a good day, people were quick to assume I felt better. It was hard enough living with the knowledge that if I felt healthy, it didn't mean the next day would be the same. Being reminded of that fact by others was a painfully close second.

The trip was, on its whole, far too easy. I should've realized that as I exited the store as fast as I could without the dizziness returning in salty waves. I should've seen the flurry of colored dresses, the elbow draped in orange that jabbed into my arm.

"Oh, I'm so sorry! Je suis très désolée."

My world swayed. Would this be the moment when my mother's nightmares came true? The ones I heard her whisper about to Papa late at night, the ones where my head cracked on the cobblestone, blood pooling onto the road?

But if fencing had taught me anything, it was how to fall with purpose. How to use my palms as a brace, how to let the wood or stone or grass shriek painfully against my skin. Palms could heal. Heads, on the other hand . . .

On the cobblestone, sugar spread out in arcs around my hunched body like an unfinished lace fan. Several eggs splattered when I fell. Stringy yellow yolk folded itself into my skirt. My knees, my feet, my head: Everything stung.

"Is she going to stay there like that?"

More flurried whispers, more piercing laughter I pretended not to recognize. I tried to stand. I shouldn't have, but I did it anyway; all I wanted was to be as far away as possible. For once, I wanted my legs not to buckle.

"Should we help her?"

"Don't you think that was a bit too far?"

"She'll be fine."

"But isn't she, you know . . . *sick*? She could die or something."

Clutching onto the outer wall, I scoffed as I steadied myself.

"See, I told you. She's fine." After she spoke, Marguerite took a step back. Was there a glint in the whites of my eyes that scared her? Had my fury overflowed, spilled through my face, like it did with Maman?

Ignoring the others, I stared at Marguerite for a hard moment. She had no idea how it felt when the girl you grew up with, the girl you once knew better than yourself, decided you were worth nothing more than broken eggs and spilled sugar.

My eyes stung as I used the wall for support and half walked, half crawled away.

"She's crawling like a baby! Baby Tania!"

Fury was building low and fast behind my sternum, a growl that ripped through my clenched teeth.

This time, when I pulled myself up, I stayed standing. The ringing in my ears blurred out all sound. I shuffled against the wall. Clung to the stone until my nails bled. Thought of Papa, of my fence, of home. Of my sword, waiting for me in the barn. All I had to do was get home.

The rest of the day was spent in my room, waiting until shadows of branches extended across the floor. Papa would know what to say. Even if we fought the other day, he would still know how to help me now. I had to believe that was true. He understood how I felt, even if he couldn't convince my mother that what I needed most was more time training in the barn and less time worrying about boys who would never be interested in me.

The path to the carriage stop was simple: one step, another step, a hand free to trail along the fence for balance, then the trees. I waited there until the light leaked out of the sky, until the ground was bathed in pinks and purples and oranges, feathery and warm against the cooling air.

I shifted my feet and peered down the road.

I waited.

I waited.

Leaned up against the trunk of a nearby tree, my eyes fluttered shut, then opened at the clopping of hooves, the clunk of wheels on road. A carriage shot into view. Probably belonged to one of the wealthy gentlemen starting the new academy; maybe they offered it up for Papa's return. But then, where was Beau?

The carriage hurtled down the road, throwing up stones and dirt in its wake. Smiling at the approach, then frowning at the driver's apparent lack of control over the horses, I launched myself out of its path. It screeched to a halt. An unfamiliar man exited before the groomsman even finished arranging the stairs.

His face was so very white.

He was not Papa.

"Oh, my dear." The man's voice was gruff. His features luminous in the darkness. "You must be Mademoiselle de Batz."

I nodded, confused. "Yes."

He took a step closer. Took one of my hands in both of his. I would've pulled away, told him how improper this behavior was, but I was rooted to the ground. Maybe if I stayed there long enough, I could become just another tree. Tall. Silent.

"My dear Mademoiselle. I am so sorry."

CHAPTER SIX

MY LEGS WERE shaking even though they were no longer holding my body: I was on the floor, my back against the wall. And wasn't that strange? Sitting had never really been a problem for me—but then, it wasn't just my legs but my arms, my chest, my head shaking, my entire body saying no no no.

The pale face.

My legs collapsing.

The return home, empty-handed.

My mother waiting by the door.

My mother's shriek.

The man explained the nature of my father's death to us slowly—rather, to my mother. To them, I'd completely curled in on myself.

But I listened: for proof that this man was wrong, that he was lying. Maybe Papa had been delayed. He'd spend the night in a village inn and be home by morning for le déjeuner, would smile tiredly as he sat at the table, would apologize for missing supper.

My eyes were as dry as the hard-packed dirt of the unused fields in summer.

"How did it happen?" my mother whispered.

A maréchaussée waited silently in the corner—he'd refused the seat my mother offered. His job as a local officer was to escort Monsieur Allard to deliver the news before returning to his unit. The unit in the region where they'd found Papa.

"Madame, it isn't appropriate conversation for a lady—" Monsieur Allard started.

"This is my husband—*my husband*—you speak of. I will decide what is or is not appropriate."

He fiddled nervously with his monogrammed handkerchief. He'd drawn it out of his pocket for her, but she'd shooed him away. My mother's tears were not made to be absorbed by fabric. They were a force in and of themselves. Her fury and grief were powerful; mine, nothing. I wished I could be that strong. My cheek rested against the wall as the man spoke, his voice so careful it burned.

Monsieur Allard: resident of a city around a day's ride from Bordeaux. One of a number of well-to-do locals who'd invested their money and ample leisure time in founding a new academy. Papa was to lodge with the wealthiest man of the group—a Monsieur Verdon. Papa had told Allard that he planned on stopping at a local inn for a drink. Monsieur Allard said they all assumed Monsieur Verdon accompanied him, but a few hours later, when the latter had no word from Papa, he rushed to Allard's house.

This was where Monsieur Allard paused. The maréchaussée was silent in the corner. Monsieur Allard must've been a wealthy man for the officer to relinquish control over relaying the facts.

My mother's words splintered when they left her lips. "Go on."

Monsieur Allard shook his head in agitation. Maman was up in a flash, nearly across the room before the maréchaussée interceded with a murmured, "Madame," his expression concealed by a wide-brimmed hat. She glanced between them. She was so small. So exposed.

"I'm sorry." Her voice cracked. "I just want—" She trailed off, retreated a few steps. "Why didn't you come right away?"

"I had to notify the local authorities," Monsieur Allard said, gesturing to the maréchaussée. "I insisted that I visit the man's family and relay the news. I can't help but feel responsible. If only I'd accompanied him to the inn . . ."

"Do you have any leads, then? Any possible suspects?"

The two men exchanged a look. "Madame, it is clear from our investigation that this was the work of highway bandits," the maréchaussée said.

"Highway bandits," my mother repeated. "You think highway bandits felled my husband? A retired Musketeer? He once dueled three men on his own. With his *left* hand!"

"That's hardly—" Monsieur Allard tried to interrupt.

"So, that's it, then? You decide it's highway bandits, and that's it?"

"Madame," the maréchaussée interjected gruffly. "Catching highway bandits is difficult—once they commit a crime, they move on to another town. Their livelihood depends on avoiding pursuit."

"Where is he? I want to see him."

Monsieur Allard's face reddened at Maman's request. "Surely that's not—"

"You come into my home to tell me my husband was murdered. *My* husband. And yet you have the nerve to tell me what's appropriate?" Had they ever been spoken to like this by a woman? I supposed things were different when grief was involved. For death, it seemed, men could forgive anything. Maman spun to face the man with the wide-brimmed hat. "Well?"

"If there were another way to tell you . . . it's not something anyone should be burdened with," he said.

"My husband is dead, and you speak of burdens! A burden greater than a wife losing a husband? A daughter losing a father?"

It was less about me and more about Maman's fury. That I knew. Still, it was as if she'd taken me by the hand and proclaimed me as her own, no hesitation when "daughter" left her lips, a solidarity that she hadn't shown me for years.

"I and two others were called to investigate a death en route from Le Rare Loup Inn to the residence of a Monsieur Verdon. We arrived half an hour after we received word, likely an hour or so after the crime itself." My mother was silent, eyes cleaved to his face, hands fisted by her sides. "We found votre mari near where the main road meets the path to the Verdon residence. Your husband wasn't immediately identifiable." She began to speak, but he continued. "It wasn't the stolen items—his sword, his clothing—that complicated matters. The bandits"—he muttered under his breath a prayer, or a curse—"cut off his beard. Sheared his hair. They weren't . . . careful."

My mother blanched. Papa's bloody hair in a killer's hands rose, unbidden, in my mind. "Are highway bandits in the habit of desecrating corpses?" she asked.

"There's no reason to assume it happened postmortem. There

were no other wounds aside from those consistent with a fight."
She didn't respond. He chanced a step forward. "You understand,
then, our hesitation for you to see the remains."

Maman was unmoored. And when she looked back at me, I
wished I had something to give her, but all I had were empty
hands, a raging heart, a mind full of memories. Her weary sigh
cracked me in two. "How do you expect me to give him a proper
burial?" she asked.

That's it? She was giving up? Three sets of eyes on me—I'd said
that last part out loud.

"Tania—" my mother began.

"No! Don't tell me to be quiet, or to mind my tongue!" I
demanded. "How can you do it? How can you believe them, just
like that?"

"You're being foolish."

"Foolish? Not to take the word of these men? You know I'm
right. You said it yourself! None of it—the inn, the walking late at
night, alone—none of it is Papa! Besides, he doesn't even drink! I
bet if it were—if it were Monsieur *Allard*"—the man in question
spluttered out an objection—"they would've already caught the
killer. Why would officers care about avenging Papa? It doesn't
matter that he was a Musketeer. He didn't leave behind hundreds of coins to line their pockets with!"

Monsieur Allard ballooned, nearly falling off his seat. The
maréchaussée regained his composure quickly enough, blinking
away shock. "Even the most pious may have a drink or two on
occasion."

"Apologize this instant." My mother swung toward me, expression scalding and burning up any of her residual tears.

"Madame, your daughter is distraught." The maréchaussée

removed his hat and held it by his left side. "No apology is necessary. She's a child; she was obviously close to her father. The outburst is understandable."

My whole body flamed. Everyone should know what this felt like; how it felt to be burning, burning. "How could you know? How could you possibly know what I'm feeling?"

I could not be my mother. I couldn't engage in her repartee, her coherent questioning of Monsieur Allard and the maréchaussée, of the scene, the motive, the suspects. I couldn't let my tears fall like musket shots, not like she did. My pain did not fit into teardrops. My anger and grief could consume whole cities, cities bustling with people who knew my father only as a retired Musketeer. They didn't know that he loved his fellow brothers more than the notoriety. They didn't know what it was to have his smile. They didn't know that he was always there to catch me.

"I'll be home by sundown tomorrow. You won't even have time to stew about how angry you are."

I threw myself at the door, smacking my shoulders against the walls, the dizziness so strong I was in a constant state of falling as I lumbered out of the sitting room and through the hallway. From far away, I heard my mother telling the men they needed to leave. She would arrive in the morning to collect the remains, but they needed to leave.

I shot through the front door. Into the sharp night. Into the sky filled with star-shaped daggers. Into this dark new world.

CHAPTER SEVEN

I LOST A SPACE of time. Short, but still. Still.

It was the sound of carriage wheels on stone, that dreadful noise retreating past the point of hearing, that forced me to emerge from myself. A few minutes at most, though it felt like hours.

This side of the house was shadowed. It had the least number of windows, the least amount of candlelight shimmering through closed shutters.

Tania.

Papa's voice. It sounded different, but it was his. I knew it in my bones.

"Papa?"

On the way to the front of the house, I rested against a tree here, a tree there. I found myself at the walkway, right at the beginning of the fence. Our house was stark against the night. Each little unshuttered glassless window with each little candle, all those eyes staring back at me.

Tania. Tania. Tania.

"Stop it!" I shrieked. I clutched my head. But the repetition of my name continued; his voice was so close, it was as if he were standing at my shoulder.

I hated him. I hated him for leaving me. For breaking his promise, for not triumphing over mere thieves.

I hated him for not giving me a chance to say goodbye.

I grabbed hold of the stakes of the fence and tried to break them into shards, pull apart the weatherworn wood with my fingers until the stakes yielded.

"Tania, where are—Tania!"

A tug at my arm and I lost balance, too dizzy, and fell back. My hands tingled.

"Tania."

I blinked. My mother was crying.

"I . . ." My voice broke. Splinters caught my skin, embroidery needles that threaded crimson across my palms and nail beds. The pointer finger on my left hand was shadowed and swollen. When I tried to flex it, the bone blistered fire.

My mother shepherded me into the kitchen, fumbling with a candle, soaking in the full sight of my hands. For a brief moment—wonderful, painful—Papa's voice was with me again. *Why be horrified by the violence your hands can inflict? You're a fencer. What did you think we did to our enemies? Clap them on the back for a good duel and send them on their way?*

She inspected the shadowy depths of a cabinet. For once, I relished the haze of the dizziness, the fog clouding my thoughts.

When the tweezers flashed, the metal darting in and out of my skin, my mother tensed. My hand—the one she wasn't tending to—reached for her trembling fist. I'd never comforted her before. I didn't know how.

"I'm sorry. I wasn't thinking." My battered fingers withdrew.

She shook her head. Blood smudged her knuckles. "It's fine, Tania. It's fine."

I retreated into myself until fresh bandages were tied neatly around my palms, until the swollen finger on my left hand was framed in a splint.

"We'll talk about this in the morning."

"Maman—"

But she walked away. Abandoned me to navigate the kitchen, my hand outstretched from habit, though there was no one to catch me now.

She used rose water to clean my hands. Sweet. Now, morning bright, as I rubbed my eyes, the cloying, sickly smell cut through the throbbing in my head.

"Maman?" My voice croaked.

The truth slammed into me. She'd told the maréchaussée and Monsieur Allard that she would retrieve Papa . . . retrieve the body. I hadn't thought she would leave me here alone. That she wouldn't take me with her. That she wouldn't *want* me with her.

The hallway was quiet, the sitting room was quiet, the entryway was quiet. The pathway leading to the house was quiet. But the remnants of the fence were loud, jagged splinters of wood. In this light it wasn't hard to discern the smears of blood on the broken stakes, on the stone.

Even the barn was quiet. A thread drew me there. Pulled with a tug at my rib cage.

Beau's empty stall glared at me. Instead of heading for the end of the row for my swords, I went to the beginning, to Papa's, to a weapon with a guard of burnished bronze. My face reflected back at me, fragmented and blurry but still mine.

The first seconds were the hardest—the sword was heavy. Bandages impeded my grip. I bent my knees, moved my feet so they were facing the proper direction. Shoulders back. Arm just so. I steadied myself. Then I thrust forward, steel meeting the fabric of the target dummy. This weapon didn't whisper memories, no, but he was there in the movements, teaching me how to advance and retreat all over again.

My right hand, all that raw skin under the bandages, screamed. And then: a shifting behind the window. A shadow along the golden slats.

"Tania?"

I dropped the sword. A few days ago, that would've cost me an afternoon of embroidery. The imprint of Papa's laughter floated round the rafters.

"How could you?" my mother whispered.

"I thought you were . . . that you went to . . ."

My mother's expression twisted. "Don't you start, don't you dare. You don't know what it was like, to have to see—"

"You could have taken me with you," I said.

"After last night? Do you realize what you could have done if I hadn't found you?" She let out a quake of a sigh when she saw my hand. "And now you've gone and opened up the wounds."

"I didn't," I retorted. "I would have felt it."

Her lips were pursed tight; even though she didn't speak I knew what she was thinking: How would I know? How could I? How could I when I'd proven time and time again that I wasn't in control of my own body?

"Maman," I tried. "It helps me. It makes me happy. Can't you see? I can fence even when I'm dizzy: Papa taught me. I'm not as good as some, but I have passion. And with more training maybe—"

"You'll be happy when you're safe."

"You mean when I'm married to someone of your choosing whom I don't care about," I scoffed.

"You know your dizziness complicates things."

"But that doesn't change anything!"

"It changes everything."

"It doesn't change what I want."

She broke the silence before I could. "There's something you need to see," she said.

We headed to the parlor. The one room that was always hers, within a house that now belonged only to her. She gestured to the seat across from her miniature desk and fiddled with a key; after a click, she pulled out a drawer hidden underneath an overhang of reddish wood. She closed the secret compartment, letter in hand. "Go ahead. Before I left, I went through his things for papers to prove who he was so I could collect . . . him. And that's when I found it."

My hands froze at the familiar handwriting.

To my wife and daughter, whom I love with my whole being: If you're reading this, it means I am no longer with you. Hopefully there will be no such need for this letter, and when one of us finds it decades from now we'll have a good laugh about the paranoia growing older is wont to bring. It is not that I am afraid of what comes after; I have stared Death in the face more times than I can count. Each time it is achingly familiar.

I don't intend to leave this world willingly. But if my death comes to pass, I've made arrangements, ma femme, for you to live the way you want.

The house is yours, however you wish it. Do not hold on to it for my sake. I know you long in your heart to be closer to your brother, to your nieces and nephews—you never wanted this life, but I selfishly insisted. I thought that loving someone meant making sacrifices, and that meant it was all right for you to sacrifice for me. But I know now that when you love someone, you shouldn't ask them to make sacrifices for you. My remedy for this is to give you a choice now without anything to hold you back. I can only apologize for not giving you the same when I was alive, and—

An extra, added fold of paper covered the next part of the letter. I made to move it, but my mother grabbed my hand. "That's private."

"I don't understand."

"I put it there."

Curiosity wrenched my throat, but as I traced over the added layer of paper with my unwounded fingers, I saw the fragile, telltale crease of dried tears. I skipped to the unobscured paragraph.

If Tania has not yet found her way, I have secured a spot for her at Madame de Treville's newly formed L'Académie des Mariées. I assume Madame de Treville's reputation, which will surely impact the school's prestige and influence, is not one that could so quickly fade since the time of my writing. Mademoiselle la Mousquetaire, embarking upon this adventure is my final request of you, passed along with all the love I could possibly give. I trust you will follow my instruction and do your duty to bring honor upon the name de Batz.

What did he mean, "if Tania has not yet found her way"? And all this talk of reputation. Papa could care less about what others thought.

My mother drummed her fingers along the desk; I used to do

that, too, but she'd told me it was unladylike. Men wanted quiet wives, quiet wives with quiet nervous habits. Not even our bad traits, our unconscious traits, belonged to us.

"I won't pretend to know what prompted your father to write this letter. What I do know is that it was in his study, in the secret drawer of that desk le menuisier lent him after the robbery—you remember Monsieur Ballou, the furniture maker from Bretagne with the son your father taught fencing to a few years ago?"

"You were in Papa's study?"

She fixed me with a look that dried up any further questions. I reread the letter. Halfway through, I screeched to a halt, eyes caught.

"Maman?" I hated how my voice shook, how my heart throbbed in my ears, hated how in that moment I felt as dizzy as if I were standing in a wide-open space with nothing and no one to catch me. "Maman, this school . . . L'Académie des Mariées . . ."

"The Academy for Wives, yes."

". . . This can't be right. Papa wouldn't want me groomed to be some stranger's wife—to marry someone who is old enough to be my father and is either a merchant who spends all his time seeking out new schemes or a gentleman who does nothing but attend parties and waste money in cabarets!"

"That is unfair. There are plenty of eligible bachelors who will make adequate husbands."

"Adequate? *Adequate?* This is the person I'll spend the rest of my life with!"

Her eyes sparked. "Don't be so naive as to not see the importance in a secure marriage."

"What is security if I can't stand the man?"

She picked up the letter from where I'd left it on the desk.

"First impressions can change. You may think a man dull, maybe even ill-suited for you, but that same man could very well be kind, considerate of your needs." She continued, not knowing how her words ate away at me. "Love can come in time—you mustn't insist on it as a prerequisite."

"But you married for love!"

She set the paper down and then looked at me, really looked at me. "Tania," she implored, softer than everything that'd come before it, "you know you are different."

I braced myself against the desk as I rose. "I won't do it."

"It's what your father wanted."

"How can you think that?"

"For once would you do what I say!" my mother exploded.

"Is this a punishment? Telling me that he thought you were right all along, that I can't take care of myself? That I'd have to find someone to trick into taking care of me?" Light flickered at the periphery of my vision, gray hills rolling over the horizon. "You're lying; he'd never do this to me!"

She shoved the paper at me. There was the familiar curve of my father's hand, the flourish of his signature.

"You must have had someone forge it." My mother's pained laugh was barely audible over the rushing of my heart. "You realize what this means? He knew someone was after him. It wasn't highway bandits—it *couldn't* have been highway bandits." I thought back to that last moment with my father: how he told me France wasn't as safe as he'd made it seem. How he wanted me to keep my sword in my room while he was gone.

The letter wasn't old. The unfaded ink, yes, but also the only time I'd heard Madame de Treville's name spoken was on that ill-fated night last week, from the mouth of Madame Chaumont herself. The academy was a newer venture, one recently introduced to the public. I didn't notice Papa paying much attention to Madame Chaumont's comments. What else hadn't I noticed?

Why write this letter now? Did he know what fate would meet him on that dark road? Was he afraid of someone skilled enough to best a Musketeer, someone with no pride, no honor? Someone who would carve his face into a mask his family wouldn't recognize?

"Please, I can't continue on like this," my mother said. "Your father knew I was worried that if anything were to happen to him, I wouldn't be able to care for you forever. So, he found a way for you to be taken care of."

I reached out my hand. She didn't move away. She let my hand touch hers. "Don't you want to know who did this?" I asked.

"Revenge isn't for everyone." Her voice was glazed; her eyes were glazed. "I'm tired, Tania. I've been fighting every day against different things and different people. And I'm tired."

She was so very lost, and all I wanted was to grip her hand tighter, to pull her through this unknown space and out the other side. If I'd known the directions, if I could've drawn her a map, I would've done it in an instant. I would have ripped up the precious books in my room for paper and used my tears for ink. I would've taken care of her like she'd taken care of me. Been the one to keep her upright and lead her where she needed to go. But that was the thing about maps—they only worked if the mapmaker knew the coordinates. If the mapmaker knew the route that would lead her through the darkness.

I trust you will follow my instruction and do your duty to bring honor upon the name de Batz.

Honor, duty. Two things Papa held closer than anything else. That the Musketeers held closer than anything.

There'd be no place at Madame de Treville's academy for a sick girl. Perhaps my father had disclosed my condition to this Madame de Treville, perhaps not, but she wouldn't want my name attached to hers once she realized the extent of my dizziness.

But a spot in her academy would get me to Paris. And Paris meant the Musketeers: the only people left in the world who could help me. If I could hide my condition long enough, hide the reason I wanted—no, needed—to be in Paris . . . then maybe, maybe when Madame de Treville introduced me to important nobles, I could gain the allies necessary to introduce me to senior members of la Maison du Roi. *They* wouldn't care that my family didn't have money to lavish on them. All they'd care about was discovering the truth of their fallen brother. That's what he would've done if the situation was reversed.

If I went to Paris, I could find out what really happened to Papa.

My father wanted me to show honor, to show duty. And I would. Even if this entire time—teaching me to fence, telling me to be brave—he thought me incapable of finding my own path, like my mother did. Even if fury and grief intermingled in my heart.

"I'll . . . I'll do it."

My mother's surprised eyes filled with tears. She squeezed my hand once, twice, and sealed my fate.

Tania. Tania. Tania.

Outside the parlor, my scorching face pressed to the closed door, I breathed in his voice.

"I love you, Papa," I murmured. "Show me how to forgive you for this. I can't spend my entire life hating you. I can't."

The voice was silent.

CHAPTER EIGHT

STRANGE, HOW SOMEONE'S life could be condensed into one traveling trunk.

In went all the things that made me *me*. They didn't feel much like me, though. Books first. An extra pair of shoes, the unfinished embroidery. When I folded the fancy blue embroidered dress, all I could see were blue eyes. But they weren't kind, no; they were haughty and proud.

My sword, the one I'd kept in my room, mocked me from the corner. A lady had no reason to keep a weapon. It couldn't be kept in a wardrobe with fine satin gowns and torturously tight corsets. And then there was the matter of propriety. Being a woman meant being soft and smooth and breakable. A husband's job was to protect his wife. For her to have a weapon would imply she thought him incapable of performing his duty.

But I wasn't married. Not yet.

When I picked up the sword, it became part of my arm, as if my skin were melded to the steel. Intricate metalwork made up the body of the guard and was crafted into the shape of spiraling leaves, so fine they were like lace. Lighter than most weapons—

better for my build. Even with the anger that clawed at any memory of my father, the moments still came to me in miniature: the first time he presented me with a wooden practice sword, my peals of laughter reverberating around the rafters, my four-year-old self dashing across the uneven floorboards littered with straw and sunlight. And then, the day he replaced the practice sword with a real one. How he'd smiled, held it to the light, even bowed as he said, "Mademoiselle, your saber."

For a split second, my father's telltale smile flashed in the flat of my blade. But then it was gone. I was alone. I stored the sword in my trunk.

"Tania?" My mother waited at the door. "Are you all right?" An achingly slow wave of exhaustion rolled over me. "Tania?"

"I'll be fine."

She stared, not really at me but through me. "Let me help you."

"The groomsman can—"

"I am not so weak that I cannot help you move a mere trunk." She used both hands, put the weight of her body behind the motion. I hurried to help. A broken girl and a broken mother might not make a whole, but we managed.

She stood carefully, unfurled her body and angry red fingers. When she stretched, her shoulder blades convulsed against the fabric. It was not just that she was thin. She was brittle.

My mother could've forced me to stay with her. Could've ripped up the letter and decided it was more important for a daughter to be with her maman. But my father wanted a life for her without me. Without having to worry about me. That was how she—he—*they* saw me—*no, no. Papa loved you. Maman loves you.*

And yet: the tear straight down my middle, the pain of fracturing. If only I were less. If only I were less of everything that I was.

It had been two weeks since Papa's death. My mother wrote Madame de Treville the day I accepted the offer. The response had arrived yesterday: I was to be in Paris in no greater than two weeks' time.

"I have something for you." My mother's voice broke through my thoughts. Papa's gold signet ring rested in her palm. "I have the wax seal. He wanted you to have the signet ring. He never took it on his trips; it was too precious."

"His letter didn't mention it," I said.

"No, but he must have mentioned the ring to me a dozen times—it's from his days as a Musketeer. The whole thing became a bit of a joke. Him reminding me how he wanted you to have it, me telling him he shouldn't talk like that . . ." Her voice faltered. "I thought maybe you'd like a chain. You could hardly wear the ring; it'd be too large." Surprise spread through me, warm. I turned so she could clasp the chain. It was long, the ring sitting well below my neckline.

An audible thump: my sword. The hired groomsman, who lifted my trunk into the luggage frame, raised his brows as I avoided eye contact. "It's so hard to properly pack shoes, don't you think?" When everything was stowed, I entered the carriage. My mother murmured to the groomsman and passed him a few extra coins. It was strange to look down on her; she'd always been taller than me.

"Tania, I . . ." She faltered. But then she sighed. "Travel safe. Lock your door at night. Your uncle and aunt will arrive tomorrow to fetch me for a few weeks away, while I decide what to do moving forward. Send word once you're settled. And be on your best behavior—this is your chance to find a suitable husband. Please try to remember that."

I searched her face, her dark irises that reflected mine, the dark hair we shared, the way her body was bowed toward me, her shoulders the crest of a wave. I did not tell her that this chance had so much more hinging on it than a potential marriage. If I was successful, I would guarantee that my father's killer wasn't free to kill again. The Musketeers would make sure of that.

"Well," she said, clearing her throat. "I need to go pack. And you need to get going so you're not late. Madame de Treville is expecting you." My mother went back into the house. As the carriage pulled away, I stuck my head out the opening. She was in the kitchen window, unmoving. Our eyes met.

She lifted her hand. And I lifted mine in return.

Finally, la France, in all its majesty: rolling fields, villages with markets teeming at the outskirts, church bells that tolled toutes les heures, on the hour. Flowers that unfurled into remarkable shapes, people brimming round every corner. Pastoral scenes that shifted to clustered towns. Everything was new, bright, brilliant.

Yes, pauvre Tania, sick Tania, was finally seeing France. And none of it mattered.

The empty space next to me gaped, an open wound. I never thought I'd travel farther than Bretagne. What reason would a sick girl have to leave Lupiac? To even leave southern France? Still, though, in daydreams, I had imagined a trip to Paris with my father. Two weeks on the road with him narrating our travels.

He'd point out each and every town he'd visited. I would've had the chance to hear stories of my father's courage and fortitude in voices that weren't his own.

"How am I supposed to fence when I'm so dizzy?"

"You're right. The dizziness is a problem."

I hadn't expected his response. *"Well, that's reassuring."*

"You misunderstand. It's a problem, oui. But one we can work around."

"How?"

"You have to be better than everyone else. You have to work harder, train harder, ensure your muscles remember the actions. You have to be in tune with your opponent so you can feel when they're going to attack, feel it when the air shifts, see how their body tenses before they lunge. Then it will not matter if you are dizzy. Because even if you're not as fast, even if you must grab onto the wall for support, even if your opponent's body is a blur, you will know exactly what to do in each and every moment."

I jerked awake, barely avoiding hitting my head against the carriage wall. The ring bounced on my chest, metal warm against my breastbone. My tenth day imprisoned in a shell of scratched wood and gold paint. Normally, it would take just over two weeks to travel from Lupiac to Paris, but my mother had arranged for us to exchange horses twice along the way—an extravagance that must've cut severely into her already limited savings. But the social season was fast approaching, and the letter we received from Madame de Treville made it clear that I'd be the last mademoiselle to arrive, months after the others. She did not strike me as a woman who liked to be kept waiting.

"Mademoiselle de Batz?" The footman rapped on the carriage roof. "We're nearly there now."

Kind, for him to give me time to prepare. Probably thought

I'd pinch my cheeks, fix my unruly hair. But I was drawn to the window. We were surrounded by orchards. Groves of trees weighed down by orange fruit—different from drawings I'd seen of oranges—fuzzier, somehow. The air was syrupy and dense with the hum of insects.

"Are you sure we—" My words died.

That was the moment. The moment entering Paris when I lost my breath. Not at the glimpse of le Palais du Luxembourg, the front so vast and me so incredibly small, not at the sight of the Notre Dame, arches so high they seemed to break the cloud line. It wasn't even when I first laid eyes upon the Palais du Louvre. No, it was the moment those wheels met stone, and I saw all of Paris spread out like a village of little dolls against the waning light of day. This Paris was nothing like the Paris of my hazy dreams.

It was loud and people-full and the smell stuck to the inside of my nose and grime was everywhere and oh, it was beautiful.

The carriage paused once at the open city gate. Wheels crackled over a drawbridge. If not for the pungent, murky water, the moat would've seemed out of a storybook. And then we were swallowed by city walls. Remnants of musket fire stained the inner stone—remains of the Grand Condé's desperate power grab that had resulted in his and many other nobles' exile from France, after which the King returned, triumphant. But the city bore the short occupation's wounds. How could it not, when a cousin of the King, the very cousin who'd helped the royals subdue a parliamentary uprising, had turned on his family?

In the muggy darkness, I was back to cool flickering candlelight: my father regaling me with stories of La Fronde, the civil wars, that gripped hold of Paris until two years ago. Stories of deception, of cowardice, of greed, Condé's name stinging on our lips. My mother used to protest. I was eleven, she said, far too young to hear what his old colleagues had written to him in their letters, but my father was adamant that it was the perfect way to illustrate to me what he'd fought for. To him, Condé was the worst kind of man. Once a loyal subject, warped by avarice and lust only sated by ruling France. Taking advantage of the monarchical system for his own greed. The true antithesis of a Musketeer. At least, my father's Musketeers. My father's Musketeers who protected the King to protect France. To keep foreign adversaries from raining bloodshed on the city. Musketeers like Papa, who knew a transfer of power meant the deaths of thousands of innocents in the process. Musketeers like Papa, who protected those who needed protection.

The Musketeers who he'd told me no longer existed.

Condé was thrust from my mind at the sight of buildings. Small ones at first: workers' residences and stalls. A man was selling roasted hazelnuts, and a young boy sneaked forward to grab a bag before taking off, the angry man at his heels. Then, an explosion of stores and residences that reached to the sky. Smatterings of cobblestone, wood planks, clouded slate.

Once we turned off the narrow, crooked side street and onto the main boulevard, everything opened and breathed. Especially upon entering Le Marais—one of the neighborhoods from my father's stories. The favored home of la noblesse. Each extravagant hôtel particulier, each grand city mansion, basked in the glow of countless street candle lamps. Ornamental trees lined the cobblestone, contorted into the most fantastical shapes and creatures: A griffin clawing at passersby. A phoenix rising triumphant from leafy flames.

There were fewer people here. But there were more guards scattered along the walkways, sabers glittering in their sheaves. The drifting shadows made it impossible to tell if any wore a Musketeer's blue cassock. When I was little, Papa had draped his over me; it had pooled around my feet like a formal gown. A bloodstain on the hem from when I'd tripped and knocked out my front teeth—got right back up, because that's what a Musketeer did. What a girl did when she knew nothing yet of dizziness, of exhaustion, of an unsteady world.

Through a film of tears, I watched a cluster of guardsmen pool together. One of them let out a loud crow of laughter, and another stumbled into him.

I yanked my head back before they could spot me gawking. Drunk, the lot of them. Not my father's Musketeers, indeed.

It was a few minutes more before the wheels slowed. "Your stop, Mademoiselle." The footman placed my trunk on the steps leading to the house with a huff. "I must be off. Someone will meet you, yes?" I nodded. "Very good. I wouldn't want to leave you here alone."

I turned, sharp heeled. "Is this not a safe area?"

"Oh, Mademoiselle, there's no cause for fear. It's just unwise to wander the streets of Paris alone at night. Especially for one such as yourself."

"I'm sure I don't know what you mean."

"Don't you?"

I spun to face my new home. L'Académie des Mariées. A smaller town house by Marais standards, pathways lined with emerald-tinted grass. And windows, real glass windows, interspersed by twos along the first and second floor. Well, one could assume—while the windows at eye level were framed by curtains, the windows along the second floor were shuttered from the outside. Maybe this Madame de Treville could only afford glass for the first floor and didn't want the rest of Le Marais to know?

Then again, based on what my mother learned from village gossip, la noblesse entrusted Madame de Treville with their daughters' futures. And from my father's stories of what he'd experienced in Paris and his brief time in the presence of my mother's father, I knew that the nobles' snobbery was second only to their eagerness to gain the royal family's favor. After La Fronde, he'd said, the nobles who weren't exiled remained on edge. Afraid of losing their titles, their positions in court, they were eager to return to the social seasons of before, near-hedonistic in their longing to distract themselves with parties and suitors and marriage prospects.

The night grew darker, the air a wet handkerchief, and still, no one came. The carriage was already gone, had disappeared into the steadily falling night.

What if the footman had the wrong address? What if—*what if* the driver deposited me at the wrong residence on purpose? What if he had an agreement with a murderer and was presenting me on a silver platter?

Although that might be preferable to Madame de Treville. I could protect myself from a killer with my sword.

With a deep breath, I ascended the two small steps. A sharp *rap rap rap* on the door. Silence. I reached to the side out of habit. With a surprised jolt, my fingers curled around a wrought-iron handrail.

Another breath, another knock. "Excusez-moi! Is anyone home?" The street was empty, but still, the feeling wouldn't shake—a pair of eyes tingling at my nape.

At long last, the distinct sound of footsteps. The door opened. Warm light flooded through the door frame.

"Bonsoir!" A woman beamed as she wiped her hands on her skirts.

"Good evening, Madame de Treville," I addressed her, blinking away the spots across my vision at the light. Hand on the iron rail, I began the perilous descent into a curtsy.

But the woman laughed, waved off my gesture, her hand pressed flat to her chest. "Ça alors! Goodness no! I'm Jeanne; I clean the house—well, the ground floor." She mistook the look on my face and continued, "Yes, yes, I know, maisons as grand as these usually have their own full-time staff . . . I presume you're the newest étudiante. What an honor to be her student! Your parents must be very proud."

"Merci. You are so kind."

"My dear," she said, positively brimming with compassion, "you mustn't be nervous. Madame de Treville hasn't chosen wrong yet. The other mademoiselles are the most accomplished young ladies I've ever encountered. Invited to every ball, every soirée—that is, the ones that matter." I swallowed my nerves and forced a smile. "In fact," she added, "the ladies and Madame are at one now. Come inside. Henri will bring your trunk to your room." I hesitated. "Well, come on, then! You don't want to catch a chill standing out there in the cold, do you? Imagine, falling ill right before the season! Mademoiselle, is everything all right?" she asked at my breathy laugh.

My voice hitched. "Yes. Everything is fine."

And, just like that, I stepped over the threshold and into the warm light.

Chapter Nine

"NOW, THAT'S BETTER," Jeanne said. "Looks like we could miss the rest of fall and l'hiver may come early to our fair city, non?" This city was not my city, did not belong to me or feel familiar to me like Lupiac did, so I only nodded.

She walked to an arched entrance. Behind it curled a thin hallway that echoed with clanging pots and pans. "Henri, fetch the trunk, would you?" I didn't hear the response, but she did; she laughed loud and full. "You are ridiculous. There's no reason to avoid the mademoiselles; you give Portia too much material to tease you with! You'll have them thinking you're scared of them! Now," she said, turning back, "you, you come with me."

She showed me from room to room, eventually landing on one off the main hallway. "Madame de Treville asked for me to spruce up this room, specifically." For all Jeanne's warmth and welcome, her voice tightened round the edges.

"Is she very strict, then?" I asked.

Her hand was steady on the doorknob until my question, then it traveled to her apron to twist the fabric. "Madame de Treville is a good woman. She has her rules, like everyone does. Those rules may be stranger than most, but"—she shook her head, face clearing—"it's to be expected that a gentlewoman who's a favorite of Cardinal Mazarin wants the highest standard from her employees. Now—if anything's the matter, call out for Henri. He'll probably be somewhere near the kitchens; always trying to sneak a bit more food, that boy. Bonne nuit."

Jeanne left me in an unfamiliar room in an unfamiliar city, my eyes darting from the window draped in heavy curtains to the daybed hastily covered with blankets. It clearly was designed for overnight guests.

I'd been so worried about Madame de Treville discovering the truth of my condition—but if this room was any reflection of how she viewed my place here, by this time tomorrow, I could be out on the street. And what chance would I have then at winning the Musketeers to my cause? I'd counted on learning where the senior officers were headquartered, making my case to them. But that was contingent on a reputation I hadn't yet earned for myself.

Once I was in bed, the ceiling wavered, dread pooling behind the hollow of my throat.

My plan's flaws exposed with only a simple, unfurnished room. I was nothing without Madame de Treville by my side. It wasn't like I could approach a Musketeer, brandish Papa's ring, and he would then convince everyone to investigate my father's murder. No, the only recourse was to arrange a meeting with a senior officer. And without cause, no senior officer would listen to a strange girl rambling about her father's untimely death.

My father never told me his brothers in arms' names, only used nicknames when he spun his stories. Their real names weren't what mattered, he'd said. The names they'd given one another, though—that's who they truly were. I'd never pressed him for more information; I'd figured there was no rush. I'd thought we had time. And I didn't need their real names, then. They existed in my mind as godlike creatures; they didn't need titles or surnames.

Before leaving for Paris, I'd attempted to find his records, ones with the names and addresses of his Musketeers, but my mother had his papers under lock and key. And I couldn't exactly tell her what I needed them for.

"Papa, what were you thinking?" The large expanse of wood gaped silently, little flecks of light, fractures of flames from street lanterns breaking through the night, leaking through the curtains.

Sleep overtook me, and it wasn't until I heard muffled voices that I blearily fumbled to the window. Brightly colored dresses flashed through the curtains: small segments of skirts, fragments of arms, the occasional sparkle of gems. Madame de Treville's handpicked mademoiselles. Three of them—the rest must've taken other carriages.

Their conversation was muted by the glass. A flurry of lights and voices, and then a pair of clear eyes locked on mine. I drew back. The curtains fell closed.

The front door opened. Next, shoes being removed, exchanged bonne nuits. The footsteps grew louder. Doubt rushed over me, as if I were trespassing on a sacred space. My sword remained locked in my trunk—no, they were girls focused on finding husbands, nothing more. The steps creaked up the main staircase.

Everything was quiet.

Back in bed with the covers under my chin, back to the glimpses I'd caught through glass panes, the shock of silver and gold against silk and velvet. The rubies that dripped down bouquets of organza like blood.

My father's face. His body on the side of the road with nobody to lift him up, nobody to knit him back together.

I twisted away from the window, pulling the blankets tight.

"Where exactly do you think you're going?"

Halfway down the hall the next morning, I stopped, fisting my hands in my skirts to keep them from shaking at the sight of a girl a year or so older than me. I hadn't met anyone close to my age since Jacques. And before then . . . well, everyone knew everyone in Lupiac. From each teething baby to every toothless arrière-arrière-grand-parent.

The girl squinted in appraisal. Against the sweep of the hallway she was an exclamation of color, the coral silk of her dress smooth against her deep gold skin. "You are Tania, aren't you? No one told me you didn't speak."

"I—I do."

"So, you thought you'd wander the halls until someone came to rescue you? Or maybe you were snooping, hmm?"

Heat pooled in my cheeks. "I'm sorry if I've done anything wrong, but—"

The girl whistled. "Mon Dieu, she's going to have a time of it." She shook her head. "Just because I was the last to arrive doesn't automatically make me the welcoming committee," she muttered.

"A time of what?" I asked.

Unimpressed midnight eyes narrowed under finely plucked brows. "Don't tell me you don't even know what this place is?"

"Of course. L'Académie des Mariées."

A slow grin spread across her face. "Well, then, Madame asked me to show you to her study." I looked down the hall, to the kitchens. "I don't have all day."

My apology caught between my teeth when the girl looked at me like she knew exactly what I was planning and would throttle me. I squared my shoulders. "If you'd be so kind as to show me the way, I won't keep you from your duties any longer . . ."

"Very well, then," she said with a sigh. "Keep up."

We walked in silence. If I had my way, I'd have peppered her with questions. But her unamused face gave me pause. I wanted to ask her where all the other mademoiselles were; the empty hallways were odd and hollow. And then, then I'd ask if she was familiar with any of the Musketeers, if she'd met any of them at social events, but she spoke before I had the chance. "This is it."

"Thank you, I—" but she was already gone, a flash of coral vanishing around the corner. Through the dizzy haze I saw my arm extend, my fist rap against a door decorated with intricately carved leaves.

"Come in."

The room was full of wood dark as tree bark at night—that shade of black that wasn't black at all. Three walls were swallowed by bookshelves filled with more books than I'd seen together in my entire life—was it possible for one person to own that many? Leather and fabric binding, the red and brown and orange of changing leaves. A woman I assumed was Madame Treville sat at a desk, her quill darting across paper. The wall facing her was adorned with a map of France as wide as a large man's wingspan. Next to it, identical in size: a detailed map of Paris. Similar to the diagrams I'd seen during my trip to doctor number two many years ago. Cities and bodies weren't that different, truly. Streets like blood veins. Parks like organs. The royal palace like a beating heart.

Ladies didn't have studies. I'd thought, perhaps, the girl had meant to say "parlor," a mere slip of the tongue. But this was no parlor.

The woman coughed, but continued her work as she spoke. "Portia mentioned I wanted to speak with you?" That was the girl's name, then. The one Jeanne mentioned yesterday, the one who scared . . . Henri, wasn't it?

"Yes, I . . ." She forcefully scratched something out, and I cleared my throat. "Yes, she did. I thought maybe I should go to the kitchens—"

"You don't think we eat meals there, do you?" She reached for more ink with her quill, returned to her papers.

"Well . . . no," I said.

She glanced up, took in my hands clasped in my skirts to keep from reaching for the open chair. "Sit down."

She wasn't wearing the fashionable style of gowns Marguerite and the other village girls fawned over—the neckline of her steel gray dress revealed only a hint of collarbone, and her low bun was unadorned with curls. Her back was so straight it didn't even touch the chair. I'd expected a great lady, one who draped herself in finery. Who else would be the talk of la noblesse? Instead, her clothes, although crafted out of fine fabrics, were practical in cut and style. No rings or bracelets adorned her fingers or wrists. All I knew of her character was that she was snobbish about where the household ate their meals, but still, wouldn't such a woman also be fastidious in wearing her wealth?

"My condolences on the death of your father," she said suddenly.

"Merci," I thanked her.

Her gaze was probing. Finally: "This is highly unusual. A girl joining us right before the social season with scant preparation time. Even Portia has had two months under my tutelage." Her eyes grazed the part of me not obstructed by her desk. "But your father insisted you were ready to continue your family's legacy."

"I'll do my absolute best," I said stiffly. *Remember Papa, remember Maman. Remember who you are doing this for.* Madame de Treville held all my hopes for learning the truth about my father. For making a name for myself. For succeeding in L'Académie—my father's final wish.

"And what if your best isn't good enough?" she asked.

"I . . . I don't think—"

"You're pretty enough, I suppose. You don't seem graceful, but we can work on that. But what I absolutely will not do is waste my time on a girl confused about her place in the world. I will not waste my time on a girl who doesn't know what she wants."

I pulled in a shaky breath, pulled back the burning tears threatening the crease between my nose and eyes, which went rosy red at the first sign of crying. "This is what I want."

"Truly? You want to be the wife of a rich, influential member of the noblesse?"

My tongue curled, tried to keep the word from escaping. But there was no turning back. I had to discover the truth. "Yes."

She was quiet for a long moment. I hadn't been effusive enough. I'd failed Papa before I even had a chance to try.

But then she spoke. And I couldn't believe what she said, except for the faint ringing in my ears, the rush that crackled from my toes to my forehead, my forearms rivers of goose bumps.

"I find that hard to believe, Mademoiselle la Mousquetaire."

CHAPTER TEN

THE RINGING IN my ears grew to a dull roar. "*What* did you call me?"

Her face betrayed nothing. She retrieved a letter from a pile of papers. A letter from my father. "Is that not what he called you?"

The tears returned with a sudden, unexpected vengeance. "That's private," I said.

"I'm afraid nothing is private here. We can't afford to keep secrets from one another."

"The possibility of scandal," I offered. "You want to know everything about a girl before you agree to sponsor her, in case it comes out she's a . . ." The only action or role of ill repute that came to mind was "fencer," or "sick girl," which were hardly responses, so I remained wordless.

"You could say that."

"I don't know what my father wrote, or why, but I'll be the perfect lady. It was just a silly name. He didn't mean anything by it." Each word I spoke was a sword through my heart.

She rose. Her posture had an air of finality, and I made to stand up with her, latching onto the desk. Her eyes lingered where my fingers tightened on the wood. "If you'll follow me . . ." She moved to the door.

"Madame," I found words again. "If you'd give me a chance to—"

"Mademoiselle de Batz, if you would accompany me, you'd realize I'm doing exactly that." Instead of taking a left to lead me back down the hall, past the sitting rooms with thick carpets and heavy gilded frames, she made a right, ushering me into an unfamiliar part of the house. Her steps were resolute. "I can hear you thinking," Madame de Treville said, though she didn't turn to look at me. "To prevent your continued struggle over deciding whether or not to ask: Yes, we are going upstairs."

The staircase was rapidly approaching. It wasn't just that my dizziness was dangerous on steps—the ever-present fear of fainting and tumbling not to the ground, but down a flight of stairs—but it was always stronger when trying to climb them, too: the blurry vision, the trembling of my legs, the world spinning round me. The general dizziness paled in comparison to the tidal wave that rushed over me when I tried to ascend stairs; it was why Papa had cleared out his beloved library off the entryway and fashioned it into a bedroom. And not because I came to him crying, embarrassed—it was just waiting for me when Maman and I returned home from doctor number two.

It was one thing to pretend to be someone I wasn't while sitting in Madame de Treville's study, but on the staircase, it wasn't up to me. It was up to my body. And when had I ever been able to rely on that?

"What on *earth* do you think you're doing?"

Hand poised at the shivering snake of a banister, feet planted shoulder width apart, I flinched. "Going upstairs?"

"Don't be ridiculous." She opened a nondescript door. Given her rank, I stalled for her to enter, long enough that she made a disgruntled cough before pushing through the doorway.

The room was cool. Only one window—the walls stretched vertically for at least twenty feet. Light pooled onto a structure in front of us: a pulley of sorts, one end with a swath of fabric wide enough to sit on. It hung from a landing that led to a shadowed door, hugged by a spindly staircase. It looked like a room that would've been used for a service staircase.

"I . . . I don't understand."

"Don't you?" Her voice echoed in the emptiness.

She'd said there was no room for secrets. But my father wouldn't have told her. He would've known what would happen if Madame de Treville discovered he was foisting his sick daughter on her, tricking her into putting the dizzy girl in a dainty dress and seeing if it camouflaged the gray pallor of her skin before she keeled over. If it masked how her legs crumpled. How her body, though able to wield a sword, was as fragile as the piece of paper that had sent her to Paris.

While I was lost in thought, Madame de Treville took the stairs—I only noticed once she reached the landing. "Are you going to stand there and gape? It's supremely unattractive," she said.

Apprehension gripped my sides as I approached the pulley. A glance at Madame de Treville was the only encouragement I had before I hoisted myself onto the fabric and arranged my skirts. "Now what?"

"We'll work together. I'll pull from this end, and you'll pull from yours."

Despite all her sharp angles, Madame de Treville was sturdy.

And with my arms toned from years of fencing, it wasn't long before I was rising into the air. I nearly fell out of the harness when I looked down, the floor wavering. I closed my eyes. This method of transportation was, after all, much better than the stairs.

When I opened my eyes again, I was level with Madame de Treville. She looped her end of the rope around a hook on the wall, then offered me her hand. I hesitated, but before further admonishments could leave her lips I grasped it and flung myself onto the landing. I caught my breath, clutching the wall for support. "A fear of heights. Interesting," she noted, rummaging in her tie-on pockets. "There we are." She produced a key from the bag, then unlocked the door.

The light hit me all in one rush. To the right was a hallway not unlike the one downstairs: carpeted floors, two sets of doors on either side. One was ajar. Laughter drifted through it; the mademoiselles. Marguerite, the girls looming above me, pauvre Tania—no. There was no one laughing at me. Not yet.

Madame de Treville stepped into my line of vision. "First we need to stop in here." She motioned to where the hallway widened on the left; instead of doors, there were large archways. We passed under the first archway and were met with a cool breath of air, as if we'd been enveloped by a ghost. The room that wasn't a room—because how could someone call it that, when one wall was practically two large archways—was easily the size of the first floor of my entire house.

"It's not usually this empty," Madame de Treville explained. "But we always clear it out for new arrivals. Gives us a good reason to clean." Her pointer finger swept away a fleck of dust that drifted along the curve of one arch; all her features curled in distaste.

"Tania, why do you think your father sent you here?"

My voice was cool, composed, everything I wasn't. I parroted my mother's words: "Your reputation is known throughout the entire country. Despite L'Académie being a new venture, girls would kill to secure a place under your tutelage."

"But not you," she inferred.

"That's not what I meant—"

"I have reached an age when listening to rambling is not merely a waste of my time, but truly vexing." My jaw snapped shut as she approached me. "You say other girls would kill to be in your position . . . but what would *you* kill for?" No telltale signs of dizziness, no symptoms that could've caused me to mishear what she said. Nothing but the cool air and the bright open space and Madame de Treville. "Perhaps I should rephrase. What would you *fight* for?" she inquired.

My gaze flicked to the two open archways. A shadow traveled across the floor. Guilt and fear roiled in my stomach. "I'm not sure I understand the question."

"Do you need an example? Let's take your father. He fought for his King, his country. Then of course for his brothers in arms, the Musketeers. He fought for his family; he fought for you—"

"Madame, you must be mistaken: My father surely never drew his sword on my account." The one time he'd had a chance, when the robbers stole into his office, he was too late. And I was too weak.

"There are other ways to fight for someone, Mademoiselle, than merely picking up a sword," she stated. All those hours spent training in the barn, the fence he'd built me, the times he'd told my mother that, even though my body had changed, I was still Tania . . . "I'll ask you again. Who would you fight for?"

I met her gaze directly. "Well . . . for my family, for the name de Batz. For my father. And for you." My voice cracked at the mention of Papa. Madame de Treville could never know what I truly meant: how I was already fighting for my father, in my own way. Discovering the truth was all that mattered. Not her or her academy.

"How flattering," she said. Her laugh was not a laugh.

"Madame . . ." I launched the words before I could talk myself out of it. "What exactly is it you want from me?"

She started toward the opposite end of the room. "By now, you must know I'm aware of your condition. The pulley was the idea of mon neveu—always tinkering and building new inventions, my nephew. A success, I'm guessing, seeing as we didn't have to peel you off the ground." I cringed, but she continued to pace. "I wouldn't go to these lengths for just anyone. But you are de Batz's daughter. We were close friends when we were young. I couldn't turn his only child away. He wrote of a girl brave enough to know she'd fall every day but who still pursued what she wanted relentlessly." Her lips tightened as she surveyed me. "But the painting doesn't match the subject. Just a girl ready to settle for a life she doesn't want and too meek to tell the truth."

I curled my fury inward. Dug my nails into the flesh between forefinger and thumb.

She clapped. I startled as the noise thundered around the empty space. "Let's get started, then."

A clang of metal, a screech of steel. All of a sudden, my sword, the one I'd hidden in my trunk, was skating across the floor, a figure scuttling back out of sight. I reached out earlier than my vision indicated—dizziness wreaked havoc on depth perception—and narrowly caught it.

I made the mistake of not squealing away like a mademoiselle should. Gave away one of my secret truths, one that would surely have me thrown out of L'Académie. But even if I wanted to put the sword down, I wasn't sure I'd be able to. It was the one familiar thing in this unfamiliar room. The steel danced in the spangled light.

"Don't think about letting go; you'll need it," Madame de Treville called out.

"What do you want from me?" I asked again, anger finally bleeding into my voice.

"What I want? I want to see if your father overexaggerated." She retrieved a sword from a corner pooled in shadows.

My father was right—an opponent would never wait for you to attack.

I parried her blade instinctively, steel meeting steel, the crash of swords sweeter than any music. Instead of attacking, I waited. Watched her movements, looked for weaknesses. When you knew nothing about your opponent, the last thing you should do was rush.

"A defensive tactician. I should have guessed," Madame de Treville said before she attacked again. I took a few quick steps back, beat her blade to the side. A lunge. Another parry. Another jump back.

Out of the corner of my vision, I felt multiple sets of eyes watching as we exchanged blows. My arm ached, but it was wonderful; it was painful, but it was like coming home.

My father's signet ring bounced on its chain as I turned and nearly caught Madame de Treville by surprise. Difficult, with no breeches underneath my skirts—I couldn't tuck the fabric back. My blade glinted as I cut once, twice, my feet featherlight on the floor. When my father had taught me the action, blade shifting right, then left, he'd said it was like a ballet. I'd laughed as he leaped awkwardly around the stables.

But the action wasn't worth Madame de Treville's approval. It was too fast, too quick, too off-balance. Black dots pooled, leached into my vision. I cursed. Tried to blink away the darkness. Kicked the hem of my skirts out of the way.

Another lunge. Another parry. Counterparry. Feint to the left. My sword was obscured in a black cloud.

Pain bloomed near my wrist, inches away from the faint hairthin scars that crossed my palms. My sword clattered to the ground. I stumbled, hands keeping me from colliding with the wall.

I was dueling Madame de Treville. Madame de Treville, the head of L'Académie des Mariées. Madame de Treville, a renowned member of Parisian high society. Madame de Treville, the lady molding girls into suitable wives for men twice their age, men who expected their wives to be ready and waiting whenever they deigned to come home, expected them to be the jeweled envy of other nobles.

Who was this woman?

And what was this *place*?

"Did she pass?" Portia's voice. Even through the haze, as my world turned in on itself, I could see, or maybe I just knew, that Madame de Treville was nodding.

The press of a cool compress to my neck. The scurry of footsteps, a door closing. I opened my eyes; I was back in Madame de Treville's study.

"You put on quite a show. The girls are excited to meet you," Madame de Treville said. "You've already met Portia, but there's also Théa and Aria. Théa's been here since the end of spring; Aria since mid-March. Seven months since Aria arrived"—she shook her head as she spoke and snapped her fingers—"flew by, like that."

When I arrived at L'Académie des Mariées, I was sure I knew exactly what it held in store for me. But those sureties had dissolved as easily as smoke. "One minute I'm being interrogated, and the next someone throws my sword at me." I grimaced at the bite of the cold compress. "A sword that was hidden in my trunk."

"I couldn't tell you the truth until I assessed your skill levels, or else risk jeopardizing our existence. If you'd failed, we would've had to make other arrangements for you." She placed her hands in her lap. "I'm sure you've guessed by now that this isn't a finishing school. At least, not one that prepares young women to become wives of lords and vicomtes. If I'm to tell you everything, you'll be sworn to secrecy."

"You have my word," I promised. Why was my silence so important? Unless . . . I sat up straighter, realization cutting through the fog in my brain.

A hint of a smile graced Madame de Treville's hard mouth. "Beginning to catch on? I train mademoiselles, but not to become docile, subservient wives." She stood and stroked her fingers down the spine of a leather-bound book, expression unblunted. "I train them to become a new kind of Musketeer. One who fights for France with her wit and charm as well as her sword."

"A spy," I breathed out.

"Far too simple a term. Under my tutelage, you'll transform into one of the most desirable young women to grace the Parisian social scene and one of the most skilled fencers to ever call themselves a Musketeer. You'll go to parties, receive the most highly sought invitations, entrance men to reveal their secrets. Distract them while your sisters in arms sneak into private offices and steal away evidence. You'll find enough information to keep them quiet. And if not . . ." She drew up her skirts to reveal breeches like the ones Papa gave me years ago. A dueling sword on her left hip, a dagger on her right. "We are not without honor. Killing another in cold blood is despicable. So, you'll duel. And when you duel, you'll win. Not only will you have the skill, but you'll also have the element of surprise: Who will suspect a beautiful woman to be one of the finest fencers this city has ever seen?"

I shook my head. She crossed the room and bent so we were level. "You're a smart girl. Did you really believe your father would send you off to be married to someone you hardly knew?"

Oh, Papa. Even though I came to Paris on his order, came as a last attempt to discover the truth, there'd still been anger burning low within me. My resentment a jagged, unsharpened blade. And yet, all this time . . .

Madame de Treville's voice was supple, slow, a whisper of a

memory. "When I was a girl, I wanted nothing more than to be a Musketeer. I insisted that your father train with me nearly every day—I had to be fantastic to have the slightest chance at earning a spot. We grew up together, fell in love with fencing at the same age . . . I'm sure our parents expected us to marry, despite my disinterest in everything marriage entailed. Thankfully, before they tried to force my hand, he met your mother—scandal followed, of course. Her father's disapproval . . . Anyway, the letter he sent was the first contact we'd had in decades, but his words brought it all back. His kindness for a young girl who wasn't what people told her she should be." She studied her papers, deep in thought. "I'm sure you can guess what happened next. None of my training mattered. The very thought of a woman in the Musketeers sent senior officials into hysterics. Now I've been given a chance, you see, to earn that respect. Not in the way I wanted, of course; it's too late for me. But not for you."

"I . . ." She waited expectantly as I stammered. "I don't believe this."

"Which part? That a woman could be a Musketeer? That she could do as much, if not more, for her country than her male counterparts?"

I didn't answer, couldn't answer that it was a combination of all these things—because how could I become the creature she spoke of? I wasn't beautiful, wasn't cunning, couldn't manipulate others to my own advantage. Sick girls did not have men falling at their feet. "You speak as if I'll be some sort of legend. A hero from a storybook," I whispered.

"You will be so much better." Insistent now, she gripped her desk as if she were crushing a throat. "You will be a siren. A gladiator. Beauty that lures evil to its side before stabbing it through the heart." Her body relaxed as she straightened. "Or you may resign yourself to being a wife to a man you'll probably know nothing about. A life without fencing."

"There is nothing wrong with that," I said, my voice trembling.

"If that is what you want, perhaps. But that isn't what *you* want, is it?"

I wanted to bring Papa's killers to justice; I wanted Maman to breathe without the weight of my world bearing down on her breastbone; I wanted to prove Papa right, that I was capable, strong, a flame; I wanted to prove Maman wrong, show her that I was so much more than she thought I was and what she'd have me be; I wanted I wanted I wanted. I wanted too much.

For a moment, a brief, blissful moment, my father's voice whistled through me, all his stories of brotherhood, divine brotherhood, brotherhood that would cross mountains and leap oceans for one another. With the dizziness had come the absence of Marguerite, my mother's lack of faith, but my father's stories had been constant. And so was the longing for sisterhood, for loyalty, for honor. The longing for something for myself.

My tears pooled in the hollow of my neck. "No," I rasped. "I don't want to give up fencing."

"What was that?" she asked. But I couldn't say it any louder. A whisper of air against my warm skin. "Tania, you have a decision to make. You can choose to forget this ever happened. Or . . ."

"Or I could stay here. Train with you," I finished.

"You held yourself well, despite your dizziness. Your father was correct: You're a talented swordswoman. But as I said before, training will not solely consist of fencing. You'll learn the manners and customs expected from a high-ranking lady: dancing, the basics of etiquette—the rules the noblesse live by. And then, of course, the fine art of wrapping men around your finger." I blanched as Madame de Treville did her best not to smirk at my expression. "So, what will it be?"

This was what Papa had wanted for me. The weight of his absence lunged once more, caught me by the throat. His voice ringing in my ears, calling my name over and over and over. His last act wasn't a betrayal, but a blessing. If I stayed, I could fence . . . and based on what Madame de Treville described, I'd have the chance to gain access to the spaces and people I needed to discover the truth. It wouldn't be so hard, would it, to appeal to the Musketeers when I was one of them?

This was what it would take, then. To catch Papa's killer. And it was a price I needed to pay. I couldn't let his murderer go free. He needed to be behind bars, where he would never hurt anyone again. Would never take another father away from his daughter.

"This decision isn't one to be made lightly, so if you need more time to—"

"I accept."

"Well, then," Madame de Treville said. "Welcome to les Mousquetaires de la Lune."

CHAPTER ELEVEN

MADAME DE TREVILLE told me to wait in the entry-way while she spoke to the other mademoiselles in the sitting room. I did my very best to keep my shoulders back, my head upright. But my cheek found its way to rest against my palm, my elbow on a side table, as I sat on a stool pushed up against the wall.

Before she left, we discussed my training regimen: fencing in the morning, followed in the afternoon by special lessons to transform me into a Musketeer. Sometimes I'd practice with the others, sometimes by myself—the latter especially when the others had social events to attend. Madame de Treville was adamant I was nowhere near ready to step foot outside the house.

Despite how that comment rankled, I was stunned to hear her so knowledgeable about my dizziness. My father's letters must've been very detailed. She knew in the past I had to work up to my skill level from back before I was sick, that my condition became more manageable when I started training again in earnest . . . I thought Papa was the only one who'd ever make the connection, but Madame de Treville also seemed to grasp how fencing helped me. She even had plans for additions to my training, in order to make me as strong as possible.

All of that had sounded fine—until I'd remembered that other, minute detail. In the moment, I'd barely gotten the words out. "But if I'm to . . . seduce," I said, my voice cracking, "these men—"

"Targets."

"Targets. If I'm to make them desire me, won't they take account of how strong I am?"

"It's not as if they'll see you in your underthings."

"I didn't mean that! I only thought if we were to dance, they would notice—"

"That your arms are more muscular than the average Parisian mademoiselle? Not to worry," she said, grinning. "When I'm through with you they won't be focusing on your *arms*."

How I didn't expire from embarrassment right then and there was beyond me.

Horseshoes clopped through the window. I examined the wall across from me in the entryway. Little painted roses. Soft pink, then mauve, then royal purple.

"Excusez-moi . . ." A cough, a raised voice. "Excuse me, Mademoiselle?"

With a jolt, I nearly fell off the stool. A boy around my age rushed to help me. But I'd already righted myself, so all that was left for him to do was straighten from his crouched position, then lean against the table—the table with an extravagant floral arrangement. The vase teetered, white lilies and all, before he narrowly caught it in the crook of one arm, his other carrying a stack of papers and a few quills. After letting out an audible wheeze, he returned it to the center of the table, then took a not-too-subtle step away. He'd left ink stains on the engraved porcelain.

"I'm sorry," I said, trying to hold in a mix of nervous and genuine laughter. "You were so quick to help me, it really is my fault—"

"It was funny," he admitted. I flushed, glanced away. When I looked back, he'd quieted. "I've only just realized—oh, I've been impolite. Such a mess I've made of everything." He adopted the appropriate stance for a formal bow. And it was silly, very much so. But his eyes sparkled all the while, as if he were aware of his awkwardness, had accepted it as immutable fact. "Allow me to formally introduce myself. Monsieur Henri, at your service."

"Why does your name . . . oh! I was wondering where to find you. I wanted to thank you."

"Thank? Me?" He enunciated each word as a separate question.

"For moving my trunk," I said. What if it wasn't him? What if I had the wrong person; what if he took offense to the thought and I'd added yet another name to the list of people who thought I didn't belong? But then who else would introduce himself by his given name, other than someone of this household? "You did move my trunk . . . didn't you?"

"You're Tania de Batz," he exhaled. The way he said my name. As if it belonged to something—someone—beautiful. "Oh, introductions! I'm an apprentice with Monsieur Sanson, the mapmaker." He scratched his head; his fingertips left a bit of ink near his hairline. A streak of black blue trailed into light golden-brown waves. "But what I really want to be is an engineer. I don't want to note down where pretty parks and palaces are; I want to plan them, how the city will work, organize the mechanics of it." His expression grew more and more animated as he spoke. Once he released the final words, he let out a breath. "It must sound inconsequential to someone like you."

"Someone like me?" I asked.

"You'll be making real, tangible change. I swear the old man's trying to drive me out the door with all the inane busywork he has me doing."

"How did you—did I say—" I croaked out.

"You didn't give it away; I already knew!" he insisted at the sight of my face. "Don't worry! It would be hard to keep the whole operation from her family, after all. Especially since I live here."

I stared up at this beaming, bumbling boy who'd nearly destroyed all the furniture in the entire entryway. "You're Madame de Treville's *son?*"

"Her nephew."

A door closed, sharp. Madame de Treville. "I see you've had a chance for introductions," she remarked while striding forward. She stopped next to Henri, then frowned and used a handkerchief to polish away the ink stains on the vase. "Don't you have work to attend to? How you spend so much time here when you're employed elsewhere is beyond me. If you don't succeed, we'll never hear the end of it from your mother." Her words might've ended in a huff, but fondness creased the corners of her eyes.

"Of course, Tante."

"Tania, there's much to be done. The tailor arrives at half past three." She turned to Henri, who was waiting too close to her shoulder. "I thought you said you had work to do?"

He stumbled over the carpet as he twisted in the other direction. "It was a pleasure to meet you, Mademoiselle de Batz! Au revoir!"

I started to wave but recognized my foolishness immediately

and made to curtsy instead—the shallowest of dips to keep the dizziness at bay.

"It's nice to see that you aren't upset," Madame de Treville said.

Midcurtsy, I glanced over my shoulder. "Excusez-moi?"

"He retrieved the sword from your trunk," she said. "I expected you to be a bit put out."

Stomach in my throat, I spun on my heel to see Henri vanish. He'd gone through my things—my books, my clothes . . . *my underthings*.

Nothing came out but stuttering. Madame de Treville sighed. "Oh goodness, Tania, of course I didn't have him go through your personal items. I had Portia search for the sword, not Henri. Besides, even if I asked, he'd be so uncomfortable at the very thought that he might never do me a favor again. But do you know what this"—she gestured to my face in all its blistering glory—"interaction tells me? No matter how much fire resides in you, I'm going to have to devote, at minimum, an entire week of training to keep you from turning the color of a tomato in front of men!"

The room was deathly quiet. Full of exquisite furniture, walls draped in lavish, thick fabrics, pale yellow and green and azure. I lifted my teacup. Took in the stony expression on Madame de Treville's face, set it on the end table. The cup clattered in its saucer. Papa surely didn't feel this way when he was meeting his brothers in arms. He might've been nervous, but he didn't have to worry about an uncomfortable neckline or being judged on a body he couldn't control.

Portia, still glaringly bright in her coral dress, sniffed, brought her cup to her lips, and sipped delicately. She'd been under Madame de Treville's tutelage for just over two months. The girl next to her, Théa, was smaller. Her ringlets took up half her head. She'd been here three months but still acted like a visitor, her dark inquisitive gaze drinking in the room. Did the others notice me doing the same? When she landed on me every so often, she smiled. The last girl, Aria, was perched on an uncomfortable-looking stool: back straight, shoulders arranged like she was sitting for a portrait. But it was more a state of awareness than good posture—as if she were constantly assessing her surroundings. If I lasted seven months with Madame de Treville, maybe I'd morph into a similar creature. Was that what it would take to catch Papa's killer?

I kept waiting for one of them to bring up how I fainted. Maybe they'd develop a new nickname for me. Another to add to the collection. Pauvre Tania, invalide . . . I kept waiting for their gazes to sparkle with derision, to look at me like Marguerite did, tell me that I had nothing, no one. That I was nothing. That I was no one.

"Tania. That's not a French name," Portia said suddenly. I startled. It didn't sound like a question . . . should I answer? I didn't know the proper conduct in such a situation. I looked to Madame de Treville, who did not speak. "Bohemian, I think," Portia continued, setting her teacup back in its saucer.

I cleared my throat. "Russian," I said. My namesake was my mother's favorite grandmère, Tatiana, a woman whose likeness graced a miniature on the mantel in our parlor. At least, it had been on our mantel. Back before the packing of trunks and stowing away of precious objects. The silence was painful. "Portia isn't French either, is it?"

She looked up in surprise—maybe even approval?

"To the important matters at hand: Théa, you'll join us with the tailor," Madame de Treville interjected, which put an end to any further questions. "You know all those strange new words for seams and threads and whatnot. Portia, Aria, you'll work on the gavotte. We can't have another fiasco like last weekend. I could practically hear the Comtesse de Gramont's snide remarks; it was all I could do not to march across the hall and inform those friends of hers how she'd gotten that fan—I know they're in the height of fashion, but sleeping with the éventailliste, now that's an unnecessarily *extreme* course of action—"

"He stepped on my foot, not the other way around!" Portia burst out.

"That very well may be, but when the Marquis du Limoges refuses to dance on account of your egregious last turn around the ballroom, adjustments must be made. The entire mission would've been compromised if it weren't for Aria." Portia sulked on the settee, threw a frustrated glance in Aria's direction. The latter stiffened but didn't meet Portia's eyes.

Théa, who was gnawing at her lip, gave a little jolt. "Oh, Madame," she beamed, "have you told Tania the story of how les Mousquetaires de la Lune came to be? It is tradition for you to tell the story during the first meeting!" She smiled proudly, and I realized she thought she was diffusing the tension.

Portia groaned, head against the back of the seat, curls crunched against the gilded wood. "You can hardly call it a tradition if it's only happened three times thus far. And you've heard Madame tell it a hundred times since then; how can you not be bored of it?"

Aria, with the muttered interjection: "Four at most."

"In fact, I have not," Madame de Treville said.

"Oh please, tell it again!" Théa said, promptly withering under Madame de Treville's reproachful stare.

"A shortened version," Madame de Treville conceded. "Tania, I found myself in a tricky situation a few years ago. Cardinal Mazarin happened upon the aftermath."

The seconds ticked on; she couldn't be finished. All of France knew Mazarin was a prominent royal adviser—how could he have anything to do with us? "But I don't—" I started.

"If you must know, a partygoer tried to accost me while I was searching for un cabinet d'affaire." My horrified gasp was met with a belabored sigh from Portia. "I said he *tried*, Tania," Madame de Treville continued. "Within a few seconds, he was at the end of my dagger. You don't have to be a Musketeer to carry a weapon at parties, you know. Anyway, Mazarin, who coincidentally was also looking to relieve himself, did me the service of threatening the scoundrel with the might of the royal household.

"If word got out, I would've been ruined. It didn't matter that the courtier attacked me. All anyone would care is that I, a woman, threatened another noble—with a blade, no less. I had no husband or other male family members to vouch for me. The nobles had tolerated me only because my mother was a favorite of Queen Anne. Few of them actually wanted me at their parties; it was Queen Anne's favor that awarded me invites. In their minds, I was barely a member of la noblesse. But Mazarin was different. He was fascinated by me, by the dagger I kept stashed in my party dress, by the story behind it, by my learning to fence as a young girl—at that point, withholding the truth was pointless, given everything he'd already seen. And then, Mazarin made the problem disappear."

"Mazarin killed him?" I asked in surprise.

"That man could be alive, dead, or passed out drunk in a ditch. Frankly, I don't care. All I know is that, despite not being involved in La Fronde, he was one of the many nobles exiled from Paris," Madame de Treville said.

"But that doesn't explain how you came to lead—"

"All that patience while bouting, but none in conversation," she interrupted with a disdainful shake of her head. "A year ago, Mazarin wrote to me about a way to serve the King, as well as prove my skills as a swordswoman, fulfill my childhood dreams. Naturally, I was intrigued. You can imagine my surprise when he asked to meet at the palace. Very few nobles are honored with personal invitations from Mazarin; not a day later and everyone in Le Marais decided me a favorite of his, the only one, in fact, and they all conveniently put aside their earlier ambivalence in favor of treating me like a new lace import from Italy to be fawned over.

"But, the meeting. In the wake of La Fronde, Mazarin knew there needed to be safeguards. Paris—the monarchy—can't handle another Condé. There'd been rumors, you see, whisperings of discontent among the remaining nobles, of a plot over a year in the making. Condé's attempt to overthrow the King might've failed, but it inspired power-hungry members of the noblesse to try to dismantle the current monarchical regime and replace it with another. Of course, with no thought for France's poor, workers, women, immigrants, all the people they'd cut down in order to achieve their *revolution*. When a King is overthrown, he is never the first to die. The ones who strive to kill him only aim to take more power for themselves and line their own pockets.

"Mazarin needed—he needs—to find out more. All previous attempts on behalf of la Maison du Roi have floundered. Les Mousquetaires, the ones the public knows about, are spirited, brave, but unrefined. Why anyone contrived to provide those boys with firearms . . . can you imagine them trying to root out the possible culprits without giving themselves away as soon as they opened their mouths? And then there's the Garde du Corps, who present themselves well enough—the epitome of manners and prestige—but have you ever seen one of them attempt to duel?"

Everyone laughed, and I wondered if I should join in, but by the time I'd decided to, they'd quieted. The other girls weren't even bothering to watch Madame de Treville anymore; no, they were all scrutinizing me. Wondering why a sick girl was allowed in their midst, surely. Wondering why the girl who'd fainted before their very eyes wasn't out on the street. "So that's where we come in: Les Mousquetaires de la Lune," Madame de Treville finished. "The Order, for short."

"I came up with that one—quicker on the tongue but so much more mysterious," Théa piped up. "It makes us sound like something out of a *novel*!"

Madame de Treville continued without acknowledging her: "You see now, why there are only four of you. I'd initially thought three was enough, but, Tania, having you as a true swordswoman will be essential moving forward. More than four would be too much of a giveaway. We deal in subtlety and secrecy. I confer with a senior Musketeer, Monsieur Brandon, who is aware of Mazarin's plans, so we can coordinate and make sure, when the time is right, we will have the full force of la Maison du Roi at our service. But, truly, I only report in full to Mazarin."

"But . . . doesn't it bother you?" I asked.

Madame de Treville paused. "Does what bother me?"

"Well, you grew up wanting to be a Musketeer. They rejected

you, cruelly. And now you're running an order of them, but no one will ever—"

"I've made my peace," she interrupted, "with my contributions going unrecognized in history. And if you do your job properly, so will you. We are not the ones who are written into history. We are the ones who ensure history exists to be written. So maybe those men won't know the truth of who that little girl grew up to be. I'm more important to France than they are—even if they don't know it."

A rap echoed from the front of the house, and she rose to her feet. "That'll be the tailor."

When she closed the door, the entire room took one simultaneous inhale, held their breaths until her footsteps retreated down the hall. And then . . .

"I'm so happy you're here!" Théa exclaimed, bounding over to me. She wrapped her arms around my shoulders, corkscrew curls smothering my face.

I stayed there, upright and still, mind whirring with Madame de Treville's story, before Aria spoke. "Théa," she said gently, "we talked about this. Remember?"

Théa withdrew. "Oh, je suis desolée. Pardonnez-moi, je vous en prie!"

Blinking rapidly at her effusive apology and request for forgiveness, I cleared my throat. "That's kind of you, but I was just startled. That's all."

Her round face warmed. "Dieu merci!" She gave me a quick squeeze before sitting at my side. "I've been so excited—"

"*We've* been," Portia interjected.

"Right, we've been so excited. Hardly been able to sleep for weeks—ever since Madame de Treville told us. It's only the three of us here, aside from her. And Henri, of course, and Jeanne, who comes by every so often, but no other girls our age who we can actually talk to, you know, really talk to without worrying about giving away our secret. Do you think you could teach me that parry you took against Madame?" Théa switched rapidly from point to point as her eyes glimmered. Not with scorn, not with disdain. Not with those familiar reactions I'd grown accustomed to. No, her face was filled with something more—something I hadn't seen since Papa left the barn all those mornings ago. "You should've seen yourself. Tu étais incroyable! Incredible, truly incredible."

"You should have seen *us*," Portia said. "I had to simultaneously pick my jaw up off the floor and stop this one from breaking out into applause."

"I wasn't clapping!" Théa insisted. "Fine, maybe I cheered, but not too much—I didn't want to distract you. Although Madame de Treville would say we need to practice dueling with distractions. It's like she always says, the world around us won't stop because we're fighting for our lives!"

"Don't think too much of our earlier apathy," Portia said once Théa paused to inhale. "Mine most of all. It's harder than I thought . . . welcoming someone new into the fold. You're nothing like what we expected." No, they couldn't have been expecting a girl who could hardly stand on her own two feet. "We knew you were a good fencer, but not like *that*." She shook her head. "And lord knows we need good fencers; if we fail, the entire operation fails with us. If we aren't ready, and we let another uprising flourish . . . they'll kill the King. And even worse: Mazarin and the Musketeers will never let women into their ranks again."

"Portia!" Théa exclaimed.

"What? As if I care what happens to some adolescent whose shoes cost more than my entire wardrobe. All the royals, the highest-ranking noblesse, they're all the same. We're the ones making a difference. We're laying the groundwork for future generations, for women to prove themselves worthy of the title of Musketeer."

A shiver shot through me. I could be part of something bigger than myself . . . or be its ruin.

"So, Tania," Théa said, watching Portia suspiciously, "you must've been surprised when Madame de Treville told you the truth! Or did you already know? I have five older brothers who are part of the military, and Madame de Treville is a distant relation of mine, and when the time came, she selected me for L'Académie. Or, well, the Order. Because I had an impressive family title to get me into parties, but also because she knew I'd grown up around my brothers and swords and that I was tough! I tagged along during my brothers' fencing lessons; my father couldn't get me to leave. The last thing I wanted was to help my mother run the estate—I know it's supposed to be a privilege, but it's so tedious—"

"Théa," Aria murmured as I fought back tears. At the mention of her father, at lessons, grief had brimmed in me, hot and painful at the surface. For hours now, I'd done my best to push it away.

"What did I do?" Théa pleaded. "I didn't mean to make her cry!"

"Not everyone has a family like yours," Portia said. "You make it sound simple that they loved you enough to let you do what you wanted. My father is thrilled I'm gone. Doesn't care how many ancient languages I've mastered nor the painting skills I've learned. All he ever wanted was a son. And now he and his new wife can celebrate their Portia-free existence and commence producing progeny by desecrating every single surface in the household. As a bonus, he thinks he'll have me married into another family by the end of the season! And don't even get me started on Aria—" Portia cut off as Aria shifted.

Théa, her lip quivering, swung back around to me. "Is Portia right? Are you upset because of . . ." She continued to speak, but I didn't hear her.

Tania. Tania. Tania.

Papa's voice. My heart beating; a call to arms. Papa on the side of the road. Papa with no one to save him.

Madame de Treville opened the door, a short man with an oversized mustache glued to her heels. They were midconversation, but she stopped short, her silhouette imposed upon the door frame. "Excusez-moi." She shooed the tailor outside and closed the door. "Is something wrong?"

"We were talking about our families, Madame," Théa said.

Madame de Treville sighed a long sigh as she turned to face me. "It didn't feel appropriate to say anything."

"Say anything about what?" Théa's tone was too insistent, too curious, but Madame de Treville didn't chide her. Perhaps she was preoccupied with how I trailed my fingers along the chain holding my father's signet ring to keep from wrapping my arms around myself.

"It's your story," Madame de Treville said. "I wasn't going to take that from you."

A story that was forced upon me. A story I desperately didn't want. "My father . . . *died*." Pain seized me around my middle. It was the first time I'd said the words out loud.

"He *died*?" Portia questioned.

A wave of irrational anger surged in me—but it wasn't her fault. She hadn't killed him. She hadn't taken his beard, his hair, everything that made him recognizable to his wife. To his daughter.

"What Portia meant to say," Aria said, "is that we're sorry for your loss. We can't imagine what you must be going through."

The retort, "No, you can't," was on my lips. But Aria's gray eyes were clear of menace and pity. Not hollow, but not full, either.

"We can discuss this later." Madame de Treville reached for the doorknob. "I trust you can hold yourself together," she said to me.

I wanted to scream. Wanted to chase after her, force her to tell me what she knew. So much wanting. I tried to swallow it down, but it only lined the pit of my stomach.

It was like the stories my father told me about life at court, with nobles and parties and gambling and vice. It was all a game. And Madame de Treville was in control of every move we made. How was I supposed to reconcile the woman who demanded deference and wielded biting comments with the woman who had her nephew design a pulley on pure faith that he'd succeed? That it would make a difference? That *I* would be worth it?

Even if I were a pawn controlled by a force not my own, I needed to be strong. Papa would want me to be strong.

And I still had moves to make.

CHAPTER TWELVE

"THE RED WILL look wonderful, especially with your dark hair and eyes." Théa swung her legs back and forth from her seat in my new room upstairs. Three times as large as my bedroom at home and infinitely grander with all its luxurious burgundy drapes and dark wood paneling, its carved vanity table and warm tapestries. Burnished silver candelabras trailed along the shuttered window ledges.

Théa was quieter when she wasn't with Portia and Aria. The youngest of the trio—*quartet*. Not yet sixteen. All that nervous energy spent trying to fit in, trying to impress.

She was even quieter when working with the tailor. Théa's eyebrows had pinched together as she discussed seam lines, careful to assure room for fencing breeches without revealing anything, enough give in the sleeves to wield a sword, enough meticulously placed trim and baubles to disguise muscled arms. The bodice couldn't be helped much—I almost cried at the mention of a corset, despite Théa's murmured consolations that truly they weren't all that bad and that she'd alter mine to allow more breath and movement. Allowing for breath seemed to defeat the purpose, but I wasn't about to complain. With the dizziness, I needed all the extra breath I could get. Behind the mirror, which was draped in yards of taffeta and lace, Madame de Treville spoke to the tailor about pricing. Outfitting three girls for the social season was expensive—outfitting four girls was outrageous. While Mazarin provided her with ample funding for expenditures, however, Madame de Treville seemed determined to come under budget.

After the tailor, after we were dismissed and Théa was instructed to show me to my new room, she took Madame de Treville's place at the pulley. As I ascended, she revealed information, unfurling it like petals from a flower that blooms only at night. Beautiful but so very strange. This, it seemed, was to be our existence as les Mousquetaires de la Lune.

Madame de Treville mentored a few other daughters of la noblesse, but they didn't live with us or know the truth of our mission. This way, even if she spent less than an hour a week with them on etiquette and dancing, they'd already secured party invites from their parents' standing at court and proclaimed to everyone they were patrons of *the* Madame de Treville. In turn, Madame de Treville's reputation flourished further, which increased opportunities for us—important, since not all our names carried the weight of wealth and prestige. My name, that is. The others were all members of the noblesse. Family rank high enough to hold sway, low enough not to draw too much attention while we worked.

"Does it feel strange," I asked her, "to let yourself be courted by suitors whom you'll never accept?"

Théa shrugged. I shrieked as the gesture dropped me a few feet before I caught myself, trembling, fingers laced through the rope. "Oh, Tania, I'm sorry!" she called. "I'm still getting used to all this!" My heart was in my throat until I reached the landing. "I haven't thought that far along, not really," Théa said, as if I hadn't almost plummeted to my death. "I suppose that once we're old enough to no longer be of much use in our current roles, we could choose among the remaining suitors we have, if we wish—maybe even continue to help Madame de Treville and the Order . . ."

My mother's worried face drifted before me; her lecturing me yet again how I needed to procure a husband before it was too late. When the Order decided me worthless, whether that was tomorrow or decades from now, what would become of me?

"Besides," Théa continued as we entered the hall, "Madame de Treville likes us to remain unattainable. The way she talks, it's as if she wants the men to not only want us, but fear us, too. Though it's different for each of us: We have strengths and weaknesses. Aria is aloof, and her targets do whatever necessary to gain a mere hint of her favor. She succeeds with the overly talkative ones—they don't know when to stop chattering and eventually they let something slip! She's an excellent eavesdropper, too; she could hear a pin fall on a crowded street corner. She's trained under Madame de Treville since March, and sometimes it feels as if I'll never catch up. I want to be as helpful as she is," Théa noted, an afterthought, punctuated with a sigh. "And then Portia can charm anyone. Un vrai caméléon! She commands attention, though, so she usually doesn't get the assignments that require sneaking into places, blending into the background. Or, well, maybe she's not a chameleon, then, because a chameleon would do rather well hiding in plain sight . . ."

"And you?" I asked.

Théa blinked with a jolt of her head. "Me? I'm silly, I guess.

Flighty. I usually end up with the ones who like women much younger than themselves, if you catch my drift. Older men," she added with a whisper.

"That's horrible!"

"I can handle myself," she retorted, full of fire under her full curls. "I may be small and young, but I can handle myself. I know what people see when they look at me, but here I get to prove them wrong, every day." Frowning, I opened my mouth again. The way she spoke . . . but she'd already cut me off with a twist of Madame de Treville's key and a smile. "If you ever dance with le Vicomte de Comborn, chance a look at his left hand."

A wave of dizziness passed. Théa waited patiently as I rested against the wall.

"Théa . . . why haven't you—"

"Asked more about your condition? I guess I thought if you wanted to talk about it, you'd talk about it. And you haven't talked about it. So I haven't talked about it! Madame de Treville did tell us the basics about how you get dizzy and sick. Normally I'd ask more questions—I don't know if you've noticed but I'm a naturally curious person—but the last thing I wanted was to make you feel uncomfortable on your first day. Oh, you should have seen Henri try to explain the pulley to us, what with all of Aria's questions and Portia's teasing! He's absolutely terrified of her, poor thing, ever since Portia first arrived. We were in another room for lessons and she mistook him for an intruder, tackled him, and pinned him to the carpet until Madame de Treville arrived for lunch! Apparently Portia tried to seduce him first and that didn't work very well, so, naturally, the tackling. But he's very nice; he listens to me, you know, or at least he lets me talk at him without complaining. Sometimes I think that's what people do mostly, when they say they're listening to me. Which is strange, because why say you're listening if you're not? It's not as if I'm a target that we're trying to impress!"

I shook my head as my world finally steadied. "Wait, you said something about a vicomte's left hand?"

"His left index finger . . . what's left of it, anyway!" With that, she opened the door to my room. What if a more powerful man tried to have his way with her? Someone she'd have to kill to keep from raining hell down on the Order? Madame de Treville had Mazarin to protect her—he would extend that favor to us, too, if there was cause . . . wouldn't he? We were his last line of defense for the King. "I wish I'd be assigned a handsome, dashing young man now and then. A soldier, perhaps—although why a soldier would be at a noble's party . . ." As Théa spoke, she pointed out my trunk and the room's features, then collapsed into an armchair. "What I *do* wonder is what type of noble you'll be assigned to."

Jacques's face flitted across my closed eyelids. His kind face that concealed a barbed tongue, a barbed heart.

To keep from answering, I went to unpack my trunk. But when I reached my cloak, it had a different feel to it, a different weight. And, when it hit the light, I gasped. Powder blue wool lined with silver fabric meant to imitate silk. Tiny fleurs-de-lis, embroidered in gold thread, trimmed the hem. It looked like Papa's cassock. That's why I couldn't find it in his wardrobe— Maman must have taken it for reference. I clutched the cloak to my chest.

Théa leaned forward to get a better look. "Oh, how beautiful!"

Maman might've thought me weak, sick, broken. A cloak wouldn't make up for that. But it was a start. The beginnings of a peace offering. One woven with my father's memories, stitched with the threads of his stories.

Perhaps I could make her believe me capable. Someday.

"Tania . . . I've wanted to say—I've been trying to say—I'm really sorry. About your father. And how I made you upset." Théa's words wrenched me out of my thoughts. She worried her bottom lip between her teeth. "What Portia said earlier was true, about how not everyone grew up like me. I understand I'm lucky."

"I know you didn't mean it that way," I said. Théa's face was partially hidden behind her curls. "And thank you." I swallowed hard, tried not to thank her for something she might not have given me. On the ground, broken eggs, Marguerite's laughing face looming above me—I blinked. "For what you said about my father, but also in general. For welcoming me."

Today was the first time I'd felt a glimmer of hope that perhaps there were people other than my parents who cared about me and my feelings—not friends, I couldn't let myself think that, but people who understood I could be strong and need help at the same time.

Théa beamed. "I'm glad you're here! So is Portia, and Aria doesn't say much, but I know she is, too. Madame de Treville was right."

Fingers curled round one of the bedposts, I tilted my head. "Right about what?"

"She said you were a chance worth taking. That having another skilled swordswoman in the Order was just what we needed."

"But you don't know me," I attested. There were so many questions I wanted to ask her, but I was tired. Her presence grated raw against my skin. And how could I explain that? That I was thankful for her welcome, for her kindness, for her support of someone she'd just met, but that there came a point when the exhaustion reached its peak and even the act of listening became painful? No—she would think I considered her annoying.

Théa grabbed ahold of the bedpost on my left, swung herself so her arm was extended, so her bright eyes loomed near mine. "Since you arrived, things feel . . . right. Like something's clicked into place. I've always liked the number four more than the number three, anyway."

This was what my father wanted for himself, what he wanted for me. This was what he wanted for his legacy. And if it meant I could fence, if it meant I could be a part of something important, maybe then it didn't just have to be about my father. Maybe I could want this, too.

"Yes," I said, though the words weren't all mine, not completely. They still cracked with a lack of assurance. A knowledge that, in one dizzy moment, all these kind sentiments could disappear. Yes, they'd seen me faint, but they hadn't seen how every morning I struggled to stand, how I used walls for balance, the way my legs could collapse without any notice. They wouldn't want me—couldn't want me—if they knew how the dizziness never abated, not fully. I couldn't have what Papa had, his Musketeers' fierce, reciprocated loyalty. Their brotherhood. Marguerite's face swam across my vision, and I swallowed. Sisterhood wasn't meant for girls like me. "Yes," I repeated. "Together at last."

The next few weeks passed by in a flurry of lessons. That didn't leave much time to ask Madame de Treville about my father— besides, I wasn't ready to question her yet. I needed to prove she hadn't made a mistake in accepting me. Once she knew I was trustworthy, surely she wouldn't see anything wrong with answering a few questions and putting me in contact with a senior Musketeer official. Maybe one would come to confer with Madame about evidence collected for Mazarin. Still, though, it was hard to focus on learning new footwork—for fencing or for popular dances—when my father's childhood friend was a few feet away.

Fencing was always in the morning, training of another sort in the afternoon. I raised my legs with rocks tied around my ankles until my muscles screamed. Practiced bladework on a target until my arm felt like it would fall off. And even then Madame de Treville had me switch to strengthening exercises that didn't require using my arms.

These weren't my father's lessons, ones where he patiently taught me how to hold the saber, thumb facing the same direction as the blade, pressed flat on the top of the grip—the arrow of a compass pointing due north. A space between the tip of my thumb and the guard. My fingers wrapped around the side, a loosened fist ready for a punch, twisted 90 degrees clockwise. No, these weren't my father's lessons, where punishment for failure would be the guilt of not living up to his expectations, and extra time spent with a needle and thread.

The stakes were different. It was more than wanting to save face in front of Papa and Beau; now I had to keep up with Portia, Aria, and Théa, had to perform with Madame de Treville's hawk-like gaze at the nape of my neck. And once she decided I was ready, the stakes would be even higher—the lives of the royals and the fate of our country.

I had to prove myself worthy. Worthy of her help in finding Papa's killer.

The first few days I wasn't allowed to bout. I was used to observing—how couldn't I be after all those days I'd been too dizzy to stand, watching my father demonstrate a perfect flunge—a lunge where both feet left the ground, where you threw yourself into the motion. It was the closest any of us would ever get to flying. He stopped practicing it when he realized I'd never be able to even try.

Yes, I was used to watching, to waiting. But that didn't mean it was easy.

When I graduated to holding a sword, Madame de Treville was brutally exacting. I was still tensing my shoulder when I parried, expending more energy than necessary. I was still struggling with blocking attacks fast off the line—my opponent would lunge almost immediately while I was getting my bearings, and everything would go gray and scarlet as they rushed at me.

A few days in, tears of frustration and pain welling in my eyes, I dropped my sword. "But I'm not left-handed! Why do I need to practice footwork on the other side?"

Madame de Treville scrutinized me from where she worked with Portia on extended attacks. Arriving only a couple of months before me, Portia had the least experience with a blade, but it was hard to tell by watching her. She was terrifying in the first seconds of a bout—imposing, making herself as large as possible—a fact learned quickly when sparring with her. But then she'd falter and leave herself open to a quick counterattack. And that was all her opponent needed.

"I don't want to hear any more excuses," Madame de Treville told me.

A flame of anger flickered to life in my chest. "What do you mean, *excuses*?"

"I told you I'd push you harder than you've ever been pushed before. I won't tolerate whining or complaining, and certainly not laziness."

The last word cut through me like the slash of a sword. "I'm not *lazy*."

Her gaze sparked. "What was that?"

I fought the urge to take back what I'd said, to crawl into myself. Instead I swallowed, straightened my back. "I'm not lazy."

Displeasure was written all over Madame de Treville's face. "I didn't ask for your opinion."

Part of me couldn't believe I was fighting back, not with Madame de Treville's approval on the line, but anger had been smoldering in my chest for weeks now. "I'll dress in expensive gowns, I'll train until my feet bleed and my hands have calluses on top of calluses, I'll sit through every lesson on etiquette and surveillance and eavesdropping and seduction, I'll tolerate it all. But I will *not* be called lazy. I am *not* lazy." My chest heaved as if I'd just fenced a duel. "Well?" I asked finally. Behind Madame de Treville, Portia gave me a nod of approval.

Our mentor sucked at her teeth. Rubbed at the bridge of her nose. For a moment, I thought I'd pushed her too far. But then: "I don't need to give you an answer," she said, "remember that. But after all those *histrionics* . . ." Her nose wrinkled. "If it's important to you, fine. Look in the mirror." She gestured to the tall glass attached to wheels so we could pull it wherever we worked to check our position; Aria used it often—not that she needed to. She fenced like water directed through a channel—smooth, so graceful it appeared effortless, while the entire time every movement was calculated by some larger force.

Doing my best not to sulk, I centered myself in the mirror, lowered into my en garde stance.

"Just stand." Brows raised, I straightened my legs, kept my right hand ready in case I needed to reach out for balance. Madame de Treville approached with her sword. Portia watched from the far-right side of the room, shook her head when our eyes locked. "Are you looking at yourself?" Madame said, inches away. Her steps were so quiet it was hard to hear her coming or going.

"Oui, Madame." For years, no matter what I saw staring back at me, I knew that wasn't what others saw. While I saw dark hair, dark eyes, curved figure, they saw a sick girl. Fainting girl. Strange girl. But everyone I met moving forward wouldn't know my story, would see me just as I was reflected in the glass: taller than I'd thought. Hair frizzing at the nape of my neck, bright red flush along the tops of my cheekbones all the way back to my ears.

Madame de Treville whacked my leg with the side of her dulled practice blade, the flat metal a bruise waiting to happen. "Your right leg is working harder than your left. See how your weight is shifted? You're prone to injury if your right side is doing extra work when you're not fencing."

I bit my tongue. I did as she said. And after a full hour of practicing as such, my left leg was a roar of fire. All I wanted was to fall into bed . . . but there were lessons in the afternoon. So I changed, then hobbled to the kitchen for an apple and hopefully some cheese. I wouldn't be able to stomach more. By the time I was finished, I was an aching mess. The throbbing space between my thumbs and forefingers, my tearing hips, the painful flesh under my rib cage, my cramped arches . . . even my teeth hurt.

Henri entered and went immediately to a side table, grabbed two rolls, and bit into one with relish. The other went in his satchel. At my cough, he turned, fumbling, a shade of scarlet I hadn't seen him achieve yet. He choked down the bread with a pained swallow.

"Mademoiselle de Batz! Forgive me, I didn't see you." Henri was in and out most days: delivering a letter here and there, running errands for Madame de Treville—with his apprenticeship, it was hard to understand how he found time to sleep. I knew that he had a room on the first floor. Madame de Treville had said something about propriety and four young mademoiselles. But Henri was one of the least frightening members of the household.

"Monsieur," I responded. Calling him Monsieur de Treville was too bizarre. "Your aunt went to speak to Aria; she's—"

"Oh, I came to see you!"

No matter how hard I tried to stop it, heat stained my face. For a moment, the pain dulled. "Me? But why?"

Henri reached into his bag. The inside was a mess: the now-squashed bread, quill nubs, broken bits of charcoal, a proportional compass for measurements, philosophy books he'd told me he used to practice his English, written by Thomas Hobbes, Francis Bacon . . .

He paused with a roll of paper in his hands, a shy smile on his face. "Local young designers are always sending Sanson their work in hopes he'll put in a good word with other artisans in the city, maybe even take them on as apprentices. He keeps their efforts in a pile which he never deigns to sort through, because of course he can't be bothered to look at these peoples' hard work"—punctuated with a scoff—"but look what I found."

I unfurled the scroll. It took a moment for the pattern of streets to become recognizable, the way the forest linked the seams of the village, the fields widening and sinking across the stretch of paper. The borders were ornamented with regional flora. I traced the outline of a vibrant sunflower. Lupiac. Home.

I wouldn't cry in front of him. I couldn't cry in front of him. I repeated this to myself, even as my eyes stung. "It's wonderful—but I can't accept it. It doesn't belong to me."

"But you must," Henri said. "My aunt told me how far away you were from home. So, we must bring your home to you. Like I said, Sanson doesn't even want it."

Through my tears, his eager face blurred. A moment later a handkerchief was pressed in my direction. Was I cursed to cry in front of every boy I'd ever meet? "I'm fine, thank you, I don't need it."

"We all need a cry sometimes." His eyes lingered on my palms, my hair-fine scars, before bouncing back to my face. The scars were faint, unraised, unnoticeable to anyone but me. At least, I'd thought they were. I'd hoped they were. "I think, well"—another breath, squaring his shoulders—"please take the handkerchief." My chest warmed. I took the handkerchief. "Oh, wonderful!"

I blinked. "What's wonderful?"

Henri rubbed the back of his neck sheepishly. Finally, he said: "You smiled. A real smile—at least, I think a real one. You've smiled very little since you arrived here. And I got the sense they weren't real ones."

That night, I fell asleep with the map propped on the pillow next to me.

Tears were harder to hide in the afternoon lessons. You couldn't explain away watery eyes when you were learning the steps to the bourrée or how often to make eye contact with a man. Too much was off-putting; too little was immature . . . the best amount—something I had yet to master—was in the middle: a coquettish dance between interest and indifference. We needed to create the illusion for our targets that our attentions could shift at any moment, that they needed to work to sustain our regard.

"Oh, Mademoiselle"—Théa deepened her voice to comic proportions, her arms akimbo—"I haven't seen you around before. Your eyes, they are the color of the trees—Oh no," she added, breaking character, "trees are green *and* brown, aren't they. Can I start over?"

"Monsieur," I laughed, more a titter than anything else, "you are so magnanimous with your compliments!"

"No! No! It's all wrong!" Madame de Treville cried. The parlor was bathed in afternoon light. Outside, children spun circles around one another, kicking up the pools of last night's rain, squealing as carriage drivers narrowly avoided them, cursing. Two weeks into living in Paris and I was beginning to understand the city's sounds, even if they were still unfamiliar.

Cheeks hot, I gripped the chair as Madame de Treville outlined my mistakes: too high pitched, too silly, too *much*. "I don't need another Théa—or Portia or Aria, for that matter. I'd rather have your innocence and nervousness peek through, rather than you come off as forced. We're honing you into a more alluring version of yourself. Not into someone else. Does that make sense?"

I tried to respond, but with the pounding in my head, the heat rising in my cheeks, I had to sit down. Madame de Treville looked like she might sigh, but then thought better of it. "How about an example? Portia, Aria . . ." She flicked her wrist.

Théa sat beside me as the other girls replaced us: Portia,

clothed in a pink gown embroidered with a delicate pattern of leaves and flowers, and Aria, striking in simple pale blue. The latter was the quietest of the entire house. Not out of nerves, but an active choice: I got the sense that she was always watching, always waiting. I knew why Portia and Théa were dedicated to the Order; Aria was still a mystery.

"Mademoiselle," Aria said. She advanced so she was only a foot away from Portia. Took Portia's delicately placed hand and bowed, lips hovering inches above the back of her hand. Aria stared up at her. "Mademoiselle," she repeated, "your eyes are the most beautiful shade of brown I've ever beheld. More than beautiful. Exquisite."

Portia's pinkie finger shook, settled. "I—I—"

Aria waited, never looked away.

"D-Do you see, Tania?" Portia stuttered out her words. "*That* is how you make someone feel like they are the only person in the room."

"Yes, but unfortunately," Madame de Treville cut in, "we can't have Tania stumbling over her words! Slight blushing: yes! Coquettish batting of lashes: yes! Stuttering: no!"

Sufficiently chastised, I returned to Théa.

Portia glanced back to Aria. "You have a little . . ."

"Hmm?"

"Your rouge. It's smudged."

"What?"

Portia took her thumb to wipe away the rogue smudge of rouge. Under Portia's touch, Aria stiffened.

"Will none of you take this seriously?" Madame de Treville exclaimed. "We do not have time to waste fixing each other's makeup!" She huffed all the way to the door. "I'm getting a cup of tea. By the time I return, you will all be ready to work!" She shut the door behind her; not as loud as a slam, but enough to creak the hinges.

For a moment, everything was hushed.

Théa giggled, clutched her mouth. But it wasn't enough, she couldn't contain it, and then we were all laughing. Me, the last to join in, but once I did I laughed so hard my sides ached. A sore, unused muscle. One I'd forgotten to train for too long.

Sometimes, like that day in the kitchen, Henri would pop in to wave bonjour before Madame de Treville pushed him from the room, muttering all the while how he wasn't setting a good example; if we thought all our targets, all these boys and men, were like Henri with his earnest, easy-to-read expression, we'd assume them easier to trample over than a carpet runner.

"He's a kind boy, don't mistake me," Madame de Treville told us, "but he isn't capable of the subtlety and subterfuge necessary to mimic these men." Portia snorted, but didn't say anything.

"And we are? Capable?" I asked.

I'd done my best to keep from talking back. Not with what was on the line. But even as I spoke, Madame de Treville shook her head, simple and stark among our fanciful curls that had begun to deflate in the sway of afternoon. She set down the stack of cards with names of la noblesse written on the front, their personal details on the back. It was essential we knew every noble, and all their secrets, before we even spoke to them.

"You aren't; not yet. But you will be. And when you are able to predict what they'll say to you—that's when you control the game. Even if they don't know it."

So I steeled my shoulders. Thought of my father. How he called me Mademoiselle la Mousquetaire with all the confidence in the world. He thought I could do this.

Late in my third week in Paris, when Madame de Treville said I'd proved capable of basic dances and manners, I was thrilled. But then we moved on to the next stage, one that made me want to curl up in a ball and vanish into the garish rug below my feet . . . how to *ensnare* men. With our words, with brief touches of hands, with whispers in ears and dangerous leans over tabletops—nothing that could be deemed untoward by Parisian society, of course. We had to maintain our reputations, keep men lusting after us, we untouchable girls.

Now I had to be the one flirting, the one ready with innuendo and intrigue—everything, as Portia remarked, that involved me hypothetically talking to or touching a man. "Tania, whatever are we going to do with you?" she asked.

And it didn't matter how she meant it as I readied myself for the fall. For the bump of Marguerite's elbow, the sear of stone against my palms. For the look you gave pauvre Tania. For the way friendship dissolved as quickly as my legs buckled.

But then Aria glanced at Portia. And Théa nudged me, asked if I could help her tomorrow with her attaque composée. A few minutes later, when it came time to switch lessons, Portia drifted by me with a little squeeze of my arm.

They were only being nice because they thought they had to be. It was their job. An order of Musketeers who didn't get along would surely fall apart during a dangerous mission. This is what I told myself as I replayed the day's events in my head. Friendly gestures, friendly words; it was important I didn't morph them into something they weren't. I was here for Papa.

The next day, business as usual. I instructed Théa, who, after a few hours, received a round of applause from everyone as she demonstrated her improved attack. She dropped her hands behind her hips, blushed and bashful, then shrieked as her forgotten sword, still in her hands, nicked her breeches.

In the afternoon, Henri brought us leftovers from Sanson's morning meeting with Mazarin: preserves sharp and sweet, the color of sunset, and a dark drink so bitter Portia railed at him: "Is this retribution? For me pinning you? Did you seriously think you could waltz in here with this foul liquid and trick me into drinking it?"

Henri took a step away from her scowl. "I—"

"Portia, leave him alone! You're going to scare him, and he won't bring us any more of this!" Théa gestured to her cup. "It's wonderful! I've never tasted anything like it!" She continued to sip at it, bouncing in her chair, chattering and laughing and laughing and chattering before Aria grabbed the cup away and poured the remaining black-brown dregs into the nearest chamber pot.

"Monsieur," I called as he made to leave. Théa was as furious as she could possibly be, which was to say mildly angry, talking at Aria as the latter watched Portia search for the powder we rubbed on our teeth with our fingers.

He halted so suddenly I almost knocked into him, and then he was apologizing, "I'm sorry, I shouldn't have turned so quickly, it's just I heard you call my name and I didn't want you to think I wasn't paying attention to you, because that's not it at all—"

"Monsieur," I cut him off, surprised by my own daring. "The others are ... preoccupied, but I know they'd wish me to pass along their thanks. For your thoughtfulness."

Nearby, Théa wailed: "But it's not fair! I was still drinking! And I feel so energized, like I could do anything—Aria, duel me! Duel me now!"

Aria sniffed as she fanned herself. "No."

Meanwhile, the tension melted from Henri. "It was no trouble."

"Thank you," I said.

"But you already—"

"I made it sound like I thanked you only on behalf of the other girls. And I wanted you to know I was thankful, too. So. Thank you."

When Henri smiled, it was impossible not to smile, too.

And so it went, this string of days, weeks. Fencing, flirting, primping, preening, the one I loved and the rest I'd learned long ago to hate all muddled up together. Aria, her nature blurry, so skilled it seemed like she'd been training for this her whole life, whether she flicked a blade or a fan. Théa with her indefatigable speech, her ceaseless kindness. Portia, ferocious and hungry.

And me. Sick Tania, dizzy Tania. Tania who didn't truly belong here, not in the way they did. But all the while, my mother's voice at my back, my father's voice ahead, the girls' voices around me, as I attempted to mold my own ice swan self into solid steel.

"Here!" Théa exclaimed, thrusting a pile of ruffles into my arms. Well into the fifth week, I was settling into the rhythm of our routine. There was a relief in the consistency, in waking up and, despite the dizziness and the exhaustion, knowing precisely how the day would unfold hour by hour, drill by drill, lesson by lesson. "Madame de Treville asked me to whip this skirt up for you to practice dancing in—it's light enough to tuck back for fencing but a good bit heavier than the skirts of our day dresses."

"But she's had me dancing for the past week!"

"Well, you had to learn the steps first. Now you're ready to take it to the next level!"

I ran a finger along the side of the skirt. The stitches were tight, uniform, no puckering around the seams. "You made this today?"

"I had time before fencing practice, and I finished during the break. It's quite plain, but then it's for practice, so all those extra embellishments aren't necessary," she explained.

"This is incredible. You should be the one making our dresses."

"Don't be silly: I can work with cheaper materials, but the embroidery skills needed to create a piece of couture? No, I'll stick to scrap fabrics!"

"Maybe this could be what you do"—she looked at me quizzically as I continued—"you know, after all this."

Her entire face glowed pink. "You really think so? There aren't many girls who design gowns, you know, and I think if women made them, they'd be so much more comfortable. And prettier, too. Not in the way men think is pretty, I suppose, but the way we think is pretty—I'm babbling nonsense, aren't I?"

"No, of course not—"

But Théa was already talking again: "Hurry up, please, and try it on, or else I'll be late for my afternoon session."

"You said I'm supposed to wear this for my lesson? Won't you need one as well?" I asked.

"It's just you today. The rest of us are rehearsing a newer court dance—apparently it's all the rage in Italy."

As I slipped into a narrow room off the main hallway, Théa called through the door, "Pull the skirt on over your gown!" The skirt *was* heavier than normal, but the enclosures were simple enough. Well, simple enough before I tried to return through the door.

"How am I supposed to get anywhere?" I heaved as the sides of the skirt hit the door frame, unable to pass over the threshold.

"Turn sideways. No, not like that . . . more of a shuffle!"

I wrenched myself through and would've landed in a heap if I hadn't been caught. "Thank you!" I looked up, expecting to see Théa.

"You're welcome. It was an honorable attempt for your first try!" I blushed as Henri withdrew from my elbow, as if he'd only just remembered his hand was there. The dizziness was right on the periphery. "Are you all right?" he asked. For a moment, his face was no longer his. Golden brown eyes transformed into unforgiving blue. A sharp gasp, a stumble step. "You're not all right," he said. "Something's wrong."

"Yes, but that doesn't mean she needs help," Théa said. My chest warmed.

"But if she's not feeling well . . ."

"Henri, you know how much I hate arguing!" Théa stamped her foot. "Especially when I am clearly right and you are not!" Her voice softened when she turned to me. "You'll tell us, though, if you need it? If you need our help?"

I hesitated, then nodded. Pausing, I clenched my toes, closed my eyes for a few seconds before opening them. The hallway was blissfully still. "I think I'll be fine. As long as someone else is around—"

"Perfect, then, that Henri's here! See you at supper!" Théa bounded away, with a smile I didn't understand. I wanted to inquire more, but she was gone in seconds. But not before she threw me a wink.

"She's something else, isn't she?" Henri said with a grin.

My heart twinged at the tenor in his voice, even though it had no cause to. I just nodded my head, unable to find the words.

She'd called him Henri. And he'd let her. Like he'd heard his name from her lips a hundred times before.

CHAPTER THIRTEEN

WE WALKED IN silence; Henri's words repeated in my head. When this was all over, when our duties were complete, perhaps he would court Théa. And that would make me happy. The kindest of our quartet, with the most thoughtful boy. Could there be a more perfect pair?

Henri came to a sudden halt. "I'm sorry if I caused any offense. I didn't mean to imply you needed my help; I—"

"Monsieur," I rushed. "You were worried about me, I understand. I appreciate it, truly." I searched the planes of his face.

He flushed and murmured in assent. "I believe ma tante is waiting." He opened the door to the makeshift ballroom. It must've been a parlor in the past, but now all that was left were a few sparse furnishings and a large, unobstructed expanse of parquet wooden floor. A harpsichord sat in the corner.

"How did you know . . . ?"

But Madame de Treville was urging us through the door. "I don't recall instructing you to idle," she said. "How is the skirt?"

"Un grand plaisir. A delight. I feel like a princess."

Henri snorted, tried to cover it with a cough.

"Now is not the time for your effervescent wit," Madame de Treville said. "Come now, get going."

Shoes scraped against the floorboards, an awkward shamble from side to side. "Tante, I hate to interrupt, but you requested me? Something about today's lesson?" Henri asked.

Her eyes lit with understanding. "Don't hide in the door frame!" He wrung his ink-stained hands as he approached her—after a pointed glare from her, he immediately let his arms rest at his sides. Madame de Treville nodded in my direction. "Tania's progressed quickly, but I'm not convinced she can actually maintain her composure around anyone besides the girls and myself. You'll have to do."

"Me?" Henri went stone-still. "But . . . but . . ."

Madame de Treville let out a great, odious sigh. "Do you question Sanson every time he asks something of you, too? Does he not find that aggravating?" The tips of Henri's ears burned through his hair.

Madame de Treville flipped through sheet music with harsh, unrestrained fervor. She'd snapped at Aria earlier today over a missed parry, had Portia grinding her teeth so hard I could hear the clench of her jaw. Théa escaped unscathed, probably because she was off sewing my skirt. Something had happened . . . *would* happen. I wasn't sure how I'd avoided her ire up until this afternoon. With a sudden lurch, I wondered if I could make it to the window before I lost the contents of my stomach.

"We'll run through a few basics," Madame de Treville snapped. "Ignore the parts requiring more than two people; I want to see how Tania can manage one-on-one interaction." After retreating to the harpsichord's accompanying bench, Madame de Treville played the first notes of a minuet. The instrument was angled for her to see us over the top of the sheet music.

Henri took a few steps toward me. I studied him, blinked. Mirrored his shaky steps. My pulse was racing; I could feel it in my wrists.

When the music reached the appropriate point, we curtsied and bowed, respectively, then started into the demi-coupé. All my lessons, all my training—those moments in the parlor, of sculpting my allure, practicing ways to reel men in. I batted my eyelashes as we approached each other before traveling in a circle, right palms pressed together.

"Do you have something in your eye?" Henri inquired.

"No, I—"

"Smile, Tania! You mustn't stop smiling! And not too big— less teeth! You're not a prancing horse!"

As the notes shifted into an allemande, I grasped his hands in mine. "I'm sorry," I said through my smile as I twirled under his raised arm. I certainly wasn't counting the beats under my breath.

"What for?" he asked.

I hazarded a glance over my shoulder, but Madame de Treville wasn't interested in our conversation, just our steps. Besides, we were supposed to keep up appearances—and whispered conversation gave the perfect opportunity to cement a target's interest. Portia did this with ease, her voice silk smooth. In her target's mind, she spoke for him, and for him alone. My attempts during Madame de Treville's lessons were painful even to my own ears. But then, Henri didn't scare me.

"What she said about . . . well, she's been anxious all day. She shouldn't take it out on you, but still. She didn't mean it, but that doesn't mean what she said is all right. I get frustrated with her, too. It's difficult, trying to prove yourself but coping with her criticism." I paused as Henri's eyes widened. This was the first time I'd seen them up close. The color of fall leaves right before they turned brown and brittle. With just that bit of gold remaining.

He relaxed his shoulders. He wasn't the most graceful dancer, but ever more practiced than me. No uncertainty in foot placement, no hesitation in how he led me around the room. Growing up in the Parisian noblesse must do that to a boy. But it was strange, this ease. As if he'd been affecting his bumbling nerves, and his true self was someone I didn't know at all.

"I feel the same way . . . but then, part of me wonders if she's right." Henri looked so crestfallen I almost stopped dancing. All thoughts of him pretending to be anything he wasn't disintegrated. "Maybe I have talent—I'd like to think so—but the only reason I had access to the apprenticeship in the first place was because someone else got me through the door. The opportunity was never truly mine to begin with."

Papa, fixing my grip on my sword. Papa, clucking over my wobbly lunge. Papa, draping me in his cassock, watching me squeal and sprint around the room.

"Don't waste it, then," I insisted.

"What?"

"You have the opportunity to do important work. Don't waste it. Prove to them you deserve it. Prove it to her. It might not be the job you want, not really, but a map can change the world. It's like the map of Lupiac you gave me: Most people think the village unimportant, unworthy. It was the first rendering of it I'd ever seen. There have to be other places like Lupiac. Written off for their size or their people or their wealth. And you have the power to teach people to think beyond themselves. To see beyond themselves."

In that next moment I became acutely aware of his hand holding mine, the two of us side by side, Henri regarding me from my left. His golden-brown eyes on my flushed face. Jeanne must've started a fire in one of the grates before we entered; I wouldn't have noticed it, too busy trying to prove myself to Madame de Treville. Henri's hand slipped from mine, ink-stained fingertips grazing my palm.

"Thank you for the dance," he mumbled. He did not step away.

Madame de Treville's loud cough startled me. "I *suppose* that will do."

I turned to meet her gaze. "Do you mean it? Truly?" Excitement bled into my voice.

I didn't think Madame de Treville was capable of looking proud. It was smugness, surely; she'd managed to shape the unshapable girl into a perfect curve. "You've proved yourself ready for this weekend."

"This weekend?"

"A smaller ball, one of the final ones before the season opening at la palais. The last nobles are returning to the city from their summers in the countryside, as are others who are finally making their way back to Paris for the first time since La Fronde ended two years ago. And then those who have been pardoned by the King in La Fronde's aftermath. All will be potential recruits for the enemy's cause. Until you're ready to take on a target of your own, you'll shadow the girls. Take extra care watching how they extract information they need from targets. It could mean the difference between your success and, well . . ." She didn't have to say it. Failure wasn't an option. Not for a Mousquetaire de la Lune. My stomach curdled, but I nodded, let the moment fill me to the brim.

Maybe Papa was right. Maybe I really could do this. I'd told myself I would succeed for him, would prove myself worthy to the Musketeers, worthy of their help in avenging him. But telling is one thing; believing is another. And maybe I didn't believe, not yet, but I didn't need belief in myself. Not with a sword in my hand and a grit to my teeth. His belief had gotten me this far; it would get me where I needed to go.

"I won't let you down, Madame."

"You have more of your father in you than I first realized." When my mother said something like this it was meant as an insult, a curse. But in Madame de Treville's voice, it was the highest praise. Papa's signet ring was warm against my sternum. I turned to bid goodbye to Henri, but he was hurrying out the door, a quick wave for me as he disappeared from sight. "Now, the real work begins," Madame de Treville said.

I half listened to her list all the tasks I needed to complete before this weekend. My eyes lit on the far wall as we exited the room. The only thing in the fireplace were cool ashes and smoke stains from last night.

If the previous weeks had been a whirlwind, the days leading up to the ball were a summer storm, a constant shriek of thunder and lightning. There were last-minute alterations on the corset, on the breeches, on the belt that would rest underneath my gown for my sword and dagger. What a blessing the current fashion of oversized skirts was—no one would discern I was hiding weapons under layers of silk, delicate lace, and scattered pearls. By the morning of the ball, my mind was crammed fit to bursting with names of key players in la noblesse and dances and all the ways to bring a man to his knees.

"Mon Dieu!" Portia exclaimed as I entered the dining room. "You look like you haven't slept in weeks!" Aria and Théa glanced up from their breakfast.

My stomach fluttered. I'd done my best to ignore the purple circles in the mirror this morning; they felt like they were pressed into my skin. I pushed my meal around my plate. Crumbled fresh bread between my fingertips. Last night, wrapped in blankets, I'd traced the outline of Lupiac on the map, traced the path my father took with Beau, all the way out of the village, all the way off the parchment until he was gone from the face of the earth. It didn't matter that I was about to be initiated into the duties of a Musketeer, that a Musketeer was supposed to put the King above all else—I'd give a thousand kings for Papa at my side. Not for the father who let me believe in his betrayal. But for the Papa who called me his daughter, all pride and no shame.

"Tania?" Théa put forward tentatively. "Asking if you're okay seems pointless, but I don't really know any other way to put it ..."

The words "I'm fine" died on my tongue; they tasted of ash and burning. My lip quivered, and I bit down hard, harder. Now the only taste was iron.

"I didn't mean it, about the circles. I can cover them up. You'll see," Portia said. "It's not too hard. Just some extra makeup."

There was a space of quiet, a strained hush. Théa shifted in discomfort. "I made a mess of my first ball in Paris!" she finally blurted out. She went blistering red as everyone turned to her. "C'est vrai! It's—it's true," she stammered. "I tripped. But I didn't fall, because Aria was dancing nearby, and she helped me find my balance before anyone besides my partner noticed. And then I completely lost control of a conversation with a visiting duke—I was so nervous I was on the verge of tears—but Portia saw me struggling and stepped in to help." Théa's eyes glistened; her voice broke, but she persisted. "We're Musketeers. We are sisters in arms. We don't let each other fall, and we never will."

"She's right," Portia said after clearing her throat, blinking rapidly. "I mean, that was all very flowery and maudlin, but she's right. Anything you'd like to add?" She positioned her body away from us and toward Aria.

Aria, face impassive as usual, examined me. "This is an annual event. It's never the most important of the season. You're making your debut, but the royal family won't be present. Neither will the highest-ranking nobles. Madame de Treville wouldn't ask this of you if she didn't think you were ready."

"Thank you," I said. "It's just that . . . I don't want to let anyone down. What if I get too dizzy and someone notices, what if I faint or—"

"You know, your hometown's ignorance has completely warped your perception of how capable you are," Portia said.

"How did you know what they—"

"It doesn't take a genius to guess how you were treated. I know what it's like to think yourself incapable of living up to others' expectations . . . to think yourself useless in general, truly. But, frankly, who cares about any of that? You're going to the ball tonight. You will be an asset to the Order. An unknown hero for your country. We've seen you fence, Tania, we've trained with you. We know what you're capable of."

Under her gaze, I swallowed, then let out a deep breath and pictured all the feathery-winged nerves escaping my body. The girls believed in me. They wouldn't let me fall.

"Right, that's settled," Portia finished, a wide grin melting her serious expression. "Now. We have a ball to prepare for."

Preparations took up the entire day. We spent hours in front of mirrors and wardrobes, holding jewels to the dips of each other's throats and placing dozens of pins in our hair. Portia blurred away the dark circles—it took nearly half an hour of awkwardly angling my head as she dotted on paint, then powder. After, she demonstrated how to bite into a halved sweet lemon to redden my lips, how to conceal the acidic sting, how to store it in my tie-on pockets for access during the ball. "You can't be serious," I'd said.

Portia had shrugged her shoulders. "If it's good enough for the Queen of Sweden, it's good enough for you." I raised my brows. "Fine, who knows if it actually works or not. But she's so dependent on it that she brought her entire stash to France a couple summers ago. I figure it's worth a shot. Worse comes to worst, you have puckered lips and better breath."

I caught sight of Henri once, when I briefly escaped Portia's clutches. But even as I called to him, he was gone, head of golden-brown hair disappearing into the kitchen before the back door closed. My mind flashed to our dance, to the familiar ink stains on his skin, to the heat of his palm . . .

I wore the first of my new dresses: sapphire silk that draped tight over my waist before flowing to the ground. A relief, to look in the mirror and still see part of myself staring back—my mother's hair tucked up and finished with a crystal-encrusted comb, ringlets framing my face. My father's smile. The bodice's plunge wasn't as daring as Portia's, but it still showed more skin than I was used to. But not so low that I couldn't wear the signet ring; it rested, safe, on its long chain beneath my neckline.

"Perfect," Théa said. Even Aria nodded her approval.

I tried not to think too much about what was waiting for me at the end of the carriage ride: A ballroom full of people I needed to impress, to charm, if I wanted to stay in Paris and have any chance at uncovering the truth about Papa.

"Madame de Treville, I really would appreciate some insight into tonight, so I know what you need of me, so I can prepare myself for—" I started as we entered the front hall to meet our mentor.

She blinked at me. "Oh, that's right. It's been a while since we've had a new mademoiselle. Into the carriage with the lot of you, and we'll discuss the rest on the way. I prefer giving assignments in the carriage. That way I can focus on your training and won't be bothered with questions about upcoming events during the rest of the week," she said, looking pointedly at me. "But, as I said earlier, you'll be shadowing the girls for the first few events. This time, it'll be Aria."

I was so nervous that I didn't work up the courage to ask more until we were nearly at our destination: the Marais hôtel particulier of a noble's son—technically he was a noble as well, just a noble whom the Order wasn't as familiar with. A new player in the upcoming social season.

"Look alive, ladies. Eyes up, chests out!" Shadows cut across Madame de Treville's face. The carriage was cramped with all of us in gowns, lace and crinoline skirts crinkled together, not even our slippered feet visible. Gemstones dripped down our bodices, our sleeves, pinched our earlobes, nested in our curls.

"This is so exciting," Théa trilled, her round face close to the carriage window. "Usually the Marquis de Toucy throws the party at his city residence, but this year it'll be his son! Just think—a new generation in charge of the season!"

Aria grimaced as her eyes darted to mine. "The Marquis's son is a notorious drunkard," she muttered. "Besides, you could hardly place him with the mesdemoiselles and messieurs of Paris; he's well into middle age."

"What was that?" Théa asked.

"Now," Madame de Treville said, drawing our attention, "assignments: Théa, you're in charge of keeping the party's host preoccupied while Portia endears herself to the Comte de Monluc's son. The Comte de Monluc has been spotted at the docks on the Right Bank three times this week alone. There's no reason for his sudden interest in the workings of the trade economy, much less for him to actually interact with dockhands and crewmen. While he probably isn't the mastermind behind the smuggling operation, he's definitely a starting point. He could barely afford to rent a Paris residence last season, and now he suddenly has the means to purchase his own hôtel particulier? On the finest street in Marais? Not to mention he's had a mysterious visitor at his home—my contacts were only able to establish that the visitor was the same person each time based on his clothing, likely a merchant, but haven't been able to discover the visitor's identity."

The others nodded, but my mind was whirling. "But I thought we were working to uncover a plot to overthrow the King?" I asked.

"Trade is never just about money; it's about power," Madame de Treville answered. "In this case, there's a quasi–black market of sorts, funneling in foreign goods that are making their way into certain homes of la noblesse."

What reason would nobles have for—wait . . . "They're being bribed for their allegiance?"

"That's partially it. But we have reason to believe those aren't the only items the ships are bringing in. Weapons, Tania," she added, sensing my confusion. "It takes one weapon to kill a King. Many more to arm the chosen nobles so they're ready at the first sign of a power vacuum."

Dry mouthed, I eased my head against the cushions as Aria finished the explanation: "The royal family can't arrest or exile the suspected nobles without proof. That would spur another Fronde. Or something worse." I remembered what Madame de Treville had said about la noblesse's lack of care for the lives of working Parisians. And I looked at Aria, and I knew. That was the something worse—not that the Paris sewers would run royal blue, but that they'd run blue and crimson.

Approval flitted across Madame de Treville's face. "A good summation. Although I'd add that the King happens to be a thrill-seeking adolescent whose greatest desire is throwing highly attended and lavish parties. That is difficult to accomplish if half your court is in exile from a prior civil war, and the remaining half are locked away because you're worried they're determined to kill you. Don't look at me like that," she added as conversation quieted in the carriage. "The fact of the matter is, our King is no older than yourselves. You must disabuse yourself of the notion that he is incapable of flawed thinking. It is our job to recognize it. Or risk getting him killed." She punctuated her sentences with a thump of her lace fan against her palm. "But we're getting ahead of ourselves. Our mission tonight is to gather information, and to show Tania what to expect from assignments. Aria, you're a special favorite of the Marquis. I want to know why he's handed over the reins of this party to his son. He loves being the center of attention—why give that up? What's he doing instead? Or, what has he been pushed aside to make room for? There's something brewing there."

"Does she think it's related to the smuggling?" I whispered to Aria as our mentor turned her attention to Théa.

"Unclear. But it's useful information to have," Aria said. I raised my brow. "We need to know every secret of this city in order to properly protect it. If the Marquis is ever provoked to act against us, we remind him of what we know to keep him quiet. Madame de Treville trusts Mazarin. But if one of us is accused in public, it could be easier for him to feign ignorance, hand us over to the guards, and rebuild an entire new order. We must work to save the King and protect ourselves at the same time."

The carriage pulled to a halt, voices and music floating through the windows on either side. "Tania, as I told you in the hall, you'll shadow Aria." Madame de Treville finally addressed me. "Théa's and Portia's targets won't be amused with another mademoiselle hanging off their skirts. And I can't afford for Portia's target, the Comte's son, to lose interest—he may have the information we need on the smuggling ring."

"I hardly see any danger in the son losing interest in me. I first met him with ruffles clinging to my neck and progressed to this," Portia said, studying her chest. "If my neckline sinks any lower, I'll be attending balls topless. The poor thing might keel over on the spot."

I spluttered, but quickly turned it into a cough at the sight of Madame de Treville's disapproval. "Portia," she chastened.

"Yes, yes, I'll acquire the name of the man who's been visiting his father every other afternoon while he spends the night with his eyes glued to my breasts." Portia sighed. "But let the record show that next time, *I* want to be the one assigned to the daily stakeout and get to spy on the mysterious merchant man. Not his contact's boring son."

Madame de Treville exited. One by one each girl left until I remained alone in the carriage. The dizziness was one thing; when combined with fluttering nerves it was an entirely new beast. One I hadn't yet learned the workings of.

"Tania, are you coming?" One of the girls, I wasn't sure which. Regardless, they were all waiting for me, outside the carriage door.

A deep breath, a clench of my toes. Then I stepped down the stairs, looked up, and hid the drop of my jaw with a smile that said I belonged here.

CHAPTER FOURTEEN

ATTENDANTS STOOD AT intervals near the entrance, directing guests in lavish dresses and embroidered satin jackets. Lanterns spilled pools of light onto the cobblestone. They overlapped so the drive that led to the mansion was bathed in one continuous glow. We were let out near the front of l'hôtel particulier and were immediately surrounded by colors and sounds, conversations, music, carriage wheels, a mess my ears could hardly pick apart.

"Madame de Treville, a pleasure to see you." A partygoer's voice, wheedling, broke through the din. Madame de Treville curtsied to the man. His partner rested her spangled hand on the inner crook of his elbow. Their clothes were ostentatious, painfully so: heavy velvet dusted with diamonds, purple-blue feathers that bloomed across his jacket cuffs and her enormous skirts, gold and silver ribbon braided for trim.

"Baron du Bellay, the pleasure is all mine," Madame de Treville said.

"Your flock is flourishing, Madame. Je vous félicite."

"You are too kind," she said. "Thank you for your congratulations."

"I believe I spy a new face. You must introduce me." It took a moment for his words to sink in, and all my willpower not to duck behind Théa, away from the leer curving across the man's face. Not a good start to my first evening out.

Madame de Treville drew his attention elsewhere. "I must say, Baroness, what an exquisite brooch! A present for the birth of your son?"

She nodded primly, lips wrinkled in disapproval. "Oui. Il est notre héritier, après tout." The mention of his heir seemed to bring her husband back to earth, cutting through his lascivious wandering gaze.

Were these people willing to sacrifice the lives of others to gain another jewel, another parcel of land? Another feather on their already plumed caps? The Order was certain that a shift in leadership wouldn't be bloodless. And even I, with my limited time in Paris, was starting to understand that the nobles would likely try to shift that burden to anyone but themselves. Particularly, those with less power. One of the many things I'd learned in my lessons.

"Girls, quick now, before we're waylaid any further," Madame de Treville muttered before motioning to an attendant, who waved us on. "And Tania," she added, "don't wear your thoughts on your face. You'll give yourself away. Not to mention the wrinkles."

Once we were inside, Portia and Théa split in opposite directions, disappearing into the grand ballroom with its sweeping arches, gilt molding, and hundreds mingling and dancing under immense starry chandeliers of crystal and gold. More attendants bordered the walls, offering beverages and small bites to eat. This wasn't a supper party, so there wouldn't be a sit-down meal, and the sole entertainment was the musicians playing harpsichord and a few other string and wind instruments. Not as ostentatious as some outdoor events, like the firework displays the King loved so well, or the masquerades where you couldn't tell friend from foe. At least, that's what the girls told me. But the party was still a crashing wave that broke at my ankles, the clash of music against voices, against laughter, against clinking glasses and the susurrus of shoes against marble.

My lungs constricted, caged by ribs, by boning, by silk. How could I possibly fit in here? How could I carve a path for myself through the clamor? The last time I felt so helpless was ... Monsieur Allard, the carriage without Papa. No, before then. Back to Lupiac, to the starless night, to the men who hoped to leave me and Maman as bloody presents for Papa to find.

Someone gripped my elbow; it was Aria. "Breathe," she whispered. "The first time is the worst. All the excess. But you have to numb yourself to it, else they win. Remember why you are here. It is not about them. It is never about them. Breathe."

Out of the corner of my eye, I watched Théa greet the Marquis's son, who appeared to have indulged in enough liquor that he could care less about propriety and how Théa was currently unchaperoned.

"Madame de Treville!" An elderly gentleman motioned from a seat against the wall, raised on a platform with a table and a few empty chairs. The Marquis. His son must've put him there in hopes he'd remain out of the way. The man clapped when Aria came into view. "Et ma belle! You have blossomed. Une vraie fleur!"

"Marquis, thank you for the invitation." Madame de Treville curtsied deeply, and Aria and I followed suit.

"Oh, please, there's no need for that," the Marquis huffed. I straightened my legs; Aria's careful hand supported me, gripping my forearm. To any onlooker, it would appear a gesture of friendship. But Aria had never touched me before. I'd never seen her on the receiving end of one of Théa's hugs. And she wasn't like Portia, whose exacting hands forced my hair into the proper shape and untied the rocks from my ankles when I was too sore to lift my head. And yet, Aria was the first girl who'd known when I needed help, and hadn't made me ask for it. "The guest list is not under my purview," the Marquis continued. "No, the young don't want us *old* men having any fun. Don't want us planning parties or organizing festivities! B-But . . . ," he stammered, as if realizing the implication, "if your names weren't on the list, I'd have cut Bertrand off as heir!"

Madame de Treville put on a dazzling smile. It was the grin of a predator. One who'd been sharpening her teeth, readying herself to dine on the marrow of the Parisian elite: secrets. "You are too kind, Marquis. May I present Mademoiselle Tania."

He smiled distractedly, his eyes darting to Aria every so often. "Bienvenue, ma fille. Another of Madame de Treville's girls?"

I peeked at Aria, unmoored. I didn't know if I should reply, if we only spoke after Madame de Treville departed. But our mentor beat me to it. "She's been a wonderful addition to the household."

At the same time, Aria muttered in my ear, "Remember what I told you. You know what to do. Even if you don't, I'll fill in the gaps."

The Marquis focused on me, brightening. "A resident of la maison de Treville? You must be special, Mademoiselle. Only the most impressive young ladies earn that honor while the rest languish in envy!"

"Please excuse me," Madame de Treville said. "I must have

a word with Madame Buteau. Girls, you'll entertain the Marquis in my absence?"

The Marquis beamed. Hadn't Théa mentioned a man missing part of his finger? I sneaked a glance at the Marquis's fingers. Intact, all of them.

"Ma belle, it's been too long," he said to Aria, and patted the seat next to his. "Join me." Aria arranged her skirts, then sat. I followed her lead. The spot provided a clear view of the expansive ballroom. Perfect—I could watch Aria, learn from her example, and take in everything around me at the same time. And, if needed, if I saw Portia or Théa floundering, maybe I could try to help them, like they had promised to help me.

"Thank goodness the summer is over," Aria said. "I understand why everyone leaves the city, of course. Who would want to melt in such heat? But it does leave one with a want of companionship." She sighed, sparing a moment on the Marquis before flicking her eyes to the dancers. She sounded like an entirely different person.

"I could not agree with you more," the Marquis said.

As they continued their conversation, I cast my gaze around the room, landing on Théa. The Marquis's son n'avait d'yeux que pour elle, had eyes for no one but her, much to the consternation of two higher-ranking nobles trying to secure a moment with him. I studied how she tilted her head, how many teeth she showed when she laughed, filed it into the part of my brain bursting with Madame de Treville's rules and teachings.

But Portia had the most important role. Her target? A noble boy, whose father had suddenly developed a friendship with an unknown merchant, despite being a complete snob who rarely deigned speak to anyone with an actual profession. It took longer to find her—she was in the middle of the crowd, her palm pressed against her target's, her dress a swirling cascade of frozen river water. Even if the rest of us succeeded, whether or not we secured the information we vitally needed tonight rested on Portia. A terrifying thought, but she seemed to thrive on it, her hard edge becoming something powerful and dangerous that drew her target like a moth to flame.

"And are you enjoying Paris?"

I started at the Marquis's question. "Pardonnez-moi?"

He smiled good-naturedly. "How do you like the city? Ma belle tells me you've adapted so well, it's as if you'd been living here your entire life!"

Of course, Aria was exaggerating, but my face warmed. "It's wonderful—there's so much to see and do."

"You mustn't wear yourself out, not with the whole social season on the horizon. Court events are a pleasure after consorting with the masses," he said, surveying the room. "Much more refined. My son insisted on inviting lower-ranking noblesse. Even a professional or two. Not all his friends, though—some are too radical for my tastes."

From what I'd heard of the King's escapades, palace events were anything but conservative, but Aria unleashed a radiant smile. "Radical, you say?"

"Yes . . . yes," the Marquis said, unable to loosen his gaze from her. "I told my son, I told my Bertrand, I'd have nothing of the sort in my house! My crest will not be marred by philosophical rantings of adolescent schoolboys who are convinced la noblesse are a blight upon society."

"I don't approve of such ideas," Aria stated, her clear eyes briefly landing on mine before drifting.

"Of course not, ma belle. And neither does my son, truly—it is those ruffians, those outsiders who are the troublemakers. Some are students and, ma belle, the horrible books they read and the philosophers they speak of!" He lowered to a strained whisper. "I even heard one of them reference . . . *democracy*." The Marquis shuddered.

"I hope I never encounter such creatures," Aria said.

"Highly unlikely. You, such a fine specimen of femininity, consorting with individuals beneath you? Non, there is nothing for you to fear."

"Are you quite sure?" Aria pressed subtly, her hand floating inches from his. "If they are as brash and bold as you say, perhaps they would disguise themselves. Pretend to be people they are not."

"Why, they are just the sort of devious persons to undertake such a thing!"

"I must say," she demurred, "I've always been impressed by your ability to read people." The Marquis puffed out his chest. "If you'd been in charge of the guest list," she continued, "surely they wouldn't be here."

"Well, I have years more experience than Bertrand. But he wants to make his own decisions. If the rumors I've heard about these ruffians are to be believed, however, I'll have to step in. For his sake. You'll keep this between us, won't you? I'd hate for someone to misconstrue my son's friendship as him questioning his . . . loyalties."

Loyalty to the King? Or loyalty to the nobles—nobles who would see the King deposed?

"Of course. You are a good father," Aria said, softer now.

"Useless trying to reason with this younger generation," he

said, patting her hand. "Not you, of course, but the others. They think we'll be content pushed to the side." He stood, stretched his neck. "On to happier matters. Would you care to dance, ma belle?" He turned to me. "Forgive me for depriving you of her company."

"Monsieur, I wouldn't *dream* of interfering with your dancing."

Aria eyed me. Maybe I'd laid that on a little thick.

"Be that as it may, we must find you a partner." He clapped his hands, and I flinched. "Ah, Richard! Richard, do come here."

A man in his forties approached our trio, features twisted in displeasure. The Marquis had interrupted his conversation with a lady in pink silk ruffles and pearls for teeth. "Oui, Marquis?"

"You absolutely must dance with this lovely young lady." He looked at me expectantly. "Monsieur Richard is a friend of my son's. One of the few good eggs in that basket. Though I suppose that's because I knew him long before then. Back when you were a little boy, not un richard!" The Marquis wheezed at his own pun, his face a wrinkled tomato.

"Oh, Marquis, it isn't necessary—" I hurried as the man's expression darkened and he offered me his hand. Aria's face showed none of my concern, her expression unreadable.

I returned to the man's dark gaze, to his reluctant outstretched hand; my resolve rose. If word got around that I'd refused a dance at my first ball, I'd be labeled an impudent brat. And it would draw attention—the kind of attention the Order didn't want.

Curtsying, I smiled as I felt the weight of my dueling sword against my left hip, my dagger against my right. "An honor, Monsieur." The words were drawn out with my teeth and tongue.

He led me to the dancers, organized in parallel lines for the minuet. Portia was near my elbow, the icy blue of her gown unmistakable.

We will not let you fall.

My body responded instinctively to the music. I could feel it deep in my bones, reverberating inside the cavity of my chest. One step forward, one step back. My palm was flat against his as we stepped forward again, turned in a circle.

The dancers blurred together in a watercolor of pastels and jewel tones, curled hair like shifting clouds. Women with vibrant rouge and lip colors, pinks and purples and reds that I didn't know the names of and were nothing at all like the natural hues of the flowers in Maman's garden. If only she could see me now. Thriving in a way she thought I never could.

I was surrounded by people who didn't know my story. Didn't know my face, didn't know my body. And even though dizziness lingered at the edges of my vision, even though my toes were clenched tight within my slippers, I was gliding across the smooth surface of a stream. It was just a bout without the swords—a bout that I would win.

The night flew by in a whirl of petticoats and drunken laughter.

Everything was too much: the sound, the sight, the world one caliginous golden pool.

I'd returned to Aria after my dance with Monsieur Richard, but I'd only succeeded in resting for a few moments before another, a young boy this time, asked me to dance. When it was over, the dizziness was no longer creeping—it was stalking.

"It's stuffy in here, isn't it?" The boy tugged at his embroidered jacket. His breath was cramped and hot. Windows closed against the cold, room pleine à craquer, bursting with people. My fan provided no relief, only moved around sweltering air.

"Pardonnez-moi," I excused myself with a hollow smile that I couldn't force into the one I'd practiced in the mirror. Threading through the thick press of guests, I managed to reach the nearest wall. Despite clenching my toes, despite the desperate gasps for air, dark gray surged in from all corners of the ballroom. Théa said they'd never let me fall. My sisters in arms. But the dizziness grew: the rushing in my ears, the rushing of my heart. I looked for them anyway, and I hated it I hated it I hated how my body betrayed me and the mission I hated how there was no one here to help me but I was still looking anyway I hated it endlessly and yet, still, the dizziness grew.

They'd abandoned me. Just like Marguerite had.

I was going to faint. Maman's nightmare, me cracking my head open, except this time my blood wouldn't pool on village cobblestone, but Parisian parquet floor.

"Tania," at my ear. Guiding me through the darkness.

"Tania, can you hear me?"

The rush, the roar, the sting of air. "Théa?" Her face wavered in front of mine. "Where are we?" The words tripped; they rang in my ears like they'd come from someone else's tongue. Swirls of gray bloomed like carnations.

"The quickest way outside is the servants' entrance." When I tensed, readying to stand from what felt to be a bench, she protested, "No, wait here, I'll get you something to drink—better yet, I'll send Portia!"

They'd caught me. They hadn't let me fall. And yet . . . "Théa?" I said. She hesitated by the door. "Are you going to tell Madame de Treville?"

"I said we wouldn't let you fall, Tania."

Tears stung at my eyes as I closed them, tight.

A scraping noise, footsteps. I looked up to see Portia through the window, a drink in her hand. She was very still, eyes wide.

"Mademoiselle? Are you all right?"

My heart scrambled. Someone had seen me; dizzy, sick. In the darkness, it was hard to discern his features. A figure: a boy or a man, though his voice wasn't rough with age. I glanced to Portia in terror. But she shook her head, then jerked it in the stranger's direction.

"I'm sorry to surprise you like this—if it makes you more comfortable, I'll stay over here," he said. A shaft of light from a lantern threw a segment of his face into relief. A hazel eye, liquid warm, a span of eyebrow, the beginnings of a strong nose. I arranged them in my mind, stomach fluttering. "I saw you inside; you appeared very ill. And I wanted to make sure you were all right. That you had someone there for you."

Portia be damned—I wasn't ready for this. "Monsieur, thank you for your kindness, but I must return—"

"That ballroom is a furnace." He searched my face. "I could locate a mademoiselle to sit with you? I'll leave if you wish it."

"Oh no, please, don't mistake me! I didn't mean to imply— that is, I don't want you to think—" I rushed over myself to return to my role. Disarmed by thoughtfulness.

But his lips quirked in a smile as I stammered. "I'm not the presumptuous sort to assume a mademoiselle's sentiments. Or the kind to write someone off who is struggling in any capacity. I only meant to convey that I won't impose myself upon you." He didn't show any signs of disgust or disinterest. He didn't know the truth, had only seen me on the verge of fainting in the ballroom . . . but the way he spoke about acceptance cracked my chest open.

"Monsieur," I settled for, my voice molasses rich, right off the spoon, surprising even myself, "your presence is the furthest thing from an imposition." And when his eyes seared across my face, my returned smile was almost entirely the smile of a Mousquetaire. Almost.

"There you are!" Portia cried, bursting through the door as if she'd just arrived on the scene, "I've been looking all over for you!"

If the man noticed her strength, how she scooped me up, her arm linked with mine, he didn't say so. "I'll take my leave now that you're cared for." He bowed. Still keeping his distance, he returned inside.

I waited until the door closed. "Portia, what was that?"

"Trial by fire. You didn't do half bad. Your nerves clearly got the best of you at the start; we can work on that."

"But who was—"

"No idea. I didn't set him on you, that's for sure. But he served his purpose, did he not?" She laughed at my expression. "He was besotted. I'm told it's a confidence boost, the first time a man shows real interest in you. And what you sorely need, my dear Tania, is confidence."

By the time Aria and I had left the Marquis, who'd pleaded with us—rather, Aria—to stay a little longer, my cheeks were full and warm with rosy flush. After Portia escorted me back to Aria and the Marquis, I'd sat for the rest of the night, Aria blocking me from the majority of the onlookers and interested dance partners, as I waited for the dark spots to fully clear from my vision.

"Quickly," Aria ground out, "before he tries to convince me to watch him gamble away all his money in the other room with the spendthrift nobles."

Tilting my head, I motioned for her to follow me into the night air. We stood by a wide torch—the lanterns only bordered the drive up to the mansion—these were for warmth as well as light. We were far enough away from the attendants and guards that no one would hear us if we spoke quietly.

"Did you learn anything?" I asked.

She nodded curtly. "We'll discuss it later."

Her profile was pale, illuminated in the flames. Shadows flickered at the edges of her cheekbones. "Did . . . did . . ." I tried to ask her if Portia or Théa mentioned what'd happened. But as I looked at her face, struck with cool focus, my words stalled.

"Did you do all right?" She finished my question incorrectly; I let her have it. Some of the iciness leaked from her expression. "You were fine. Good, even. It's how he talks about them—the students. He's so dismissive."

"But I thought that was what we're trying to suppress? People attempting to attack the foundation of our—"

"There's a difference between those wishing to overtake France for another monarchy and hopeful young men and women who don't want to cause harm, merely wish their countrymen had enough to feed their families and roofs over their heads instead of starving while the royals gorge themselves on food and drink. Not to be shut out of decision-making because they don't have a drop of blue blood in their veins. Those specific rumors he spoke of, those are no use to us."

I stiffened at the malice in her voice. "But isn't your family part of the noblesse, too? Are you trying to say you are antiroyalist?"

"Keep your voice down. You'll get us both killed," Aria hissed. Once she led us to an even quieter spot, near where we'd meet the others, she continued. "I don't think of things in terms of such labels. It limits a person to one goal."

"So, you want the country to be for everyone, but you don't care what form of government that takes?"

A flash of surprise crossed her face. "Perhaps. You'd be wise to conceal that quick thinking of yours. In our line of work, to be smart is to hide our wit. We women are not meant to understand such things. It's why the Order is so effective. No one sees une Mousquetaire de la Lune coming until it is too late. We have their reputation, their hearts, their lives in the palms of our hands . . . on the edges of our swords." Aria paused, her gaze drifting to the open doors. "There's the carriage now. And the others," she added.

I turned with her, scanning the crowd. But I stopped when I felt eyes boring into me. When our gazes met over the torch flame he smiled, slow as velvet. Hazel irises warm in the flickering light.

"Tania, are you coming?"

I jerked toward Théa's voice. She was waiting at the carriage steps, the others already inside.

"One moment," I said, sneaking a glance back at the crowd of people.

But he was gone.

CHAPTER FIFTEEN

"TELL ME AGAIN, Portia, what your target told you," Aria whispered.

I flattened myself against the wall. Two days after the ball, my grainy vision was finally starting to clear, my body loosening the knots it'd contorted itself into.

"I've repeated it a thousand times—" Portia complained, too loud for our position near the gate of the Comte de Monluc's Paris residence. The three of us were pressed tight to a stone wall, Aria peeking around the corner every so often in case our target appeared. The empty side street had been busy, a convenient location for food and flower deliveries, but in the afternoon, the only noise wafted in from the main street it connected to.

"Portia . . . ," Aria coaxed.

Portia dropped her eyes to the ground, then lifted to a spot over Aria's shoulder. "The Comte's visitor is Monsieur Verdon's younger brother—the one who went into business instead of the military and subsequently got himself written off by his entire family, except for Monsieur Verdon. Quelle horreur, indeed."

While I hadn't mentioned what happened to Madame de

Treville that night, not with the threat of losing her support, the other girls were worried. Aria had stared at me, long and slow, as Portia recounted the circumstances behind my chance encounter. Not hurt that I hadn't told her, no, more a look of examination. Like she was studying me.

Despite the girls' acceptance, there was still that current of fear that shocked through my veins; all those years of doing my best to pretend nothing was wrong had stitched a permanent mark into my skin.

Aria flicked away a stray hair as Portia finished. "Interesting how you omitted everything he mentioned about the money—"

Portia scoffed. "It's not relevant to the task at hand that he prattled on about the increasing size of his coffers and coupled it with euphemisms that I won't sully sweet Tania's ears with; she'll light up the entire alley with her blush. But you know full well that boy would've told me he had a key to the King's jewel vault if he thought it would win me over."

"Well, then," Aria tossed back, "I suppose it's lucky you're not easily won over."

"What is that supposed—"

Aria cut her off with a hiss. "He's here."

"Are you sure?" I asked. I caught the glimpse of a waving cloak's hem, its owner already past my sight range.

"Servants use the side entrance. Besides, his chin does resemble that of his older brother, Verdon senior," Aria noted. "Before you ask, Portia, yes. That was all I could see. And yes, I still have that handy ability to remember a face that I've seen before."

Beside me, Portia scowled. I rubbed at my temples. Ever since I'd first heard the name Verdon, a memory had scratched at my subconscious, along with a distinct, uneasy sensation.

As thrilling as it was to be part of a mission that didn't involve seduction, the minutes we waited felt like hours, each second slowed to a trickle. With the sun at its zenith, heat beat lazily against the back of my neck and my forearms. Paris might've been on the cusp of winter, but the frozen sun was a miserable beast to bear in a wool cloak.

"Tania, cover me," Portia said, and I turned, reaching for my hidden dueling sword, to see her hike up her skirts. I shrieked and covered my eyes. "Oh, pardonnez-moi, please point me in the direction of the conveniently located cabinet d'affaires that only you seem to be aware of."

Grumbling, hand against the wall for balance, I stood in front of Portia and blocked her from the view of any curious Parisians as she relieved herself.

"I think this has been a real bonding experience for us, don't you?" Portia said after she finished.

Aria flapped her hand at us. "He's leaving." Once the coast was clear, Aria took a step back with a sigh. "Now, Tania."

I cupped my hands around my mouth and whistled out a birdcall Papa taught me when I was a child. The next moment, Théa emerged from her flattened position atop the town house across from the Comte's residence. She squeaked along the roof, climbed down a decorative trellis, then scampered across the street, narrowly avoiding a trundling carriage.

Reunited, we walked a ways down the main street, acting as if we were on a mere diverting stroll. Not breathing in the fumes of garbage and muck.

"The younger Verdon had papers in the folds of his cloak; I saw them when he entered, when the fabric shifted as he went through the gate," Théa said. "I didn't see them there when he left."

My shoulders tensed at the clatter of wheels, but it was only Madame de Treville's carriage. "Mesdemoiselles!" she proclaimed through the window, loud enough for any passersby to hear, "I decided to join you; let's travel to la Place Royale together. It's the perfect day to view the statue of Louis XII—Tania, you're in for a treat."

We filed into the carriage. Madame de Treville's feigned smile fell off her face as quick as it appeared and morphed into a frown as we recounted what we'd learned. As she listened, she handed me a cool wet cloth from a bowl at her feet. I draped it on my neck with a sigh.

". . . He's the right age for Verdon's brother. And while I didn't get a full look at his face, it was enough," Aria finished.

Portia picked up where Aria left off. "Verdon's brother is based in Marseille. Weeks away from Paris, which means that, if he's been frequenting le Comte's home every few days, he has to be staying somewhere nearby. He left the Marseille port when he should be finishing up business before the winter storms. And now he's delivering papers, too?"

Madame de Treville stared at the carriage wall. "He must've been introduced to the Comte by the elder Verdon, although given that the younger is the money-making black sheep of the family, it does seem plausible they could all be involved in the plot. It's the easiest way to connect their dots, but we can't prove it. Yet." Her voice quieted as her eyes darted between us, landed on me for a beat longer, as if she could see the dizziness lingering, then out the carriage window. "We could try to discover where he is staying . . . but that would be like trying to find a chestnut shell in all of Paris. Not to mention how much of our time it would take up, time that could be spent investigating known locations of suspects."

Théa's drowsing figure heaved. Her sleeping head flopped onto Portia's shoulder. Portia motioned to Théa, rolled her eyes in dismay. I hid a small smile, however, when Portia didn't wake her.

The carriage slowed to travel over a rut. In that moment, I caught sight of an archway in the shadows. A wide hole gaped between two rickety buildings. Through it, a road extended down a steep hill and out of sight. "Where does that lead to?"

"That," Madame de Treville said, nose upturned as if she'd caught a whiff of garbage, "is La Cour des Miracles." I ducked my head through the window for a glimpse, but her hand clawed me back. "It is unbecoming for a lady to gape," she sniffed.

Aria, ever observant, tapped her skirts—a sign to wait. When Madame de Treville was sufficiently distracted instructing Portia on how to fidget less at formal suppers, Aria bent over, feigning a dropped handkerchief. "The Court of Miracles is not what it sounds like," she murmured, eyes flicking up to greet mine. "It's almost entirely populated by beggars. Ones who return home after long days on the streets with their ailments miraculously vanished: the blindness, the bad legs . . . Les malingreaux, les piètres, les francs mitoux. Different names, united by pretense."

My chest ached as I thought back to the first doctors Maman had taken me to, the ones who told her I was acting out, that I wasn't actually sick. "But surely not all of them are pretending. Why condemn a whole group of people?"

Aria's typical impassive expression broke into bewilderment. "You really don't get it, do you?"

"Get what?"

"La noblesse. They hate the beggars. Anything that reminds them the world is not perfect and beautiful. They detest any reminder of their own mortality. Beggars are the perfect target to blame for any and all social ills. Even Madame de Treville derides them, despite us working to protect them from the potential aftermath of the King's murder. Whether their ailments are real, aren't real—it doesn't matter to them. Think about it. The nobles will probably blame his death on the Court's inhabitants. All the usurpers have to do is proclaim they've solved the crime. They'll point their fingers at the beggars, and then assume power as a means of enacting justice. No one cares what happens to the Court. Nobles can have beggars hung for stealing a loaf of bread." Her impassioned speech, combined with the flash in her eyes, piqued my curiosity.

"How do you know so much about this place? About the attitudes of the lords and ladies?"

"You ask too many questions."

"But isn't that what we're trained to do? Find answers?" I countered.

She smiled sharply, thin lips almost disappearing. "I was worried when you arrived. I thought your moments of ferocity were too infrequent. Your ability to find embarrassment at every turn. But you're not meek, are you? You're burning for answers to questions you don't even know yet.

"I won't apologize for my misjudgment. I wasn't wrong to be skeptical. Any threat to our work's secrecy is a threat against me. Besides, apologies are worthless. A person can only truly prove her intentions through actions." She surveyed me a beat longer, then let out a breath. "As an offering of good will . . . the reason

I know is because of personal experience." She straightened in her seat, finished with the conversation even if I wasn't.

A moment later another question burst through my lips. "But I don't—"

Aria's gray irises were all stone and steel. "You do not grow up in La Cour des Miracles without understanding how despised you are."

What Aria said . . . it didn't make any sense. Madame de Treville used the other girls' names and family titles to her advantage. One mystery mademoiselle in L'Académie baited the nobles' curiosity; any more would provide unwanted attention.

Aria couldn't be from La Cour des Miracles. She was noble born. She had to be.

In the bright on-the-brink-of-winter light, I studied Aria's face. Aria, for whom Madame de Treville had an endless wealth of praise; Aria, who never second-guessed any move she made . . . who had Aria been before all this?

When we turned onto our street, exhausted and stomachs growling, the carriage faltered a few hundred feet away from the house. I lurched out of my seat, saved by Portia's lightning-quick arm across my torso. Théa fell forward and woke with a snort.

"What in the world . . . ," Madame de Treville said. She craned her neck out the window. In the next moment, she iced over.

"Madame—"

"Wait here." Our mentor cut Théa off with a look that could

cut a diamond clean in half, gathered her skirts in her fists, and let herself out into the cooling air.

"What do you think it could be?" Théa wrung her hands.

Aria leaned out the carriage window like Madame de Treville had. "There are horses tethered outside," she murmured. "I can't be sure. The saddles look like they have a Musketeers' seal—"

I didn't wait for the rest, just scrambled out of the carriage with Portia at my heels. We sped through the open doorway. Nearly fell head over feet at the sight of our mentor and a man in a full cassock, high boots. For a moment, a brief, glorious moment, I thought it was him. I thought it was Papa. Come to revel in how far I'd come. To tell me he was proud of his Mademoiselle la Mousquetaire.

But then the candlelight bent—his profile, his dark hair, the furrow between his brows, none of it was my father. Their words were quick, hurried. Probably one of the senior officials Madame de Treville mentioned that very first day in the parlor.

By the time his eyes grazed across us, we were ready. Waiting to curtsy demurely, gazes lowered, Portia let out a breathy apology, all the while keeping her hand at my elbow: "Excusez-nous, we didn't mean to interrupt."

When the man shook his head his curls shifted under his plumed hat. "Don't worry yourselves. I was just leaving." He bowed shallowly and stepped aside as Théa and Aria joined us, red cheeked and curious.

"Madame." He nodded to our mentor. "Souvenez-vous, le temps presse. Notre roi est bouleversé et—"

"Dites-lui que c'est sous contrôle."

There wasn't time to wonder why time was short, why the King was worried, why Madame thought we had everything under control, because the man was leaving, and I couldn't let that happen. Not a man who might've protected France with Papa. Not a man who could help me find out what really happened.

"Monsieur!" I cried out. He turned on his polished heel. "J'aimerais prendre un peu de votre temps. Only a brief moment of your time, please."

"Ladies, leave us," Madame de Treville said. Aria had already exited the entryway; Théa was at the door frame. Portia huffed in frustration before pulling Théa into the hall and closing the door.

"Cette fille," he asked Madame, "this girl, she is the one? The daughter of de Batz?" Madame de Treville nodded, but she didn't interject. Removing his hat, he crouched down, as if I were a small child. I recoiled instinctively. But still, this could be my father's friend, so I forced a receptive smile, readied for him to wax on about Papa, willed my eyes to be dry as forgotten bones. "We mourn your father's loss with you," he declared.

Time stretched painfully before he stood up with a groan. "The body of an old man, I have. Should've stretched while I had the chance!"

Papa's laughter hit me with a slap; his jokes about his aching knees, his badges of honor. I blinked and the man was walking away. "Monsieur! His death was suspicious. Wasn't what the maréchaussées painted it to be."

Madame de Treville stiffened, a small angry breath escaping her lips.

On route to his head, his hat paused midair, brim gripped by scarred fingers. Those weren't fingers flayed from breaking apart a fence; he'd earned those scars. That's what Musketeers did. Earned their wounds. "I didn't know your father as well as I would've liked; when he left for Lupiac I was only beginning my duties. But what I did know about him, from what I observed and from stories, was that the Musketeers' duties? He fully embodied them. Honor, duty, sacrifice. We sign our lives over in service to the country. And our King, Mademoiselle, he is in danger. We can't afford to draw attention—we don't have the resources to investigate every retired Musketeer's death."

"Papa did everything to protect his King, and this is how you repay him? The King will always be in danger," I retorted, the weight of it leaving me breathless. Madame de Treville burned livid beside me.

For a brief moment, I wondered if he'd curse at me. But instead, he returned his hat atop his curls, shadowing the hard lines of his profile. "Precisely, Mademoiselle. Our King will always be our priority." He looked to Madame de Treville. "Perhaps it would be wise to remind these girls who exactly they're fighting for."

My breath, my heartbeat, they all rushed in my ears. "I assure you," Madame de Treville gritted out, "my Musketeers are well under control. In fact, I'm about to write to Cardinal Mazarin about the girls' discovery today." I opened my mouth to speak, desperate to further plead my case. But Madame de Treville's hand came down on my shoulder, tightened, as she said: "Au revoir, Monsieur."

At the sound of the front door closing she spun me around, face gleaming with fury. "You foolish girl! Have you forgotten everything I've told you? Your very purpose in being here?"

"I told you I wanted to fight for my father—I didn't know that fighting for the King meant giving up fighting for Papa!"

"Don't you see, Tania! Can't you see!" Madame de Treville's

face was warped with uncharacteristic emotion. "Fighting for the King *is* fighting for your father."

I shook my head, strands of hair threaded with tears. "I have to speak with another officer. One who knew Papa, knew him better, knows . . ."

"Knows what, Tania? What do you know that they don't?" The cloaked robbers, Papa's overturned desk, Beau's empty stall. Papa on the side of the road, Papa a piece of stone they carved into, Papa Papa Papa.

"I have to try."

"Let's say you go. What makes you think they'll take you seriously? Besides Monsieur Brandon, who does not take kindly to being insulted, none of les Mousquetaires du Roi know about us. And Brandon is the most understanding of the lot! If you told them, you'd compromise Mazarin's purpose for us. And they wouldn't even believe you—remember, I know these men. I know what they say about determined young women. I will not let you throw away everything we have worked for. Everything you have worked for." Head thumping, stomach churning, I clawed at the side table for balance. Some of the heat leached from Madame de Treville's face. "Believe me when I tell you that the best thing you can do is help find the traitors. Especially now."

Through the dizziness, through the haze, my mind tightened. "Especially now?"

"To the parlor; I don't want to have to repeat myself." Madame de Treville went to open the door but was forced back when Théa and Portia tumbled through the frame. "Practicing eavesdropping for the upcoming ball, I see."

Skin acrawl, I prepared for the questions. But Théa slipped

her arm through one of mine, Portia the other. And we stayed like that until we sat down in the parlor, waiting for the news.

Madame de Treville sank into the chair nearest the fire. "There's been an . . . incident." She withdrew a letter from her tie-on pocket; the Musketeer must've given it to her when he arrived. The gold wax seal stark against the creamy paper. The King's seal.

Rage and grief mingled deep in my chest, but there was room for guilt there, too. Guilt for my impulsiveness. For my inability to comprehend the gravity of the situation we'd rushed into. What was bad enough to warrant a message from the King?

"An incident?" Portia prompted.

"His servant didn't know any better and called for the guards. Our King was curious about the commotion in his dressing room, so of course he decided to march right in before anyone had the sense of mind to shut the damn door. The last thing we needed was the King terrified his own quarters aren't safe—"

"Madame, what was *it*?" Aria asked.

"Someone completely drenched one of the King's ceremonial crowns in blood. Smeared a message on the mirror while they were at it. *Votre règne se terminera pendant la nuit la plus longue. Vive La Fronde.*"

Your reign will end on the longest night. Long live La Fronde.

"Blood?" Théa forced the words out, teeth cracking together. "You don't actually think someone—"

"Non, they must have procured it à la boucherie." Madame de Treville's mention of the butcher calmed Théa, but one glance at Aria's unconvinced expression was all it took to know that Madame was merely placating her. Trying to keep images of metal and gemstones drowning in thick red streams from invading her thoughts. My nails carved unstrung bows into my palms.

"It's a clear threat," Madame de Treville continued, "given the crown's symbolism—not to mention l'artiste had access to the King's private quarters."

"You think someone inside the palace is involved?" Aria asked.

"We can't be sure, although anyone who had the means to commit the act was fired. New servants will be vetted by the King's personal guard."

Again, just like Aria had told me. Again, working Parisians suffered for the greed of the noblesse. Someone was likely murdered to deliver the message. An innocent life, snuffed out because of them.

They'd be alive if we'd discovered the coconspirators. I told myself I hadn't had enough time to make a quantifiable difference, not yet. But that didn't alleviate the choking guilt.

"Why warn of a date? What do they have to gain by revealing part of their plan?" Théa asked.

"They want him scared, to cancel festivals and celebrations and public appearances. It'll lead to angry nobles, angry merchants . . . angry Parisians. He's already on thin ice. Some think he's spending too much; others think he's not spending enough. There are nobles who would've preferred the outcome of La Fronde to be something very different," Madame de Treville said. "Our job is to uncover the truth; that hasn't changed. But there can be no more hesitation, no more waiting: The time for less dangerous missions is behind us, now that we know there's a deadline. Choosing the winter solstice is no coincidence. They'll have the added cover of darkness for their uprising, and it's in the middle of des fêtes de Noël. Can you imagine the chaos they'd rain down upon Paris, upon all of France, if they not only killed the King, but killed the King *then*?"

Horror struck Portia's face. "Mon Dieu . . . isn't that the day of the Winter Festival? The banks of the Seine will be packed. You don't think they'd attempt anything there? Or after, at the ball in the palace?"

Théa shivered. Portia looked to Aria. And I sat there, staring at the gold wax seal, unable to keep it from shifting and transforming into a bloody golden crown that sat atop my father's head, little strands of gray peeking through his brown hair.

The intimate garden soiree was so very different from last week's ball. At least, it seemed like it was; it was hard to tell as lookout. My position at the window afforded me a view of the office entrance, a few paces over from where I was posted, as well as le Jardin des Tuileries, which bloomed across the Seine. The guests' daytime party gowns were mere pastel dots along the northern terrace of the gardens.

"Have you found it yet?" Portia asked from the office door. Our target this afternoon was the business partner of the younger Verdon. As Madame de Treville had predicted, there wasn't enough time for us to discover the younger Verdon's location. But his business partner's was another story. The partner's office in Paris was bright, airy—and today, empty of bustling merchants and vendors as he laughed and chatted and did whatever else one does when likely trying to convince nobles to betray their King. But even though I could not see her, I knew Théa was entrancing the man to her side, hindering his subterfuge and providing us time to work.

"Aria," Portia gritted out, "I hate repeating myself . . ."

"Got it." Aria riffled through the book. "Records for the past two calendar years. There's a chance I might need to find earlier records to compare . . ."

"Everyone down!" I whispered. I peered over the sill while Portia and Aria ducked to the floor. After a closer glimpse of the man weaving through carriages, I sighed. "It wasn't him. Only someone with the same unfortunate taste in hats."

"Normally I'd be furious at you for making me worry," Portia said, dusting off her pleated skirts, "but that might be the first funny thing I've heard you say, so I'll allow it. Next time you won't be a beginner on lookout duty, though, so take this as a warning."

Aria cleared her throat, scrawling across a fresh sheet of paper with a piece of charcoal. "Does no one remember that I've found what we're looking for?"

"Go on, then," Portia said.

"Well, *now* you have to wait for me to copy it—"

Portia's eyes glimmered. "I swear, Aria, sometimes you make me want to—"

"And . . . finished." Aria tucked the copy into her cloak. "A sudden, though nonetheless large increase of livres on the books in the past two months," she told us as we rushed to return everything to the way we'd found it. "Not to mention the shift in imports earlier this year. Chocolate, Seville oranges. And then some abbreviations, but we can figure out those later. Suspicious, *non*? Luxuries that the nobles would love to get their hands on. Perfect for bribes."

Sneaking out the back entrance was easy enough. Théa had a stash of threadbare clothing she tinkered with in preparation for missions like these; the three of us were draped in dusty brown wool. If anyone suspected us to be other than servants, we had our swords. But I hoped it didn't come to that.

Once outside, we squeezed the cloaks behind empty barrels. Portia rearranged her garden dress underneath her real cloak. "I thought I was going to suffocate. Théa has all the luck."

We'd been careful. Hadn't left a book out of place. I might've been new, but I had Portia and Aria with me; they wouldn't let anything go wrong. But to stave off suspicion, we crossed the Seine and inserted ourselves into the garden party, taking care to greet a handful of nobles each.

Théa was to stay with her target. We might've gotten the copies we needed, but if Théa could wriggle more out of him, maybe we could put an end to all this today. Protect the displaced palace workers, the derided inhabitants of La Cour des Miracles, before the nobles even had a chance to spill blood in the streets. I thought back to Aria, when she spoke of how the nobles would blame members of La Cour for the death of the King. People who were told their illnesses, their conditions, were worn like masks.

Portia, attached to my hip in case the heat of having worn two cloaks proved too much for my dizziness, led the way. But not without watching Aria melt herself into a raucous group of young men.

There were Parisians being told they were lying about their illnesses—and yet here I was, dizziness and all, listening to a noble drone on about his portrait gallery's latest acquisition. Why was I the one who was chewing on a pastry so delicate it could very well float off my tongue? Were there other girls, other girls like me, who were starving in La Cour? "I swear," Portia said, smile miraculously somehow still intact, as he finally left us, "if I had to spend one more minute listening to that pompous man explain the importance of art, mon Dieu, I would've cut out his tongue. Doesn't he realize he isn't my tutor? He completely butchered the significance of Nicolas Poussin's use of color gradient. And worst of all: he made us *late*! Oh, I hope he's part of the plot, if only to have the chance to see him cower at the end of my sword."

We made our way back to Aria, who dallied near the riverbank. Lacy parasols bobbed like multicolored birds through the air. Laughter floated over deep emerald hedges and ornamental trees arranged in miniature groves.

"Shouldn't Théa be back by now?" I asked Portia, voice hushed. "Wasn't that the plan?"

Portia didn't tease me; her dark eyes reflected my concern. "Aria, where's Théa?"

Aria tensed. "She went with her target after he said he saw you two in the hedge maze. She was wondering where you were, and—"

"Merde." Portia shot off in the direction of the maze, swooping between lone hedges to remain out of sight.

"Go with her," Aria said to me. "I'll wait for Madame de Treville, tell her what's happening."

If something was wrong, if something was really wrong—not accidentally-stepping-on-someone's-foot-during-the-minuet wrong, not snorting-out-a-laugh-when-a-target-proved-himself-a-foppish-fool wrong—what could I do to help, truly help? Draw away attention by fainting? "But I—"

"Go!" Aria repeated. "Théa has Portia to help her. But who will be there to help Portia? What if she . . ." Aria's voice broke.

I hurried after Portia. Stopped every so often to rest my palm against a tree, a hedge. Waited for my vision to clear enough to continue.

The maze towered above me, green bushes solid as stone. I didn't see Portia, but I could hear the shuffling of shoes against dirt, of branches against silk. I found her scrunched against an interior wall, eyes narrowed, ears pricked.

"What's going on . . ." Hands slapped against someone's chest. A voice scratching at the air, warped with panic and almost unrecognizable. Almost.

"Wait here," Portia whispered. "Keep anyone from coming down this path." With that, she thrust herself around the corner of the hedge. "Get your hands off her!"

Théa needed us. Which meant not rushing after Portia—no matter how much I wanted to. This was how I could help.

Indistinguishable words in a placating tone. A flurry of voices, a loud exclamation.

I peered around the hedge, clapped a hand over my mouth. Portia's dagger was poised at a man's throat—Verdon's business partner and Théa's target; I could tell even in the dim. Portia's teeth bared in a snarl. Théa was hidden in the shadows. Pulling back, I rested against the greenery to calm the wild thrum of my heart.

When Théa and Portia appeared, we didn't stop, just powered out of the maze, running through the trees for cover until we reached Aria, who led Théa to the banks of the Seine.

He hadn't followed us.

Portia made a sound of disapproval as I took a small step toward Théa. I searched for the outline of my sword under my dress. The familiar feel of it was a balm in the flush of fear and the running and the sound of Théa's voice that also wasn't Théa's voice at all. "You used your dagger . . . ," I said.

"He won't turn me over to the authorities, if that's what you're worried about. No gentleman would admit to being bested by a lady—think of what la noblesse would say about his strength and honor. Besides," Portia said, adjusting a crystal earring that had slipped out of place, "who would believe him?"

"But what happens when someone doesn't fear social ruin?"

Portia hesitated as she brought a hand to her brow to block the sun's glare. Her eyes drifted over Théa's and Aria's huddled figures, softened. "Hence why weapons are a last resort."

"Then you haven't dueled anyone before?"

"Now, I didn't say that. A month or so before you arrived, we closed in on a murder suspect—we thought he might've been affiliated with the smugglers. He wasn't, though we didn't know that at the time. Just a man who enjoyed the feeling of silencing a pulse. Aria and I cornered him outside a party and pretended we were interested in . . . you know . . ." She trailed off, then refocused. "It was easy to lure him into a secluded alleyway." She snorted, but her eyes glimmered with something stronger. "He confessed to the murders, two of the King's favorite personal attendants—he was sure I'd be dead at his hand moments later. I left him bleeding and broken and knocked out cold."

"Did he . . . did you kill him?"

"Les Mousquetaires du Roi saw to that. His execution was a spectacle; it's how they dissuade possible treachery." She studied me intently. "But if I had to, I would've killed him."

"You say it like it's so simple."

"But that's just it, it *is*," she insisted. "I won't sacrifice my life to keep my hands clean. I meant what I said about leaving a legacy. About making things better for us and all the Mousquetaires de la Lune who will come after us. I won't have them think me weak, incapable of doing what is necessary, because I'm a woman.

Being part of the Order means proving that women are just as capable as men and protecting our sisters. Don't worry, Tania. Like I said: a last resort."

"Girls!" We started at Madame de Treville's voice. She waved us toward the carriage. Aria and Théa were already inside. "Quickly!"

Théa had closed herself into a corner. Madame de Treville wrung her hands in her lap, the copies from the office pressed between them on the bench. "Did you take care of it?" she asked Portia.

"He wasn't going to back down."

The rest of the ride was silent.

Madame de Treville didn't wait for us to exit before hurrying out of the carriage. We descended the small steps and entered the front door to see a flash of skirts round the corner to her study.

"She's regrouping," Aria told me. "Making sure we have enough information to move on to the next step of investigating, so we don't have to interact with him at any future events."

In my room, with a hiss of relief, I removed my shoes. They were padded for comfort, and to make fencing easier, but that didn't change the fact that slippers weren't designed for chasing down assailants.

When I went into the hallway, Portia and Aria were arguing by Théa's door. Portia's midnight eyes flashed, dagger sharp.

Aria paused when I was still halfway down the hall; Portia didn't acknowledge my approach until I was a few feet away. Her gaze didn't leave Aria's. "Théa wants to talk to you."

I rapped my knuckles on the door before heading in, feet raw on the carpet, blinking away the dizziness. Once it was manageable, I released the doorknob.

Théa sat on her bed, so very small. Her eyes were swollen. I bit away tears. This wasn't my pain and I wouldn't claim it for my own, even though my chest was flayed open.

"You must think me such a liar. So weak. All that talk of being able to take care of myself," Théa sniffled.

"That's what you wanted to talk to me about?" I went to sit beside her. The pale blue bed coverings crinkled under us. "Théa, you're anything but weak. You're hurting. That's different."

"I know better, though, I do! I was ridiculous to believe him. That he truly had seen you and wanted to help me find you and Portia." She blew her nose before crumpling up her handkerchief. "I didn't lie about the Vicomte de Comborn, though. I *did* cut off part of his finger. It comes and goes, you know? Sometimes it's as if I'm over it; I won't think of it for weeks. But other times . . . if a person's behind me, and I can't see where the touch is coming from, it's like I'm frozen. I'm back to that one moment. That one memory. It doesn't matter how long it's been. Everyone else continuing on, time continuing on, but I'm frozen." When I made to pull back, to give her room, she shook her head vehemently. "This helps. Being close to friends and having it be my choice." The flash of memories, on a loop: Théa's brimming happiness at my arrival. Aria's gentle reprimand about personal space. Théa's concern, which seemed to border on pain. "The Order was the best way to prove I was past it, but I'm not, and maybe I never will be, and maybe I have to accept that, but I have all of you, and that is wonderful, is it not?"

I smiled at her and did not cry. "Yes. It's wonderful."

Théa nodded, worrying at her lip. "It was before Paris, before . . . that is, I . . . ," she started haltingly.

"You don't have to tell me."

"It's not that I don't trust you, it's . . ." She exhaled deeply. "Thank you." She pulled me into a tight hug and withdrew when my arms had lost all feeling. "I think—no, I know—I'd like to be alone now."

I paused at the door. "Théa," I said. "I meant what I said . . . about you not being weak. You're one of the strongest people I know."

After I left, I leaned against the closed door, guilt and frustration bitter on my tongue.

How could I tell my friend to trust her strength if I couldn't even trust my own?

Chapter Sixteen

TWILIGHT FILTERED THIN through the permanently shuttered windows on the second floor; my bedroom was no exception. Sheets of paper overflowed to the carpeted floor: all abysmal drafts of letters, all for Maman. She'd only written to me once, a few weeks after I arrived in Paris, to tell me she'd made it to my uncle's safely. I'd replied to let her know I was settled, too. Other than that, no missives had passed between us. I didn't want to write her—no, I didn't *want* to want to write her. There was everything to tell. And nothing. The Order's secrets weren't for her eyes. But there was this yearning in me, mellow and so smooth that I'd hardly noticed it until it was lapping at my throat. The need to tell her that I was proving myself. Even with the stumbles, the setbacks. How hard I worked, how I would craft myself into someone strong enough for the Mousquetaires de la Lune, strong enough to find Papa's killer. How I wasn't broken. How every day I transformed further into steel.

Fat salty drops blurred the sentence I'd agonized over for an entire hour. A simple attempt to thank her for the cloak.

Barefoot, I padded into the hallway in search of a water jug.

There was usually a spare one kept by the . . . I paused. Someone was walking silently through the training room.

"Henri?" His given name flew out before I could stop myself. My mind flashed to the empty room, the way his hand grabbed mine. Heat rose in my cheeks.

"Mademoiselle de Batz! Forgive me; I didn't mean to startle you."

"It was my fault. I didn't expect to see you up here so late— are you all right?"

"Tante sent me to gather notes she left in the fencing studio by mistake. I dropped a few," he added, and scratched at the back of his neck. I'd seen Henri bashful: when I'd thanked him for bringing us treats, when he gave me the map of Lupiac. But this felt different, as if he were nervous.

"Do you need help? It must be difficult, without a candle or—"

"No!" I flinched. His cheeks were splotchy even in the dim light. "I—I didn't mean it like that," he stammered. "I've already got them, see?" He held up a few before tucking the sheets into his jacket. "I better go—Aunt was insistent."

"Wait! I—" but he'd already turned toward the staircase. Hurt bloomed in my chest. Maybe he was angry—I'd insulted him, using his first name.

It wasn't until I was back on my bed, staring at the draped canopy, that I remembered Madame de Treville had left hours ago to meet with Monsieur Brandon.

Two weeks. Two weeks of parties, of laughing in gardens and ballrooms, of eavesdropping on whispered conversations, and one particularly painful attempt to distract a lord while Portia flirted secrets out of his valet, until Madame de Treville announced I'd be assigned a target of my very own.

We prepared for the season's first ball at the palace all week, and now that we were less than a day away, it was time to rehearse out kinks in the more popular dances. Portia mocked how the royal ladies held their fans, how certain twists and turns in a left or right hand could mean flirtation, rejection, a warning to a paramour of being watched. Théa and I laughed as she waved the instrument as if she were attempting to swat a bug. "Mourez les mouches! Mourez!" Aria hid her smile behind her fan. Théa ran, squealing, as Portia darted toward her, fan thwapping through the air. "No! Not the fan!" Théa tripped over the edge of the carpet and fell onto one of the room's many, many cushions.

"Ahem." Madame de Treville stood in the doorway. "I'm going to pretend I walked in on you practicing the tempo changes like I asked."

She only got a few sentences into her explanation before I couldn't help but interject. "You think I'm ready?" I asked her in amazement. After the confrontation with Monsieur Brandon, I'd thought I might never get a target of my own. I'd just be there, off to the side, the fourth Mousquetaire. Waiting and watching and supporting.

"You have to enter the inferno at some point. Shadowing the others helps, but no amount of practice and training can adequately replicate your actual duties as a Musketeer. All that said, I *believe* you're ready . . . more importantly, you're needed for this assignment."

"You need me?" It was impossible to keep the pleasure out of my voice.

Madame de Treville assessed me coolly. "You're an unknown. Unlike the others, you haven't been attending balls and parties for months. By introducing you to a select few, we heightened interest, added mystery. And that is what we need for Étienne Verdon. The son of Verdon senior," she added.

"Lucky!" Théa exclaimed. "Your first assignment and he's not old enough to be your father!"

"Don't mistake youth for a lack of danger," Madame de Treville chastened. "This is why I like to wait to inform you of your targets; too much gossip and your ability to focus goes out the window!"

"You think he's involved with the ring like his uncle? Maybe even his father?" I asked.

"He's not influential enough with the wealthiest noblesse to be anything more than privy to useful information. But you must endear yourself to him. If we fail to unravel the scheme via his uncle, we need another way to monitor that family. And chasing Verdon senior directly is too complicated; he spends little time in Paris, and we can't waste an entire month coming and going from his estate. Not to mention his wife is reportedly ill. He hasn't taken social calls in weeks. But his son is still on the social scene; that's how we get close to him. Do you remember the papers Aria copied?"

"But, Madame, we've already analyzed those. The Spanish goods and the money increase have to be linked to Verdon's brother's relocation to Paris. Somewhere near Paris. Or wherever he is that gives him easy access to the city," Portia said from the chaise she'd draped herself over.

"We waited to investigate the abbreviations until we had more information . . . we have that information now." We all froze. Even

Théa put down her fan. "Don't get too excited," Madame de Treville cautioned, "it's more of a suspicion." She lifted a bound leather journal with the seal of les Mousquetaires du Roi. "This is the unofficial Musketeer's weapon encyclopedia; one of the newest Musketeers was a scribe before La Fronde. He's kept an official record, based on letters Musketeers have received from our forces stationed in other countries, of every weapon la France has encountered. Mazarin is lending it to me. Normally such a treasure trove of information wouldn't leave his sight, but given the circumstances . . ." She trailed off to examine the paper flags stuck between the pages. "The abbreviations all map onto—which again, mind you, is not a given—kinds of weapons."

Aria shook her head. "If they're being smuggled into Paris and then distributed along with goods and monetary bribes to nobles . . . imagine a Paris full of nobles with caches of hidden foreign weapons. Ready for when the King is murdered to take control of the power vacuum left in his wake."

Madame de Treville nodded. "I won't risk returning to that office. Not after what happened to . . ." Her eyes darted to Théa, then she shook her head and continued. "We don't know where the Verdon brothers, if they are indeed working together, are based out of. And that is why—"

"And that's why Étienne Verdon is my target." I swallowed bubbling nerves. "What else do I need to know? What would you have me do?"

"You know," Théa said from her seat, "I do think I've heard his name whispered by some of the ladies at court."

Madame de Treville's forced laugh prickled at my arms. "I wouldn't be surprised. He has friends in many circles, especially the local university students. But he's not just some errant, handsome schoolboy who thinks philosophy is the answer to the plight of the poor and disenfranchised. According to my sources, he's smart, sharp even, but he revels in it. Use his overconfidence against him. I laid the groundwork at every party, practically whenever I saw him or one of his friends nearby. Don't give him your last name. He'll like a chase."

"And you think he'll like me?" I wasn't someone who boys chased after. But then, I wasn't who I was, not anymore.

Portia brought a hand to her mouth but couldn't keep laughter from spilling. "Oh, he won't just like you . . . he'll *want* you."

A month ago, I would've squeaked. Now, however, I kept my reaction limited to my widening eyes, the frightened churn of my stomach. Théa smiled encouragingly at me, and the nerves dimmed.

"That's enough," Madame de Treville said. "He's not some philandering wastrel who preys on pretty girls. But he *is* charming, and from what my accounts say, unpredictable." She took another step toward me. I had to crane my neck to see her, could feel the insistence radiating off her in waves, and when she bent down to take me by the shoulders, I didn't look away. "Tania," she said, "you mustn't let him slip through your fingers."

After rehearsal, I stopped in a side hallway at the sight of a familiar figure, awkward and out of place amid the delicate rose wallpaper. "Henri!" A few hours left before the ball, and I was idling downstairs to prolong the time I wasn't tied into a corset.

But I hadn't had a chance to apologize to Henri. I hadn't managed to get ahold of him, despite the fact that we lived in the same house. And as much as the idea stung, I had to consider his avoidance was intentional and that it was my fault.

He glanced up, a substantial pile of papers under his arm. "Mademoiselle de Batz," Henri said. I tensed at his unfamiliar, controlled expression. But when he bowed, his work flew out from under his arms, hung on the air for a split second before rustling to the floor. I rushed to gather everything that fell on the side tables, on a few of the chairs, ones that weren't on the carpet—attempting that would risk me being too dizzy to attend the ball.

But they weren't diagrams for work. They were sketches. Half-drawn birds poised midflight. One of the sun low over the Seine—though it was hard to tell whether it was the sunrise or the sunset; everything was in black ink. But there was that distinct half globe disappearing behind a wavering riverbank. Numberless times I'd seen the Seine, and yet, it was never so beautiful.

"I didn't know you could draw like this!" My wonder dried up my planned apologies.

His blush traveled to the tips of his ears. His hair had brightened in the past month. He must've been spending time outside and away from the house.

"They're nothing—I shouldn't even store them with my papers. But if there's a lull in assignments, or if I'm taking notes for a meeting but nothing's happening, I sketch. Despite Sanson's *genius*, he and his colleagues waste an impressive amount of time debating aesthetic value." He scooped up the papers and restored them to the stack. "It's like none of them see the bigger picture or how their work matters to those with less than them. It's like you told me: Maps can change a person's perspective. Whole villages, towns, cities, they can all be erased from public perception if they're not included." His movements were sharp, frustrated. Angry.

I extended the remaining drawings. Our fingers barely grazed, but he still withdrew as if he'd been shocked. "They're very good. Truly."

Henri stared at me for an extended moment. "Thank you, Mademoiselle de Batz." A cloak draped itself over us, a pall of seriousness.

"We are friends, are we not?" I tried to sound upbeat. "Must you be so formal?"

Madame de Treville's voice thundered down the staircase. "Tania! Where are you?"

"She doesn't usually yell like that." Henri couldn't contain a nervous laugh, and I smiled, glad that some of the tension had eased.

"I'm leading the mission tonight. For the first time, that is. If only she'd understand I'm nervous enough for the both of us." Maybe that could make him laugh—a real laugh this time.

Instead, his expression grew worried. "Be careful tonight. The palace is beautiful—but beautiful things are usually the most dangerous."

"You've been to the palace before?" I asked.

He shifted uncomfortably. "Yes, Sanson has sent me there on occasion. I suppose it's aesthetically pleasing, but what it's used for . . ." He shook his head. "Just, be careful tonight," he repeated.

He left me trying to unpack how strangely he'd spoken, how unlike himself. Was he truly that worried about the success of my assignment? Yes, he'd mentioned the palace, but it wasn't some living creature; it could not pick me up and swallow me whole.

It was just another building. Just marble and stone.

"So? Do I look all right?" I asked tentatively.

They were silent. I reached for the décolleté bodice, but all at once the others rushed into a flurry. "Don't you dare touch that neckline!" Portia shrieked.

Théa pried my hands from the scarlet fabric as I bit back the fear of failure. Of once again being the girl forced into a dress, a child playing dress-up as she watched a boy walk away from her. But then they coaxed me in front of the mirror.

It wasn't like when I wore the blue dress the night of my first Parisian ball. Whether this gown was different, or I was different, I didn't know—but someone had replaced me in the mirror.

She was blazing. Blistering. Collarbones melted into red silk that hugged her curves. Molten gemstones dripped from her ears. Her skirt one large flame reflected in the glass. She was the gladiator and siren Madame de Treville spoke of.

She was a Musketeer.

"I don't think we'll have to worry about your target being interested. He won't be able to keep his eyes off you. Although," Portia continued, finger tapping against her bottom lip, "if he drools on your gown, Madame de Treville might kill him herself. Silk shows everything. It won't do to have slobber on your bodice."

My face turned the color of my dress. Ah, there I was. That was something familiar to hold on to.

The palace was a dream. A dream wonderful and terrifying all at once. Marble arches and columns that extended as far as the eye could see led into a courtyard, an enclosed street only the finest noblesse could enter. We gave the horses a wide berth, not wanting to risk our shoes and hemlines, and nodded at the copious number of guards and attendants as we passed through the designated entrance.

The ballroom—one of many—opened into a portico, glass doors revealing a party at its onset. The sheer volume of people was overwhelming. Their hair, their gowns and jackets, the light bouncing off all the crystals. Laughter tinkled over clinking glasses. It was like the first ball, but everything was ten times larger, ten times more extravagant. And taking into account the number of armed guards, ten times deadlier. Even the party guests were sharper, more defined—lip colors like violent wounds across their faces, gold and silver jewelry pricking at their wrists, their throats. The air was cloudy with perfume and sweat and the bite of alcohol.

The wide room descended into whispers as an attendant cleared his throat. "May I present His Royal Highness, Louis XIV, par la grace de Dieu, Roi de France et de Navarre." Théa made to stand on tiptoe, but Madame de Treville yanked at her sleeve. Everyone was fixed on the King. They paid little attention to the rest of the royal family's introduction. Less than a year older than me . . . and yet, it was hard to reconcile all this grandeur, this pomp and circumstance, for a boy. Even if you traded his palace finery for farmer's clothes, though, no one would mistake him as un roturier, a commoner. Not with his slight frame and dark hair arranged in artful curls past his shoulders.

This was the boy we'd sworn our lives to protect. Face pale from powder and lack of sunlight. When was the last time he'd left the palace? Seen the streets of Paris? Been to La Cour des Miracles?

I clenched my fists. His life was at risk. One didn't parade around Paris, didn't examine workers' conditions or the noxious state of the Seine when assassination followed every conversation and every word, shadowlike. But could I say that if things were different, if he were safe, that he would care more, would care better, for his people? He was just a boy with a crown.

I thought back to the night of the first ball, to Aria's insistence that none of this was about "them." Perhaps this wasn't about the King, either. It never was—at least, not all of it. Because to Papa . . . to me, it was so much more. It was sisterhood and brotherhood. For the girls like me who were told they were wrong and lying about their bodies, but who didn't wear pretty gowns or have swords strapped underneath their skirts.

The dancing resumed. Courtiers had scant interest in gawking, but guests observed him from spots along the wall. He retreated to a secluded corner along with his brother and a few others. An official taster waited at the King's side, only retreating once he'd poured himself a sip of red wine. At the taster's nod, the King secured his own full glass, said a few words that spurred the group into raucous laughter.

The four of us were clustered off to the side of the rotating couples. Théa was swept away by a stammering fellow who barely managed to ask her to dance. He hardly noticed that her eyes remained on the King. Portia was midsoliloquy regarding the royal portraits when Madame de Treville's fingers tightened on my elbow. "He's here." She withdrew her hand. "Oh look, Duchesse de Piney! What an exquisitely crafted gown—I must procure the name of her dressmaker immediately." Our mentor nodded as she left with Portia. The signal. The target had seen us: Madame de Treville and her new, unfamiliar-faced pupil. The mysterious girl Madame de Treville's contacts told him about.

I let out a shaky breath. Uncurled my fingers from the scarlet fabric.

"Mademoiselle," someone said from behind me.

Verdon, half-bowed, was not what I'd expected. A bit older; from Théa's insistence, I had guessed he'd be in his midtwenties. Wasn't as handsome as I'd assumed, either—though it was wrong to think such things. Perhaps it was the lighting, or the crush of people. And at the end of the day, it didn't matter. I wasn't here for that.

"Enchantée, Monsieur." I let the word linger on my tongue as I curtsied. His tongue shot out to lick his lips. He was right in front of me, too close by anyone's standards.

"Ma chère, how beautiful you look. Like a perfect porcelain doll." His finger grazed my cheek, and I tried not to gag, tried not to wipe my sleeve where his fingers touched.

"Monsieur Baldec." A voice, mocking and steel all at once, rang from a few feet away. A young man with a smile fixed on his face as if it were sculpted there. Memories of the first ball rushed back to me, of hazel eyes that melted above the torchlight.

No, not just any young man. The one who'd seen me struggle. The one who'd sought me out, who wanted to help, who spoke about people like me with an empathy that scorched.

The man with the hazel eyes clapped my frozen admirer on the back. "Perhaps you'd have better luck if you did not compare the mademoiselle to a child's toy?"

Monsieur Baldec flushed as red as his mustache. "Monsieur Verdon. I thought this party was for guests of the royal family."

Verdon's eyes locked on mine. And then his smile grew wider, genuine. He remembered.

"I believe your wife is searching for you," he told Baldec. "She was quite frantic, in fact. She thought you were lost on your return from paying respects to the King."

"Merci," Monsieur Baldec said through gritted teeth, "Monsieur, for alerting me of my wife's distress."

When he didn't move, Verdon hardened. "My pleasure. Given last month's *incident*, I said I'd go and find you right away."

The two stared each other down before Monsieur Baldec blinked. "I must attend to my wife. A pleasure." A shallow bow in my direction, then he hurried off—but not without a scowl for the man in front of me.

Verdon's clothes were not as ornate as most. No gaudy baubles or overdone embroidery.

I recalled what Madame de Treville had told me about my target. He wanted a chase, and I'd give him one. "I suppose I'm to thank you for playing my savior? I'm quite capable of saving myself," I said. I wasn't the shrinking mademoiselle he'd first met. I had to make sure he didn't see me as the dizzy girl. Just the dizzy girl.

"Playing, Mademoiselle? You wound me. Here I was thinking I'd acted my part and appeared confident without betraying my distress. But you saw right through me. A pleasure, to finally become acquainted. Monsieur Verdon, at your service."

A memory itched at the back of my mind like it had when Madame de Treville first told me his name. *Verdon. Verdon.*

As I continued to stare up at him, it dawned on me. My composed expression nearly broke; it took everything in me not to shout or scream, to only curl my lips in a coy smile. A good thing, that he couldn't hear the roaring of my heartbeat. How was this even possible? "You wouldn't happen to know a Monsieur Verdon? I believe he lives near Bordeaux?"

"I assume you speak of Monsieur Hubert Verdon?"

"Are you of any relation to the man?" I asked.

He laughed in response, full, from behind his sternum. It sounded how his smile looked: charming—maybe even sincere. "You could say that." I raised one brow. Madame de Treville encouraged this, said it drew attention to my eyes, dark and luminous against my skin. "Why do you ask?"

"My family's originally from a town nearby." This line of questioning was dangerously close to revealing personal information, so I pivoted. "His name was spoken on occasion. In conjunction with the highest praise, of course: How generous he is for donating his time and means to provide instruction for future service members of la Maison du Roi."

His gaze was hard and deep. "Hubert Verdon is my father," he said eventually. "I'd much rather talk about you, though."

"Me?" I asked, hand to my chest.

"You sound shocked anyone would find you intriguing."

"On the contrary," I replied, "I'm merely surprised I've piqued your interest. Especially considering I've cut in line."

"Oh?"

I glanced pointedly over his shoulder. He followed my gaze

to the two women glaring at me. Both their gowns were inlaid with expensive crystals, scattered around the hems and edges of the bodices, catching the light of nearby candles. He turned back with a gleam in his eyes, but not before I caught a glimpse of Portia inserting herself between the women, drawing their attention away. "I am my own man, society protocols or not." He searched my face before extending his hand. "But if you insist: Mademoiselle, may I have the honor of this dance?"

"But what will they say?" My question sounded earnest, even to my own ears, even though I'd practiced it a dozen times, even though I already knew what his answer would be, how his breath would hitch. "Think of the gossip. Dancing with an unknown lady in a room full of nobles?"

"Me, worried about association with the woman who's drawn the attention of everyone here? The mystery only lures the court-iers in."

I placed my outstretched hand in his. "And you?"

He wrapped his fingers around it, pulled gently so I had to take a step forward. A step closer to him. "Me? I love a good mystery. The best part is solving it." His fingers were warm, his thumb skating along my knuckles, leaving a trail of heat in its wake. "Mademoiselle," he murmured, only loud enough for me to hear. "If your hesitance to dance is informed by what happened the last time we met, we could sit, if you wish."

"Monsieur, we are at a ball—at the palace, no less. I am sure you would prefer dancing."

"Sitting can be much preferable to dancing . . . depending on the company."

"Étienne!" I pulled my hand away as a man approached, and

the two greeted each other. "I'm loath to intrude on you and your enchanting companion, but I really must insist," the man said.

A shadow passed over my target's face. "Business calls." He grimaced. He found my hand again, cradled it. "We'll have to dance another time."

"Of course, Monsieur Verdon."

"That's my father's name," he said.

I nearly balked then and there at his forwardness. At his unsettling, disarming nature: not predatory, not leering, but very, very warm. "Of course, Étienne."

His gaze drifted along the curve of my lips at the sound of his name, so soft only he could hear it. The courtiers wouldn't know what was passing between us—what he believed was passing between us, that is. "I'm afraid you have me at a disadvantage."

I paused, remembered the smile the girls had practiced with me in the mirror, the one they said would dwell in his mind even after we parted. "My name is Tania."

"Tania," he repeated. He pressed a kiss to my hand, still in his. And all the while his eyes remained on mine. They were darker than they'd been in the torchlight, that color between brown and green melting to a shade deeper. "Until we meet again, *Tania*."

CHAPTER SEVENTEEN

"UNTIL WE MEET again, *Tania*?" Portia scoffed. "Did he present you with a sonnet in your honor to top the whole thing off?"

"He really said you'd drawn the attention of everyone there?" Théa interjected from atop the bed, chin in her hands and ankles crossed behind her. "That's the same as calling her beautiful, non?" She looked to Portia for confirmation. "Has she managed to win herself a suitor?"

Portia, making faces in the mirror, immediately perked up. "Upon further consideration, Tania, I *do* hope he pens you a collection full of sonnets, which, of course, I must be allowed to perform to the household via dramatic reading."

"Don't be silly," I cut in gently, removing the rubies from my earlobes and returning them to the vanity. Gentlemen showed interest in ladies all the time without any intention of actually pursuing them. He wasn't really interested in me. He was a flirt. He didn't know any of my secrets; the knowledge of merely one would send him running.

But I needed to know his father's secrets, his uncle's. As much as I wanted to ask Madame de Treville about the connection I'd discovered, ask if she'd known, I couldn't. That would mean revealing I'd almost given away information about my background—a definite offense for the mystery mademoiselle she'd have me be.

"Please, Tania, don't deny me this! I bet he's a rhymer," she said, turning to Théa, who nodded. "He was enamored with you. And he obviously made a poignant second impression," Portia continued as I finished taking off the jewels I was draped in. "You've practically said nothing since we got home!"

"You've hardly let her get in a word as is." Aria was propped against the door frame.

Portia shrieked. "How long have you been standing there? You know I hate when you do that!"

"It's not my fault you weren't listening," Aria said.

Portia huffed and plopped down on the edge of the bed. "It's not fair you can sneak up on us like that. Madame de Treville says my steps are loud as a horse on cobblestone."

"Practice helps," Aria said gently. She continued to watch Portia, but the latter's focus had already shifted.

"Yes, Verdon is over-the-top, but I'd still rather have him as a target than distraction duty," Portia said. "I had to listen to that woman go on and on. Mon Dieu, how many times can one hear about fabric and cut before she loses whatever remains of her mind? No one wants to hear about your newest gown, Babette!"

"It wasn't even that well made," Théa said. Portia looked at her, stunned. "What?" Théa asked. "It's true! The embroidery placement wasn't even flattering—what's the point of going to all that trouble if you're going to plop that stitching on the fabric with no care for appearance?"

Despite the agony in my feet and the dizziness cool around the corners of my vision, I laughed. Then I thought back to earlier, before the ball, a shadow passing across my face in the mirror.

"Tania, what's wrong?" I met Théa's concerned gaze.

"It's . . ." The memory of the hallway, Henri watching Théa retreat . . . the way she'd said his name. "Have you noticed anything the matter with Henri?"

Aria and Portia were too busy bickering about something or other to take much notice. Théa's nose wrinkled. "What do you mean?"

"He seems—well, he seems frustrated. And angry."

Théa placed her hand on my shoulder, peering into the glass. "I think we're all frustrated, don't you? Everyone in the house knows we're just a step away from the King . . . oh, it's too horrible to even think about, let alone say out loud. And I think Henri is taking on extra work at Sanson's. He really doesn't want to be an apprentice forever." She studied me. "Are you sure you're all right, Tania—I could make you a cup of tea if you wished it, although I'd have to be sneaky. Madame hasn't let me near the teapot ever since the antique-lace-and-chamber-pot incident." I shook my head. Smiled at her to show everything was fine. Yes, I shook my head—and yet my neck itched all through the night, as I lifted my head up, expecting to find a set of eyes staring back. Watching.

Madame de Treville declared my first lead mission a success. Now was the time to spur the youngest Verdon to action. So, I did as I was told. Donned a dress the color of the twilight sky, distracted the son of a vicomte recently returned from exile while Portia flirted with his father, kept him occupied to provide time for Aria and Théa to sneak into the Vicomte's private quarters, his cellars, anywhere he might hide smuggled goods he'd brought back to Paris. I was getting better at this part. It was easier when I remembered what I was doing this all for. Not for the King, but for the people who would be hurt in the aftermath of his death. Sometimes, at least—other times it made me lose focus, had me picking at my fingernails and laughing too loudly, at the thought of protecting a king when Papa was gone, even if I knew there was a greater purpose. And when my gaze drifted up, it met with Verdon's as if he knew my laugh, had heard it, had his eyes at the ready for me.

I woke the next morning with Portia's voice barely audible over the throbbing in my head. "Hurry up! We're supposed to train together today, or did you forget?"

I tried to sit up, but immediately regretted it.

"Tania?" Her voice was closer; she must have come into the room, must have been standing somewhere near the edge of my bed.

"I overworked myself."

There was a pause. "But I thought . . ." Another pause, and when I shifted, her face doubled. "You were fine yesterday."

I wasn't fine yesterday. I was never fine. But even if I had been, it wouldn't have meant today would be the same. She didn't know, couldn't know what her words meant, how they felt. "There are good days and bad days. I've had more good ones lately—which I'm sure Madame de Treville attributes to training until my body is mush—but a bad day was bound to happen."

Portia sat near the far bedpost with a creak. "That must be hard: the uncertainty of going to sleep and not knowing what it'll be like when you wake up." That was a profound understatement. She was trying; it was written all over her face. But I was too tired to acknowledge it, too tired to tell her what it meant to have someone actively attempt to place themselves in my shoes. "What do you want to do?" she asked.

"It's not what I want to do, it's what I can do," I snipped. Guilt immediately bloomed in my chest. And fear; the fear of her face morphing into Marguerite's. "I'm sorry, I didn't mean it like that."

"Don't be. I deserved that," Portia said. "I'll do some drills on my own. We'll work together soon."

Once she left, I tried to fall back asleep. But every time my eyelids shut, faces swam in front of me: Papa, Maman, Madame de Treville, and the other girls . . . Verdon appeared occasionally, and whenever I recognized his profile, my stomach tumbled over itself. Yes, he was handsome and charming, but I'd prepared for that. So why had his words unmoored me? "*Sitting can be much preferable to dancing, depending on the company.*" "*I'm not the presumptuous sort to assume a mademoiselle's sentiments. Or the kind to write someone off who is struggling in any capacity.*" What did it matter if he wasn't the rake Madame de Treville thought him? I groaned and stared up at the canopy.

Months ago, the aftermath of overusing energy would have rendered me bedridden for days. But I made it to the dining room for a little supper, and the next day I even managed some footwork. I wasn't any less dizzy than before, any less sick. But my legs were stronger. They were fighting for me. All the same symptoms, but no fainting. The day following, I was ready for Portia when she arrived in the training room, a twinge of a smile on my lips. It wasn't without pain, no. But it was fully mine and it was true. It wasn't there to make myself look appealing. It wasn't there for anyone but myself.

Amid all the parties, all the dancing and flirting and spying, fencing was like coming home. The clash of steel against steel. Knees bent, eyes narrowed. The crash of a parry riposte.

Portia laughed as she countered my attack and nearly swept my sword out of my hand. But I was craftier and waited until she attacked. Waited until she thought she'd won before I jumped back, out of her lunge's reach.

Théa cheered from somewhere nearby. Portia's face scrunched in concentration.

She lunged again. My blade met with hers. And there it was.

It wasn't anything I could control. At the sight of sparks, my sword clattered to the ground. A sob wrenched from my throat.

Swept into the memory of Papa and me, in the barn: morning light through holes in the rafters, motes of dust in the air, me spinning to meet the clash of his blade.

"Papa!" I'd shrieked, dropping my sword at the sight of sparks, bright and sharp and gone in an instant.

But Papa hadn't been angry, no—he'd laughed. "Don't be afraid. Look how powerful you are, ma fille. Look at what you've created with your own hand and sword."

I'd glanced with trepidation at the blade. My father had reached to pick it up, and then presented it to me. "Your weapon, Mademoiselle la Mousquetaire."

The very first time he'd called me that.

"Mon Dieu, did my sword catch you? Are you bleeding?" Portia grabbed at my arms, frantically checking for wounds.

"Papa," I managed to say, but then my breath hitched again,

and again. I was underwater and trying to take a breath. Expecting air but finding liquid that filled my lungs.

I wept whole histories into my hands.

Arms draped around me, led me from the light, the noise. I was shepherded into a seat. When I finally opened my eyes, they revealed Madame de Treville's study.

Our mentor handed me a cup. "Here." I took a few slow sips and waited for my breaths to ease, to stop pulling and tearing at my rib cage.

"Where are the others?"

"I requested they give us some privacy," she said as she examined me. "You've done so much to suppress what happened. Honestly, I'm surprised you haven't broken down before now."

"It's just . . . when the swords . . ."

"You don't have to explain," she said with a kindness I wasn't expecting.

I drank more, then set the cup on her desk. Fear wormed into my chest. "Please, don't remove me from the next mission. I know it seems like I'm broken, but I'm not. I can handle this."

"For someone who believes everyone questions her capabilities, you do a lot of questioning yourself." Madame de Treville paused. Something was eating at her. She let out a sharp breath, nodded to herself. "I haven't been completely forthright with you. At first it was a matter of protecting the Order. You refused to truly address your sorrow—and I know that everyone grieves differently, but you stoppered it up so tightly . . . then, as time went on, I didn't want to provide further distraction. Even with your reservations to joining and the complicated reasons why you eventually did, ones I'm not sure even I know the extent of, you've taken to being a Mousquetaire de la Lune in a way I never foresaw. I thought I'd do a kindness for your father. That maybe you'd be helpful to the others, ensure missions were successful, but would never have your own targets. But you are an asset in your own right; you are as essential to our mission as Portia, Théa, and Aria. Your dedication to and passion for fencing is a rare gift, one that makes you passionate in all areas of the rest of your life. And I didn't want to threaten that. But now it's clear the truth will be what stitches you back together . . . and what ensures your dedication to the Order." She rubbed at her brow. Fingerprints left a red-pink trail across her forehead.

"I'm not sure I understand," I said.

"There's reason to think Monsieur Verdon, the elder that is, is more involved in the plot than we initially believed. He doesn't have a title, so Mazarin and I thought the Comte de Monluc—Portia's target at your first ball—was a likelier suspect, since he holds sway over more nobles. But when we learned the younger Verdon brother was visiting him, we started to realize that perhaps the very fact that Verdon senior doesn't have a title gives him motive. When the King exiled scores of nobles after La Fronde, he redistributed some of their titles to those he perceived loyal. But Verdon received nothing. He could've been planning this for years. Do you see now? It's like I told you before: Verdon senior is too difficult a target to approach head-on. We need to use the son to get to him. That's why he's your target." She was adamant, fervor in her face. "And if we can get to Verdon senior . . ."

I let out a short breath and fought to keep from rubbing at my temples. "I wish you'd told me your suspicions when you learned of them. But I know I'm new to the Order. And I suppose I haven't been the most obedient. And it's your prerogative to . . ."

A gruff voice echoed in my memory. *I and two others were called to investigate a death en route from Le Rare Loup Inn to the residence of a Monsieur Verdon . . .* Madame de Treville's meaning of keeping this from me, of what it had to do with my father, it all fell into place. "No. It can't be." My tongue choked me, sealed against the roof of my mouth with tears and spit, cheeks freezing hot. "Verdon was supposed to host my father. But he was the one who notified the others when Papa didn't arrive."

There was pity in Madame de Treville's eyes.

"I don't understand . . ."

"You are thinking like a daughter. But you must think like a Musketeer," she said softly.

The throb of my heartbeat was loud, loud, loud. The maréchaussée and Monsieur Allard said Papa's body was found on the road between Verdon's estate and the village tavern . . . *think like a Musketeer . . .* it wouldn't have been difficult for Verdon to feign distress for his guest's safety. He could have met Papa en route and attacked him on the dark, empty road. Who's to say that, instead of rushing to Monsieur Allard at my father's absence, Verdon didn't kill Papa, cover his tracks, and then search for help in order to clear himself of any implication of wrongdoing?

I raised my eyes, horrified, to Madame de Treville.

"I see you've happened upon the same possibility I did. But it's important we don't view conjectures as truth. There is still so much work to be done."

My fingers—white, bloodless—gripped my chair. "Verdon was involved in Papa's death? Why . . . how could you think that? The bandits. What they did to him. Cutting off his beard, his hair . . ."

"That's the first I've heard anything of the sort," Madame

de Treville said. "Although"—she hesitated—"it's not surprising it hasn't gotten out. That's something everyone would've done their best to keep quiet."

"Well, it happened. What reason would he have for killing Papa like *that*?"

"Perhaps he wanted to shame your father. Or have him serve as a warning to anyone who might follow in his footsteps," she said.

"What do you mean?"

"Tania, your father wasn't traveling to discuss the opening of new fencing academies. Well, he was, but that wasn't why he went to those meetings. He was gathering information on the plot to overthrow the King. For the Musketeers. For France."

CHAPTER EIGHTEEN

FURY UNFURLED WITHIN me. "You had no right not to tell me. He was my father. *Mine.*" My fingers rested above the ring trapped in my bodice.

"I should have told you. For that I am sorry."

"That's all you have to say? You kept what you knew about my father to yourself. You've been lying to me all this time. And Monsieur Brandon, he treated me like some silly girl . . ." The memory knifed through me, his patronizing expression framed by a chapeau and cassock, how he'd stumbled over his explanations . . . "That's why he hesitated," I said, watching Madame de Treville for any sign of remorse. "He concealed it by saying they didn't have enough resources to investigate. But really they don't want to draw attention to the fact that Papa was spying for them."

More memories rebounded, of nighttime and open doors and cloaked men stealing through windows. They weren't looking for Maman's jewels. They were looking for Papa's secrets.

How much of what Papa told me were lies? I'd known there was more to it than him humoring nobles, but I'd thought all the traveling was an excuse to see his friends . . . mais non. They weren't just his friends. They were still his brothers in arms, no matter if he was no longer reporting to them and instead to Madame de Treville and Mazarin.

"How . . ." I trailed off, unsure of how to ask all the questions running through my mind.

"What I know is this: Your father was released from his duties after his father-in-law forced the Musketeers to do so. He left for Lupiac thinking his days serving his country were behind him. But that was before La Fronde. The Musketeers needed spies stationed throughout the country to provide intelligence on Condé's supporters. That's when your father was contacted by la Maison du Roi and offered the opportunity to rejoin the Musketeers in secret. His role continued after La Fronde's resolution, and even involved gathering information for the current mission to save the King. I wouldn't have known the full story if it weren't for his letter requesting a place be made available to you. He explained the situation, how he feared what your life would be like in the event he passed."

"That doesn't excuse the fact that you didn't tell me," I said, cutting off Madame de Treville when she opened her mouth. "Yes, I know, you worried that I'd break. You care more about the King's life than my father's. But I'm not fragile."

"I was wrong, Tania, and I've apologized. But I will not tolerate being spoken to in such a fashion." She relaxed her arms but continued to struggle with an invisible weight fixed to the nape of her neck. "As hard as it is, your duty is to France. Don't you remember what I told you after Monsieur Brandon left that day?"

Fighting for the King is fighting for your father. At the time, the implication had seemed straightforward: Papa's final wish was for me to serve the King. And I tried to accept his love of country as my own. But that wasn't what Madame de Treville had meant at all.

The blistering fury dimmed, overtaken by a small bit of hope that flashed bright behind my eyes. "Can it truly be that simple? Discovering the names of those who plot against the King, finding proof to arrest them, could lead to finding Papa's murderer? Could even be one and the same?"

She eventually met my gaze. "I believe it's your best chance. Perhaps your only chance. And you'll only know the truth if we succeed."

Up until now, I'd thought I was doing my best. But I wasn't—I could harden myself further; I knew I could. Turn myself fully into steel, become the creature the Order needed. That France needed. Because France meant Papa. And Papa meant everything.

"What happened? I thought I hurt you!" Portia said when I exited the study. They were waiting for me. My Musketeers.

"*We* were worried," Aria added quietly.

My gaze fell to the floor. "Promise me you didn't know."

"What do you mean?" Théa asked.

"My father. He was spying for the Musketeers. Madame de Treville thinks Verdon might've murdered Papa after he learned too much about the plot to kill the King."

"Your target!" Portia's eyes were sharp as a pair of dueling swords. "He murdered your father, and she assigned him as your—"

"No, not Étienne. His father," I said.

She fell silent. Even Aria was taken aback.

"What are you going to do?" Théa said finally. "What can we do?"

I willed my insides into hammered metal. The girls were staring back at me, waiting. "We're going to take them down . . . and then we're going to make them pay."

Portia, Théa, and Aria weren't the Musketeers who populated my childhood stories. They weren't Papa's Musketeers. But they were warm enough to thaw the dark Parisian night that squeezed at my throat, the fear of how somewhere, out in the cold, there were traitors who plotted the King's assassination. Traitors whose hands were already stained with Papa's blood.

They may not be the Musketeers I'd imagined. But they were better, because they were mine. And I knew, as I looked at them and saw the cold steely resolve inside me mirrored in their eyes, that I was theirs.

I thought the next time I'd see Étienne would be at a party. But instead, he appeared the day after the sparking swords in the form of a broken wax seal: a lion rearing on its hind legs.

"Tania, you have a letter," Madame de Treville said.

Théa, hunched over a slice of bread and wrapped in sleep, sat up ramrod straight, her shoulders pushed so far back it was stunning they didn't stick there. "A letter?"

Madame de Treville placed the envelope next to my plate. I pushed my cooling cup of tea aside; her expression betrayed nothing. "It was delivered this morning. Henri's been sorting the post before he heads to Sanson's for the day: If I didn't know him any better, I'd suspect he wanted to be part of the Order!"

Mademoiselle Tania,

I hope this letter finds you well, and much recovered from our first encounter. I would have enquired this of you from my own lips, but I didn't want to be an imposition. It seems propriety has managed to latch its claws in me after all. Balls are such stuffy affairs, all decorum and no substance, but meeting you was like a breath of fresh air on the most crowded street corner.

A ball is no place to get to know someone. Which is why I respect-fully request your presence as my guest at the Gramonde theater opening three evenings from today. Madame de Treville and the other mesdemoiselles under her care are of course invited as well.

Your humble servant,

E. Verdon

"You must say yes." Madame de Treville's voice was insistent.

"You know what it says?" The seal was broken; of course she had opened it.

"Obviously I wouldn't give you a letter I hadn't closely examined first," Madame de Treville said. "And under other circumstances, I would want to know what exactly he means by 'recovered.' But given everything that happened yesterday . . ."

I squared my shoulders. "He doesn't know the truth. I handled it."

I mentioned nothing of his kindness. Madame de Treville was wrong about the finer points of his character. Her betrayal of my privacy, her incursion on the first letter I'd ever received from a man, stung more than I cared to admit. It wasn't a love letter—his words showed fondness, not adoration. Not that it mattered; I just never thought I'd receive a letter like that. That I'd have a man interested to the point where he set quill to paper and revealed a thin underlayer of his heart. A man who didn't believe dizziness was a sign of inferiority.

Madame de Treville informed me how to accept his request, and what words to use: It would be short notice, and apparently I had "other engagements" earlier in the day, but I would "make time."

Nose wrinkled, I fiddled with my cup's saucer. "But won't that make me sound indifferent?" I asked.

"Not indifferent, in *demand*. It's for that same reason we won't send your response until tomorrow. Remember, Tania, he's playing a game like we are. A different one, to be sure, but a game nonetheless. You mustn't let him think he's won before he's played all his cards."

On the night of the theater opening we waited outside, breaths crackling in the air. Winter was not too far off now and nipped at our ears . . . and neither was the Winter Festival that the King refused to cancel—Madame de Treville had posited the idea to Mazarin, who in turn was met with a resounding *non*. Plus other words not fit for gentle ears. Madame de Treville said it was exactly what she expected from him—a whiny adolescent threatened with losing his favorite event of the season. I burrowed further into my cloak. Protecting the King wasn't about proving my worth anymore—I had to uncover all the nobles and proof of their treachery to solve Papa's murder. If the worst happened, surely that would mean the end in my quest for the truth . . . and the death of innocent people. I looked at the girls with a pang in my chest. It would mean the end for other things, too.

Portia shifted her weight and cursed under her breath before plastering on a smile. "Wonderful night."

"A bit crisp, perhaps," Aria said. "Did you forget your gloves again?"

"Non, they're in my tie-on pockets, and my fingers are too frozen to—wait, what are you doing?"

Aria had grasped Portia's waist and was busy loosening the ties of the pockets. "Getting your gloves, obviously." When Aria had retrieved them, she looked to Portia, whose wide eyes were framed with dozens of curls. "I suppose you'll need help putting them on. Since your fingers are frozen." Portia nodded emphatically and held out a hand, the other fisting the skirt of her dress. Aria took Portia's hand in hers, slid on the glove finger by finger.

"What was that?" Aria asked with a jolt. "Did you hear something squeak?"

"Carriages!" Portia said. "A carriage wheel!"

The familiar sound of hooves rang on stone, and we snapped to attention.

Madame de Treville descended the front steps, frowning at the cold sky before focusing on us. "Now, as we discussed: the three of you in our carriage, while I ride with Tania and Monsieur Verdon. You will handle yourselves with the utmost decorum."

The carriages screeched to a halt. A groomsman bounded down to open the unfamiliar carriage's door and place the block of steps. Étienne exited, jacketed in navy and silver. The cold wasn't so bitter now. Théa's teeth were chattering, but I didn't hesitate to lower my hood.

He strode toward us, stopped in front of Madame de Treville, bowed. "Madame. You honor me by accepting my invitation." As he rose, his gaze darted to mine. Strange, how I didn't feel the cold but it still made it difficult to draw breath, to find air in the ice.

The girls curtsied as they were each introduced, then retreated to their carriage. Étienne's hazel eyes were dark under the night sky. "After you," he said, taking my hand in his as I ascended two steps to the open carriage door. My knuckles warmed.

Conversation was sparse in the carriage with a chaperone. Madame de Treville only once inquired after his family, so as not to be seen as suspicious. Étienne ever polite, but not to the point of fawning. At the mention of our first meeting, he lightly tipped his head to the side, eyes gleaming in amusement as they darted toward me.

Madame de Treville coughed, playing her role. He tensed, drifting his gaze away from mine, and I hid my smile behind my floral-patterned fan.

But once we exited, once he took my hand again, he beamed. "Finally, a chance—"

"Monsieur Verdon!" Étienne shook his head, groaned. "Monsieur Verdon!" The man reached us, cherry-cheeked.

Étienne introduced him as one of the theater's main investors. "We have him to thank for such fine seats," Étienne added.

The man laughed and readjusted his spectacles. "Monsieur Verdon is modest to a fault. The opening tonight wouldn't be possible without his father's generosity. A shame such a charitable man couldn't attend the first performance." Étienne's jaw hardened, but the next moment, it was gone.

We were buffeted by the crowd, the other girls joining us along with Madame de Treville. The foyer was grander than l'amphi-théâtre itself, with carved renditions of Greek Muses, the sisters frozen midlaugh creating symphonies and sonnets and lounging on the white stone riverbank. Portia pointed out a few of the depictions to Théa, detailing their artistry, as the latter hid a yawn behind her gloved hand. A flurry of voices, different languages, different accents . . .

We were in a private galley above the standing audience members in the parterre and the mass of spectators onstage. Théa distracted the investor, who tried to glom on to Étienne, by asking about the play—a comedy—penned by some up-and-coming playwright with a name that sounded a bit like "man-teau." "I know nothing at all about theater, Monsieur. Oh please, do explain to me what to expect. Is there anything very trouble-some depicted on the stage?—I must prepare my nerves, you see." She threw an exaggerated wink over her shoulder as she pulled him away.

My seat wasn't so close to Étienne's that it was improper, but still, when he sat beside me, a nervous tingle started at the base of my spine. Madame de Treville hid her expression well, but I'd learned how to read her: She waffled between outrage at his presumption and relief that she didn't need to contrive a way to bend customs to force us together.

But none of it mattered once the curtain rose. Once the audi-ence hushed. Traveling performers came to Lupiac every year around la Noël, but there was something different in watching actors with elaborate costumes laugh, fight, and love their way across an amphithéâtre stage. Papa would have loved it; Maman would have called it ridiculous, hiding her secret smile at my father's awestruck expression. The lead was particularly strong, and every time he lamented his fate, separated from his love by familial interference, my gaze cleaved to his face. Was this what my parents had dealt with? My father, brave hearted but too poor for the very noblesse who filled this theater? My mother, giving up everything she had ever known?

An hour into the show, I felt Étienne's focus on me. *Bide your time*, Madame de Treville had said. *Let him come to you.* Up until now he hadn't let his gaze linger more than a few seconds. This time, however, it was over a minute before I finally acknowledged him. "You're not watching the show," I chastised, mellowing it with a small smile.

"Maybe not. But I'm watching a wonder infinitely more entrancing."

Warmth flared in my limbs. I kept my eyes trained on the actors. This wasn't like sitting in the garden with Jacques. Nothing had spooled between us, no matter how much I'd willed it. But now, it was hard to focus on the scene. I was so acutely aware of every movement my target made: the way he drummed his fingers against his knee, the crinkle of fabric as he shifted in his seat, his gaze like a brand, the lack of air . . . the second I shut my eyes I was met with the vision of Papa's body, cold on the edge of an unmarked road. I opened them with a snap. Streaks of blood were replaced with red velvet cushions, a stage teeming with performers and standing audience members.

"Is everything all right?" His expression sincere, his words sincere; everything about him seemed sincere. But none of that mattered. Not when Papa was dead.

"I'm a bit overheated—and dizzy." Lies were best when mixed with truths, sounded smooth and sincere on your tongue.

Would he purse his lips? Decide me a weak girl with a pattern of frailty? Or was my theory right? Was he more than others thought?

"Allow me to accompany you for a breath of fresh air."

"Sir, it would be improper to be alone together unchaperoned." My voice was light, teasing.

"I'm hardly inviting you to gallivant about Paris. A quick stroll. Or we could sit, if you prefer. We won't even leave the theater grounds." He offered his hand before I had the chance to worry about standing. Before I had the chance to answer. In any other situation, I'd barely put any pressure, wouldn't take what I needed; I'd regret it later when I was confined to my bed. But when my fingers squeezed his arm, his face remained unchanged. Before we left, unbeknownst to my target, Madame de Treville signaled to Aria.

Étienne led me back into the foyer—mostly deserted aside from a few last-minute stragglers—and then to a door, which opened to reveal a courtyard. Green-tipped topiaries and gentle murmurs of grass a step away. Aria's presence was muted, subtle, almost unnoticeable. But she couldn't pass over the threshold undetected. With two fingers, I tapped my skirt; to the ignorant observer I adjusted my dress. The secret signal used if, despite appearances, we were sound and steady and didn't need help.

This wouldn't be like the first ball. I was stronger now, smarter.

"See? We didn't have to leave the theater," he said, shutting the door. "But I've neglected our purpose. I thought it would be best, the next time we saw each other, if I had an easily accessible cool place at my fingertips. Since heat is a problem for you, I've gathered. Are you feeling any better?"

I returned my hand to his arm, ignoring my shiver at the brisk air, at the warmth of his arm through the thick embroidered fabric, hid my shock at his consideration. "Much better," I said. "You were right, the air is doing me some good." His lips pulled into a satisfied grin. Étienne was thoughtful, but he was still a man. Like all our targets, he wasn't without pride.

"Are you enjoying the show?" he asked as we wandered around the edges of the courtyard. The breeze sighed against our faces.

"Very much. Thank you again for extending your invitation to the other ladies. They were so excited."

"Surely you must know it was all for you. Your companions are charming, yes, but it was *you* I was desperate to see." He misread my expression and paused, halting our progression. "That was forward of me."

"Yes."

His brows furrowed. "Say you'll forgive me."

I curved my lips just so. After practicing these past months it no longer felt uncomfortable, not like it had when I first arrived in Paris. His sharp inhale melted into the night. "I don't know, Monsieur Verdon. Honor and virtue are a lady's most prized possessions, after all."

"Have I regressed to *Monsieur* Verdon? Who would've thought my name had such capacity to wound? Mademoiselle, I beg you: Accept my apology."

"Well, if you're begging . . ." I paused; he waited. "Very well. I accept."

"That was devious." He laughed and the tension dissipated.

"I almost gave it away. You were so upset."

"Upset?" Étienne inquired. "You're mistaken." My face burned. "I was devastated." The burn became a full-on flame. "As pretty as that blush is, I didn't mean to embarrass you. Let's talk about something else. How do you like living with Madame de Treville? You've been there a few months now, yes?"

How could I possibly describe what that place meant to me? The fencing lessons, the nights spent preparing for another event in an endless parade of parties, the sword and dagger at my hips under many layers of fine silk. Girls at my side who would never let me fall. "I like it very much," I settled for.

"I'm glad to hear it. I've driven by the house on occasion: It seems like it could be large and lonely, with only the four of you and Madame de Treville."

I was about to correct him, then paused. Étienne didn't know Henri. But then, perhaps I could use that to my advantage. Madame de Treville did say he liked a chase. I performed my very best, belabored sigh as I trailed my free hand along a bare tree. "Well, there's her nephew. But he's been so busy," I said with a frown. "The past few times I've seen him have been under the strangest of circumstances." Lies *did* go better with truths. Henri had been busy of late.

Étienne listened intently before speaking. "Well, I can't say I'm disappointed that a potential rival has ceded his time with you, but I'm sorry for anything that brings you distress."

I let his tense words hang between us for as long as I could, then shook my head, staring up at him through my lashes. "You are mistaken; the Monsieur is just a friend," I said. Étienne's expression thawed. Instead of speaking further he started walking again, modulating his strides so it wasn't necessary for me to take three steps for every one of his. "May I ask you a question?"

"It seems only fair, non? A question for a question," he said.

Wetting my lips, I thought back to Madame de Treville's instructions. To the way Étienne's jaw hardened in front of the theater. "Earlier, when the theater investor brought up your father, you seemed troubled." He hardened into stone. "I'm sorry. I didn't mean to pry—"

"Don't apologize." Some of his dark hair had fallen from its tie. In another place, another time, maybe if I were another girl, one who wasn't trying to wriggle out secrets for the Order, one whose unsteady legs weren't swallowed in dark waves, I'd stand on tiptoe to tuck the strands behind his ear. "I want to be my own man. Not renowned for my father's coin purse, but for making a difference. It must be difficult to understand, but—"

"I don't think it's difficult at all." He regarded me in surprise, and I fought the urge to cut myself off midthought. "To live up to everyone's expectations, but also wanting to make your own way. To never feel like you'll be good enough, not in the way they want you to be."

There was a new emotion in his face. "You speak as if from personal experience."

"With Madame de Treville as a guide, how could I be a stranger to those feelings?" My laugh was breathy, a stalling tactic. "Are there other family members who might understand your plight?"

"My uncle sought to make a business and a name for himself through trade. He would be the likeliest to comprehend my position . . . but I've never discussed it with him, not truly. Not like I do with you now."

I swallowed. Tried not to break away from his intense gaze. He said he didn't mean to make me blush, and yet . . . "He must be very busy with making deals and supervising ships and such."

Étienne smiled, as if he were fully aware I knew what he meant but had chosen to interpret it differently. "I was surprised when he said he'd come support the opening, and, frankly, thought it was too good to be true. And I was right. After I wrote you, I received a letter from him apologizing for the late notice, but that he needed to prepare for unloading his last shipment of the year. He should have had one of his men stand in ... then again, right now, I find I can hardly remember ever being frustrated." He looked down at me, and I looked back up at him, trying to discover the danger in his face that his father had hidden there, the danger I couldn't seem to find.

I masked my intake of breath as a cough. But the sound continued, melted into shouts that echoed from somewhere outside, spilling over and trembling into the starlit courtyard. "Did you hear that?"

His brows rumpled. "Nothing to be concerned about. Probably a latecomer who's upset about not being allowed inside."

I tucked my hand back into the crook of his arm just before we heard the scream. High pitched and isolated, it floated on the smoky night air. Then it cut off abruptly.

"We need to get back to the others," Étienne said. I clung onto his arm for balance as he pivoted sharply toward the door.

"Tania! Oh, thank goodness!" Théa exclaimed as we stepped over the threshold. She was tiny against the clustered audience members, many of whom had flooded into the foyer. "That scream ... I worried—not to say, Monsieur Verdon, that I thought her in danger—"

He cut her off, not unkindly: "I understand. I'm glad to know Tania has such devoted friends." Théa's eyes flitted to mine at his casual address. "Mademoiselle," he continued, "has there been any word as to what caused the disturbance?"

"One of the audience members—all he remembers is stepping

out into the foyer, and then a searing pain to the back of his head. He came to for a moment, but passed out not long after, and then a pedestrian outside said they saw someone running out of the theater like a fire was at his heels. And now a few men, there, by the main entrance—they're organizing a search party of sorts, to investigate," Théa recounted.

His focus flickered to me, to the double doors, back to me again. "I won't leave if you're feeling unwell."

"Madame de Treville won't let anything happen to us," I said with a tight throat, a tight chest. The way his gaze roved over me didn't make me uncomfortable, but still, I took a step back, a step toward Théa.

The resolution wavered in his face. "Promise me you'll stay with the group until the guards arrive."

"I promise." There was no reason for me to feel guilty. And yet. He stared at me for a beat longer. And then, with a brief, firm kiss to my hand, he was off to join the search.

"Quickly." A tug at my elbow—Théa. Her once-frightened expression was all edges now, sharpened at a whetstone. She pulled me to Portia, Aria, and Madame de Treville, who waited in a secluded archway.

We followed our mentor around a crescent-shaped wall, through a back exit, into the night. Voices spilled out of the theater, then went silent as the door swung shut. Madame de Treville checked our surroundings as Aria spoke: "An attack on the opening night of a theater mostly funded by a discontented noble. *And* he doesn't attend the first performance? What's more important to him than flaunting his wealth?"

"You think the opening night was a cover," I guessed.

"A distraction to sneak something or someone into the city.

Or transfer something already here to a more secure location. The attacker fled to draw the guards' attention. They'll only be focused on finding him," Aria said as she paced back and forth, turning every five steps, each time she reached the alley wall.

"That still doesn't explain the crash. A body falling to the ground doesn't make that much noise," Portia noted.

"Well, something didn't go according to plan," Aria said. Her clear gaze struck down the next street. "Perhaps the victim was in the wrong place at the wrong time? Maybe the attacker was interrupted in his task by a civilian? Maybe he didn't intend to harm the victim."

"You don't know what they did to my father," I bit out. "These aren't people who care who they hurt. The attacker probably didn't even hesitate. He probably *enjoyed* it."

I spun at the sound of a boot catching on stone. A few blocks over, indiscernible shouts echoed, would-be detectives going from door to door. But everything faded into the background when the shadows shifted.

"Tania, do you—"

I held up my hand for silence; I wasn't sure who spoke. I watched, waited, willed myself into the night—there. A man darted out from behind a pile of overturned barrels and squeezed into a nearby alley.

"Portia, Théa, tail him!" Madame de Treville ordered. "Aria, go around back and approach from the opposite direction. I'll guard the front of the theater in case he tries to blend in with the search party. Tania," she said as the others sprinted away, "stand guard here. On the chance he doubles back, you'll cut him off."

"But . . ." She was gone before I had a chance to finish.

My gaze trailed the shadowed crevices, the pools of murky

rainwater, the muddy cobblestones. Beady eyes glowed in the dark corners, followed by scuttling claws and the sense of being watched. No one was here. No one but me and the rats.

A door creaked open, closed. Shoulders nearly to my chin, I took a few steps toward the overturned barrels. Another shift. Nails on cobblestone.

Only one man had appeared from the pile of weathered wood containers. But what if he was distracting us from something else? Someone else?

Just a quick check behind the barrels to quiet my nerves— once I was a couple of feet away, I used a section of wood for support to lean around the side.

A fist, whizzing toward my jaw, stark against the night. I ducked. The air parted with a whoosh; my world blurred. I steadied myself as a shadowed figure raced away from me.

I scrambled after him, tucking aside my skirts to give my legs more room. He weaved in and out of the shadows, veered to the left, paused with his palms against the back of a fine shopfront with painted windows.

What on earth was he thinking? I wouldn't have been able to catch him before, not with the black dots staining my vision and the weakness in my legs, not if he'd kept running. But, stopped, I had the chance.

He threw his hand in the air, in the direction of the roof. Metal claws screeched against shingles, sent some flying after finding purchase on the chimney stack. Horror unfurled in my chest as he started to climb a rope that now hung down the building's facade.

I tossed myself at the stone wall, fumbled for the rope's end. The man was dangling midair. The rope cut into my palms. As I hoisted myself up, my foot connected with a glass window. My stomach dropped at a crackling; that one window probably cost more than anything I'd ever owned.

The man looked down, caught a glimpse of me, swore. He hurdled over the edge of the roof and climbed to the chimney stack, a flash of silver in his hand—the hook.

I felt the give in the rope before I saw it. For one mind-numbing, stomach-chilling second, I was in freefall. But my fingers latched onto a shingle, which shifted as my body swung. I grabbed with my other hand at the roof's edge.

The man was gone.

"Tania?" Théa's voice, but all my breath was leached from me, nothing there to let her know where I was.

The shingle wasn't made to support my weight. I barely got hold of another before the first slid and crashed to the ground. Twenty feet? Thirty? This wouldn't be like falling in the village square. It wouldn't be egg yolks on the cobblestone, not this time.

"Where did that—oh, mon Dieu. Portia, Aria, hurry!"

Everything was blistering, burning. My arms wrenched from my sockets with fireplace tongs. My fingers screamed.

"Hang on!" Portia cried. "The theater should have a ladder!"

"There isn't time!" Aria's words, a fear-laced dagger.

"What choice do we have?"

Running footsteps. The wall and the few shingles in my line of sight undulated in front of me. "Hold on, Tania!" Théa's voice, high and sharp, barely pierced through my heart's roar.

My fingers shook. The vibrations rocked my bones.

The shingle slipped from underneath my left hand, scratched against my healed wounds from breaking the fence. Too drained to reach for another grip, I dangled by my right arm. Papa's voice rushed in my ears.

Hold on, Tania, hold on.

Teeth clenched, I watched the shingle under my right hand slide ever so slowly.

A little longer. A little longer and the others would be back with the ladder and everything would be fine, I'd be safe, and— the shingle flew into the smoky night.

Too late. Much too late to frantically grasp for purchase, but I tried, my fingers closing around air. The world falling, plummeting, and . . .

"Oof!"

One elbow seared against stone. The other met the soft flesh of Théa's stomach. She hissed as she caught the majority of my fall, drew me to my feet, gripped me by my shoulder as the world spun. Shards of air punched through my lungs. When I could finally take a breath without my sides shrieking, I looked at my flustered companion. Dirt and dust marred the skirt of her dress, one sleeve torn at the wrist. She winced as she shook out her arms, her legs.

"What happened?" I croaked out.

"I caught you," Théa said, then frowned. "I'm quite strong: Aside from scrapes and bumps, and maybe a sprain or two, I should be fine."

"No, I didn't mean—thank you. But the man I was chasing, and the one you and Portia were trailing, did they escape?"

"Portia and I caught him . . . wait, did you say there was another man?"

My laugh turned into a wheeze. "Scaling buildings isn't my idea of fun."

Portia and Aria struggled through the back exit, the ladder

they carried on their shoulders falling with a clunk. "Tania!" Portia exclaimed as she rushed to my side. "Are you hurt? Injured?"

"What? She fell on *me*!" Théa said in disbelief. "Where's the concern over *my* potential injuries?"

"Tania fell! Off a *roof*!" Portia said. "When you do that, *then* you can expect sympathy from me." Despite all her bluster, Portia still pulled Théa toward her after examining me, tutting over the scrapes and scratches on Théa's arms.

We limped back to the theater, Théa grimacing and my arms useless by my sides. As they pressed me between them, Portia and Aria explained how they'd apprehended the other man—the man who hit the theatergoer—and cornered him on the other side of the theater. The two of them kept me upright through the dizziness, their hands at my elbows. Outside the theater, I tried to scan the street for Étienne. But the others hustled me straight into the carriage.

At Madame de Treville's insistence, I recounted what happened as best I could: the man, the rope, the barrels. And before: Étienne in the courtyard. His disdain for his father. How he let slip mention of his uncle's final upcoming shipment. His genuine surprise at the disturbance. How he almost didn't leave out of concern for my safety.

"Men, thinking they're heroes." Madame de Treville snorted. "They're still on patrol; I saw them on my way to find you. Don't fret," she continued, "they were too busy investigating the other street to even consider searching the back alleys. Great search-party work from the lot of them."

"The Musketeers must be on their way," Aria noted. "They can't avoid a public disturbance. Not one with so many nobles as witnesses."

Madame de Treville nodded. "Brandon is already there; he came after I alerted him. He'll do his best to rein in the more enthusiastic recruits and will question the assailant himself. He'll send a report to the house before the night is through." Then she sighed, taking in my drooped shoulders. "Blame is a pointless emotion that will get us absolutely nowhere. We possibly caught a member of the smuggling ring tonight. With interrogation, we could learn who he's working for. Biding our time is a nuisance, yes, but it's a necessary element of our profession. As far as the one who disappeared . . ." She sighed and pressed her fingers to her temples. "Well, we must pray he isn't the more important of the two. And that he doesn't leave the city before la Maison du Roi find him."

I settled back into my seat. Let the angry throb of my arms overtake my vision until everything was pulsing black and red.

He'd slipped through my fingers as easily as the roof's shingles. And no matter how strong I'd become, all I could do was watch him disappear into the dark bloom of night.

CHAPTER NINETEEN

THE OTHERS INSISTED on staying up with Madame de Treville until she received news on the second man's identity. I dozed on and off in a velvet stuffed chair, arms wrapped in warm towels. Aria bandaged Théa's ankle with wide strands of linen. Henri hadn't come out of his room to help us; Madame de Treville said Sanson was making him come into work very early, and he needed his sleep. It was strange to see her occupy the role of concerned aunt when she spent most of her time picking us apart during lessons.

"The man Aria and Portia caught was brought on as brute force, likely by nobles who didn't want their hands dirty." Madame de Treville folded the letter twice, three times as she continued, light slipping off the paper from the fireplace. Its roaring flames were the only thing staving off the beginnings of the freezing Parisian winter. "Apparently, he was hired off the docks. A cloaked figure offered him a purse full of livres for guarding another man—a messenger, probably—the man you chased after, Tania. The attack was planned. Paired with the commotion from the theater opening, it was a perfect distraction. But what the distraction was for . . . now, that remains to be seen. We don't have the other suspect for questioning. Based on the information you've acquired, I'm inclined to believe there was a large transport of weapons, something of vital import that would've been too noticeable on the Parisian streets if most of the guards in le quartier weren't distracted."

Pain throbbed behind my eyes as I spoke. "But what about the shipment Étienne referred to? The one his uncle is supervising?"

Even as I wondered aloud, Portia fumed: "This man didn't think to inquire why everything was shrouded in mystery? He just took the money?"

"He needed it," Aria snapped. Théa winced as Aria yanked the bandages on her ankle tighter. "That's a good enough reason. Dockworkers are paid next to nothing. That money was more than he makes in a month. It's almost winter. People who live outside Le Marais feel cold, too."

Portia started to protest, but Madame de Treville quelled her with a glare. "We don't have time for this." She flipped the letter over. "To Tania's point, perhaps the distraction was a distraction in more ways than one—have la Maison du Roi so focused on tonight's dealings that they'll be investigating this when they should be watching the docks. Did your target say anything else? Anything else we could use?" she asked me.

The warmth of Étienne's arm. Supporting me. Lifting me. I blinked. "Not exactly. Ét—my target and his father aren't on good terms. He knew about the shipment because his uncle snubbed an invitation to the theater opening. Even if he isn't wholly ignorant of his father and uncle's treachery, I don't see how he could be aligned with a father he speaks of with such loathing."

Aria observed me, features narrowed, as if there were something I hadn't disclosed. True, I didn't recount the entire interaction, from subtle glances to the way his profile looked when drenched in starlight, but none of that held anything for the Order, anything for our mission. I was making him want me, like I was supposed to. Madame de Treville didn't need us to regale her with every detail of our seduction, every specific line of flirtatious banter.

Madame de Treville contemplated the roaring fire, the shards of wood engulfed in blue flame. And then she shifted to face me. Approval in her features, between the exhaustion and frustration. "What a journey you've had since arriving on my doorstep. And you have a way to go . . . but I know you're dedicated to uncovering the truth. If you believe you're unlikely to glean more information from him, I'll find you another target, maybe two. There's always his uncle, his father's friends. In addition to Verdon's son, of course. If there's any chance he knows more than he's given you cause to suspect, we can't let that information slip away. But I won't waste valuable time squeezing information from a dry rag."

My chest ached. The soreness from climbing was catching up with me.

"You're all free to go. Aria, now that we know about the hired hands, the mission I mentioned will be of the utmost importance. Théa and Portia will provide distraction. And take Tania with you—she has the quickest hand."

Once Madame de Treville left, we rounded on Aria. "Mission? What mission?" I asked.

A rare smile graced her lips. "I hope you like fish."

"This wasn't what I thought you meant!" I whispered through my sleeve, trying not to gag on the pungent smell of brine and guts as Aria and I cautiously sneaked across the Port of Paris. Shadows hid our bodies from workers unloading large crates that groaned and rattled as they were lowered to the ground. Every so often, a wooden plank would creak under my feet. I'd freeze. Press myself firmly against the back wall of a tavern or warehouse. Hold my breath and count to ten, waiting for raucous laughter, or a dockworker singing sea chanteys, to know it was safe to continue.

I might've not grown up in lavish mansions, not like my sisters in arms, but even the lake I'd once traveled to near Lupiac didn't smell this way. Maybe it was the city—a thought that made me chuckle, because it was exactly what Papa would think. That Paris, and the deceit and grime of la noblesse, had corrupted the very water.

Aria shot me a quick, amused glance. "I didn't want to spoil the surprise. What did you think I meant, anyway?" Initially, when I saw the vêtements, I thought she was joking. But this was Aria, so I took the clothes and transformed myself into a proper Parisian boy. I thought perhaps we were going to a cabaret or a market or somewhere that served or sold fish.

Now, slinking along the docks, this new attire was certainly more convenient than unwieldy gowns and corsets. The jacket even had pockets, including one for my dagger. And my sword was more accessible without all those layers of fabric, easily concealed in an unadorned sheath at my hip. We even managed to pass by pubs like L'Auberge de la Félicité and The Gryphon, ones with men swaying and spilling out the doors, without them calling out to us, leering at us.

Maman would be horrified.

It was wonderful.

With the information I learned from Étienne, combined with intelligence from dockhands and other merchants, it wasn't difficult to determine which day his uncle's ship was making port. What we hadn't expected was the wait. The crew docked in the afternoon, yet hours elapsed with hardly any motion. Aria insisted on us being silent, hardened professionals for the first hour, but she finally relented once she realized there was no visible end in sight. We exhausted talking about our families—well, I exhausted talking about my family; Aria replied to a few questions with clipped, one-word answers and was adept at changing the topic—then I made a game of pointing out ships and guessing where they were from, with Aria then telling me why I was wrong. Over the course of our conversation, the sky shifted from clear to milky blue to inky night.

"Spain!" I dramatically thrust my hand at the port's latest arrival.

Aria scoffed. "You think every ship is from Spain."

"Condé is there. What if he's trying to make another play for the throne?"

Aria shook her head. "Don't you think we've addressed that possibility already? No. He's busy licking his wounds."

I let out a *humph*, arms across my chest, seated on a forgotten cargo box. "Well, *I* think that—"

"Hush now."

"Don't tell me to hush! I have—"

Aria pointed to the ship we'd been waiting on as two gentlemen boarded and went below deck. A few minutes later, members of the crew started bringing up box after box from the hold, preparing to unload cargo.

"Oh my! Is there a gentleman to be found?" Portia's voice carried toward us. "My slipper fell into the port! Oh, what I wouldn't do for the kind, courageous fellow who retrieved my favorite slipper! I think, no, *I know*, I'd be the most grateful mademoiselle in all of Paris!"

Aria and I scuttled forward, peered around the ship. Portia was gesturing animatedly to the crew members who debarked via the gangplank. She and Théa were dressed in the most outrageous fashions, wigs, and veiled hats we could find in our collected wardrobes. A little rosette slipper bobbed twenty feet out from the dock. What a throw.

I pulled up the brim of my hat, which kept slipping, and stopped when Aria raised her hand. The signal. The gentlemen were above deck.

"My sister insisted we go for a walk, but I think we may have gotten ourselves lost," Théa called to the two gentlemen. "Maybe you could be of assistance, while your workers retrieve her slipper?" She smiled up at them, doe-eyed, took an additional step to erase some of the distance between them.

The gentlemen muttered to each other, then strolled down the gangplank and onto the dock, a few steps away—not ideal for a covert boarding, but the only chance we'd get. With their bodies turned, Aria and I edged out from behind the ship. We rolled onto our backs at the end of the plank. Then we gripped onto it, hands and feet precariously balanced, and shimmied our way toward the deck. Barnacled wood encompassed my vision.

With a tug, Aria flipped over and onto the deck with not so much as a creak. My descent was less graceful, but the noise was covered by the lapping of waves and Portia's crowing.

We dashed behind the cargo boxes just in time: A crew member crossed the deck, whistling, a few feet and boxes separating us. I chanced a look over the side of the ship. Nets made from ropes thick as my wrists clung to the wood, grimy with salt and seaweed, like strands of oversized pearls in the shadows.

Aria raised a finger to her lips as workers lifted a box fifteen or so feet away. She crouched down, crept closer. I could discern some words exchanged between the crew, muddled by Portia's and Théa's ministrations. Stories of long journeys, aching joints, sea salt air, and the tremor of the water. I retrieved parchment and charcoal from my jacket pocket, focused on Aria's hands. She gestured to her clothing, then to an object lodged in one of the wooden slats. It took a moment to realize what she meant. A bolt. So, they were transporting fabric. But how many bolts? She held up two fingers, then rounded them together to make a zero. I started writing the number before she held up another zero, formed with the fingers on her other hand. Two hundred bolts of fabric? Were they planning on sewing a blanket to smother all of Paris?

Ear cocked toward Portia and Théa, careful not to miss potential warnings, I watched Aria use a sharp flat of metal and a dagger to pry open a box. I winced at the splintering. Portia covered the noise with a shriek. One of the crew had started to paddle through the water toward her slipper. His friend had hold of one end of a rope, the other tied around his middle, presumably to reel him in if he started to go under.

Aria motioned for me to join her. "Hold the lid while I move the fabric."

The box wasn't full. A strange sight on a merchant's ship. But if he wanted not to tip off crew members with too-heavy boxes . . . Aria riffled through layers of brocade and silk. Then she stopped. I followed the line of her arm. There, even in the dark, steel glinted dangerously. Weapons—just as we'd thought—given the abbreviations on the ledger notes. Squinting, I made out the sharp angles of muskets. At least, what I thought were muskets. I'd never seen one up close. Papa had gifted his weaponry—other than his swords, of course—to his brothers in arms when he left with my mother for Lupiac. I'd asked him why once. He said he hated the things. Made it too easy to destroy without remorse. That he preferred the sword: the weapon of a gentleman. And, he'd added with a bop on my nose, of a gentlelady.

The lid came down on my knuckles as the box was tugged from the opposite side. Aria flung herself at me, shoving us behind another box.

Knuckles pounding, clutching my throat, I waited for the flash of a knife to my neck. A musket to my temple. Aria sagged against the cargo box. "We need to get off the ship, now," she whispered. "Won't be any boxes left to hide behind soon."

I crawled under the gangplank first. When feet thundered above me, I gripped the board tighter, desperate not to fall into the murky water. My neck and hands ached. My knees throbbed with each slap of waves against wood.

Somehow, I successfully reached the dock. When it was safe, when the two gentlemen and other crew members were fully distracted by and were facing Portia and Théa, I crawled back into the shadows of the hull.

A loud crash. A sickening thump, shattering wood. Fragments rained down on the dock. Portia and Théa squealed, hurrying out of sight. One of the gentlemen shouted at the crew unloading the boxes: "Can't you keep your men in check?"

I surveyed the crate's remains. Probably the one Aria tampered with; it would explain why it came apart. The gentlemen rushed the workers to gather the fabric. Bolts had fallen into the water, some light enough to float, others sinking like drowned water nymphs. The ones wrapped around muskets, most likely. A purple silk, stained dark with salt water, was close enough for me to touch. But there was another object floating among the unfurling yards of fabric: a piece of paper. A few other sheets had already met a watery grave, glimmering as they sank into the murk. I adjusted my hat, glanced at the workers. Back to the remaining paper. The ink would dissolve. And Aria, debarking the ship, was in too precarious a position to reach for it.

I crept forward. Winced as a plank creaked, but kept going, extended a hand, fingers pale over the icy depths . . .

"You there! What are you doing?"

I snatched the paper from the water. When someone grabbed at me, I fought back: biting, rearing, scratching. Every kick, every flail of my fist for Papa—I wouldn't let them take me, wouldn't let them carve me unrecognizable.

"It's me!" Aria's voice slowed my heart enough that it wasn't jumping out of my throat.

The dockworker who spotted us was shouting, pointing with one hand, a lantern in the other. "Halt!"

I sprinted across the dock with Aria by my side. Salty wind against my face, on my tongue, in my eyes. The pounding in my ears wasn't loud enough to drown out the running footsteps, so much heavier than ours. Their strides so much longer.

We darted around another warehouse. I braced myself against the wall, panting. Everything churned; the wood was water beneath my feet.

As I did my best to keep from swaying, I stared at Aria until she came into focus. "We have to split up. Portia and Théa should be gone by now," I said.

"I won't leave you. Not like this," she said. Her gaze darted to my legs, to my eyes that were looking at her but not really seeing.

"We'll have a better chance if we meet back at the house. I can do this," I added at her uncertainty, forcing my shoulders back, my chin high.

She threw a look over her shoulder before speaking. "Not the house. It's too risky. We can't compromise the Order. We'll meet at The Gryphon." We'd passed the pub on our way to the docks.

Another angry shout, a rush of footsteps. "Go. Now!" I whispered. She gave me one last look as we parted: her to the left, me to the right. I ran down the pier, furiously sucking down the crisp air. My boots thwapped against wet wood.

"Catch him!"

I raced around a warehouse that stored extra boat parts, oars. Skeletons in the dark. No matter how many breaths I took, my chest rose and fell rapidly, my heartbeat a thunderstorm just overhead.

"That way!"

At the sound of retreating footsteps, I sighed, my head falling back against the wall. This area of the dock was calm. Lanterns swinging slowly, ships large as buildings bobbing in the cloudy water.

"Now, what do we have here?" I fumbled for my sword, drew it as I spun. My fingers warmed the cold steel. One of the gentlemen. He must have stayed behind, split off from the others currently chasing after Aria, or a shadow they'd mistaken for her. His angular features prompted no recognition. "What kind of common street rat has a sword like that? Steal it, did you? What were you doing, then, sneaking around the ship?" He took a step closer, and I raised the weapon in line with his heart. The blade blurred in my vision.

"Let me go, and I won't hurt you." I deepened my voice. Thrust out my chest, because that's what I'd seen men do, then retracted—had he noticed the curve of my breasts under the loose shirt?

"You're a funny one, I'll give you that . . . no, you're not going anywhere. Didn't your mother teach you it isn't polite to sneak around?" Another step closer. Was he planning on trying to rush at me?

"I won't warn you again," I threatened, unable to stop the tremor in the words. But when he attempted to approach farther, I bent my knees into my en garde stance.

"Brave," he spat as he reached for his dueling sword. "But bravery won't keep you from bleeding out on the docks. The gulls will be picking at your corpse before anyone has a chance to miss you—though I doubt any such person exists, fils de pute."

I lunged. Steel met steel. He barely recovered from his surprise, blocking my sword at the very last second. Returned my attack with a thrust so quick I had to jump out of the way. His blade whizzed across the space where my stomach was less than a second ago.

Our blades met again and again.

My opponent slashed at my uncovered arm. A rent in the fabric. The sting of blood rushing against skin. I didn't look at the wound; my concentration had already cost me once. Instead I took a difficult parry, channeling all my strength into the action.

He tried to recover, but it was too late. It was just like what Papa told me. Yes, I was dizzy; yes, his body swayed before me like the rocking of a ship; yes, my legs felt as if they'd collapse at any moment. But I knew the rhythm of this bout. It was in my bones, in the throb of my wounded arm, in the beat of my heart.

With a cry, I thrust forward. My sword sank into his side. His hands went to the flowering splash of blood spreading across his shirt. He staggered backward, but not before I yanked out my sword. A gruesome tug-of-war with abdominal muscle. He fell against the wall with a wheeze.

A rustle of fabric. I whirled, my entire body shaking, my sword dripping a pattern of crimson onto the shadowed planks.

Aria: red-cheeked, focus darting from the sword pointed at her face, the sword I couldn't seem to lower, to the man slumped in the corner. "It's over," she said as she moved around the blade, pressed against my upper arm until the muscles released. My blade clattered to the ground. It was cold, but I was covered in fabric, had been fencing; sweat tears dripped down my cheeks. So why was I shivering?

After wiping my sword on her pant leg, Aria presented it to me. It took a few attempts to sheath the blade. My teeth cracked against each other.

"We have to go." She watched as I hesitated, locked on the man puddled into the wall. "It's not a fatal wound. I lost the dockworkers a street over and doubled back. But they'll come looking for him soon. He didn't discover who you were, right?" I shook my head slowly.

She tugged at my arm. For a second my body resisted, but I followed her. Looked back over my shoulder, once. From here, the man was only shadows and blood.

We ran until I doubled over, until my insides were melted flames. Aria stopped and surveyed our surroundings. Pain flared through my arm. "How bad is it?" I asked.

She examined the wound, taking care to touch only my shirt-sleeve. "Probably won't need stitches. Only a bandage. Don't move your arm too much."

The empty street was quiet, dark. "What happened to meeting at The Gryphon?"

"I heard what sounded like a duel. Thought I'd check. I'm glad I did."

"Aria, when you startled me, I—"

She shook her head. "Your first duel—a real one—is . . . difficult." There was no strength left in me to protest. "Come. We'll take the long way back. Just in case."

We stumbled across the house's threshold an hour or so later. Though it was hard to tell time with the rushing in my ears, with the wave of dizziness threatening to swallow me whole. When Henri opened the door I nearly fell into his arms; he almost dropped me in surprise.

"What are you doing up so late? Where are the others?" Aria asked. I'd wondered the same, but I was in no state to ask questions, the inquiries flying from my mind in a plume of blurry smoke.

"I was helping my aunt," he said defensively. "Just because my apprenticeship keeps me away from the house doesn't mean I don't believe in her—your—cause. I'm allowed to want to do more, be more—" I stumbled, and he was quick to grab my arm. He withdrew when I whimpered in pain. "She's wounded!"

"It's not deep," Aria said.

Henri seemed personally affronted by Aria's lack of concern; then again, everything was so fuzzy that I couldn't quite tell whose expression belonged to whose face.

"She's right. I'll be fine . . . ," I reassured him as my vision tunneled. My words slurred as dark waves, the same ones rolling and tumbling against the ship's hull, crashed over me. Pulled my body out into a pitch-black sea.

Someone forced a cup to my lips. I drank a couple sips of cold tea.

A few minutes later, I opened my eyes—and there was the rest of the Order. A blanket was tucked underneath my body so blood wouldn't stain the couch cushions. A bandage gripped my left bicep.

"I heard you had quite the adventure," Madame de Treville said from across the room. I prepared myself for her anger. Or worse, disappointment. "Aria said you confirmed there were weapons on board, that you even won a duel. It's not enough for an arrest, but it's close. What we need now is evidence that connects the weapons to the nobles, in addition to the merchants—

along with confirmation of the main nobles in charge. Verdon, if we're right. And we'll come in ahead of schedule!"

My thumbs pressed hard against my eyelids, against the approaching headache. All I could see was that man slumped against the wall. Aria said I hadn't killed him—was that true? Or had I taken a life? A life for a life . . . had Papa slumped like that, chest crumpled over hips?

There was a difference between day-to-day training and actually dueling. Knowing that, in order to keep your life, to protect others' lives, you must endanger someone else's. Maybe even take it.

Aria had retrieved the notes from my jacket pocket and was going over them with Madame de Treville. With a jolt, I felt the other scrap of paper scrape against my chest. Pulling it out gingerly, I swallowed. It was brittle. As if the very paper might disintegrate in my hands.

"What I can't figure out is how they saw us," Aria considered.

"It was my fault." Everyone turned to stare at me after I spoke, my eyes still trained on the paper, on its contents; I could feel the weight of their gazes.

"Excuse me?" Madame de Treville said.

I held out the paper, shoulders quaking. "I saw papers floating with the fabric and grabbed one because I thought it might be important. Why else would it be packed with the muskets? But it's not," I said, unable to stop the tears. "I risked our lives for an *inventory slip*!"

Madame de Treville plucked the paper from my grasp, read it fervently. "No, Tania." She wasn't upset. She was beaming. "No, you brilliant, foolish girl. It's not an inventory slip. It's a code."

CHAPTER TWENTY

MADAME DE TREVILLE banned us from her study after we flocked around her desk. Well, the others had—I remained by the door, clutching the frame for balance. "Allez!" she cried. "Shoo! I need to make copies before the ink fades from the salt water. How can I finish anything with all of you breathing down my neck?"

Portia leaned her head against the wall next to the study's closed door and groaned. "Nom de Dieu . . . first I miss Tania's duel, and now *this*! What if there's a secret message triggered by water? Or by the oil from fingerprints?"

"The latter is impossible," Aria said. "The former, highly unlikely. You'll be fine."

The muted thud of a door. My head snapped up, but I wasn't seeing the hallway. I didn't see my sword stuck in a stone, a lake, a hill. It was lodged between ribs.

Henri came into focus: frazzled, jacket rumpled. He zipped down the hallway, unable to keep from knocking into the sole unoccupied chair. "Mesdemoiselles," he intoned, bowing his head.

"Your aunt is inside her study and isn't here to enforce protocol, so if you think I'm getting up to curtsy for you, you're about to be *very* disappointed," Portia said, examining an embroidered flower coming loose from her sleeve.

Théa let out a little squeak as Henri blushed. "I didn't expect you—it wasn't my intention . . ." For some reason, he looked at me, searching. Was he embarrassed at the thought of making me stand up to curtsy for him? With my dizziness? I shook my head and smiled. But my gesture didn't have the intended effect; his flush darkened before he knocked on the study door.

"What exactly are you still doing here?" Aria asked Henri, her eyes narrowed.

"Aunt asked me to help." Confusion furrowed his brow at her insistence. "And I want to. I want to help." He recovered quickly, lighting his gaze on mine before he entered. Madame de Treville greeted him faintly, and the door closed behind him. All was silent.

"Is everything all right?" Portia asked Aria after a brief pause.

"If you want to wait here and do nothing, fine. But I'm going to bed," Aria said.

Once Aria left, Théa asked Portia tentatively, "Is she okay?"

Portia scoffed, fiddled with her sleeve. A stray thread snapped. "How should I know? Ask Tania—*she's* the one who's been with *her* the whole night." Portia's words frosted, the beginning of winter when the air starts to change. After a moment, she tempered. "Get some sleep; you can tell us about the duel tomorrow. I want to hear everything," she told me.

My mind was back at the docks. Back to the dizziness, the salty waves of black ink that threatened to drag me into the deep. To the blood flowering on the man's jacket, dark, the water lapping at the ship's hull, darker. A wave passed over me that had nothing to do with dizziness. I couldn't swallow it down; it was still there in the corners of my eyes, echoing in the velvet crush of my ears. "Yes," I said, voice hollow. "Yes. I'll tell you tomorrow."

"How much longer is it going to take her?" I asked.

Aria tapped her foot. "We're not supposed to draw attention. Stop speaking so loudly."

"We're two unaccompanied girls idling near l'Université du Paris. How exactly is that subtle?" Students milled around the university square, studying philosophy and practicing Greek at café tables, flirting with visiting sweethearts . . .

"We can't wear men's clothes if it's the middle of the day. Not where people could recognize us. We just have to wait for Théa. She'll get the cryptography texts we need. Then we'll be on our way."

We were all would-be code breakers now. And code breakers needed proper foundations. We couldn't afford anyone knowing what books we needed from the university library. And that's where Théa came in, with her unassuming manner and no less than three admirers among the faculty. We'd return the books as soon as possible. Sometimes, stealing was necessary. I thought to Henri, to the map of Lupiac, my throat closing.

Arching my back, rib cage fighting against the bodice, I grumbled. "Do you ever get used to this?"

"Returning to gowns after the clothing we wore the other night? It takes years."

I froze midstretch. Aria came to stand beside me. "Did you see Théa? She's wearing a red plume in her hair, remember."

"You said it took years . . . but you've been with Madame de Treville for a much shorter time than that," I said.

"Mesdemoiselles."

Aria and I turned at the clearing of a throat, me flustered, Aria ever calm. Étienne. My stomach jumped to the base of my throat. "Monsieur Verdon," I murmured. Aria and I curtsied in unison. Our skirts swept the ground; her hand was at my elbow as we both straightened. She made it look as if she were squeezing my arm to let me know she had to leave.

"Monsieur, what a wonderful surprise. I'm off to meet my cousin. He traveled home recently and has a letter for me from my aunt. But, Tania, you must stay," she insisted. "You were so kind to accompany me. The least I can do is let you two have a few moments of uninterrupted conversation."

I opened my mouth to protest, but Aria quelled me with a look that glued me to the spot. The last time I'd seen Étienne, he was pressing a kiss to the back of my hand, worried eyes on mine. Madame de Treville hadn't prepared me for this interaction. I was on my own now.

"That's a shame." Étienne didn't seem very disappointed. "Are you meeting here?" At Aria's nod, he smiled. "We'll be sure to stay in the square. I wouldn't want you to think I was absconding with Tania."

Other than a subtle arch of her brow, Aria didn't acknowledge his familiarity. "A true gentleman."

As she made herself scarce, I tried not to watch Étienne's expression for signs of excitement. What did it matter if he wanted to be alone, other than it meant I was doing my job properly? Besides, it wasn't like we were truly alone. Just far enough away from the students that, if he were to whisper to me, no one would hear a thing. The thought flushed scarlet down my arms.

"How I wish I knew what you were thinking," he said.

"Monsieur, I'm quite sure my uncomplicated musings would be of no interest to a gentleman of your education and standing." The mocking words tangled on my tongue as his hazel eyes bored into mine.

"Tania," he said gently, "we've been over this: it's Étienne." There was no witty retort on my lips, no coy flirtation at the ready. He was right; he *was* Étienne. Unlike the other men we were trained to manipulate and seduce, he made it clear that he cared what I had to say. Cared how I felt. Wanted to help me when I was ill. He wasn't anything like my mother had made me believe young men were. How could his father produce such a son? "Are you enjoying your excursion to the university?" he continued.

"I suppose," I demurred. "Now that you're here, though, I'm enjoying it much more."

There; there it was. It was in the stretch of his fingers, in the way he held his jaw, and it didn't matter that it was a reaction to a false version of myself, because the way he looked at me, it was as if he saw through all the artifice and still liked what he found.

Étienne's hand grazed my forearm. His fingertips pressed against the fabric, so very light. But it wasn't until his hand traced over my concealed dueling wound, accompanied by a blister flash of pain, that I stepped back with a wheeze.

"Is everything all right?" A dozen things flashed through my head, questions and emotions all jumbled, all overwhelmed by a sudden surge of panic. My muscles eased when he withdrew.

"I apologize. That was forward of me." A slight, frustrated frown crossed his lips. "I seem to say those words to you a lot lately."

"Apology accepted," I said, even through the conflicting twinges of irritation and yearning for things to be different, to step forward, to feel that whisper of a touch. Even if it meant that bit of pain, too.

His intense expression lightened as he glanced at the nearby clocktower. "I want to speak with you further, but I'm afraid I must leave."

"So soon?"

"My mother requested my presence." At my raised eyebrows, Étienne laughed. "She thinks I've spent too much time away from home. Neglecting familial duties, as it were."

"And what duties might those be?" I wanted to ask him how she was—I knew that she was unwell; Madame de Treville had told me. But he didn't know I knew that. He didn't know that I could tell, despite the casualness of his tone, that he worried about his mother.

He looked at me curiously. "Attending to matters of the estate. I'm the eldest. But I'm sure you already knew that." The last bit was offhand, his focus drifting to the students.

"What is that supposed to mean?"

"Only that everyone is acutely aware I'm my father's only son and due to inherit his titles and burdens. Strange, how my parents paid for my education to have me use it 'being a gentleman.'"

"I don't know what you mean to imply, but—" I started.

"I intended no slight. I was complaining; I'm acting like a child, I know—"

"I don't think it's childish at all," I broke in. Now was my chance. "It's like you told me: You want to make a name for your-self, to do good on your own terms. That's not the problem. The problem is that I still know next to nothing about you other than what you *don't* want to be. I don't exist for your amusement. I am not a toy. If you don't want to be thought childish, prove it. Tell me who you are, Étienne. Who you are and what you want."

The air had gone very cold. The response had sounded right in my head, as a way to force his hand, but when I laid it all out, flesh side up, bare to the elements, it rang with emotion I hadn't expected. Oh Dieu, what had I done?

But then his expression opened, warmer than I'd ever seen. I wanted to reach for his hand but stopped as I remembered Madame de Treville's instructions. He had to chase me.

"Tania," he whispered my name like it belonged on his lips, like it had always belonged there. I closed my eyes briefly against his, against the sharp light and sounds of the university square, the thick pain of betrayal rolling in my stomach.

A shadow fell over us. Nearly time for Aria to return from her feigned meeting, surely . . . but even she wasn't tall enough to douse us in darkness. For the first time since Étienne approached, I felt the cold rush of wind, air on the cusp of winter.

"Father?"

Not now. Please, not now. This was a trick, a joke, a prank. It wasn't possible to summon a person by thinking about them. If it were, Papa would be by my side. "I told Mother I'd return today—isn't sending you to fetch me a bit excessive?" he said.

Steeling myself, I spun to face the man who might have mur-dered my father.

I'd pictured his face often in the past weeks; it came to me in my nightmares, the ones that left me drenched in tears and my throat sore from screaming. There was so much of Étienne in him. The sharp jaw, the dark hair ... thankfully his eyes were icy green, held no resemblance to Étienne's hazel ones.

"Not that you have any reason to be privy to such information, but I'm here on business—I figured you'd return to your old haunts. Besides, must I have a reason to see my only son?" His words were cool. "Now, then, aren't you going to introduce me to your lovely acquaintance?"

It would take less than five seconds. Less than five seconds to retrieve my sword and dagger from under my skirts and flay him from navel to nose. My fingers itched for my saber. I grasped a ruffle of my skirt instead. This wasn't me—I wasn't eager to hurt others. There was something scary in how the eagerness stemmed in me, the unfamiliarity of it. But then, this could be Papa's killer. This wasn't an innocent civilian, wasn't even a man on the docks with his sword pointed at me.

"Father, I present to you Mademoiselle Tania."

His gaze roved over me, clinical. "Just *Tania*?"

Did he recognize me? Did he see my father's face in mine like I saw Étienne's face in his? "*Mademoiselle* Tania," I emphasized, a bit too much bite in my response.

He studied me for what felt like an eternity. *Murderer* ringing in my ears, my pulse. Finally, he returned to his son. "Interesting. Étienne, bid adieu to your companion. You're clearly prone to distraction, and I won't risk you forgetting your promise to your mother."

The sentence echoed in my mind; Maman had said something eerily similar before. She always had me making promises she knew I couldn't keep.

Étienne tried to speak. "Father, I—"

Verdon hardened. "I shouldn't have to remind you of your duty, Étienne. To your family. To *me*. I'm feeling generous, so I'll give you a moment to gather yourself, but you *will* be in that carriage in five minutes. Understood?"

Flames licked at the corners of my vision as Verdon retreated to the street corner a few hundred feet away. His steps were quick, meticulous. He couldn't have been older than Papa—but while Papa's movements had shown the creaks and cracks of a body worked to the bone, Verdon's motions were unencumbered from vestiges of injuries. It would've been easy for him to quietly sneak up on Papa in the paling twilight, to hide under the sound of Beau's hooves, to silently dispatch my father. That is, if he'd deigned to do the bloody work himself. After conversing with a groomsman, he disappeared into a waiting carriage with a lion emblazoned on its side, reminiscent of the seal on Étienne's letter.

"I'm sorry," Étienne whispered close to my ear. I shivered and tightened the hood of Maman's embroidered cloak. "I know how my father comes off—I'm sure he does, too, but he doesn't care. I meant it when I said we didn't see eye to eye. I'm working on that, though. I'll do whatever it takes to make him understand that other people matter. That *we* matter." My face warmed under his concern. "We will speak more when I return, of what you talked about. I promise, no interruptions."

Once he was out of my vicinity I could breathe again. When he was next to me he took up all the air until there was so little left that I had to take searching, gasping breaths, hoping to catch a wisp of air to pull myself out of the haze.

I felt the presence of my sisters in arms before I looked up—

Aria and Théa at my shoulder. "Did you get what we needed?" I asked.

Théa nodded, gleeful, and pointed to her frilled skirts. "I strapped the books to my legs, Tania—to my legs! Have you ever heard of anything so scandalous?"

Aria tugged at my arm before we set off. "I didn't mean to spring him on you. But I didn't see any other option. Did you get new information?"

The heat of Étienne's hand on my arm lingered even after we parted. The ice of his father's gaze burned in my mind. "Yes. Yes, I think I did."

"*Familial duties?* Really?" said Portia after we returned. We were clustered in the parlor, chairs pulled close to the fireplace for warmth. "Why else would his father suddenly appear in Paris? He's obviously taking him home to resume plotting the King's murder."

I responded before Portia finished. "You didn't hear him: He hates his father. And the feeling is mutual. On the slightest chance Étienne's involved, he's being coerced."

"What does it matter if he can give us the information we need?" Portia asked. "And why are you so set on defending him?"

"Because I've spent time with him, Portia! He's thoughtful, not selfish. His father, on the other hand—"

"Girls," Madame de Treville warned. We ceased bickering. Aria's eyes remained on mine a moment before she returned to leafing through one of the books Théa had acquired.

"We don't have time for this," Madame de Treville continued. Her ever-constant refrain. With December around the corner, every interaction with her was fraught, sharp. "Tania, get Verdon to open up more when he returns. Procuring the shipment information from him was brilliant; who knows what else he has to offer? Maybe we can even get him to confide in you about his father's plans."

"I can try, but—"

"You did well laying out your cards when you told him you weren't to be trifled with. Now is the time to force his hand. We'll assign you a different target for the first party after he returns."

Unfamiliar emotions swirled through my chest. "And what exactly will that accomplish?" I asked.

"Isn't it obvious? You're going to make him mad with jealousy. He'll see you flirting and he'll have no choice but to spill his heart to you," Portia answered before Madame de Treville could.

Aria stood at the mention of flirting, before Portia was even finished speaking. "I'm going to bed," Aria said.

"As you all should," our mentor announced. "Get some sleep. We're almost at the end, girls. I can feel it. We're going to accomplish what even les Mousquetaires du Roi couldn't. What all those men couldn't. We're going to be the ones to save the King."

CHAPTER TWENTY-ONE

IT TOOK HOURS for me to reach the brink of sleep, to latch onto that numbing haze, and then: the sound of a foot placed carefully, but not carefully enough. A clench of floorboard against floorboard. The wheeze of wood panels creaking under pressure.

The noise spurred a series of images: Papa dead and alone in the dark. The man bleeding on the docks. The men who'd gutted Papa's office and left us to pick up the pieces. The men who planned to kill me if they had the chance.

I rose from my bed. Did my best not to rush, did my best to wait until I became accustomed to the pitch and fall of the world. It was probably Théa, searching for her chamber pot. Or Portia, pacing in her room, as she did when she was unraveling a particularly obscure problem.

None of these reassurances kept me from arming myself with my dagger before stepping into the hallway.

Empty. There was nothing. All of it, imagined. Théa's snores thundered under the crack of her door, only partially muffled by the carpet.

But then my stomach plummeted, fine hairs vertical on my

arms when something shifted in the dark. No, *someone*. "Halt!"
I said. "Arrétez-vous!" I wanted to cry the words, but I was too
surprised, too unsteady on my trembling legs to raise my voice
louder than it would be when speaking in the parlor.

A masked figure, covered head to toe in black, paused, boots
inaudible on the carpet as he rotated to face me. "Bonsoir, Mademoiselle la Mousquetaire." Words gruff, he spiraled his hand and
draped himself into a parody of a bow.

My blood went cold as I scrambled for my dagger. "What did
you call me?"

"You believe no one has discovered your secret?" The way he
spoke, the forced harshness—he was altering his voice.

I fought to maintain my grip on the sweat-lined dagger handle.
"Well, you know who I am. Why don't you tell me who you are,
and we'll call it even?"

"I don't think that wise, but I applaud the effort."

I caught a glimpse of a sheaf of papers. "If you give those back,
I won't alert the guards."

"Ah, but that is a lie. Look how you tremble in fear."

"Even if I were afraid, I'm braver than you could ever be," I
ground out.

"Continue to tell yourself this, ma chère. I bid you adieu."

"Wait!" I stormed forward to find an object held right under
my nose, his arm outstretched. Coughing, I waved away the sudden pungent fumes. But then I lurched. Grabbed onto a dresser
as the floor pitched, tumbled, transformed into a roiling, angry
sea. This wasn't the dizziness I knew; this was something else,
something foreign and monstrous. Something that flared across
my vision in large swaths of onyx.

After a long, painful stretch of time, my vision cleared. The hallway was empty. Everything as it had been, aside from the smell scorched into my nostrils. The thief had vanished.

Heart pounding, I knelt, not heeding the warning that spotted across my vision. Just clenched my toes as I felt along the carpet for anything that could've produced my symptoms, anything he might've left behind. But I only found flecks of dust.

"Tania?" Aria stood in the threshold of her doorway holding a candlestick, delicate light pooling into the hallway. She coughed, cleared her throat, her words gruff at first. "I thought I heard . . ." She set down the light before padding over, bare feet against carpet. "Did you faint?"

She helped me up as the floor tilted under me. "There was a thief. He knew what I am—what *we* are," I said.

She scanned the length of the hall. "Where is he?"

"He had papers. I tried to stop him, but he—I don't know what he did, but he held an object up to my face—a vial, maybe? And the smell . . ." Hearing it out loud made it sound ridiculous. "You don't think me foolish?"

Aria took up the candlestick once more, half her face illuminated in its buttery glow. "Would you lie about this?"

"Of course not," I said.

She let out a deep breath, her gaze traveling along the creaks and corners of the hallway. "We need to investigate. Did he have a rope? Un rossignol?" I stared at her blankly. "A picklock, Tania. To get inside. Though the house's locks are reinforced. He could've climbed. But then he would've entered through a window." She paced, unaware of my growing shock. "Not impossible. The risk of breaking glass, however. Any thief worth their salt would know better."

"Aria," I said eventually, "how?"

"How what?"

"How do you know all of this? Does this have to do with what you told me that day in the carriage? About La Cour des Miracles?" She hesitated, but she didn't tell me to stop, or cut me off, so I forged on. "I want to understand. How to assess this aftermath, how to think like the intruder. If I understand, I can help you figure out how he got in—maybe even who he is. Please, Aria," I added to the statue who'd replaced her.

At long last, a crack: a release of her rocky shoulders, an unclench of her sharp jaw. "You remember our conversation?" she asked.

"Of course." Madame de Treville lecturing Portia, the shadowed alleyway, Aria whispering from across the carriage . . . "You said you grew up in La Cour. But I don't understand how that's possible."

She drew me into her room and shut the door, resignation flooding her face. "Sit." She motioned to an armchair and studied me before returning the candlestick to her nightstand. "What I'm going to tell you remains between us. Théa must never know. Or Madame de Treville, for that matter."

"And Portia?"

Aria's face smoothed, expression tender. "She knows."

"Is it that . . . are you worried Théa or Madame de Treville would treat you differently? Your past is part of you; our past is part of each of us—but that doesn't mean we're not ourselves. It doesn't mean you're not still Aria."

Her cool eyes remained unchanged, but her body tensed. "Théa would insist on knowing everything. She doesn't know which questions not to ask. I can't deal with that. I will be in control of what I tell and what I don't. And Madame de Treville would never forgive me. She thinks she is the same as us because she knows struggle. That her rejection by the Musketeers gives her heightened understanding. But she doesn't comprehend what it's like to be pushed aside for other reasons than just being a woman. You must promise, Tania. Promise you won't tell them."

What could I do but nod? She took a deep breath. "I'll start from the beginning. I have to start from the beginning.

"Until I was ten, it was me and ma mère. We shared a small appartement within La Cour des Miracles with another family. A large family. My mind's erased most aside from my mother's voice. Her smile . . ." Her gaze was distant. "She did what she had to. Made sure I had clothes on my back and food in my stomach, however little."

A pang went through my chest. Maman, with fury in her face. Maman, with how she let my fingers bite into her arm when I needed to stand. Maman, who wanted me to be safe even though she didn't—couldn't—understand that maybe I could be the one doing the saving. "She sounds strong."

"And she was. But there are things that don't take strength into account. Even the fiercest of warriors can't battle invisible predators."

"She fell ill?"

"Consumption. She died a few weeks before I turned ten." The darkness in Aria's face kept me from speaking. Condolences weren't what she needed. To imagine: if I'd lost Papa before I was ten. If I'd lost him before the dizziness. Before he could teach me I was still strong, still Tania.

"I had no one else. No one who had the money or room to take me in. There aren't many ways to make a living in La Cour when you're ten. I wasn't any good at begging. So I did what

I was good at. First, it was pickpocketing." Portia's exclamations rose in my mind, her frustration at Aria's ability to enter a room unheard and unseen. "But I got cocky. I learned how to pick locks. Which doorways led to kitchen pantries and which to empty hallways. And once that wasn't enough, I decided to press further. To rob a house in Marais. If I succeeded, I'd never have to steal again.

"I chose carefully. I passed it daily on the way to the center of Paris in my attempts to outpace the rest of La Cour. It wasn't that large, but it was beautiful. White walls with portrait windows. A door so grand I could barely reach the knocker. I sneaked through the servants' entrance. The lock was weak. Jiggle it a few times with a hairpin and it'd crack open. I gathered whatever fit in a pillowcase: a jewelry box, coin purses, imported honey to barter with. A man stopped me on my way out. A candle in his hand. 'You should've gone for the painting in the study. It would fetch a hefty sum from any reputable dealer.'"

Aria paused; a hint of a smile ran along her mouth. "I didn't run. I sat in the chair across from his. We talked until the candle had all but burned away." She raised her eyes to mine. "I'd never had a father. Lost my mother less than a year before.

"The sun was beginning to rise when he explained his idea. Instead of handing me over to the guards, which would mean prison or worse, he offered to take me in as if I were his own. I was intelligent and resourceful. Admirable qualities he saw little of in the Parisian noblesse. Talents he could teach me to use. He'd provide all the tutoring I could ever want. Opportunities I'd never dared dream of. It sounds strange. An older man offering a young girl room and board, his protection . . ." She trailed off, steely gaze on mine.

"That was the furthest thing from my mind," I said.

"He withdrew from court life after the birth of his daughter. Her mother—it wasn't a love marriage, but they respected each other—died in childbirth. He was all the baby had. He never liked court," Aria said, an afterthought. "Couldn't stand the parties and the endless niceties. He stayed with his daughter. Raised her to be headstrong and independent. She loved poetry as much as she loved fencing."

"Loved?"

"She died when she was eight. Fell out of a tree and hit the back of her head. My father was heartbroken. He blamed himself for not telling her to stop climbing. For not running fast enough to catch her. He didn't leave his house for years. Then, one night, there I was. He said I reminded him of her." Aria folded her hands in her lap, let out a breath. "Given his absence at court, none of the noblesse knew what his daughter looked like. Or that she'd died. Not to mention his wife. Neither of them were close with their family. He told friends that they were going on an extended trip across the continent and didn't know when they'd return. That perhaps they'd even settle down somewhere else.

"It's a strange thing, to spend your life as one person, then go to sleep and wake up as someone else. I was no longer Danielle, an orphan from La Cour des Miracles. I was Aria d'Herblay. I'll never be able to repay my father for what he did for me." Her words broke. But then she laughed. "He hates that kind of talk. I'm his daughter. Fathers don't expect daughters to repay them for their kindness. That's what he tells me."

I sat, transfixed even after she finished speaking. "I think Papa would've liked him very much. They would've bonded over how much they hated court." Aria snorted, then covered her mouth and nose, as if she were surprised at the sound. I hesitated, unsure how to ask the question I needed to. "Would . . . would you prefer it if I called you Danielle?"

"That's not my name—no, my name's Aria. I chose it and it chose me." She paused, and in that moment I couldn't help myself, couldn't help the words from tumbling out.

"Are there people like me there?"

"What?"

My breath was shaky, my hands were shaky, and yet my mind was crystal clear. "In La Cour des Miracles. You told me how nobles deride the people who live there. That the people who pretend to suffer illnesses, they call them les francs mitoux. But they can't all be faking. Aria, are there people . . . *like me*?"

"It's been years . . ." She hesitated. "But yes. I'd imagine there would be."

Other girls like me. Girls who knew what it was like to be unsteady on unsteady ground. I'd imagined that there might be others like me, but I had tried to temper my hopes, had tried to remind myself that I was already lucky enough to have the Order—I didn't, shouldn't, need more. And was it fair to hope there were others who meandered through the same dizziness? Was it fair to wish that burden onto someone else for my own comfort? For the knowledge that there were people out there who understood what it felt like to be me, living in my body?

"I must ask something of you now," Aria said.

"Anything you need, say the word."

"Tell no one."

"Of course—but Aria, I already promised I would—"

She shook her head. "That's not what I'm talking about."

I drew in her meaning with a gasp. "Not tell the others about the thief?"

"I won't be the reason Théa has more nightmares. And Portia has never slept well. We share a wall. I can hear her shifting. It's gotten worse since the weather changed. She doesn't do well without the sun."

"What about Madame de Treville?" I asked. "The thief had papers—what if something important was stolen?"

Aria hardened. "Madame de Treville, with all her talk of womanhood and strength, is still a snob. Remember how she turned up her nose when we drove past La Cour? The only reason I'm here is because she thinks my father trained me. That I was the same little girl she once was. But she learned to fight out of passion. I learned to fight to survive."

"But what does that have to do with the thief?"

"Someone appeared in the hallway, Tania. No commotion, no trail. And then, the docks. Those men were tipped off. There was no reason for them to think us anything other than dockworkers. But they knew." My mind caught on Aria's words, fabric against a splinter of wood, an exposed nail, the blade of a knife someone had dropped, forgotten.

Oh Dieu. I took in a deep, heaving breath. "No. Not her."

"I never said it was her," Aria pointed out. "But this thief has to be an inside job. It wasn't you, wasn't me. Wasn't Théa—the very idea is ludicrous." Aria's assertion was punctuated with a nasal snore, muted somewhat now we were out of the hallway. "Thank goodness for the carpeting to muffle her," Aria said. "Or else we'd never sleep at all. And Portia—well, it *isn't* Portia."

"And that leaves . . ."

Aria held out her hand, ticked off her fingers as she listed the names: "Henri. Madame de Treville. And Jeanne, though that's a reach, since she doesn't have keys to the second floor."

Their faces danced in my head; I shut my eyes tight, clawed at my temples. "You're wrong. How can you say that Madame de Treville . . . or Henri . . ."

"Madame de Treville was shut out of what she wanted most. That's enough to prompt anyone to revenge. Maybe the nobles made her a deal. She feeds them information on Mazarin's plans to protect the King, on what leads the Order has so far. They let her into the Musketeers. The ones that the public actually know about. Perhaps those are the papers you saw the masked thief with."

"Do you think she lied to us? About Verdon?"

Aria pursed her lips. "Madame de Treville is smart. She'd want to play both sides. Make sure that, when things unfold, she comes out on top."

"And . . . and Henri?" My voice broke.

"I've heard how he talks about his apprenticeship. How he wants so much more than he already has. And . . ." Her whole body tensed as she spoke. "Haven't you noticed how odd he's been acting? Running away to keep from talking to us—and not just when Portia is around, either. He lives here. Yet I can count on one hand the number of times I've seen him in the past month."

I opened my mouth, closed it, a cool flush running over me. Hadn't I observed the same thing? I swallowed. "Well, yes, maybe he's seemed out of sorts, but he wants to be a civil engineer for the good of others, too. He doesn't want more only for himself."

I cut myself off, aware of how Aria watched me, dissected me, peered under my skeleton to the meat and marrow.

"Boys will say anything to girls. Anything if they think it will get them what they want. You know that, Tania." I recoiled. "Was there anything else? Anything the thief said, or did?" Aria asked.

How he turned on his heel. That horrible, satisfied smirk. How he'd called me Mademoiselle la Mousquetaire. How I was terrified that his voice would replace Papa's in my memories. That I would forget how lovingly Papa said the name.

But then I looked back at Aria, saw something stunning: a hint of fear.

"No." My voice was tight. "No, there was nothing else." I shied away from her prying gaze. "I should get to bed—I'm very tired. Good night."

I won't be the reason Théa has more nightmares. That's what Aria had said. But who was keeping Aria from her own fears, from needless worrying about a kind boy who was a bit busier than usual? A boy who I wanted to protect like I wanted to protect Aria?

I shut the door behind me. In my mind, I watched as the masked thief bowed, mocking me. The piece of hair that had escaped the confines of his wide-brimmed hat.

One single, golden-brown curl.

Chapter Twenty-Two

"TANIA?"

I jerked, then winced as tea splattered onto my hand. "Sorry," I said, rushing to dab up the liquid.

"You've been like this all week. As if you've seen un fantôme, non?" Portia asked, looking to Aria in curiosity, but the latter tilted her head to the side in ambivalence.

"We're close to apprehending the nobles smuggling weapons into the city. I'm surprised we're not all looking over our shoulders," Aria said with a firm glance in my direction.

Madame de Treville entered the room, pausing inside the open door. "Girls, have any of you seen some of my papers about? A few are missing from my office. Letters, mostly, nothing of too much import. I keep vital information on my person. But I thought I'd ask. I already checked with Jeanne, just in case."

Could she see the worry in my face? The possibility of betrayal? Why would she ask about the papers if she was the one who stole them away—was it merely a matter of throwing us off her trail? I shook my head. Once Aria had spoken her ideas out loud they'd seeded in my mind, taken root and bloomed over the nights I lay awake in bed, sleepless. Whenever I slept, my dreams brimmed with nightmarish versions of Madame de Treville, of Henri, of the other girls, each of them taking turns stabbing Papa, his chest a patchwork of dagger wounds. And then, one by one, each of them taking that same blade and thrusting it into my back as I crouched over Papa, trying to clean his face and make it recognizable for Maman.

"What kind of letters?" Portia asked Madame de Treville.

"My personal correspondence is none of your business."

"I haven't seen any letters, Madame!" I blurted out.

Aria kicked me under the table.

"Thank you, Tania, for being the only one of my Musketeers who can answer a simple question," Madame de Treville said.

"Maybe it's worth asking the Cardinal about? Since today is your weekly meeting," Aria said.

Madame de Treville turned to Aria, a little taken aback, then controlled her expression. "I shouldn't be surprised you've observed me enough to know my schedule. For the record, however, the meetings are now every other day. There's only two weeks until the solstice deadline."

"Has the Cardinal made any headway on convincing the King to retreat from the city? At the very least, not attend any of the upcoming balls or festivities?" Portia asked.

"Negotiating with the King is like negotiating with a child—he *is* a boy." Madame de Treville sighed as she ran a hand down her face.

Aria's eyes met mine. *Tell no one.*

The coded inventory slip, the possibility of betrayal. Papa bloody on the side of the road. Maman's diminishing frame as the carriage pulled away. My Musketeers. My Musketeers who were supposed to change everything. My Musketeers who I needed to protect.

I dropped my head into my hands. Dropped my head into my hands, hid my face, and screamed, mouth open, no sound.

The kitchen was the only room that felt anything like home. More lavish than any room in any house in Lupiac, of course— but with the sunlight and the fire smoke, the color and heft of the air was familiar.

I'd been avoiding the others all day. I couldn't bear to look into faces that had grown so dear to me and wonder if they were in fact masks worn by traitors. With another gulp of air, I rested my chin in my palms, scars to thin skin.

And then Henri, through the kitchen door. And somehow that made the uncertainty grow stronger. The scrattle and scrape of door against floor, worn boots against floor. He stopped when he saw me, blush rising in his cheeks. "I came to deliver another cryptography book I found in Sanson's library; I thought it might be useful in your decoding attempts." His eyes wouldn't meet mine.

I cleared my throat. "I can take it." He would talk to me, even if I had to make him. Even if I found a truth too horrible for words tucked under those curls.

"Oh, I should give it to my aunt; she's—"

"She's in a meeting." A lie that rattled my teeth. I tightened everything in me. "I'll take it."

Henri paused, as if debating with himself whether to listen. And still, he wouldn't look at me, only at the wilting purple asters on the table. "Well . . . all right." He fumbled in his bag. I tried to peek inside, but he was too quick. "Here," he said. He pressed a book into my hands.

Clumsy Henri, bumbling Henri, kind Henri. Henri who blushed bright enough to give away any mistake. Henri who stole me a map. Henri, who might have stolen this book.

Henri, who wanted so much more than what he already had.

I placed the book on the table. "Is there anything else that you—"

"I'm sorry, but I have to go—so much work to be done—"

"Henri, wait—"

But the door slammed shut. The flowers continued to die on the table.

Only a few minutes later, another sound—this time, at the opposite end of the room. And even though I knew it wasn't Henri, couldn't be Henri, I still let myself imagine that he'd returned to explain himself.

"Tania, might I speak with you?" Madame de Treville asked.

I followed her into the office, awash with fear. She knew. When I looked up, I expected a furious face, eyes like shards of glass. But it was the opposite. "How are you?"

I stared at her, blinked. "Fine . . . I guess?"

"You guess you are fine? Or you are fine?"

"I am fine." This was an easy lie; I knew it well.

"I didn't want to say anything in front of the other girls. But the letters—they were from your father." My stomach sucked in, and still, the bodice felt too tight, no air. "This is an opportunity, Tania, for you to tell me if you took them. I wouldn't begrudge you for wanting to know more about him and his work."

"His letters? They're . . . they're gone?" My voice trembled.

"So you didn't take them, then." I clutched at my wrists, tears building. "There's no need to fear your identity being compromised. Your father never referred to you by name; he knew better. A spy knows how to protect his family. But"—she grimaced—"I'm afraid his longer letters, the ones in which he wrote of his unnamed daughter's talent and skill . . . those are gone. I suppose I could have misplaced them. There is a first time for everything." She didn't sound like she really believed it was a possibility.

"It's not that . . . it's just"—I settled on something simpler, something true—"I would've liked to read them."

"It's not the same as reading it in his hand, but know that your father thought the world of you." A hint of a tremor. Was she remembering how he trained with her? How he believed in her when no one else did? Or was she regretting her betrayal? "To be clear, you haven't seen anything out of the ordinary, correct? Anything suspicious?"

How could I be sure of the intruder's hair color? It was one curl. And it had been so very late. So very dim. Shade and tone and hue all crumpled together in the dark.

And even still, there was Henri, pressing the book to my palms, warm golden-brown eyes under warm golden-brown hair, the memory a sickening pang in my gut.

"Very well," she said. My head jerked, but Madame de Treville was already onto the next issue, a beleaguered expression on her face. "Tell me right away if you notice anything." She ruffled through some papers on her desk, then paused. "Go see Théa. She wasn't able to fix your breeches—you'll need a new pair. What were you thinking, trying to duck before taking a parry? And in practice, too?"

I was thinking that I needed my sword in my hand, the clash

of steel against steel. That I needed to stop seeing traitors around every corner, wondering if our mentor or Henri was secretly working to betray us. That I needed to stop hearing Étienne cradle my name on his lips. That I needed to stop hearing Papa's reproachful voice, telling me that I'd never improve if I didn't focus. That when I fenced I had to fully give myself to the bout, and nothing—and no one—else.

It was funny, really, how Madame de Treville told me on my very first day in Paris that we couldn't afford secrets. Funny, now that secrets were all I seemed to have.

"What do you think it's like?"

"What?"

Théa rearranged the spools of thread in her sewing kit—a wooden box perched on carved blocks, all stained a rich deep brown. "Kissing." I spun to face her, and she clucked at me. "Don't rip my work!"

"Oh, Théa dear, have you been reading novels again?" Portia tutted. She and Aria drilled a parry sequence nearby. Madame de Treville had been especially hard on all of us of late when it came to working on our weaknesses outside of training sessions. According to her, there was no such thing as free time, only wasted time. Portia's eyes were bright, sparkling as her blade swished from side to side. "Please tell me you've given up on *L'Astrée*. You'll be an old maid by the time you've finished. How anyone has the conviction of will to read five thousand pages . . . you've made your point, D'Urfé, you're obsessed with shepherds in love! Can you imagine that as your legacy? Five thousand pages of odious pining?" Aria slipped through Portia's defenses, nicked her sleeve. "That was uncalled for."

"You're not paying attention. There's no point in drilling if you're not going to pay attention."

"Well, I think five thousand pages dedicated to love is romantic," Théa stated with a pout. "The characters love each other for who they are, and they are so kind and gentle." She frowned at my legs as she passed a needle through the gaping hole in my breeches. The thread snapped like an icicle. "I don't think I can salvage these. We'll have to send Jeanne to buy fabric and say it's for Henri—trying to buy breeches with your measurements from the tailor is asking a lot of his silence, don't you think? N'est-ce pas? Try these on for size," she said, handing me another pair.

Stepping behind the screen, I shimmied out of the ruined breeches.

"Five thousand of anything is obsessive," Portia said. "What would you say if I suddenly acquired five thousand pairs of gloves? Or five thousand evening gowns?"

"You would never do that. You'd spend that money on paintings. Landscapes. Portraits. Not on clothes," Aria said. "You'd start your own gallery. Give tours during which you'd reteach all the nobles whose tutors didn't understand color gradient."

I slipped on the pair Théa handed me, fabric taut. My legs felt stronger, vision clearer. Even the dizziness was a little better. When I exited, the pants were so tight I was forced to totter over, feet splayed comme un canard. Portia looked flustered, but she still snorted. "Look at you, walking like a duck! Théa, are you trying to torture the girl?" She cocked her head. "Odd. You're grayer at this point, usually."

"It's strange—I think it's the breeches. Maybe because they're lightweight? My last pair was heavier."

Théa's brows pinched in that familiar line of deep concentration. She muttered and plucked at the fabric near my knee, but didn't say more, just returned to her scraps of fabric and started sketching.

Aria and Portia saluted each other, signaling the end of their drill. Portia wiped beads of sweat from her forehead. "I almost had you on that one." Her eyes sparkled, scanned Aria's face with expectation.

Aria bit down an uncharacteristic chuckle. "Continue to tell yourself that."

Portia's laugh was a clear, loud bell. "Comme tu veux. As you wish."

Aria hesitated, gaze never leaving Portia. But then her eyes darted to me, to Théa, and she nodded. "As it should be."

Portia's light faltered. She gestured to the spot across from her, then looked pointedly at me. "Mere days until the next ball. If Madame de Treville assigns you another target, who knows what kind of trouble the youngest Verdon will cook up."

Nerves raced down my spine. "I told you, I really don't think he—"

"I never said anything about the traitors! No, if Verdon starts a duel it'll be over your honor." She smirked, sword glimmering dangerously. "Make sure he sees you touching the new target. No, not in that way," she laughed when I nearly dropped my sword mere seconds after retrieving it. "I meant dancing. Or brushing your hand against his—you know, casual flirtation . . . now, if you want greater impact, you can trail your fingers down his chest. Draw it out, slowly. Just take care you're not seen by other nobles." She winked.

"Tania, are you all right?" Théa asked as she rejoined us. "You've gone red."

"Fine," I cried louder than necessary. "Everything's fine!" Portia chuckled at my glare, as I readied myself for her attack. I didn't think about what Étienne's hazel eyes would look like when he saw me dancing with another man. I didn't think about the way he said my name. I didn't think about how, when Théa asked me what I thought kissing was like, my mind had shot to his imagined lips ghosting over mine.

No. I did not think about any of those things.

The next few days, every time we saw Madame de Treville, she was scrunched over the coded message. A copy of it, anyway, marked up with ink and charcoal. Crossed through incorrect ideas, entire squares of black and blue ink bruising the paper, matching the circles under her eyes.

Madame de Treville had allowed us to each make a copy to puzzle through. I stared so long at mine that all the letters blurred together. Hopeless. Portia hunched over her copy at mealtimes. Théa was on her third copy after spilling cups of tea on the first two. And Aria held hers close during every carriage ride.

I woke eight days before the Winter Festival with fear roiling in my gut. Papa's face faded, despite how I clung onto the dream haze. Ink stained my fingertips, the base of the candle at my bedside, the ripped remains of yet another draft of a letter to Maman. Would she even believe me, even listen to me, if I told her France was in danger? It was December now. The air was cooling, and the letters of the message swirled on the inside of my lids whenever I closed my eyes.

"I've had it," Portia said as I exited my room in a hurry; I was late for our breakfast meeting. I nearly jumped out of my skin. "Merde. Did I set off the dizziness? Should I find you a chair?"

My heart thrummed frantically; I didn't move as I waited for my heart to settle. Finally, I shook my head, told her I was fine with a sigh. "You've had it with what?" I added.

"With Madame de Treville acting like everything is fine when we're eight days away from losing our only chance for equality! Don't look at me like that," she said crossly. "Fine. Us being Musketeers might not be a revolution, but imagine what it could mean, what it could lead to. For all womankind!"

Portia made it sound so easy. Yes, it would—could—lead to so much. But I had to keep my sisters in arms safe first. What was a legacy if it came at the expense of the people I cared about?

She continued her impassioned speech as she lowered me in the pulley, and as we walked down the hallway to breakfast. "...And yes, I suppose I'd feel bad if the King died, but that's not the point! He's our way to assuring a place for every woman who comes after us. I'd protect a pigeon just the same, ces monstres dégoûtants, if it meant changing how men saw us." She shuddered. "Dieu, now I'm going to be imagining those winged rats sitting on the throne all day."

"Bonjour," Henri said. I hadn't even heard him approach.

My shoulders tensed under my cloak. I'd taken to wearing it everywhere, as if it would shield me from whatever sneaked its way into the house. Or whatever was already inside it. Silly, and yet . . . with Papa and Maman surrounding me, the terror whispered rather than roared.

"Bonjour," I managed. My eyes drifted from the cryptography books in his hands to the golden-brown curls framing his face. I swallowed.

Portia tugged at my elbow and started walking again. "You froze—are you worried he'll say something about my outburst?" Portia snorted as we turned the corner. "That poor boy doesn't even know how to gossip. I can count the number of times he's spoken to me or Aria on one hand. And I've been here half a year now!"

Madame de Treville glanced up as we entered. Théa and Aria were already seated. "Nice of you to join us." I squirmed; it was my fault Portia was late, since she'd been the one on pulley duty. "As Théa and Aria already know, I've eliminated over ten possible ciphers known to the Musketeers. They couldn't map onto the coded message, or the results were gibberish."

Théa stared intently at her cup of tea. "We've run out of time— who can we apprehend now? We know the Comte de Monluc has had suspicious meetings with Verdon's younger brother. There's the increase in capital for the latter's business partner, the initials that represent weapons, the muskets Verdon's younger brother shipped in along with the coded message. Verdon senior invested in the theater opening, which was a cover for bringing something into the city, possibly more weapons. Doesn't that all point to Verdon senior?"

"We don't have direct confirmation that links everything together, not yet. That's why Tania's task is so important. We need information from Verdon's son. We can't arrest the lesser players before we arrest Verdon senior. If he really is behind this whole ordeal, is feeding money and supplies and weapons to la noblesse via his brother and his brother's colleagues' ships, then he'll need to be here for the finale to fill the power vacuum he created . . ." Madame de Treville's jaw clenched. "Non. We must wait. It's what the King wants."

"The King is a child," Portia said.

"He's the same age as you," Aria muttered as she pulled apart a slice of bread.

"A *child*," Portia continued, "with no conception of reality: He isn't immortal. So what if we don't catch all the nobles and Verdon. If we arrest the nobles, Verdon won't have the backing he needs. And there's, you know, the added bonus come the Winter Festival Feast that the King won't be *dead*."

"It won't last in the long term," Madame de Treville retorted, her usual composure absent. "We must verify all the nobles involved before pursuing their arrests: cut off the heads of the beast to ensure its true defeat, otherwise risk it returning more powerful. We can't afford a would-be king killer slipping undetected through the streets."

"What if we all ran lead in the mission tonight?" Portia asked. "Tania will take Verdon's son, obviously, in addition to the other target she'll use to make him jealous. Théa will take Monluc—if his son shows his face, even I can't explain away flirting with his father. And then Aria and I could take a name each from our list of potential nobles involved in the plot. No one would run interference, and no distraction duty." Théa was nodding along by the time Portia finished.

But Madame de Treville's face hardened. "It's too risky."

"We're Musketeers," Aria noted. "Our lives are the very definition of risk."

Madame de Treville slammed her fist on the table. Teacups rattled in their saucers. "What happened to Théa won't happen again. I won't let it."

"Madame," Théa said hesitantly.

But Madame de Treville forged on. "I sent the three of you to the office and left Théa on her own."

"We knew the risks when we joined the Order," Portia said. "We're not ignorant farm animals trotting off to slaughter. Even Tania, who was a veritable naive lamb who blushed at the slightest hint of innuendo when she arrived . . . why, she's got to be a half a year old now, at least." I huffed in my seat. "You want this as much as we do, don't deny it," Portia insisted to Madame de Treville. "To be respected by the other Musketeer senior officials, for them to know all you've done for the throne."

"Madame," Théa tried again. She reached across the table to tentatively touch our mentor's hand. Like how I'd reached out to my mother that night. But no blood streaked across Madame de Treville's knuckles. "Madame, you don't need to worry about protecting us—you see, you taught us how to protect ourselves," Théa said.

"Oh Dieu, I think she might cry. Do you think she can?" Portia muttered next to me.

Madame de Treville blinked, taking in Théa's earnest face. She cleared her throat. And finally, after a tense, held breath, she nodded.

Aria glanced at me, my thoughts reflected on her face: Madame de Treville wanted her revenge, wanted her glory. But she wanted us safe, too. She couldn't be the inside informant.

Portia handed over a teardrop pendant; I slipped it over my head. It sank to land right between my breasts. Papa's ring was on a long, unadorned chain, so it wasn't difficult to hide it under my bodice.

"Isn't this a little . . . revealing?" I asked.

"What, you think because we're celebrating the Feast of the Immaculate Conception that you have to look as virginal as the Mother of Christ?" She didn't give me time to respond, simply rounded on Aria, hands at her hips. "Well?"

Aria, frothy in drifts of lace, sat straight backed in her chair. "Is it enough to attract Verdon? And the other target?"

Portia shrugged. "Other than having her strut in toute nue? Oui, I think so."

"I am not going anywhere naked!" I hissed as Portia tapped a thoughtful finger to her chin. A knock at the door, and we jolted. "Enter!" she called out.

"Ma tante wishes for you to know the carriage is ready." Henri's words sneaked under the door.

"We'll be down in a minute," Portia answered, then snickered at the retreating footsteps. "By the way that boy acts, you'd think him scared to face us. He's really never going to let that whole intruder debacle go. I apologized; what more does he want? I had absolutely no desire to pin him down then, and those sentiments haven't changed. I certainly don't intend on repeating the ordeal." She went to help Théa with her rouge, but Aria stared at the door with a look she reserved for her most difficult targets. Cold-blooded calculation.

Portia and Théa were caught up in preparations, but Aria

caught my eye. "I changed my mind about these earrings. Would you let me try on one of your pairs?"

I swallowed down my questions. "Of course. Let me—"

"I'll come with you. There's no point in bringing them all the way over here if they clash with the yellow satin," Aria said.

She thought Henri was the intruder, the spy . . . but that couldn't be true. Not Henri. It didn't matter that I thought I saw his hair—I hadn't been thinking clearly. I was dazed, dizzy. The masked man was cold, composed. And Henri . . . Henri was not.

I sat on my bed as Aria sank into an armchair. "I'm tired," she said. "I'm tired of seeing evil and deceit in every passing shadow. And I keep questioning my own observations. Did I really experience a moment? Or was it my imagination? And even if I did experience it, does my experience reflect what actually happened? I've thought through every possibility. Madame de Treville . . . you know I'm not swayed easily, but the look on her face, Tania. The look on her face when she talked about Théa."

"This is Henri we're speaking of, sweet and kind—"

"You can't let feelings cloud your judgment," she bit out. "You care, Tania. You care deeply about others who give you any cause, and you long for it to be reciprocated. That helps when you have a new target. You are true and genuine. They sense it. But it will be your undoing if you don't learn to control it."

My tongue was leaden, throat soldered shut. My fingers gripped the bedpost for balance even though I was seated. Even though I was safe. The dizziness wasn't the reason for my hot, unshed tears. "My feelings aren't things I can turn off. And even if I could, I wouldn't want to!" I didn't let myself think of the loss I tried to push away, tried to force out but somehow still managed to return in blistering, blazing glory each time two swords met just so. I didn't let myself think of Marguerite tormenting me, the face of the girl she once was, absent. I didn't let myself think of my mother growing smaller and smaller from my spot in the carriage until she was no larger than a speck of dust. I didn't let myself think of Étienne, my gratitude at his understanding, how he never recoiled.

I didn't let myself think of Henri, the kind boy who might not be kind at all.

"Tania," Aria said softly. "I know you've been left before. That you've been hurt. You must understand, we'll never leave you. We're Musketeers. We never leave our own. But you can't count on that loyalty from others. None of us can."

Words were words were words. Words were doctors shrinking away from my mother in corridors. Words were childhood promises of everlasting friendship. Aria couldn't promise me anything. Being sick meant, at any moment, the people I cared about could decide I wasn't worth the trouble I put them through.

But then: the first time the other girls saw me faint. And all the times I was dizzy: the second time, the third, the fourth . . . they had stayed. And they still stayed. Henri had seen me injured, yes. But he hadn't seen my dizziness, not really. He hadn't been there during those early mornings, the ones when I couldn't get out of bed. He designed the pulley for me, but he'd never been the one at the top of the staircase, lifting me up.

"Tania," Aria repeated. "Regardless of how you care about Henri, he isn't one of us."

I choked down a laugh at her knowing gaze. "Don't be ridiculous; we're friends. Besides, he likes Théa."

"What?"

"The way he talks about her . . ."

"So, you don't like him, then." I swallowed, and shook my head. Aria didn't speak, face clouded. "Well, then . . . I never thought I'd be relieved that you were attracted to the youngest Verdon. However, he seems to be the less dangerous option. As long as you keep your distance. As much distance as one can keep from a target, that is." I stood there, speechless. "If Madame de Treville were here, she'd tell you to close your mouth. She'd say it's unbecoming."

I took a deep breath. "First you're convinced I have feelings for Henri, and now Étienne? You're losing your touch."

She smiled. But it was tired. "You might be able to fool yourself. But you can't fool me. It's like I said before—you crave care in return. I can't make you believe we're enough. I can't undo the hurt done to you. I know it will take time for you to understand and accept that we care. But, in the meantime . . . promise you won't get too far in over your head. We can keep you from falling if you're too dizzy. We can help you regain your balance. We can even offer you a hand to pull you out of the water. But if you don't accept it, if you let yourself fall even farther in . . . then saving you from drowning? That's beyond any of our abilities."

Tucked into the corner of the carriage, the clack of hooves and lacquered wheels steady underneath our seats, I watched the dark depths of the Paris night morph the curtain print into strange, fantastical shapes. A phoenix immolating itself in flames of liquefied gold. A gryphon clawing at the ground, galloping toward me before dissipating into clouds of smoke. As the figure shifted, and the lion's mouth opened, I squeezed my eyes shut.

"What are you thinking?" Théa's voice drew me back with a lurch. Four sets of eyes, all on me.

Papa's ring glowed warm and solid and I pressed my hand to my chest so it was over my heart. *Tania, Tania, Tania,* beating in perfect time, my own heart a call to arms. "Planning how to catch a killer."

Théa squeezed my hand. I imagined my feelings turning off. Lights fading. Candles being extinguished.

There was no more upset, no more shame, no more yearning. Only Papa on the side of the road and my blistering, furious heartbeat.

The carriage went under a bridge. We were plunged into darkness.

CHAPTER TWENTY-THREE

ENTERING THE ROYAL palace the second time should've been like the first—I'd seen all the splendor before. And yet it wasn't. The monstrous gates, the colossal columns, the hedges sculpted into terrifying mythical beasts, the crystal chandeliers and wallpaper adorned with gold leaf like the inside of the Dowager Queen's jewelry box—these were all the same. The mirror-laden walls reflected back every version of you, even the ones you tried to hide. But now I knew the extravagance was a distraction from the secrets that whispered on the air with every flick of a mademoiselle's fan.

Madame de Treville went to announce our arrival. Théa found the Comte and left us quietly, but not without a look back over her shoulder and a glimmer in her eyes. She could feel it, too. We were close.

When our mentor returned, she insisted on finding the man Étienne introduced me to that night at the theater—he was Aria's target. The pair disappeared into clouds of embroidered damask and feathery lace. Portia linked our arms, drew me a few steps away to point out a figure. "Ah, there's my target. Monsieur Janvier."

I nodded. "I recognize him from Madame de Treville's lesson cards." The curling blond mustache, the wide gesticulations punctuating his words, the velvet cuffs catching the chandelier light.

Portia's smile was genuine. "Well done, Tania. Do you remember the rest?"

I paused, mind whirring, sweat and spice heavy on the air. "His grand Paris residence was a casualty during La Fronde. He never recovered his wealth or standing."

Portia nodded along, her voice a whisper under the strain of music and laughter. "Although his appearance has undergone a dramatic shift. As if he's suddenly acquired beaucoup d'argent, n'est-ce pas? Or perhaps that fabric you found on the ship had further uses than mere musket coverings."

We split off, Portia ingratiating herself with Monsieur Janvier's group while I watched the throng of couples. Waiting for the sight of my target, Lord DuVerlac—the man I'd use to make Étienne jealous.

"They let anyone into these parties now."

My eyes drifted, my body tilted toward the main expanse of the ballroom. A man and woman stood side by side, observing Portia with thinly veiled disgust as she simpered and batted her eyelashes at something the messieurs said.

It couldn't be . . . the last time I'd seen this man, he was barking orders to dockhands. Was his companion here, too? The one I'd left bleeding, slumped against a wall—the crush of salt water, the thick of night. Pretending to be engrossed with the spectacle of dancing couples, I stepped back and to the side, then trained my ears on their muttered exchange.

"It's a shame to see the palace polluted in such a way," he said. Closing my eyes tight against the rush of anger, I opened them to the bright golden sway of lights and air so heady with perfume and alcohol I could hardly tell which scent was which. "Things will be righted soon; eventually the King will understand ces bricons do not deserve his generosity. Fools, the lot of them."

Maybe the King would understand . . . if said understanding were reliant on being buried in la Basilique Cathédrale de Saint-Denis.

"One can hope," the woman said with a sniff. "I noticed your wife didn't attend my gathering this week?" Her tone was casual, but her eyes glinted dangerously.

"She was sorry to have missed it."

"Is that so? You know, it is time-consuming, custom ordering fans. I had hers waiting. I thought she might appreciate the style; I know all the other ladies did. If she's changed her mind, however, I'd be happy to return it to the éventailliste if she no longer approves of the craftsmanship."

"N-No," the man stuttered. "She was—she was unwell, and—"

"Busy. Interesting."

"She'll retrieve it tomorrow. You have my word."

"That won't be necessary." The woman opened one of her tie-on pockets and pulled out a gilded fan. "I assume I can pass on your appreciation of the detailing to the appropriate party?"

The man pulled at his collar. "I'd like nothing more."

The woman twirled her own fan, an extravagant thing of filigreed paper and lace, over in her left hand. Ice licked up my spine. Madame de Treville had tested us on every minute movement. Every intricate tilt of the instrument, every coy smile that meant anything but. A fan in a lady's left hand, turned over . . . *We're being watched.*

Her eyes belied nothing. His, however, darted to Portia. "I'm quite parched," the woman declared. "Go fetch me a drink before you return to your wife? Doubtless she's missing your comfort during her convalescence."

The man balked and started in the direction of the drinks. I tried to get Portia's attention, but she was too busy charming Monsieur Janvier. Squaring my shoulders, I took a deep breath. Timed my movements so that, as the man strode purposefully across my path, I thrust myself forward.

We collided with a crunch. And then I was falling. Back to the main square, back to fiery skinned palms and skirts strewn with eggshell and yolk and Marguerite's laugh seared into my brain. But then a hand gripped my elbow. Portia.

"Oh, pardonnez-moi!" I exclaimed.

He looked down at me, at Portia, at the feigned apology plastered on our faces. He blinked, his face all scrunched. And then, a sneer. No hint of recognition. To him, we were silly girls in pretty dresses. As he reached down I caught a glimpse of the open fan. A true work of art. Fine calligraphy letters, gold and delicate and folded between the fan's ribs and floral lace . . . wait a moment. Letters? No . . . *words.*

"Racaille," he muttered. I shifted over, trying to get a look under his hat. His voice was different from the masked intruder's—then again, hadn't it sounded like the intruder was altering his voice?

"Qu'est-ce que vous avez dit?" Portia inquired, all sugar and silk. "What did you say? I must have misheard you."

He bowed curtly as he tucked the ornate fan into his jacket.

"C'est de ma faute. Excusez-moi." He followed his apology with a grimace.

I fought against the crashing gray waves, the scramble of my heartbeat. His partner brushed past, presenting us with a frosty look before they both disappeared into the crowd.

"He was with the Comtesse de Gramont?" Portia asked.

"That was the Comtesse?"

"Bien sûr. And one of the gentlemen from the docks. Was that why you bumped into him?" Her dark irises blazed. "At first I thought you were dizzy—"

"She gave him a fan, Portia. A *fan*. For his wife."

A whisper of a breath escaped her lips. "What do you think it all means?"

I thought back to that very first day in the parlor, how Madame de Treville had chastised Portia for stepping on a target's foot, how snide the Comtesse de Gramont had been ... "*but sleeping with the éventailliste, now that's an unnecessarily extreme course of action—*"

"Perhaps the affair with the éventailliste wasn't about fashion after all." I lowered my voice, ready to tell her about the letters.

"Excusez-moi." A man interrupted us and bowed low, the sleeve of his jacket almost brushing the floor. He bounced up on the balls of his feet. "I wanted to inquire after your hand. For the next dance." He nodded to the couples milling about as they awaited music—the performers were taking a short break. "I have it on good authority you're an excellent dancer. Madame de Treville informed me you were looking forward to the gavotte this evening."

I placed my hand in his. "I'd be honored ..."

His free hand met his forehead and left an uncomfortably

bright red mark. "You must think me so rude! Lord DuVerlac, at your service."

I smiled my best smile and fluttered my lashes. Ah, there. There was that familiar sharp intake of breath as our gazes found each other. If only Maman could see me now. "My name is Tania. And I assure you, the pleasure is *all* mine."

Chapter Twenty-Four

LORD DuVERLAC WAS more of a gentleman than most. His hands strayed no lower than what propriety dictated. He even listened when I responded to his occasional question. His only sin was being a tad dull—then again, that was likely why Madame de Treville chose him: enough of a presence to make Étienne feel threatened, but easy for me to manage and navigate.

"And are you enjoying the season?" As he spoke, my focus drifted to Étienne. He'd arrived almost an hour after the ballroom opened, and spoke to the theater investor, but Aria was quick to draw the latter away and into the throng of dancers. Étienne had stood there, his eyes roaming around the room. Was he looking for me?

He was with a group of other young nobles now. There was a woman, too, whispering to him, hand covering her mouth from sight. Heat surged under my skin. But as if he sensed it, he glanced up, hazel gaze intent on me. Her hand touching his arm, her smiling at him and him smiling back—the vision shifted so I was in her place. No intrigue, no deception. The two of us under the twinkling lights refracting through crystal . . .

"Mademoiselle?" Lord DuVerlac asked.

I pulled my focus back to my partner and forced a placid expression. "It appears I'm still a bit overcome . . . by the general splendor, you know."

DuVerlac nodded sympathetically. "It took me many seasons to grow accustomed to it. Quite a shock, at first."

"May I cut in?" Étienne stood at Lord DuVerlac's shoulder, a flickering flame that sucked all the air out of the room. DuVerlac wasn't just a member of the noblesse, but also a gentleman—despite the interruption, he wouldn't refuse the request, even for a lower-ranking noble.

"Monsieur Verdon." I stumbled over his name. Étienne took hold of my hand. I started at the sudden contact, at the feel of his skin, at the crackle of heat that passed from his fingertips to mine. "What do you think you're doing?" I asked.

"You still owe me a dance. Truly, a travesty of epic proportion." As we spoke, he urged me forward, until we were in the rows of dancers. "And you seem to be feeling better."

Annoyance shot through me—he hadn't asked; had just assumed based on how I looked. But then he didn't know that I could look fine but feel anything but, even if he were kind when I nearly fainted. I couldn't be frustrated with him for things he didn't know.

"I thought you'd be dancing with that mademoiselle," I said sweetly. She sneered over at us; irritation clung to her like perfume.

His laughter reverberated in his hand. In my hand. "Why? Are you jealous?" His gaze lingered on mine, searching. And I stared back, felt myself leaning forward, pulled by some invisible thread, only to blink and right myself at the last second.

"No," I retorted, "merely surprised. I was in the middle of a conversation."

"With DuVerlac? You'd have a better time conversing with a brick wall. The man is uncommonly tedious."

He couldn't fool me, not anymore. The blatant arrogance was a show for la noblesse. I knew the Étienne who checked to make sure a sick girl was safe. "On the contrary," I said, "the conversation was stimulating. Perhaps his wit requires an adequate partner to flourish." His hand tightened on mine. As the candlelight shifted, hazel darkened to deep brown with a hint of green. "Jealous?" I parroted back.

"Jealous? Of DuVerlac? Hardly." His hand dipped to my waist, and I jerked. "It's the dance," he explained. "A new style from Italy. Look." To my dismay, each man placed his hand flat on his partner's back. There was more than a foot between them, but still.

"I . . . well, th-then . . . ," I stammered as his palm found the small of my back. We'd walked side by side and sat next to each other at the theater, but this was different. From here I could see his chest expand with each breath he took, could feel his arm curled around me. Could sense his chin near the top of my head, the warmth radiating onto my scalp.

Like a statue, I was still. Even when the music started. I couldn't do this. Not with him. It was a ruse, I knew that, but my heart was racing at a breakneck pace. The world was whirling, fast, fast, fast, and nothing I could do would slow it down.

"Tania." He said my name tenderly, encouragingly. As if he were coaxing me out of the shadows. We were closer than the dance required. Madame de Treville's teachings echoed in my ears. But then his hand flexed on my bodice, only a few layers of silk and petticoats and boning between his skin and mine. "I won't let you fall."

And then we were dancing. For so long, I thought I'd never experience the sensation of flying, that I couldn't—my body would never let me flunge. That I'd have to be satisfied watching others complete a flying lunge, gliding through the air, goddesses of the wind.

Yet, I was flying. And the dizziness was there, but so was his hand at my waist. His strong nose, a hairline crooked. His fingers grasping mine. The steps were unfamiliar, but the way he led wasn't. When he pulled me into a twirl I laughed, kept laughing even as the gray waves across my vision crashed and blurred. Even as my legs threatened to give way.

"Tania?" I stopped short, my cheek below his shoulder. Not now. Not again. Tears pooled at the corners of my eyes, my surroundings spinning so I couldn't tell the dancers from the room, Étienne from the dancers. "Here," he murmured. My feet no longer supported my weight. Movement, a cool wash of air, solid arms enclosed around me.

Time, slow, and then: The world righted itself. A balcony, a stone bench beneath me, fragrant, sweet-smelling winter pansies budding around stone pillars. My skin welcomed the rush of wind. Étienne knelt and captured both my hands in his.

"Étienne, please, think of how this must look." Any passerby would see how close we were. It wasn't like before, that first time we were alone, when he maintained his distance in the shadowed half-light through ballroom windows. The calluses on my thumbs knew the feel of his skin now—achingly familiar.

"We're the only ones here." He was right; the balcony was empty, the partygoers' laughter muted by marble and glass. The only other sound was the occasional gust of frigid wind singing through branches. He moved to sit on the bench next to me. A less compromising position, but now his arm brushed against mine. Frustration coursed through me at him for not listening, at myself for not being stronger; Aria's warnings: for me to protect myself, to protect my heart. But wasn't this what Madame de Treville wanted? For Étienne to open up? For us to assure his father's involvement in the plot?

"You said my name," he observed, facing me, knees grazing my skirts.

"What?" Remnants of dizziness clouded my mind. My words weren't catching on my tongue because of him. My thoughts weren't languid and slow because of his proximity. It was the dizziness. Only the dizziness.

"You . . . it's nothing. Are you all right?" His expression transformed in worry. "You seemed unwell, like you are sometimes. So I brought you out here." He studied the empty balcony overlooking the grounds, dark green hills black under the moonlight. The anticipation of approaching snow thickened the air. "But it *is* cold."

"I'm not cold," I said.

"You're sure, ma tourterelle?" Blood rushed in my ears. As his thumb traced patterns on my palm, I shivered. "You're shaking," he murmured, the tips of our noses brushing together. His other hand cupped my cheek.

"Not cold." I was going to say something else. Should say something else. But the words were lost before they began. Lost in the exhale of breath as his lips met mine, soft at first, his thumb featherlight across my jaw. One of us sighed. In the next moment his hand drifted from my face to tangle in my hair, his other arm looped low around my waist. He drew me closer, breathed me in, his lips burning against the cold air, a low noise escaping the back of his throat.

I was wrong, before. *This* was flying.

The minute our chests crushed together, the minute two heartbeats pounded in sync, I wrenched away, took a gasping breath. He bent to press kisses along my jaw.

"We shouldn't have done that," I said, voice faltering as I disentangled myself. I ghosted my fingers across my lips.

If someone saw us, the entirety of the Parisian elite would know by the time they returned to their carriages. And what would that mean for me? Surely a girl already accounted for, a girl seen kissing a man, would be of no use to the Order. No other targets would want me. Or worse—they *would* want me, in ways that I wouldn't ever let happen.

I looked up at Étienne's face, at the sharp line of his jaw, at his slightly crooked nose. At his curved lips that were just kissing mine. "I'm sorry to disappoint," he said. "I for one thought it was fantastic."

"Étienne, I—"

"Tania." He dragged his thumb across my cheek. "I'm teasing. You asked me to make my intentions known, so I am."

Months of training had readied me to seduce targets, to uncover secrets, to duel enemies until I was standing above them, triumphant. But none of it could have prepared me for this. Someone who wanted me. Someone who I wanted in return.

No matter how many times I told myself Étienne didn't mean anything to me, couldn't mean anything to me, that didn't make it true. Aria was right. Yes, he was kind. Yes, he knew I was different and still wanted to kiss me in the starlight.

I had feelings for him, but that didn't matter. Because I chose the Musketeers—I chose myself. The girls cared and I trusted them. I trusted myself. They thought I was enough. I thought I was enough.

Now: blink back tears, square my shoulders. I was a Musketeer. And a Musketeer did not run from anything or anyone. "Kissing someone hardly reveals your intentions for them." There. I'd found her again. Tania, Mademoiselle la Mousquetaire—or at least, enough of a glimmer of her to bolster me through this with my heart intact.

"You think that doesn't reveal my intentions?" he asked. "At first, I was intrigued by your abrupt arrival in Paris, the girl in scarlet who stole everyone's breath. But that changed as soon as you opened your lips. You're more than that, Tania, so much more. I don't have any ulterior motives when it comes to you. How could I, when you are who you are?"

"Truly?"

"Let me prove it. Ask me whatever you wish."

He stared at me, guileless, gripping my hands in his and gazing at me like I was the only one he would ever—could ever—want. *Is your father plotting to kill the King? Did he have a hand in Papa's murder? Has he forced you to become a part of the plot? What do you know? What do you know what do you know what do you know?*

"You didn't want to tell me about your family before. So tell me now."

He seemed perplexed but took it in stride. "A strange request, but anything for you. What do you wish to know?"

I needed to be careful. Craft my questions with the precision of a sharpened blade. Something that would give me evidence, or lead me to evidence, that directly connected his father with the plot to kill the King. "What are your parents like?"

"We've never been particularly close."

"But you left Paris the other afternoon at your mother's request?"

"Since I finished schooling she's wanted me at the estate more. But that's born from her worry that I won't live up to expectations more than any real desire to see me."

Maman, an explosion of fury. "*For once would you do what I say!*" My failure etched into the lines in her face.

Oh, Étienne. I wanted to tell him he wasn't alone, that I knew the burden of being a disappointment, the deep, near-painful yearning to prove worthiness to the person who bore you into the world. But his mother wasn't who I was after.

"That must be difficult," I responded cautiously. "And your father?"

"It's like I told you: We've never seen eye to eye." No matter how meticulous his word choice, his emotions flashed venom across his face.

I observed him in perfectly arranged confusion. "Really?"

"He has his own ideas on how best to serve the country. Foolish, foolish ideas. You're sure you're not cold?" he added as a shiver ran through me.

I leaned closer to him for warmth. "You're different from your father, then?"

Étienne let out a whoosh of a breath. "Very."

"How so?"

"You're asking a lot of questions about him."

My smile froze. "I'm just interested about where you come from. About your family."

"You mentioned my father the first time we met," he said.

"My home is not far from Bordeaux, so I'd heard of your family before. It's a wonder we never encountered each other."

"My parents shipped me off to school when I was ten. My mother visited for the holidays, but my father never did. He didn't want me home; he thought I needed to be tougher, and that traveling home would defeat the purpose of school in the first place, make me weak."

And the thread unwound: his father's insistence on solitude, a period of time when he could do whatever work he pleased without fear of interruption. Like balancing ledgers . . . or planning a King's assassination. Perhaps this had been in the works before La Fronde. Maybe he stayed neutral during the scourge, lying in wait for the opportune moment. I just needed Étienne to keep talking. For him to let further information slip. Could I ask him where his father was, right now? Or would that be too much of a giveaway?

His hand found mine. "It's a shame I wasn't at home more—perhaps we would have met sooner. In the countryside. In the sunlight." He toyed with one of my curls. "It was overcast that day." I blinked in confusion. "At the university. It was overcast. I've never seen your hair in the sunlight—in candlelight, yes, but it's not the same."

He leaned in again. A muffled crash shrieked across the empty balcony, and I jerked toward the noise.

"Someone must've dropped a glass." Étienne's fingers found my chin, pressed gently until I turned my face to his. "We should return to the party before we're missed. I'll call on you Monday afternoon; I know I promised no more interruptions, but whatever you need to say, tell me then . . . we won't have to hide any-more."

I'd asked him to reveal his intentions—but I had never let myself believe they were honorable. The very thought of him entering the Order's headquarters shot ice through my veins, colder than any Parisian winter. None of it could happen. Not the courting, not the kissing. None of it.

But what if it could save the King's life?

He placed a lingering kiss on my forehead. Grinned at the blush he thought was for him, unaware of the guilt that had its fingers around my throat. Papa's face flooded into my mind, cov-ered in blood. I nearly retched.

After we wound back through the columns, Étienne kissed my hand. Then he walked around the corner and disappeared from sight. I shivered, finally aware of the bitter cold leeching under my gown.

"I can't care about you," I tried out, resting the words on the cutting night air. They twisted into rings of smoke, dissolved into the darkness, and became part of the endless Parisian sky. At the next gust of wind, I shook my head. Waiting here until I froze was the last thing a Musketeer would do. So, I returned to the warmth.

As I passed over the threshold, I could've sworn a fragment of pale yellow fabric fluttered around the corner, near the balcony. I blinked, and it was gone. A trick of the light.

CHAPTER TWENTY-FIVE

SURELY, THE OTHERS would see it in my face, would see the echo of it on my lips—the betrayal of my father, of my new sisters, of our mentor.

And yet the world continued on. The party guests danced and drank and laughed until they were red in the face, the same shade as their painted mouths and cheeks.

"Where have you been?" Madame de Treville surprised me at the edge of the ballroom. Was my hair mussed? Makeup smudged? "Well, that's no matter now. Portia told me everything."

"She did?" I squeaked.

"Yes . . . ," she said, lowering her voice, "about your observation of a particular accessoire? And the writing on it?" I gaped at her. "Did you speak to Verdon? Did our plan work?"

"Yes," I breathed out. There was no time to explain before I was shepherded into the carriage.

Our mentor waited for the groomsman to close the door and the steady clop of hooves before she spoke. "Portia's already informed me you saw the Comtesse de Gramont with the man from the docks."

I recounted their conversation: the Comtesse's odd interest in why the man's wife hadn't attended her party, their weighted language, how she'd brought a gift to a ball, of all places. "There was writing on the fan. Hidden between the ribs. It shimmered a bit, too, like it was made of metal."

"Probably to ensure the writing doesn't fade. Perhaps it's a letter? It has to be the same as the one she had custom made, non?" Portia wondered.

"Maybe . . ." I stopped, then continued on. "Maybe it's connected to the coded message I found?"

For the first time in weeks, Madame de Treville looked like she wasn't shouldering the weight of all of Paris. The strain was still there in the hold of her neck, the furrows of her brow. But hope alleviated the worst of it. "I think it's time we paid the éventailliste a visit. Well done, Tania." Her voice was so full of pride that I wanted to melt into the seat cushions. I didn't deserve it, not when I'd been kissing my target less than an hour ago.

She could never know. Not if I wanted to discover the truth about what truly happened to Papa. And she wouldn't have to know—it wouldn't happen again. It could never happen again.

"You and Portia will question the éventailliste tomorrow."

Portia's eyes were brilliantly bright; her smile nearly glowed in the carriage's dim interior. "We won't let you down, Madame."

In the corner of my vision, I watched Aria lean forward, as if unaware of the motion. And then, a *thud*. "Sorry," Aria muttered, retrieving her own fan from the floor, body halfway off the seat and cheeks uncharacteristically pink. "I lost my balance."

"Now, the next matter at hand—what did Verdon say?" Madame de Treville asked.

The carriage was already small; now it felt minuscule. "His

father spends a great deal of time at home without family present. If Verdon senior wanted time to plan, to discuss the plot with other local nobles, or even host exiled persons, he had the opportunity . . . but this started well before La Fronde."

"Did he reveal anything else?"

"He only reinforced that he and his father are very different men."

"And?" Madame de Treville said. "How did you leave things?"

"He wants to call on Monday."

Théa let out a little gasp. Portia grinned. Aria remained motionless.

Madame de Treville furrowed her brow. "Now *this* presents an interesting dilemma."

"How so?" Théa yawned her words, trying not to fall asleep. "Tania was supposed to make him fall for her, and she did! Look at all the information she's found for us!"

"Information that means nothing without verbal confirmation. If we're wrong, if Verdon isn't the leader, we'll risk everything we've worked for." Each of Madame de Treville's words was an executioner's noose that tightened around my neck. *Traitor. Traitor. Traitor.*

I fisted my hands in the skirts of my dress to hide my trembling fingers. "It's difficult . . . he's difficult."

Madame de Treville grimaced. "That one's as slippery as an eel. If I thought we could get away with having you call on him, I'd send you over there in a heartbeat. Propriety: what an unfortunate hindrance to assassination investigations.

"We have our work cut out for us. Tomorrow Portia and Tania will question the fan maker. Aria, Théa, you'll accompany me. One Madame has wanted to meet my pupils for a while now, and since she's a friend of the Comtesse's, I think it's high time she does. If Tania gets the information we need on Monday, we might even have a few days to spare. Especially if that cryptography book of Henri's is as useful as it purports to be."

Aria tensed against the corner she'd burrowed herself into—that is, as much as one could wearing a gown.

The lull of the carriage's sway was deep in my bones. My limbs ached like we'd spent another night escaping the docks.

"It'll be over soon," I said to Aria, who was watching me. Her disbelief of Henri's loyalty. The fear that, because of our inability to confirm the plot's leader, a horrible fate would befall the King, that innocents would be blamed and their blood shed, while the nobles reaped the reward of an empty throne. When we saved the King, we'd have leverage. He'd owe his life to a girl from La Cour. That had to mean something: Surely Mazarin and the rest of the royals would pay dearly to keep it from getting out that we accomplished what the other Musketeers couldn't? We could leverage that into something greater, something that could help future women in the Musketeers, like Portia wanted, but also help La Cour. Maybe even girls like me.

Soon, the man who killed Papa would be locked away in the Bastille.

Aria's exhale drew me back to earth. "Yes," she said. "It'll all be over soon."

Portia yanked me to her as a cart trundled past us on the busy street.

"I don't see why the carriage couldn't let us off in front of the shop."

She sighed theatrically as she avoided a steaming pile of horse droppings, twirling in a wide circle so her shoes met worn stone instead of dung. "What would we do if customers were inside? Even the most oblivious Parisian would notice a carriage loitering outside a shop with its riders peeking through the curtains. Remember, Tania: *spies!*" she whispered, her fingers spread like stars.

Once we reached the storefront and determined the shop was empty, I followed the swing of Portia's skirts as we entered to bells jingling.

"Un moment, s'il vous plaît!" A voice carried from behind the register. My gaze roamed around the store, halting as Portia rearranged the front of her dress, her cleavage spilling out of her bodice. I rolled my eyes, but she looped her arm through mine and pinched the inside of my elbow.

The store, while small, was the finest shop I'd ever been in, with its wood paneling and framed fans on the walls. No price guide to be found, but then, that was common with la noblesse. Money did not matter the way it should, and to have reference to it, out in the open, would be seen as uncivilized. To think: The money spent on such fragile things, paper light and delicate as feathers, easily ripped and ruined, could feed a family for weeks. Months, even.

A man emerged from what looked to be a storage room. "Bonjour, Mesdemoiselles—" His words cut off as he traveled the length of our bodies. He scrambled to put the material clasped in his arms on the counter. "How may I help you? I assure you, my shop has the finest fans in all of Paris. Whatever you search for, you will find it here."

"Oh, we are well aware of your reputation," Portia demurred, trailing her fingers along the edge of the counter that separated them.

"My lady is too kind. Is there anything in particular she *desires*?" But his gaze wasn't focused on Portia. It was focused on *me*. Even more so when Portia pushed me forward.

"One moment, please! I must discuss my . . . fan-ly desires with my sister," I blundered, pulling Portia away. "What was that? I thought you were running lead?" I whispered. The man, confused, stared at us as he rearranged scraps of fabric on the countertop.

"Apparently he's not a breast man. Such a shame." She glanced down at her exposed cleavage and sighed. "You look wonderful today; it's that mean man's fault. Even you, Péronelle." She tapped her left breast with a fond sigh.

"You *named* them?"

"You haven't? I'll have you know that Péronelle *earned* her name. Little stone indeed. Do you know how difficult it is to get a dress lacing right when one breast is noticeably smaller than the other? And Péronelle is very sensitive to chafing. Padding is out of the question."

"I just . . . I . . ."

Portia took the opportunity to push me back to the countertop. "Go on! Time to fly, Tania!"

I clunked into the furniture. The man looked up, his whole face brightening. "Mademoiselle. You're back!"

I flashed him my most dazzling smile. His fingers tightened

on the countertop, Adam's apple bobbing as he swallowed once, twice. "I heard from a particular Comtesse that you created exquisite designs for her."

"A unique circumstance. We went through many personal consultations—I wanted to be sure I gave her *exactly* what she wanted."

Oh, pour l'amour du ciel. For the love of God. But I didn't escape through the door—instead I let my hand rest mere inches away from his on the countertop.

"Perhaps we too can come to an arrangement. Though I'd like to see what I'm paying for first."

The man extracted a fan from one of the displays. "This is too simple," I said, frowning at him. "Nothing like what the Comtesse has. I don't want to be thought unfashionable."

"Of course not, Mademoiselle! The Comtesse's fans were couture, made specially for her. This is the base design."

"What was so special about them?" I breathed.

"W-Well...," he stammered, patting his forehead with a handkerchief and pulling his eyes away from the length of my neck, the span of my collarbones, "she had me inscribe a poem between the ribs. I did the calligraphy myself. Nothing too ostentatious, but it turned out beautifully, if I do say so myself."

"What kind of poem? A love poem, perhaps?"

"A lullaby her mother sang to her when she was a child. I copied it as requested, but she still read it over three times before she deemed me—I mean my work—satisfactory."

I forced down bile. Replaced my innocent smile with a coy smirk I'd been practicing for months. "Do you remember the lyrics? I've been told I have a *wonderful* voice."

"We did it! Or, really, Tania did!" Portia crowed, waving her own fan in the air as she skipped through the front door.

Théa, in the middle of mending a dress, screeched. "Tu m'as fait sursauter!"

"Oh, je suis très désolée. I'm very sorry for scaring you," Portia sang, arms floating as she danced to imaginary music. "I suppose you don't want to know about the lullaby the Comtesse has written on her fans, then?"

"Portia? Tania? Is that you?" Madame de Treville popped her head into the hallway.

"A lullaby?" she said once we'd summarized our findings to her. "Let's hear it."

"Do I really need to sing it?" I used to like singing—nothing too showy, childhood tunes—but that was before the dizziness. Before every extended note was a potential fainting spell.

"There could be a clue in the notes," Madame de Treville said.

Shoulders tight, fingers laced together, I took a breath.

Dors bien, mon trésor

Fais de beaux rêves

I winced at the missed note, sharp and scratchy.

Et, si tu as peur

Rappelle-toi ces paroles:

Tu iras loin

Si les petits cochons ne te mangent pas

I exhaled after the last line, winded and relieved.

Théa broke into applause. I jerked—the noise came from opposite corners of the room. At the other end, hands clapping soft together, face lifted from a stack of papers and nose smudged with ink, was Henri. As soon as he noticed me noticing him, his applause died.

"I'll map the notes onto the coded message, to see if there's any possible key to be found," Madame de Treville said, humming to herself as she marked down the score. "A fairly common musical pattern. Familiar enough that even if you missed a few of the notes, we can predict the rest."

"The lyrics seem fairly innocuous. Are we sure it's related to the plot?" Aria's voice was tight with contemplation.

"Obviously they'd want it to seem innocent, wouldn't they? Perhaps it's in code, too," Portia said.

Théa repeated the lyrics, words a shimmer, buoyant, not singing but still sounding better than my attempt:

Sleep well, my treasure
Dream sweet dreams
And, if you are afraid
Remember these words:
You will go far
If the piglets don't eat you

Madame de Treville tensed. "Repeat that last bit?"

"Si les petits cochons ne te mangent pas."

Portia perked up, alert. "It's a saying; it means 'you'll go far if nothing gets in the way.' But why use it in the first place? That's practically the opposite of a reassuring thing to sing to a child before sleep—and for that matter, going far if obstacles don't get in your way doesn't have much to do with dreaming at all. Why not say that the cauchemar, her nightmare, isn't real? Or that her mother will protect them?"

"I know it's a saying, but maybe it's meant to signify something more literal?" Théa wondered. "Maybe some of the goods smuggled in were pigs? Les petits cochons?"

Aria frowned. "Too risky. Aside from the weapons, we think the goods are used for bribes. They'd stick to items they have control over. Fabrics, luxuries . . ."

"But what about the ball, the one where the host served oranges and chocolates?" Théa asked.

"Still less likely than live pigs to carry disease. Or make a ruckus when unloaded."

We all fell silent. The quiet cloaked us. Madame de Treville sat back in her chair and surveyed the jumble. "I'll cross-reference the lyrics with my library . . . maybe there's a clue to be found." Her tone wasn't hopeful. A gust of air escaped between her teeth, a grimace distorting her mouth. "I'll send a request for music-specific texts from Mazarin. Maybe send for the King's favorite composers, and others who've studied music."

"What about your visit with that Madame? Was she of any use?" Portia asked Madame de Treville.

"We didn't have the chance to speak with her; apparently she was 'out.' But her attendant let slip she was at a gathering hosted by the Comtesse earlier this week. And then, when we were entering the carriage, I swear I saw her observing through one of the upstairs windows." The masked man's taunt echoed hollow in my ears. *Mademoiselle la Mousquetaire.* Perhaps he wasn't the only one who knew our secrets. "Well," Madame de Treville said. "While I contact Mazarin: Each of you, take an encyclopedia. Search for phrases, anything that can be linked to the lullaby. Definitions, the terms themselves—everything is fair game." Her half smile held the weight of countless sleepless nights, of long hours studying the intricate maps on these very walls. Portia groaned as she was handed a stack of books. "Start with these. Go read them in the main library, though, so you don't disturb me."

We trudged into the library. As soon as I opened my assigned copy, I pressed my fingertips to my forehead at the cramped font, at words segmented by comma after comma with no period in sight.

"So, *this* is what they think our courses are like," Portia quipped after a few minutes. She let out a horrified gasp as she turned the page. "Oh, now, *that's* disgusting. How could anyone think our insides look like that?" She showed an illustration to Théa, who pushed her away with a shriek.

We had all of tonight, tomorrow, and then . . . Monday. The day Étienne promised to call.

When I felt the weight of someone's gaze, I looked up. Aria's eyes darted away. But not before I saw the worry lingering behind her irises.

CHAPTER TWENTY-SIX

WE SPENT TWO days poring over every encyclopedia Madame de Treville owned. The entries were tedious. Descriptions of medical theory, the four humors, *hypochóndria*, so many different words and entries for women in pain that wasn't believed. I powered through entries on bloodletting, oleum dulce vitrioli, medicinal treatments that, according to the text, resulted in dizziness more often than improvements in health. I was on the latter's entry when Portia took note of my expression and swapped books with me, carrying on reading as if nothing had happened. This new encyclopedia's entries were tedious. But I'd take the tediousness over the rare exceptions. The painful ones.

"Tania!" Théa rushed over to me in the library, slightly out of breath, her mass of curls going every which way. "I finished!" She thrust a bundle into my hands.

"Finished what?"

"Oh, I didn't tell you, did I? I just went off and started sewing, I'm sorry; I tend to be like that when I'm working . . . you know, nothing else matters, have to get my thoughts down before they fly out of my head—that sort of thing!"

Her words jolted a memory: me trying on torn trousers, her sudden steely veneer of focus, Aria's insistence that I didn't disturb her. "New breeches? Merci!"

Expression keen, she smiled. "Well, I don't think I'd use *that* terminology."

"I don't understand—"

"Try them on," she urged with a giggle, hustling me out of the library and into the room where I'd tried on the skirt all those months ago. I laughed; it felt wonderful. Even when I had to rest against the closed door when my legs wobbled. It'd been so long since I'd actually taken time to breathe, to not worry about the mire swirling around us. Papa had his brotherhood, but I couldn't imagine any of the Musketeers from his stories sewing him new breeches, searching for the finest materials, taking care with every stitch.

After Théa helped me unlace my gown, she turned away for me to remove my stockings, and I put on the blouse from my dock's ensemble so I wouldn't be standing in my underthings.

"What are *these*?" I choked out as I unfurled the breeches. My hands ran over the lightweight fabric. Nary a buckle or a clasp to be found.

"Try them on," she repeated, still facing the door.

They clung to my skin, leechlike, so tight my legs compressed. I struggled them up and over my hips. "They're nearly as tight as those breeches from the other day," I panted.

"Exactement!" Théa whipped around, clapping her hands in delight. "But these you can actually walk in, non?" Skeptically, I took a step forward. While the initial pair of breeches was stiff, unyielding, these gave way with no resistance. "How do you feel?"

I didn't dare answer. Only walked around the room, steps halting, trying to quell the ember of hope blistering in my chest. But when I'd completed the circuit, the spark had fanned into a full-on flame. I was still dizzy; that would not disappear anytime soon. But my balance was better. The pools of gray lingering at the edges of my vision further off. And oh, my legs: They felt steadier. "Oh, Théa, they're better than any couture gown!"

She blushed. "It was nothing. I had a hunch after you tried on that other pair, so I researched fabrics with more give."

When she gestured for me to look in the mirror, I shrieked and fruitlessly made to cover myself with my hands. "I can't be seen in these! They're so, they're so . . ." I chanced another glimpse at the black stretch of fabric. They hid nothing. Absolutely nothing.

"That's why you'll wear them under your dress, silly!"

"But if there's time, in the moment, I'll tuck up my skirts to duel," I said, unable to tear away from the fierce line of my legs. If Maman saw me now, *she* would be the one passed out on the ground.

"At most they'll see the front of your legs—and besides," Théa said, "if they're looking at your legs then they're not looking at your sword—there are benefits all around."

"Théa," I rushed at her crestfallen face, "please don't think I'm ungrateful. It's a lot to take in. But you're right, of course you are."

"Perfect! You can wear them under your gown when Monsieur Verdon comes to call this afternoon and I'll go fetch you a necklace so you won't have to take the pulley again and oh this is perfect, just perfect!" She beamed, upset erased in an instant, and shut the door behind her.

Did she just . . . was she pretending to get me to . . .

Henri hurried through the door, walked all the way to the lone bookcase before he noticed me standing there, horrified. Before he noticed what I was—or wasn't—wearing.

"I—I'm sorry!" he stammered, clapping his hands over his eyes before knocking straight into the wall. "I'm so very sorry!" Books tumbled to the ground, and he scrambled to pick them up, all the while trying to shield me from his sight. "Ma tante couldn't find a book, and there's a bookshelf in here, and—"

"Henri!" He paused in his efforts, and I fisted my hands to keep from grabbing for my dress to hold in front of me. I was a Musketeer. And a Musketeer wasn't afraid of someone spotting her in clothing that was, well . . . snug. "You've seen me in breeches before. Remember, when Aria and I returned from the docks and—"

"That was different." He pulled himself to his feet. His eyes darted over my frame, the shape of my thighs, the curve of my calves. I coughed. He blinked, then straightened.

"How was that different?"

"I don't know," he said. "But it was different."

I cleared my throat. Why did this feel more embarrassing than the afternoon at the éventailliste? "You said you needed a book?"

"Yes . . ." He hesitated, then launched into speech. "Are you planning on leaving the house like that, because it's very cold outside and they don't look at all warm—"

"They'll go under my gown. Théa wanted me to try them on. To see if they fit properly."

"Oh." His voice cracked. "Théa made them, then?"

"Designed them and everything." I let my fingers run down the sides, reveling in how much clearer my vision was. "To help with the dizziness." At the sound of choking, I looked up in concern. "Is something wrong?"

"No," Henri said. "It's good that they help with the dizziness."

"Right," I said.

"Right," he said, too.

We both stood there awkwardly, his gaze fastened on a spot above my head. But then he let out a gust of air and closed the gap between us. "Listen . . . there's something I need to—well, that is—"

"Yes?"

His face was only a foot away from mine. Why was he so nervous . . . had Aria been right all along?

I watched his mouth. Waited for his words. And I tried to ignore how this was the first time he'd made any attempt to truly speak or look at me in weeks, and how much that hurt. Because he was still the boy who had brought me the map, the boy who made me laugh that very first morning in Paris before the city became as familiar as my sword in my hand.

"I brought the necklace . . ." Théa entered, examining the chain she carried. "I think it'll work with your dress, but you should try it on to be sure—imagine if the colors clashed!" She finally looked up as Henri lurched away. "Oh, I hadn't realized you were here!"

He flushed under her attention. What would that feel like? To blush when you saw someone, to be attracted to someone . . . to like someone, and for it not to be a betrayal? "I came for this," he said shakily. He held up a book. "I should go; I'm late for work as is."

"Be sure to leave through the back entrance; that way Monsieur Verdon doesn't catch you on your way out," Théa said.

"Monsieur Verdon?" His gaze slid to me as Théa answered proudly.

"Oui! He's calling on Tania this afternoon, and you should see how he looks at her; she's done such a magnificent job."

Henri's eyes never left my face. For some inexplicable reason, my lungs constricted. "Congratulations on a job well done, then." His expression was unreadable. I waited for him to say something else, but he turned and left through the open doorway.

Théa stared after him in shock. "Did I upset him? What happened while I was upstairs?"

I blinked against the bite of tears; stress, surely—of Étienne's rapidly approaching visit, of what I must do, how desperately we needed a direct link between the evidence and the suspects . . . "He was embarrassed to have barged in here. With me not having on a gown."

Her pert nose crinkled, sending her freckles into disarray. "Oh, I'm sorry, I'm so sorry, Tania, I shouldn't have left—"

"It's not your fault. Don't worry. It's not anyone's fault." Even as I spoke guilt bloomed in my chest, a morbid, misshapen sunflower. Unspoken for and foreign behind my breastbone.

"I don't want to be inconsiderate—please don't think me inconsiderate—but, Tania, it's getting late, and, well, are you going to start getting ready?"

"Yes," I said. "Help me, please?"

And so she helped me back into my gown, looped the necklace, all crystalline gemstone and silver lattice, over my head. At the last minute, I pulled the ring out from underneath my bodice. The chain didn't glitter like the fine jewelry, but it hummed with something stronger. Today, Papa's ring, the chain: They would be my anchor.

"Madame de Treville? What's the matter?" I said immediately upon entering the parlor.

She stood near the window, twisting her hands. "It can wait until after the visit." Portia and Aria were on a settee, conversing quietly. But at the edge in Madame de Treville's voice they looked up with a jolt.

Dread seeped through me. "Please, tell us."

"How are your new breeches? Do you feel better?"

"They do help some—but an item of clothing isn't about to cure my dizziness. Now, what are you keeping from us?"

Madame de Treville went very still. Studied me before letting out a splintered breath. "It was the éventailliste. Mazarin sent a messenger to let me know."

I gripped Papa's ring. "What happened?"

"He never returned home Saturday night. His wife only contacted the guards yesterday; she presumed he spent the night finishing a rush order . . . but that was disproved this morning when a local fisherman reeled in a corpse along with the fish. His body, his face . . . well, from what you told me, Tania, it sounds like he was given the same treatment as your father. When officers investigated the shop, they found this," she said, and pulled something in a handkerchief out of her tie-on pockets. When she unwrapped it, Théa gasped. Aria looked worriedly at Portia, who'd sucked in a breath she had yet to release. "Mazarin had it delivered less than an hour ago. He . . . isn't pleased by the latest developments. He tried arguing with the King about the festival again, and that went as well as could be expected."

A fan, intricate, like the ones the Comtesse had designed. But, in place of a lullaby, a different message was written. Some of the letters were difficult to read; the red ink—I couldn't think of it as anything else—had started to flake and peel away.

Arretez-vous maintenant, et nous vous épargnerons.

Stop now, and we will spare you.

We'd visited the fan maker two days ago. Portia and I could've been some of the last people, besides his murderer, to see him alive.

"It's the work of the nobles," Madame de Treville continued. "They know we're onto them."

I screwed my eyes tight against the image of Papa, bloody and beaten. His face morphed into Aria, Portia, Théa. Henri. Étienne. Madame de Treville. Maman.

A rapping sound echoed from down the hall. "He's early!" Madame de Treville gasped, bustling about, arranging the four of us around the room—fruit in a still life. Théa and Portia practiced embroidery in the corner. Aria in her usual spot at the miniature table and set of chairs. And I was in the center of it all, emerald green skirts spread across the cushions, a fan of lush leaves.

Jeanne eased through the threshold—it wasn't usual to have a maid greet guests, but Madame de Treville wasn't willing to hire more staff and risk exposing our secrets. And Madame de Treville had offered Jeanne extra livres for her participation today.

"A Monsieur Verdon here to call on you, Madame."

"Send him in."

We rose when Étienne entered, me slower than the rest as I

braced for dizziness. It was muted, yes. But still there. Always there. Étienne stared intently at me. Madame de Treville coughed. He hastened to face her. "Madame, thank you for permitting me to call."

"It's our pleasure." Her gaze flickered to mine, and his eyes followed hers. "Girls," she said to Portia and Théa, since Jeanne already left per Madame de Treville's earlier instructions, "will you tell the kitchen to put on some tea? Claude never remembers to steep the leaves long enough." Claude, I'd gathered, was our fictional chef.

That left four of us. With the fire roaring everything was warm, flushed, soupy. I should've worn a more extravagant gown; it was easier to face him in my armor.

"Please, take a seat." Madame de Treville motioned to a chair.

"I hope you've been having a pleasant season," Étienne said as he arranged his jacket tails.

"Exceedingly pleasant. More so with our newest addition to the household."

His eyes concealed the warmth I knew lay beneath their surface. "You're not the only one grateful for her presence."

Madame de Treville cleared her throat and stood. "Where are they with that tea? Monsieur Verdon, I apologize for our lack of prompt hospitality." Under other circumstances, a chaperone would be wary to leave her charge unattended in a man's presence—even with the company of another young lady.

But Madame de Treville was no ordinary chaperone. And I was no ordinary charge.

Madame de Treville closed the door behind her. Étienne threw a concerned look Aria's way, but she'd located a book, likely one of the encyclopedias. Multitasking, always multitasking. "It's all right," I reassured him. I gestured to the space on the love seat next to me and swallowed down my heartbeat.

"What an interesting necklace," he said once he was seated.

I patted the silver latticework. "Merci—" but he'd already reached forward to curl his finger around my mother's unjeweled chain. His thumb brushed against my exposed breastbone. My heart stalled, skipped, stuttered. "A family heirloom," I said, pleased by how steady my voice was. "Truly, it's fine," I insisted as he glanced over at Aria again.

Only then did his body relax. "A miracle, truly, that I managed to wait this long to see you."

"It's only been a few days since the ball," I demurred.

"Still." He grazed his fingers along my cheek. When I shrank away, he returned his hand to his lap in confusion.

"Étienne, what happened the other night . . ." Aria was either engrossed in the book or doing a very good job at pretending to be so.

He took one of my hands in his, held it like it was some delicate, rare flower. I wanted to pull back, to keep my heart safe, but I couldn't. I had to fulfill my duty to the Order. To my sisters. Even if I knew it would hurt. "Tania, I'm sorry. I haven't treated you properly, haven't courted you properly. I've gone about this all wrong." Étienne was fervent.

"Please, you mustn't feel that you've done anything wrong." I was proud of my measured response. I was proud I didn't act on the little surge of anger, unfamiliar, surprising, that flared deep in my marrow. Why was it that, whenever we were together, he was apologizing for something he'd done to me?

"I let my emotions get the best of me. But I promise I won't let that happen again," he said.

The sound of a book closing. "But I thought . . ."

"I wanted you? I do. I do want you very much, which is why I intend to write your father for his blessing." I stared at him, unshed tears clinging to my lashes. "Have I misread our situation? Don't you want this?"

"No," I stumbled over my words. "No, I do—I do want this. I just, I don't know how to tell . . . well, I can't—that is, first, I need to ask you, I need to know—"

The door opened in a rush with only a brief knock as warning: a harried courier, followed by a frazzled Jeanne. "Monsieur Verdon, a letter," the courier gasped out.

"Whatever it is, I don't—"

"It's urgent."

Étienne retrieved the envelope and thumbed open the flap. As he scanned the letter, his expression shifted.

"Étienne? Is something wrong?" I asked.

"It's my mother. She's unwell," he said.

"Unwell?"

He returned to me, tucking the letter into his jacket. "My father told her he has to stay in Paris for business. At least, that's what he'd have us believe. More likely he's drinking in some pub, trying to fool himself he's part of the masses by not going to cabarets. But, Tania . . . even when very ill, she hardly complains—if it's bad enough that she needed to write me . . ."

"You're sure you must leave?" He'd opened his heart, placed it in my outstretched palms; he'd answer any questions about his father. About Verdon senior's business in Paris, about the Winter Festival, only a few days away.

Shame rushed white-hot. If I had a chance to speak with Papa before . . . Even if Étienne wasn't close to his mother, he still loved her. The woman who visited him at boarding school, who sent for him whenever she felt him drifting—the one parent with his true interests at heart.

"Étienne," I tried again. Imagined myself a girl of metal, and nothing more. A girl who cared only for her duty. "Please, I need you to stay, I need to know—"

He pressed a kiss to the back of my hand. Sighed my name into my skin. As he left, the door closing behind him, I drew that same hand to my chest.

Aria thrust her book back onto the shelf with so much vitriol that I jumped. She looked at me like she had no idea who I was.

"Aria," I started. But I couldn't continue: Her face held no surprise, no shock. Only the truth.

"I didn't tell anyone. I thought it a one-time occurrence. That you were so desperate to find evidence that you tried something outrageous. But I was wrong. I see that now. You were going to tell him. About you. About us. You . . . you *care* for him. Deeply. I told you we couldn't save you if you're intent on drowning."

"The ball was a mistake, but today wasn't like that. You don't understand, I wasn't going to tell—" I tried again, tears flowing now, but she didn't respond. She removed herself from the room like it was some infected place.

The crash. The flash of pale yellow. It was her.

Aria knew everything.

CHAPTER TWENTY-SEVEN

"ÉTIENNE VERDON IS no longer your target." Madame de Treville didn't bother to look up from her work as I entered the study.

I knew something like this would happen when Aria left me in the parlor yesterday. I'd waited for it through the night, sleepless, waited through the morning, the afternoon, part of the evening. Images slamming into me of Papa, alone, of Maman, alone, of Étienne, alone by his mother's bedside. But that didn't numb me to Madame de Treville's anger. "We only have two days until—"

"His use has been expended. That's abundantly clear."

My failures multiplied with every breath I took. The Order. My sisters in arms. Papa. "I know what Aria thought she saw," I said after a shivering breath, "but—"

"Tell me, then: What exactly were you doing?"

The moment returned to me as quickly as a thunderclap: the roar of wind, the roar of my heartbeat. "Aria saw us kiss, yes. I only meant she was mistaken yesterday—I would never let myself get too attached or tell him about the Order. If you give me a bit more time, I can uncover the truth; I know I can. He's distraught: his mother's ill and I didn't have a chance to interrogate him further, but now he's just outside Paris. Maybe I could go see him?"

Madame de Treville set down her quill, disappointment hardening her features. This was worse than her anger. Worse than her criticism of a poorly taken parry. Worse than her glare at a misstep during the gavotte. Shame crawled up my body. "Despite insisting you'd keep our secrets, there's still the terrifying matter at hand that you have developed feelings for a target. Even if you never acted on them again, how am I supposed to trust your judgment?"

"That's not what—I never meant for—"

"What did you mean, then? You've always let your emotions rule you, but you've never been so dangerously foolish. Not until now." I made no move to wipe the tears gathering along my cheekbones. "You couldn't even fulfill your most basic assignment. Because of your inability to keep your feelings in check, Aria had to distract your first target at the ball. You were gone for so long with Verdon, DuVerlac thought you were being taken advantage of. Do you understand the irrevocable damage to your reputation, and mine, for that matter, if he'd found you?"

I couldn't help but flinch; Madame de Treville's words were hot coals against my skin. "I'm not saying it was a good idea. But it was only a kiss—"

"That's not what the gossip-hungry nobles would have called it. By the time the news traveled across social circles, they'd have had you with your skirts around your waist, straddling him in the middle of the palace garden. Tell me, who would take you seriously then? Who would take *us* seriously? Do you think Mazarin would believe us capable of anything after you'd ruined the

Order?" Madame de Treville's words reached a fever pitch, her knuckles clenched bloodless. "Were you so desperate for affection that the second someone showed the slightest bit of interest in you, you swooned? Because let me make things absolutely clear: he doesn't care for you, Tania. He doesn't even know you."

I wrapped my arms around myself to keep from shaking. To keep myself from fracturing. Little pieces of fragile Tania all over the study floor along with everything else I'd already lost or was about to lose. No—no. I'd spent too many months hardening myself. Too many months of strengthening my legs, of laughing with the girls, of dancing gavottes. Too many months becoming myself to lose her.

A muscle ticked near Madame de Treville's jaw. "That was harsh of me," she said. She paused, as if the words pained her. "Harsh, to insinuate you were pathetic . . . I know you have a different history than the others. But that doesn't excuse the fact that you've jeopardized our mission."

The legends on the maps warped and spun. Bookshelves tipped over, righted themselves, tipped over again. The nausea and fear stormed together, consumed me, banded round my chest, my stomach, my heart.

"I forget, sometimes, how very young you all are." My eyes focused down near my feet, tracing the cracks in the floorboards; I didn't move. As if a whisper of a breath would be my undoing. "Being a young woman can be as difficult as being a Musketeer. You know parts of my history. Not enough, however, to know how desperately I fought to be where I am at this very moment. How many years went by as I watched, and waited, and yearned. I never wanted a marriage. I never wanted a life with someone else. I wanted to be a Musketeer."

My rib cage was squeezing, trying to crush me into dust. I thought back to the day I arrived in Paris. The day I saw this house for the first time, entered what I thought was my worst nightmare. All I had to lose then were the clothes on my back, the sword in my trunk. But now I could fill entire worlds, oceans and all, with what I stood to lose: My love for my new family. My joy at knowing I'd never have to give up fencing, at knowing I finally had the chance to make Papa proud. That I'd found my purpose and my people, all in one place. That Maman was wrong, that I could be loved. That I'd found my strength.

A long moment passed before I was able to speak. "On my very first day, you told me you wouldn't waste time on a girl confused about her place in the world, her duty. That you wouldn't waste time on a girl who doesn't know what she wants. Maybe I was that girl then, but I'm not anymore. My duty is to my sisters. To the Order," I said.

Madame de Treville took up her quill. Then put it down. A drawn-out sigh. "If . . . *if* you are to stay in the Order, nothing remotely similar to this can happen again." My head shot up, stomach tumbling in surprise and even a little hope. Another sigh, long and low and more of an exhale. "I can't afford to lose a Musketeer. Not now. Not two days before an assassination threat. But you are on probation. You will do exactly what I say. You won't argue. And until we have the message decoded, you will be glued to the reference books. You will not leave this house. Once this is over, if there's still an Order to speak of, I'll decide what to do with you. Do I make myself clear?"

I nodded, my heart swelling. I wasn't forgiven—it wouldn't be that easy. Nothing ever was.

But it was a start.

Exhaustion trailed me from the pulley under Madame de Treville's watchful gaze to the hallway, all black and gray, the shade of doves buffeted in a snowstorm. Théa's high-pitched laughter echoed through an open door. She was probably laughing at something Portia said while Aria sat in the corner quietly, watching it all unfold.

I'd been so close to losing this. I still could, if I wasn't careful.

Halfway to my room, the sound of my name. I paused. Aria with her arms at her sides, feet hushed on the carpeted floor. Any vestiges of relief flew from me instantly.

"What do you want, Aria?" Her impassive veneer cracked slightly.

"I hope you understand why I had to tell," she said. She didn't block my path, but walked with me, following me.

"You didn't even ask. Didn't even ask if I knew it was a mistake, if I wasn't going to let it happen again. Didn't have faith in me." I bit back the anger and upset and guilt. "Everything you said about trusting you, about not letting me fall. Was that all a lie?"

Her mouth remained set in a hard line as I spoke. The laughter in the other room had stopped. "Even if you decided to end things, it doesn't matter. It's hard to understand now. But I was protecting you," she said. "You were going to tell him. About the mission. About who we are."

"Protecting? Like when you insisted I not tell Théa and Portia about the masked thief? No, you like knowing secrets and lording them over us. You only ever protect yourself."

Aria pulled me into her room. "Did you think that was some form of justice?" She shook her head. "They could have heard you. Besides," she argued, "you've been doing the same thing. Wrapped up in your own self-interest. You kissed him, Tania. You fell for him. You chose him over us."

"I would never. It was you who nearly cost me the Order, the truth about my father, my new family . . ."

"Telling them now isn't going to undo what you did," Aria shot back. "You can't stand for anyone to be mad at you. You want to come clean now. Have our anger done with in one fell swoop. But anger doesn't work like that! We don't have to forgive you just because you're sorry."

"Well, I could say the same for you—except you haven't even apologized!" Aria's eyes flashed as I spoke. Something tore inside me, ripped from the hollow of my throat all the way to my navel. "I've kept all your secrets, even the ones you never told me."

Aria's mask dropped. For the first time, for the very first time, she looked as young as Madame de Treville had made me feel. "I don't know what you mean."

"I'm not oblivious, Aria. I'm surprised she hasn't figured it out herself."

"Now I suppose you're going to tell me we're the same. But we're not. She's not my target. Madame de Treville might not . . . I don't know how she would feel about it. If she would let me stay, or would throw me out. But the fact remains it wouldn't jeopardize our mission—"

"I know it's not the same."

We stared at each other, crumpled in defeat. "You won't tell her?" she whispered.

"Of course not." I made for the door. But I couldn't leave, not yet. "You should tell her, though—at least, consider it."

"What?" Aria asked.

"I've seen the way she looks at you, too. At least"—I stopped, started—"at least give her the chance. I know how you feel about me, about what I've done. I know I failed. But do you truly think I ever *wanted* this? What I wanted was to make all of you proud, to be the best Musketeer I could be. And it doesn't matter that Étienne couldn't have known about his father and mine, because rejecting him is the right thing to do. Did you really think I'd let it continue? When I touch him, I feel like I'm betraying everyone I have ever and will ever care about"—*the theater, the shift of his leg against mine, the crush of red velvet like Papa's blood*—I swallowed. "Everyone other than him. And that's not worth it. Regardless of whatever's between us, that's not worth it to me. But you failed me, Aria. You failed me, too."

Tears accumulated around Aria's lash line, and the very thought that I'd caused them was almost enough to get me to stop, but I couldn't, not now. She had to know. I had to make her understand.

"I'm not the girl newly arrived in Paris, grieving my father and a body I thought would keep me from being whole. I've changed. And honestly, if it hadn't been for all of you, I never would've been able to fall for him in the first place. Or realized that what happened at the ball could never happen again."

"Are you blaming me—"

"It's hard to explain," I broke her off. "Please, listen. When I finally accepted I had feelings for him, I was never worried about him rejecting me because of my dizziness. Yes, he cares for me, and even though he has helped me, has seen me sick, that's not why I wasn't worried. It's because of all of you. My sisters in arms. The three of you made me realize that whatever this dizziness is . . . well, maybe it's never been the real problem. It's horrible and it hurts and it makes me feel fragile in a way I never wanted, but it's not the thing that tears me apart. The problem, the real problem, is the people who decide I'm unworthy because of it."

Suddenly, I tilted, grabbing on to the door frame before I fell. Théa's breeches helped, though they did not cure. Aria spoke. But I was too full to hear her—ears full of roaring waves. Head full of the steady pulse of a white-hot sun.

CHAPTER TWENTY-EIGHT

A BLUR OF colors. Multiple sets of hands on mine, lifting me, carrying me, helping me. And then everything was still.

Portia's bedroom. Théa knelt in front of the chair I was in. Aria rested against the window frame. Portia, arms akimbo and a familiar, steely determination in her face, let her eyes travel from Aria, to me, then back to Aria. "Well," she said finally, "what is this I hear about a masked *thief*?"

"I should have told you—"

"*We* should have told you," Aria said, cutting me off. "We share the blame."

"Oh, so you kissed Monsieur Verdon, too, then?" Portia asked archly. An uncharacteristic stammer escaped Aria's lips before Portia shook her head and turned to me. "Well?"

Once I started speaking, it was impossible to stop. Even if I could, I wouldn't want to—after everything that happened, after how strong they'd made me, they deserved the truth. We were sisters in arms. The four Musketeers. No more secrets.

Portia and Théa remained silent for the most part, interjecting every so often with a question—Théa's questions accompanied by animated shock or horror at appropriate moments. She also valiantly defended Henri when Aria voiced her suspicions of him being the masked thief. "How could you say such a thing? After everything he's done for the Order? You're wrong; I know you're wrong!" Her small face contorted under her corkscrew curls, freckles brandishing themselves like weapons.

But all Aria responded with was, "I don't trust him."

"We still haven't heard about Verdon," Portia said as Théa sucked in another breath. Aria looked to Portia with a tentative smile. Portia's eyes widened, and she turned away. "By all means, argue with Aria later. I want to get caught up before something else exciting happens we're not privy to."

Théa huffed but didn't complain as the subject moved on to Verdon, as I unraveled the tale's thread as best I could. When I arrived at my evisceration in Madame de Treville's study, Théa frowned. "But how did she find out?"

The answer stalled between my teeth. But Aria squared her shoulders. "I told her."

"I don't believe it," Portia said. "No, wait, I *can* believe it; it's just like you to jump to conclusions."

"I didn't have an option. I have to jump to conclusions."

"What a ludicrous thing to say," Portia retorted.

"As a Musketeer, I lose no matter what," Aria said. "Protect the King: let the monarchy flourish. Let La Cour continue to struggle. Don't protect the King: be responsible for the nobles blaming La Cour and hanging the 'traitors.' And then the deaths that would follow in the power vacuum. I might not agree with Madame de Treville on most things, but she's right about that. About who will be the first people to die when nobles decide they want more power. The fan maker, Tania's father, the blood

on the King's mirror . . . either way, I betray what I care about."
Her breaths tightened; she looked like she might cry. "But my
father's face when Madame de Treville came to him with the
offer . . . he was so proud. He will never let me repay him. But I
can give him this. A daughter in the Musketeers . . ." She wiped
her tears, cleared her throat; Théa had looked very confused
during the last part of Aria's speech but now seemed distracted
by her display of emotion, such a rarity. "So I picked the choice
with the fewest immediate casualties," Aria finished.

"It's not just about those things, though," Portia said emphatically. "Tania isn't some casualty. You've forgotten there's a third
thing to fight for. The most important."

"What?"

"Us," I answered for Portia. "That's who we fight for. Us."

Silence stretched paper-thin. Théa glanced at me in discomfort. Aria looked at Portia like Portia had run her through the
heart.

"Maybe . . . maybe you're right," Aria said finally.

"What was that?" Portia's eyebrows nearly reached her hairline.

"I should've let Tania explain first."

"Your inability to trust anyone nearly resulted in her being
thrown out of the Order," Portia retorted. "What kind of Musketeer does that to a sister in arms? We never let each other fall."

"Even when one of us falls for her target?" I whispered.

Portia snorted. Her gaze was forgiving, though. "Especially
then. I wish you'd come to us . . . we could have helped."

"What could you have done?"

"I don't know," Portia answered truthfully. "I can't say I've
ever thought about what I'd do in these kind of circumstances—

I've never been attracted to a target, not even the reasonably polite and handsome ones. Even thinking about those men in that way . . ." She shuddered.

"Although Portia might not be able to imagine herself in your place," Théa said, taking over, "she would've helped you. I would've, too—I mean, I don't know how, but I would've tried my very best!"

"Tania knows what I meant," Portia grumbled. "So, Verdon," she said. "You love him?"

The question hit me like the flat of a blade, and I blinked as I struggled for words. "I don't know—I'm not exactly sure what that's supposed to feel like. I have feelings for him, I do, but I'm not sure how to explain them."

"Can I ask a question?" After I nodded, Théa continued. "What did it feel like? You know . . . the kiss? Was it like the stories?"

"I thought it was," I said. "At least, when it happened, I thought it was." I chewed at my lip.

"He's seen me dizzy before. He's helped me before: That's why we were outside in the first place. He knew how to help me. He's thoughtful, attentive. He knew I wasn't feeling well. And yet, that's when he chose to kiss me—and when we kissed, it's not like I could have pushed him away and risked him never speaking to me again, never telling me the information we need to know. And I don't know how I feel about that. Because I care for him, I do—"

"Did he try anything untoward? If he forced you I'll—" Portia started.

"No, Portia," Théa said firmly as she looked at me. "Tania," she said, more softly this time, "it's okay to not know how to feel."

"Why don't we—"

"It's fine; I'll be all right. Truly," Théa said, cutting off Portia's worried interjection. "Well, maybe *fine* isn't the right word, no." She stopped herself. Took a breath, her expression settling in surety. "But you don't have to protect me from this, Portia, I won't fall apart if we talk about these things. I want to be able to help Tania like you helped me."

Portia stood and smoothed her skirts, but not before she grabbed ahold of Théa's hand, squeezed it, and helped her to her feet. "Right, then. We trust each other, from here on out, with everything. No more secrets?"

"No more secrets," we all repeated. Portia was too caught up in worrying over her hair to notice how pained Aria's whisper was. How her eyes followed Portia collapsing into the seat before her vanity and yanking a strand of hair away from her forehead.

Théa retreated to the full-length mirror to check her recently mended hemline. Aria leaned against a bedpost, arms folded. And Portia stabbed hairpins through her locks. Sighed loudly each time.

"Is something the matter?" Aria asked finally.

Portia met Aria's eyes and blushed. "I haven't gotten a full night of sleep in weeks. And it's *showing*. Dieu, I hate winter." She gestured to her face.

"What are you pointing at?" Aria asked.

"Well, you know . . . it's all well and good having these"—she reached into the dip of her bodice to adjust her breasts—"for distracting targets, but my lips are dull, even with rouge. And I think this puffiness may very well be permanent." She touched the skin below her lash line and winced. "Alas, my bright youthful beauty might never recover, but at least I sacrificed it in service of a good cause."

"Don't be ridiculous," Aria said.

Portia spluttered as she twisted to see Aria: blistering, indignant. "That's easy for you to say," she finally choked out. "Look at you!"

"Would you listen to me for once?" Aria shouted. "You're beautiful. Always have been. Always will be."

Portia flushed. "I don't think you're—"

"Well, I *do* think!" Before there was time to blink, Aria strode to the vanity chair, pulled Portia to her feet. There was a beat. And then: Portia's arms around Aria's waist, Aria's hands in Portia's just-fixed hair, kissing each other like they'd been waiting to for months.

"What was that new design you wanted to show me in the other room?" I asked Théa.

"Design?" Théa squeaked. "What des—oh yes, *that* design!"

We exited quickly; Théa gaping back over her shoulder, giving me her arm for support when I stood. She finally unleashed a slew of words at the end of the hall: "I had no idea! Did you have any idea? They're always arguing, and I thought they didn't even like each other, but people who don't like each other don't do *that*!" Her eyes were as wide as supper plates.

"No," I said with a laugh. "I suppose they don't."

Théa fidgeted. "Oh. I've gone and ruined things, haven't I—I didn't mean to bring up the whole—that is, we already talked about it and you shouldn't have to explain yourself over and over—"

"I'll be okay."

"Tania," she said, very serious all of a sudden. "You should know that we would've never let Madame de Treville turn you away, no matter what you did. We are Musketeers, and we'll stumble at some point, but we'll always find our way back to each other."

A bang reverberated around the room, like the sound of many doors opening and closing all at once, combining together to make one thunderous crash. The noise reverberated in my throat, my ribs.

"Everyone! Come quickly!" Henri.

I looked at Théa in horror. We had talked through the evening; it had to be nearly midnight. Why would he be calling for us now? Unless . . .

Théa flew to the rack on the far wall. I hurried after her and took two swords, including my own, from her extended hands.

We met the others in the hall. "What on earth was that?" Portia asked.

"Henri called for us," I explained.

"We didn't hear anything but the crash," said Aria as she gratefully accepted a sword from Théa.

"Your fault for being so distracting," Portia countered as she took the remaining sword.

"Please! Hurry!" There was Henri again.

Aria headed to the adjacent door. "I'll help Tania with the pulley."

"But if we're being attacked, if the trade ring has sent soldiers or spies or assassins or even worse, you're a better duelist than me," Théa insisted.

"Something worse than soldiers, spies, *and* assassins?" Portia said. "I certainly hope not. What's left . . . dragons?"

Théa threw a frustrated scream back at Portia as we raced through the door, her fingers locked round my arm. I arranged myself in the seat. She lowered me down as usual. "Faster!" I shouted up to her.

The next moment, I was plummeting. I scrunched my eyes shut, heart near my throat. It wasn't an honorable death, but at least it'd be over quickly. At the very last second, the pulley tugged sharp at my waist. I stopped a few feet from the ground. Everything was pounding, crashing, tumbling.

"Sorry!" she yelled.

"The second time, Théa. *The second time!*"

As soon as I extracted myself, I shot to the door. I was ready for whatever was on the other side. Papa's guidance in my heart, my sisters' voices surrounding me, I withdrew my sword and forced myself into the unknown.

"I thought I was going to have to come and find you myself!" Madame de Treville announced as I rushed through the doorway. "Mon Dieu, child, put that sword away. You know you're supposed to keep the point down if you're not fencing. You'll take someone's eye out."

"But I—we thought we heard," I stammered. Théa burst through the door with a roar, knocked into the side table, and sent the familiar porcelain vase flying, lilies making a wide arc before crashing to the ground. Splinters of ceramic and decapitated blossoms littered the floor.

Madame de Treville grabbed us by our elbows, pulled us toward the library. "Théa, cease your antics before you break everything in the hallway."

"Does that mean no one's attacking us?" Théa asked breathlessly.

"What gave you that idea?"

"The crash," I said. "We thought there might be a duel, or—"

"Henri bumped into a bookshelf and somehow managed to knock three of them over. He reverted to dramatics, what with the shouting and carrying on, but I suppose it's understandable, given the excitement."

"Excitement?" I asked.

We arrived at the library. Bookshelves gutted on their sides. Henri looked like he'd been run over by a carriage. Ink smeared across his forehead, his chin, his hands; even a few curls were doused navy blue black. He waved to us with hands full of papers. Which, of course, sent them flying every which way.

Madame de Treville sniffed with displeasure at Henri as he scrambled to grab the papers, before she turned to us. "Henri believes he's cracked the code."

CHAPTER TWENTY-NINE

"YOU WHAT?" PORTIA asked once we assured her we weren't in immediate danger. Aria's eyes still darted from person to person, as if she didn't trust what she saw and heard.

"Tell us," Madame de Treville said to her nephew, who was scurrying around the room, trying to get a handle on the stray papers. "It's not as if it's the midnight before a likely assassination attempt."

The crown dipped in blood. Papa's bloody face.

My chest constricted. Had we found the answer?

Henri grabbed the last paper from the carpet, straightened, and tried to rearrange the pages into a semblance of a stack. "My first step was reviewing the academic source texts Théa got from the university library—they're brilliant! You were all searching for a direct link between the lyrics on the fan and other sources, so I thought the most helpful thing for me to do would be to focus on the proverb's history: who first said it, that sort of thing. While I didn't find who the proverb is attributed to, I did discover a compilation of famous proverbs. I saw his name in it—Bacon. And that's when I remembered." Henri reached for one of the books on the table, lifted it reverently. With a start, I realized I'd seen the book before—the day Henri had given me the map of Lupiac. One of the philosophy texts he used to practice English. *Of the Proficience and Advancement of Learning, Divine and Human*, by Francis Bacon.

"Are we supposed to be looking at something?" Portia said.

Henri was confused. "Don't you see?" he said. "The lullaby! Pigs. Bacon. The line about the pigs is a tip-off to use Bacon's Cipher. Now, the book is dense. I hardly understood most of it at the time. But I did remember the discussion of ciphers . . ."

"Why?" Aria cut in sharply. "What makes ciphers so interesting? What use do you have for them?"

Henri blinked. "The theory of puzzles is fascinating?"

"Henri," Madame de Treville cautioned, "please continue with your initial train of thought."

"Right. So once I made the connection, I went back to my own book and found the page I remembered. And then I read it what felt like a hundred times, until I got a firm grasp on the concept."

"Bacon's Cipher . . . is it complicated?" I asked, moving to look over his expanse of shoulder. I felt him tense beside me. A lump rose in my throat.

Henri cleared off the table, pushing aside stray books and parchment before fanning out the papers in one large arc. We crowded together, skirts fighting for space. "With a Bacon Cipher, each letter of the alphabet is represented by a five-character sequence comprised of 0s and 1s—in the case of the inventory slip, 0s are capital letters, and 1s are lowercase letters. So *T*, for instance," he said. "*T* is any five-letter sequence that can be translated as 10011. Bacon created a whole list of sequences that map onto the alphabet."

"So that's why the Comtesse gave those fans away?" I said, my words sounding like a question, but the threads were weaving together as I spoke. I sat in one of the chairs surrounding the table.

"Right." Henri flipped the page over, growing more animated as he explained the process. "Since the information was hidden in an inventory slip, and not formatted in full sentences, the 0s and 1s are harder to distinguish between. And even if someone were to note all the capitalized letters that seemed out of place, the resulting text would be gibberish."

"They were for the nobles in on the plot," I breathed out. "Everyone who received smuggled goods could've received that inventory slip; there were a handful in that one box alone. But the nobles at the top of the scheme probably wanted to be selective as far as who could decode the message on the slip, so they didn't let anyone know which cipher to use until the Comtesse's gathering. The lullaby on the fans. It was a signal!" A horrible thing to be happy about—and yet I was beaming at the realization that my brain could pull it all together.

"That means I was right, you know," Théa said. "About the pigs being literal."

Portia rolled her eyes. Next to her, Aria was grasping and releasing the hilt of her saber. Her shoulders taut. "You're lying."

Henri startled, dropped a piece of charcoal, which Madame de Treville caught before it tumbled to mark the carpet. "What?" he asked.

"Aria, he figured out the cipher," Théa tried to say.

But Aria wasn't finished. A sharp glare to match her knife of a tongue. "That's what he wants us to think. We'll fritter away our remaining time using the wrong cipher. We'll be left with no message. No information. Not enough hours before the Winter Festival to do anything other than wait for the King to breathe his last breath."

"Aria, what on earth are you talking about?" Madame de Treville said.

Aria hesitated. And then she looked to me. She needed me. If Madame de Treville knew we hadn't told her about the thief, if Madame de Treville knew it was Aria who insisted on keeping it all a secret because she suspected her . . . she would be the one in our mentor's office, waiting to hear if she had a future with the Order. My sister in arms.

"Aria and I were speaking earlier today about the possibility of an internal leak. You mentioned missing papers, Madame." I neglected any mention of the thief.

Aria mouthed "Thank you" to me.

Madame de Treville gaped at us. "Oh, mon Dieu. And you two thought it was Henri?"

A gasp—as if someone had been punched in the stomach. I looked up to see Henri's gaze locked on mine, brows broken, paper slipping from his hands.

Madame de Treville's brows furrowed. "Aria, we don't—"

"Non, Tante." I hardly believed it. But there was Henri. Standing tall, shoulders straight, golden-brown eyes latched onto Aria. His fingers were still trembling, though. "I know I can't fence and I'm not a Musketeer like the rest of you . . . but I have my own strengths. I want to help—the last thing I'd want is to harm any of you. Or to anger my aunt," he added, with a fearful glance toward Madame de Treville. "I think helping organize a power grab would be grounds for my expulsion from the house. And then Aunt would write to my mother."

"You're damn right I would," Madame de Treville muttered.

"We know that, Henri," Théa said, glaring at Aria and elbowing Portia in her side. "Don't we, Portia? He wants to help, not hurt. We know that, *right*?"

Portia startled. "Oh, for the love of—that's not fair!" Théa tapped her foot. "Fine," Portia grumbled. "Perhaps I've been a little hard on you, Henri."

"Portia," Théa said, frowning.

"So help me that is as much as I am going to give you! Ask Tania if you want maudlin declarations."

I swallowed, my eyes not leaving Henri's. "We believe you. I believe you."

Henri looked at me, and the room went very warm. Madame de Treville stepped forward, as if to touch his cheek. But she never raised her hand. Just cleared her throat. "Henri, are you sure about this? Are you absolutely sure?"

He nodded. "I can go through my entire research process, step-by-step! It all started over two thousand years ago in Sparta; they developed these wonderful instruments called scytales—"

"Might I remind everyone that while we stand here arguing, power-hungry nobles are plotting the demise of the country?" Portia announced. "With the way Théa has us blathering on, we'll be finished decoding the message at the King's funeral."

All the flush leached from Henri's face. "That won't be necessary! I've already started decoding, see? You have to verify the pattern with the original document—but I've made progress!"

I leaned forward to examine the paper. *M.*

"That's it?" Madame de Treville asked in horror. "That's all? One measly letter?" She collapsed into a chair. "Théa, ready the tea. It's going to be a long night."

Half-drained teacups littered all surfaces of the library. The dark was on the brink of shifting the sky, a crack in the night, a brief morning haze creeping at the horizon. Papa loved this time. I'd hear him through the walls, huffing about, pulling on his shoes for his early trek to the barn to groom Beau and then practice footwork he knew I couldn't do. That way I wouldn't have to sit and watch him perform actions I was too dizzy to try. Or at least, that's what I'd thought then. I might never be able to perform a flunge. But now . . . now I could do so much more.

I reached blearily for another sheet of paper, hand bumping into a saucer. Théa snored until Portia flicked her ear. She cackled when Théa woke with murder in her face.

Henri had offered to procure more of that dark drink he'd brought us over a month ago, but Madame de Treville insisted he stay. A good thing, too, and not only because the prospect of Théa bouncing off the walls might be more terrifying than facing down a hundred armed nobles—the hours wheedled by and still all of us worked, candlelight throwing shadows onto the walls, the fire ebbing till one of us rose to stoke the embers.

We each had a copy of the message and our own assigned section. Maybe if we were well versed in code breaking, we'd be finished already. But we were forced to spend time rechecking for missed letters, meaningless words.

I held up what we'd managed so far to my tired eyes. I'd slept for a few hours, knowing how important it was that I wasn't falling asleep as well as dizzy during the festival, but my sleep was restless. Dreams of Papa kept me near the surface.

Messieurs,

Rendez-vous du quartier général. Demandez au patron.

Instructing others to meet at "headquarters" wasn't actionable material. And it wasn't clear if patron meant "boss" or "man of the house." Context would be key. If we ever acquired any.

There was no time to be caught up in frustration. And yet, every moment brought the looming knowledge that perhaps by this time tomorrow, I would know the identity of my father's killer. The anger, the fury, all of it fueling me . . . and I'd finally be forced to reckon with it.

"Zut alors!" Henri cried. Ink flooded over a fresh ream of paper, knocked over by his elbow. Madame de Treville and Aria rushed for towels. Henri strained, beet red. "Please excuse my unconscionable language—"

"I think," said Portia, "we've reached the point where you can curse in front of us without fear of damaging our fragile female sensibilities."

"Now, then," Madame de Treville said, once everything was cleaned and we were seated again. "Théa, what do you have?"

I tried to catch Henri's eye, but he was lost in his notes. When he finally looked up, he saw me staring at him and a hint of a smile passed across his face. Relief washed through me. After those months of mistrust and worry, after his declaration and the way he looked at me when I said I believed him, the air between us felt different, somehow. Closer to when we first met, but slightly altered, like one changed note in a piece of music.

"I'm not sure it makes sense," Théa said. "*Vous trouverez notre camara de régimend?*"

"Here, let me see." Portia took the paper, scanned it, gaze stuttering every so often over an underlined letter, an errant comma. She started scratching at the paper with a piece of charcoal.

"Wait! What are you—"

"You missed a few letters. It's not *camara*, it's *camarades*." With a final flourish, Portia straightened. "*Vous trouverez nos camarades de régiment.*"

"How did you do that so quickly?" Théa asked in awe as she went back through her notes.

"I didn't. You missed some letters, so I considered the possible words that could be completed, and selected the only ones that made sense. *You will find your fellow servicemen.*"

"You're brilliant, you know that?" Portia flushed at Aria's murmured compliment.

I looked to the window, to the sky glowing with painted purple cinders, the orange rising sun. In the palace, the King was still asleep. A wave of anger crested, pulsed. If only he had canceled the festival. If only he were more King than boy.

"*I'll be there to meet you.*"

We hushed at Henri's words. "What was that?" I said.

He fumbled with his papers. "That's the next line, the one I just finished. *Je serai là pour vous rencontrer.* But who is *I*?"

"It's probably at the end of the message," Aria said. "A way for the reader to be sure it's from a verified source. Since there's a cipher, they wouldn't expect anyone other than their intended recipients to be able to decode the name."

"Well, whoever *je* is, they must be the leader, non?" Théa piped up. "No one else would have the authority to make such plans." She yawned, extended her arms wide, fingers outstretched.

I turned to Henri, anticipation in my throat. "Is there much left? To the message?"

"I don't think so." He squinted at the harsh light, blinked. "Oh, morning already?"

Madame de Treville glanced to the window, her face flooded in light. "Quick, change into the gowns I brought down to the parlor. And although I sincerely hope this reminder isn't necessary, try not to forget your swords."

"But, Madame—" Théa started.

"The King won't make an appearance at the procession, but it's chaotic and packed and the perfect place to distribute weapons to other nobles without spectators taking note."

In the haze of tea and codes, there was no time to admire the extravagant festival gowns, the jewels, the matching slippers. We all helped one another: Portia drew up my hair while I sorted through gemstones that Théa then dropped from our earlobes. Aria found the correct shoes and placed them at our feet.

"Venez, Mesdemoiselles!" Madame de Treville's voice echoed down the hall, under the door. "Venez! Come! You need time to scout the perimeter before the noon rush." Aria burst through, me at her heels, Portia and Théa not far behind. Madame de Treville fastened the clasp of her silvery cloak, pulled on her gloves with a snap of leather. "We'll finish on the way. Henri, get your things."

Through the open library door, Henri's expression grew wide, hopeful, his arms full of papers. "I'm . . . I'm coming with you?"

"You want to be part of the Order? Don't slow us down," she retorted, yanking open the front door and exposing us to a wintery blast of air. "Another set of eyes won't hurt."

There was a moment's pause, and then everything was a flurry of gowns and dueling swords and whispered prayers. Someone gripped my hand, fingers lacing through mine like the ribbons of a corset, tight. I squeezed back without knowing who, because it didn't matter. We were together; we were one. And soon, I would finally know the truth.

I winced at every bump, every pause of the horses.

Le Marais was home to la noblesse, many of whom wouldn't attend an event as common as a street procession. But a few servants were out and about, off work for the day, ribbons in their hair and a bounce in their step. Once we left the neighborhood, made our way to the heart of the celebration, the roads bristled with festival goers. Cramped market stalls housed vendors selling winter fruits and ladling steaming thick brown liquid—chocolat chaud—to customers bundled in cloaks. And then, the screaming children looping around carriage wheels, adorned with faux tinsel crafted from loose thread and masks that resembled animals and mythical beasts. Some painted wood, others sculpted from feathers. Mothers and fathers looked on, or didn't look on, cupping flagons of mulled wine, laughs frosty in the air. In the darkened corners, a few eyes peeked out, a few smudged hands. Hungry children. Hopeful children.

These were the people we needed to protect. These were the people who would suffer if nobles used bloodshed to replace one King's rule with another.

"These other conspirators. The ones who weren't already in Paris for the season . . . if they're all staying in one place, how are they managing to keep a low profile?" Aria asked.

"The message on the King's mirror did mention the solstice. Theoretically, everyone could show up on different days as long as they arrived before that deadline. They could easily pass themselves off as visitors to the city, or merchants here to examine goods. Or participants in the festival," Portia added.

"Henri, how much longer?" Madame de Treville gritted out.

"We're getting close. We'll run into the procession."

He reached for his bag, presumably for another piece of charcoal, his hands stained black gray, but it was out of reach. Portia grabbed it, riffled through the contents.

She retrieved a charcoal, and with it, a small unbound stack of papers. "What's this?"

"My personal sketches—wait!" Henri cried out as Portia flipped through them eagerly.

"Tania, here's one of you! How sweet—look, you're in the gown from your first ball! Didn't I tell you it was divine?"

For all the times I'd seen him blush, I'd never seen Henri so embarrassed as he was at this very moment. It was just a sketch—like the sunset on the Seine, like the doves in flight. And I wanted to look at the paper Portia was gesturing to. I wanted to know how Henri saw me. But I couldn't tear my eyes away from his flushed face.

Madame de Treville took the papers right from Portia's fingers. "Focus! The cipher is what's important, not Henri's artistic abilities." She nodded to Henri, who returned to the code, scratching away, the tips of his ears pink and surrounded by curls.

"We're almost there," I warned from my spot at the window.

Madame de Treville rapped on the ceiling; we'd make the rest of our way by foot. Portia grabbed my arm to prevent me from falling into the street headfirst through the window opening as the driver screeched to a halt. First out of the carriage, her nose wrinkled as she avoided an unidentifiable pile of sludge. Aria was next, then Théa. They were waiting for me, but I couldn't move. I was rooted to the seat by Papa's voice.

Tania. Tania. Tania.

Back to that night. Back to the windows like eyes, Papa's voice, following, the sound of the fence and my heart crunching underfoot.

"Tania." A hand on my shoulder. Madame de Treville glanced from me, to Henri marking up the page with charcoal, and back to me again. "Whatever happens, this won't be the end. We'll find out whoever killed—"

"I have it," Henri announced.

I reached out to him, hands shaking. Held the paper close to my face.

Two lines. The first, a parting. Sincèrement. As if it were only a letter. As if I were writing to Maman.

And there was the second. A name.

Verdon.

CHAPTER THIRTY

"IT'S HIM." I thrust the paper at Madame de Treville. "It has to be. The man who killed my father."

Tania. Tania. Tania.

The truth of it hummed in my bones. I'd already known, hadn't I? But the name on the paper, that was real. The confirmation the Order had needed all along: Verdon was the mastermind behind the plot. And now, now we could arrest him. Save the King. And . . . and I would finally learn the truth. Would finally know if he was responsible for taking Papa from me. Now that the moment was so close, the anger I thought I'd tamped down flared in my chest; it had morphed into something disciplined and wieldable like a sword. Verdon. Verdon had killed Papa. It was his fault Papa was gone.

Madame de Treville's eyes darted to the paper, to my face, to the trio standing outside the carriage. "We'll have Musketeers sent to Verdon's Paris residence, as well as the residences of the Comte de Monluc, the Gramonts, everyone implicated. All at once, so they can't let the others know what's coming. I'll try to get hold of Brandon in time for him and his men to make the arrests before the festival gets too far underway. The streets will be packed."

"And if Verdon senior isn't there? What if he decided at the last minute to go home, to be with his wife and son?" Portia questioned. I'd wondered this, too . . . but my mind was full of Papa. Of Maman's broken face. Of Monsieur Allard and the maréchaussée, how they'd looked at me like I was a little girl, just some little girl with anger that didn't belong in such a breakable body.

"As I've told you before, he'll be skulking about the city, lying in wait to take full advantage of the chaos. But I'll have Mazarin send the Musketeers' two fastest riders in that direction. I'll make sure they're heavily armed, too. And stay safe," she reminded us. "I don't know if they have any other tricks planned." She made to close the carriage door but stopped when I latched onto her arm. I needed to go with her. I needed to be the one to deliver Verdon's fate. See the look in his eyes as he recognized the echoes of my father's face in mine. And yet, that didn't feel like enough. He hadn't spared Papa's life. I imagined Verdon, how he must've stood over Papa as he bled into the unforgiving night. I wanted . . . no. It didn't matter what I wanted. I was a Musketeer. Not some executioner. And I was needed here. I stepped back. Stepped back into the line of my sisters in arms, who radiated heat, strength.

For the first time since learning of the kiss, Madame de Treville smiled at me. Or, at least, her version of a smile. "Your father would be proud."

"Cheer up, Tania. Try some of, well, whatever this is." Portia thrust a sticky, bun-shaped pastry at me. "For someone who saved France, you sure are frowning a lot."

"We didn't save France. We stopped the King from being assassinated," Aria said. "Technically, we haven't even done that. Not yet, at least."

We staked out the perimeter of the festival center once Madame de Treville and Henri left. We listened as traveling performers sang of the glory of France. Watched the throngs of people cluster, disperse, cluster again. Children accompanied by their parents begged for livres to buy sweets.

"That very well may be, but if you think I'm going to say that in front of Mazarin or, truly, anyone affiliated with the King, you're mistaken. We have to be better than them for even a chance at being considered true Musketeers. And if I don't start practicing now, who knows what I'll blurt out when we meet him? Probably something about how he should be prostrating himself before us." Portia grunted as yet another person jostled into her. "Maybe you have the right idea, Tania. It's starting to get miserable here."

Aria, the tallest of us, searched for a spot of refuge, but even she had to stand on tiptoe. "The entire bank is packed," she sighed as she settled down on her feet.

My stomach churned. I returned the half-eaten sticky bun to Portia, who grimaced. "Come, now," she said. "It's over. At this very moment Musketeers are swarming Verdon's residence and taking him out in chains! The only downside is we're not there to jeer and throw rotten vegetables."

I swallowed. When would Étienne hear the news? Would he

be at his mother's bedside when he received word his father was arrested? Could his mother handle such a shock?

My foot caught on a stone. Red liquid oozed around my feet. I made to scream, but Portia clapped a hand over my mouth. "A crushed tomato. Breathe, Tania."

She attempted to press through, to get us to the edge of the Seine, but the crush of people pushed us sideways. I almost fell into Théa, who leaned back, kept me standing, and I regained my balance. Tightened my toes, my calves.

Music drifted over our heads: the procession. The echo of drums, lutes, string instruments overtook the din. In the next moment, an opening forged itself, people struggling aside, escaping the parade path. Acrobats leaped and somersaulted over the icy cobblestone, bells tied to their wrists. Masked actors teased the crowd. I flinched away from a wooden, leering face. The frost bit at my cheeks so I pulled my hood up, the sight of the embroidery softening my heartbeat. I was a Musketeer, in my Musketeer's cassock.

The crowd shifted, and I toppled into the path of the open carriages. Masked figures waved and pointed as I braced my hands against the frozen ground. Another yank, this time at my cloak's hood, and I was pulled back, back to standing, the carriage wheels narrowly missing my fingers.

Gasping for air, I fumbled with the clasp, hands immediately going to my neck, and spun. "Madame de Treville?" I asked. She was gasping, too. Her perfectly coiffed bun skewed, bedraggled. "Madame, where's Henri?"

The crowd overtook us once more. I reached, barely made contact with her gloved fingertips. The wave of people crashed around the performers. Whoops, cheers, everything culminating in one roar. Noise. All there was: noise, noise and my heartbeat.

Suddenly, Portia was there. Aria, too—we huddled together. When the crowd thinned, we pushed forward. Madame de Treville and Théa had managed to find an alleyway, and we hurried toward them.

"What happened?" Aria asked clinically as she surveyed for stray onlookers or eavesdroppers.

"He's not there," Madame de Treville finally gasped out. "Verdon. No one can find him. The only thing I got from a servant is that he went for a drink before a scheduled 'business meeting.' I sent Henri with a sealed message asking for Monsieur Brandon to acquire reinforcements from Mazarin. Then, I notified every Musketeer on my way back to search the city cabarets."

"He's not at a cabaret," I breathed out.

"What?" Madame de Treville said.

"He won't be at a cabaret," I said, words coming quicker, "he'll be at a pub. Étienne mentioned before he left that his father would spend his time in pubs instead of doing business . . . but what if they're one and the same? What if their headquarters isn't somewhere lavish and comfortable?"

"How are we supposed to know which pub he'd choose? There's hardly time to send word for the Musketeers to change locations, and we're not likely to be able to reach them in this." Portia gestured to the crushing people, the slurp of wine, of beer, of sweat sluicing over cobblestones and into the Seine.

Madame de Treville gripped me by the shoulders. "Think, Tania, think!"

But there wasn't any time; there never was. Not enough time

with Papa. Not enough time to avenge him, to prove Maman wrong, to prove the worth of my body. Of myself.

When our mentor twisted, I caught sight of a flash of paper within her cloak. I snatched at it. "This is the original? Of the coded message?"

"Oui, but why does that matter? You all have copies of the text."

I traced the edge. INVENTORY SLIP—DECEMBER SHIPMENT. I went through the list of items again. The descriptions of fabric, the diagrams of each item, labeled and clearly drawn. I skimmed over the drawings, hooked on the rendering of the fabric pattern. Birds, clawed birds. Those weren't on my copy. Only with squinting were the faint lines of eagles discernible. I stared at one, stared hard. My legs were billowing. Dizziness on the cusp. The eagle's wings blurred. "That's it," I murmured.

"What's it?" Madame de Treville reached for the slip.

"An eagle. And Verdon's lion—I saw it on the carriage, the day I met Verdon senior. It's part of his crest. When you put them together . . ."

"A griffin," Aria finished. "The Gryphon. The pub we passed. The fabric pattern was part of the code."

A pause. And then we broke. Kicked away the empty refuse in our path as we raced down the alley. Lungs throbbing with each step; our breaths seared sword sharp.

When we hit the opposite side, the clear street, Madame de Treville halted. "Wait," she wheezed. "I have to tell the nearest King's Guard post to send a group to The Gryphon and have the rest spread along the far edge of La Cour. If traitors escape, their only choice will be to head in that direction—not enough of them to man a large vessel; anything smaller than a merchant's ship won't hold up against the winter waters. Follow them. Occupy them to give me time to reach the post, and the Musketeers time to surround them."

"Shouldn't one of us go with you?" Théa asked through labored breaths.

Madame de Treville shook her head. "I'm not splitting you up again. I learned my lesson. Keep each other safe. We all know our duty to throne and country, but I swear if I learn you took unnecessary risks I'll kill you myself."

"A funny way to say you care for us, but I suppose it'll do," Portia quipped.

Madame de Treville laughed once. Maybe it was a sob. A croaking breath. As we made to leave, she grabbed my upper arm. Just like I had with her, before I'd accepted I wouldn't be the one to apprehend Papa's murderer. Every feature of her face hardened. "No matter what that man says or does, you can't kill him. The King will want him alive for questioning. If Verdon has outside influences, foreign powers helping him—that's not information we can afford to lose. And if there are other splinter groups and assassins to step in if he's discovered, we have to know." I hesitated. The rage reared in my chest again, the anger at this man, this horrible man, for taking Papa from me before he even had the chance to see what I'd become. "Promise me, Tania." I refocused on her worried brow, the lines that streaked sunbeams to her temples.

"I promise, Madame. I promise."

CHAPTER THIRTY-ONE

THE DESERTED ALLEYWAY'S cobblestones were strewn with discarded barrels and excrement. Flies swarmed in lazy clouds, indistinguishable from the dim if it weren't for the incessant buzzing. The sky was obscured with clouds. The prospect of the first snowfall of the year bit bitter at our ankles. The tight breeches under my dress helped with dizziness but didn't provide much warmth.

"Charming," Portia said. "Nothing says la guerre finale quite like the smell of sewers."

The ten minutes it took to reach the rear of The Gryphon was enough time for the frantic edge to wear off, adrenaline replaced with gnawing anxiety, the threat of what was to come. We formed a circle against the cold, salty air. Three familiar faces peered back at me, wavering a bit as I clenched my toes against the dizziness. Théa spoke first. "I can't believe it's finally happening." Her tight curls escaped her cloak's hood. She wrenched the fabric forward; it shifted back.

Portia pulled the ties of her cloak tighter. She attempted a grin, but her lips couldn't seem to stay there. "We have each other, though."

"Un pour tous, tous pour un," I whispered. Just like Papa had told me in bedtime stories, just like I had wished those months ago, in the barn with the hay-smelling sun and the yearning for something greater than myself. I hadn't thought it possible, but I had my band of sisters now. Like he'd had his brothers.

Portia repeated it. She grabbed ahold of my hand, squeezed. "One for all, all for one." We murmured it together, voices crashing, nowhere near in sync.

"We'll have to practice." Théa's shaky laugh evaporated into the prefrost. "I love you all, but that sounded horrendous!"

"I'll hold you to that," Aria said. "I'm holding all of you to that."

"We'll live to see another day. To question the monarchy another day," Portia added with a laugh, fingers linked with Aria's.

"Oh, I've had a wonderful thought: Perhaps we could be independent Musketeers for hire!" Théa exclaimed. "And we could give the funds to Parisians who need them! We'll be like Robin Hood, except without the stealing—although I suppose I stole those books from the library . . . so yes, we'll be just like Robin Hood!"

Aria softened and smiled at her. "We'll have negotiating power. The girls who saved the King."

They talked like there was no chance of defeat. No chance of the four of us becoming three, two, one . . . I didn't want to consider a world without them. But then, I hadn't been able to conceive of a world without Papa, either. And now he was gone. And yet, somehow, he was everywhere. In the way I lunged with my arm just so. In the anticipation coursing through my veins. In the knowledge that people were relying on me and, for maybe the first time, their trust in me didn't feel like a mistake, but a right I'd earned.

I turned to face The Gryphon. The others moved up to meet me. "All of that will have to wait. There's work to be done."

The Gryphon wasn't what one would call a fine establishment. Fitting for the crime of killing a king—less so for the title-obsessed nobles plotting to do so. Even with the lure of power, of titles and wealth, it was difficult to imagine Verdon here. Not with his regal stature. Not with the way he looked down his nose with those ice green eyes, as if my mere presence was enough to warrant incinerating his clothes.

When we entered, the raucous laughter that greeted us fell silent. The wooden floors were sticky with alcohol and spit. Outlines of tankards were stark against the tabletops, like someone engraved the rings with a knife. There weren't many patrons; two or three benches were occupied by men hunched over their drinks—jowls loose, stubbly; wrinkles dangling under their chins. Portia removed her cloak with a flourish, draped it over a hook so rusty it could've been there since the Battle of Châlons, strode up to the bar, and flashed a brilliant smile to the man gathering tankards from a lower shelf. "Bonsoir. Am I correct in assuming you're the owner of this splendid business?"

"Non, Mademoiselle. Puis-je vous aider? Can I help you?" As they spoke, we removed our cloaks, put them wherever we found free space. I forced the clasp open, unwound myself from the warm familiarity, and winced as the blue fabric hit the sticky bench. But it wasn't as difficult as I thought it would be to pry my fingers away. I didn't need the cloak to be strong. I was strong enough on my own.

"As much as I'd appreciate your assistance, it's a matter of a *private* nature. Un sujet délicat. What sort of woman would I be, betraying a client's trust?" Portia gazed up at the man through her dark lashes. Aria started, jaw thrust forward, hand fumbling for her sword—I grabbed her arm.

The man glanced at my stone-faced companion but returned to Portia when she trailed a finger down his sweaty cheek. "He's in the back managing the b-books . . . ," the man sputtered, "but I could ask him to come out front? If that would please you?"

"Would you? I'd be ever so grateful."

We joined her as he retreated down a narrow, bedimmed hall adjacent to the bar. "What do you think you're doing?" Portia said through clenched teeth. "You almost blew our cover."

"The way he looked at you," Aria muttered. "It was—"

"Plenty of men have undressed me with their eyes before, and it wasn't necessary for Tania to keep you from skewering them."

"I don't like it," Aria said shortly. "Just because I know it's going to happen doesn't mean I have to like it. It is disgusting."

Portia's brow quirked. "Take heart, ma crevette. There is no need to be jealous."

Aria scowled. "I am not jealous. And I'm the tallest one here!"

"Tush, it's a common enough pet name. My little shrimp. My little shrimp with gray eyes and pink cheeks."

I peered into the hallway. There were stairs off to the right, easy to miss in the shadows. "Should we wait?"

"There have to be at least six or seven rooms. It would take too long to check them all. By then someone would hear us," Aria said, still glaring at Portia.

The barkeep returned with a beaming man, and we withdrew.

"Mesdemoiselles! What an unexpected pleasure. Beautiful ladies such as yourselves rarely grace my business."

"We were sent for from Madame Roubille's house. By a Monsieur V?" Portia lowered her voice. She must have chosen a real brothel given their looks of recognition. "The messenger requested four of the finest mesdemoiselles our house has to offer. Something about a larger party of gentlemen? A way to pass the time and decompress before a meeting?"

The owner's discerning gaze swept over us. "He didn't mention sending for des femmes de mauvaise vie."

I pushed forward as Portia hesitated under the flickering candlelight. "He mustn't have wanted to share—that's not fair, if you ask me. If we hurry now, though, I'll be sure to reserve some time for you after we're finished upstairs," I said. For added emphasis, I placed my hand, featherlight, on his chest. His ribs constricted under my touch.

"Well, then," he said, throatier this time, "I wouldn't dream of keeping Monsieur V waiting. Follow me."

As the barkeep trundled away, I retracted my hand from the man's sternum, lips curled into melted sugar, and trailed him. Only pausing when Portia squeezed my shoulder, sniffling. "That was beautiful. I don't think I've ever been so proud."

At the base of the staircase, I froze. The stairs extended, a mountain. Portia edged around me and took my spot behind the owner. In the next moment, I was airborne. Aria's face strained as she trailed after Portia, me in her arms.

"The ceiling and stairs are too narrow for him to see anything behind him but Portia," Aria said.

"But how will you—"

"I'm fairly strong. If you haven't noticed," she grimaced as we hit the halfway point, Portia keeping up a steady chatter to cover our voices.

On the landing, Portia used every inch of her frame to block our movements. Aria set me down as discreetly as possible on the next-to-last step while Théa spotted me from behind. "I should contain my praise, but oh, I can't help myself: You have one of the finest taverns in all of Paris," Portia cooed, waiting until I crested the stairs to move aside.

"I'll send up more wine straightaway." He fumbled with a key ring fixed to his belt. "I'm the only one with access. They'll know it's me," he announced proudly. He chanced on the correct key and slid it into the lock.

The click of tumblers paused as Théa, who'd draped herself in the far wall's shadows, brought the guard of her sword down over the man's head. "Sorry!" she squeaked to her victim as it connected with the back of his head. "I had no choice!" He crumpled, and she jumped back as his skull thudded against the dusty planks. "What?" she whispered indignantly at Portia's heaven-ward glance. "It's not like he tried to kill us! He could be completely innocent, minding his own business and making a living, not knowing he's renting out a room to a murderer!"

"For all we know he's as much a part of this as the men behind that door," Portia muttered. I helped her grab the passed-out man by the ankles and drag him into a darkened corner.

"Hurry," Aria said. "We don't have all night."

I wiped my hands on my dress and joined the others near the door. Théa's hand trembled. She took a breath. Turned the key.

"François, is that you? We need more wine!" someone sang out.

"Quiet," another voice reproached. "We're not here to drink."

Portia strode into the room, and we accompanied her: slow, quiet, smiling shyly at anyone who locked eyes with us.

A man stood quickly, chair scraping against the floor; he knocked one of the dirty plates off the table. The rest of the room's occupants were bundled in a cramped seating area. "Now . . . *who* exactly are *you*?"

"Compliments of The Gyphon for your patronage. We are the very finest Madame Roubille's has to offer, Monsieur . . . ?"

He visibly relaxed, and by the time Portia finished speaking, he regarded her like a child with their nose pressed up against a pâtisserie window. "You, mon chou, may call me Guillaume."

Two men were fully visible near the fireplace. One arranged papers across the well-worn carpet. As soon as he felt my gaze, he scrambled, returned the sheets to a leather-bound folder. All I could see of the men in the large armchairs were their dark hats and the slope of their shoulders.

"Relax, Antoine," he told the man with the folder. "C'est seulement des putes." Guillaume mistook the shine in Portia's eyes as lust. He could not see the spark for what it was: brilliant, incandescent rage. But I knew her expressions like my own now. And, more importantly, I knew that any man who said *pute* in her presence wasn't long for this world. "How many ladies are we hosting this fair evening?"

Portia's eyes crackled over him. "Three others. The last is a bit shy." Théa stepped forward, hands clasped behind her back, readying to tuck up her skirts. "Be a dear and close the door, won't you? These handsome gentlemen surely won't wish to be disturbed."

Three of the men from the opposite side of the room, Antoine included, approached eagerly. But I watched the one who remained in his chair, did my best to search for the green eyes that had haunted my nightmares since that day at the university.

"Verdon, aren't you coming?" Guillaume asked.

There was no time for an answer. One of the men lunged at Portia. Grabbed a handful of her skirts, of her stockinged thigh.

"Remove your hands before I remove them for you." Aria's expression matched the steel she held to the man's throat. And then. And then the screech of metal. And then the rip and crush of fabric folded and pulled aside and tucked away.

Our adversaries hurried to arm themselves. Knocking over stools, they scrambled for their swords in a state of half shock, half fury. Aria slashed a rent in her opponent's vest, not deep enough to do any significant damage, but the man still crashed into the table and sent a tankard flying, wine dregs splattering across Guillaume's face.

One man hands shook. I vaguely recognized him from a party—some lord or another; I'd only seen him in passing. He stared at Théa like she was a creature from the darkest depths of his nightmares. Théa's entire body tensed, and I thought for a moment she'd frozen like that day in the maze. But the next second she unleashed a guttural cry, raining a series of attacks down on him, each one more vicious than the next.

A flurry of color shot from the armchair. Hands unlatching window shutters, then lifting their owner's body out and over the sill. I caught a flash of dark hair, of green. With a cry, I wrenched through the duelists to where he'd disappeared. Verdon.

Behind me, les Mousquetaires de la Lune whirled like children's tops. The room was ablaze with their clashing swords, with their colorful skirts mixing together and wrenching apart. Portia and Aria fought back-to-back, their blades never ceasing, Portia even laughing as she knocked an opponent's sword clean out of his hand.

"You can't let him get away!" Théa shrieked at my hesitation. She sidestepped to parry an attack that would've cut her clean through.

"But you're outnumbered!" I returned, kicking aside an injured man, groaning, who tried to pull himself up from the floor with a nearby chair for leverage.

Portia hissed loud enough to hear even over the crash of metal. Blood stained her sleeve, dripping onto her bare hand, but as I started toward her, she let out a pained shout. "Je jure si tu n'y vas pas, je te botterai le cul!"

Portia didn't make idle threats. If she swore that if I didn't go, she'd kick my . . . well . . . I cursed. Pulled myself through the open window, curled my fingers around the sill, and counted one, two . . .

Fencing taught me how to fall. And oh, how I had ample time to practice what to do when my feet would no longer hold me. When my body fell prey to the pull of the earth.

It was over quickly. Teeth rattling in my skull. Flames singeing my feet. My bones groaned beneath my skin. The dizziness crashed over me as I waited for my world to steady itself.

There. A flash of coattails flapped behind the adjacent building, dissolving into air thick as ice. I sprinted after his blurry figure, barely registering the cold that had become part of my blood and bones.

The others would be fine. They would hold the conspirators off until the Musketeers arrived. But it would all be for nothing if I didn't reach Verdon. Didn't stall him until he was surrounded. And I wanted to see the look in his eyes when I told him who I was. Wanted to see the fear as I held my blade poised at his throat.

We flew down one street, then the next. I crashed into a wall as dizziness stained my vision, staggering before I continued down a shadowed alleyway, refuse from the nearby boulangerie littering the dark cobblestone. The alley was whispering my name—no—crooning. *Tania. Tania. Tania.*

La Cour des Miracles.

Precariously tilted buildings, rotting rafters, rags stoppering up empty door frames and holes in the walls, they all shook around me. My dizziness leveled them all.

I ran under a crumbling archway, leaped over a dangerous patch of ice, narrowly missing a girl my age. I gasped out an apology. One of her hands was pressed against a wall—was she using it for balance?

Aria had said that she thought there might be people like me, girls like me, here. Aria, the girl from La Cour; me, the sick girl . . . neither of us would've been accepted if it weren't for our fathers. How strange, that the way we could help people like us was pretending not to be like them at all. To dress in gowns, to act like nobles, in order to create something better for all of us.

I shook my head to clear it and pushed onward.

Stars burst gold and onyx at the edges of my vision by the time I purposely looped far to his right, once we reached the edge of

La Cour. Just like I'd planned, he darted left, to the bridge over the Seine. He thought he'd bested me. But what he didn't know was, under Madame de Treville's instructions, there'd be Musketeers waiting on the other side. Hidden away in the shadowed square.

He stopped short on the bridge. Merde. He'd probably realized that running on the streets of Paris, without the protection of La Cour or the docks, he'd surely be spotted. I reached for any last vestiges of energy. Willed my body into steel.

By the time he searched his surroundings, ready to double back and find other means of escape, I'd closed the distance to a few yards. With fire running through my veins, I reached for my sword, muddled through the gray waves. My fingers found the grip. Triumphantly, I unsheathed my sword, drew it on the man who plotted to kill the King. The man who killed my father.

"Monsieur Verdon, you are a traitor to your country. Not only have you conspired against your King for your own self-interest, but you have taken lives freely and without restraint."

He froze. He was a bit shorter than I remembered from that day at the university, the outline of his body stark against the bridge.

"My name is Tania de Batz. You killed my father. Prepare yourself, sir. I will not ambush a man with his back turned. I have honor . . . unlike *you*."

He finally turned, arms outstretched as he sank into a bow. He straightened with a good-natured smile.

"Oh, Tania. Always with the formality. I thought we agreed you'd call me Étienne?"

CHAPTER THIRTY-TWO

WHAT A CRUEL trick for my dizziness to play on me. Yet again making me see and hear things not truly of this world.

But when he approached, that fantasy came crashing down. A stroke of lightning followed by a thunderclap. Étienne, with the same smile he always wore, with his hazel eyes that melted even the coldest air. Hadn't I seen green flashing through the window at The Gryphon . . . or was that only what I'd wanted to see? With a groan, I noticed Étienne's hat, threaded with a green ribbon. No.

My lips cracked against the frost as I pried them apart. "But . . . I don't understand. Where's your father? Why aren't you with your mother—shouldn't someone be with her? She shouldn't be alone, not when she's so sick."

"Tania," he said. I'd done my best to forget how he said my name like a caress. Like he'd been saying it for years and years. He glanced at my weapon. "Why don't you put that away before someone gets hurt."

"I don't understand," I repeated. "I don't understand. Why are you here? Don't come any closer," I added when he attempted to shorten the distance between us. My sword was steady.

"We both know you won't use it." Another step. His voice was soft, placating. Like when he'd coaxed me to dance with him. The night he took me in his arms. The night when I learned the sound of another's heartbeat could be as musical as the strains of a minuet.

I shook my head. "You're always so sure of yourself, aren't you?"

"You couldn't manage to fight me last time. Why should today be any different?"

Confused, I watched his words spiral and swirl, smoke signals in the frosty air. And then that night came back to me. The darkness, the dizziness. "The masked thief . . . it was *you*? But I thought—"

"It was Henri?" The curve of his lips was horribly familiar. "All you needed was a little push. Me calling you Mademoiselle la Mousquetaire when you were sure only you and your friends knew about that name was enough to plant the seed. I'd overheard your friend use it—the blond one with the sour expression—outside the Marquis's party. And then, the wig: the finishing touch. I'd seen Henri hours before I collected you for the theater, when I was examining the house for possible entrance points. None of you even considered that I sneaked in right after you returned from the theater, before the doors were locked for the night. All I had to do was wait for everyone to fall asleep. I knew it wouldn't be too difficult to frame Henri, especially not after what you told me at the theater. Only one or two curls needed to slip from under my hat to convince you of his guilt. For a while, I was worried your friend was catching on, but she completely took the bait."

I swallowed hard. "That's awful," I said, fighting the urge to grip my waist at the memory of Henri's betrayed expression.

"Is it? You believed it, didn't you?"

I vehemently shook my head, even as thoughts pressed at the back of my mind. "Of course not."

He continued on like I hadn't spoken. "The masked intruder kept you preoccupied chasing after dead ends. I'd hoped you'd tell the others what you'd seen, but, well, I'd come for the letters, first. Not for creating discord. That was a helpful, if unintended side effect. I was skeptical about *oleum dulce vitrioli*, but the alchemist was right: no real harm but with all the intended effect.

"In truth, I thought your father's letters contained intelligence he obtained while undercover. I never would've risked it otherwise. But I suppose it wasn't all for naught." His face softened, and for a moment he looked like the man I thought I knew. "While I enjoyed reading about your childhood, the sections that detailed how to help you through your dizziness were quite instructive. I'd already intuited much of what I needed to do, through our conversations and overhearing what you told your friends, but it was nice to have my efforts confirmed."

Sweet oil of vitriol . . . where had I heard that name before? And then it hit me—Madame de Treville's encyclopedias—a substance people breathed in, even swallowed, that made them dizzy or lose consciousness, all in the name of health. Portia had taken the book from me, had tried to keep me from reading more entries that hurt my heart. But she hadn't taken it away quickly enough.

He'd known the entire time about the Order. He'd known

about my dizziness. A kind man. An open-minded man—that was what I'd thought. In reality, a man who had weaponized my dizziness against me.

He took that moment of silence to reach for me. As if he were going to fold me into his arms like some delicate little bird with brittle, brittle bones. "Oh, Tania. I had no choice but to make you doubt yourself. You were so wrapped up in uncovering the truth that you didn't see what was right in front of you."

"And I suppose that was you, was it?" I retorted.

He surged forward, gripping my free hand before I could pull away. I kept my fingers wrapped tight around my sword. Could I bring myself to use it? Madame de Treville's warnings not to kill him echoed in my ears. But Étienne's frantic hazel eyes dragged me back. "Yes, *me*. One of the future saviors of France. The man in love with you."

Stomach clenched, body blistering, I wrenched my hand away. Once, I thought I'd never hear someone say those words, not after they knew the truth of my body. But now all I wanted was for him to take them back. "You don't even know what love means."

"But I do. It's the way I feel when you enter a room—everything narrows and my point of focus is you and only you. It's the way you look when I say something surprising, how your lips part, that crinkle of skin between your brows if you don't agree. It's the way you go through your life, unaware of how truly brilliant you are." He grabbed the hand I'd pulled away, placed it flat against his chest. "See, Tania? I can't be a heartless beast if my heart races every time I see you."

My hand burned on his sternum. He grinned down at me like he'd won something. Like he'd won me. "Tania, you don't have to pretend anymore. You love me, and that's what matters."

"I never said I cared about you." I yanked my hand from his chest, lowered my sword to clutch at the low stone wall. My world swayed. "The balcony," I whispered in horror.

"You really thought I left right away? I waited behind one of the columns. And"—he grinned—"even if I hadn't, your answer now is enough. You don't deny you care about me—you only say you never *told* me."

My fingers tightened on the stone. The water and ice cracked below, blue and black and draped in crystal shadows.

I cared for him once. But this wasn't love.

Love didn't make me feel guilty for knowing my duty. Didn't manipulate my emotions. Didn't wait to kiss me until I had no choice but to kiss back.

"You can't love me," I settled for, pleasure rushing through me as his confident veneer fractured. "You knew who I was the whole time, were getting close to me to help yourself." His lips drew together as I spoke.

"The monarchy needs fresh blood," he said. "Whoever is chosen to wear the crown will be a symbol of hope; no one needs to know he'll be a mere figurehead. We're giving the people what they want: someone powerful enough to protect them and the ability to start afresh. You know what it's like, Tania, to feel like you'll never be good enough for your family. My father was devastated after La Fronde. Loyalty to the King got him and my family absolutely nothing. But look at us now—we've proved them wrong. We've written our own destinies. The new King will give me whatever honorific I wish. I'll never be looked down upon again, and I'll have a title I earned, not from sitting around at balls and drinking wine, but by fighting for it."

"Do you even hear yourself? Replacing corruption with more

corruption doesn't help France. Monarchies don't replace monarchies without a price. How many innocents have to die for your ambition?"

"All death is unfortunate . . . but in this case it's for the greater good. Are the lives of beggars and bastards really such a high price to pay?" I willed down bile. There was truth in what Aria told me the night of my very first ball—protecting the King and protecting our country were two separate things. But Étienne didn't want a revolution for the people. Étienne wanted a revolution for himself.

"And"—he cleared his throat—"as for the first matter. My love for you." The icy Seine creaked below us. Tear-stained lashes from my unshed tears freezing to icicles. "Falling for you wasn't the plan, but that hardly means my feelings aren't real—need I remind you, you fell for me under a similar level of convoluted intrigue."

"It's not the same! My intentions weren't only about my own self-interest. I was fulfilling my father's legacy, and—" My breath hitched, words trapped. Next, I should've listed, "protecting my country." But those words were hollow. Because deep down, my duty was to the Mousquetaires de la Lune, Madame de Treville, Henri: my family.

"You don't need to explain yourself," Étienne said, velvet voiced. "It's one of the things I love most about you, your strong sense of what you believe is right. Even if you can't see the other possibilities. My possibilities.

"I owe your father a debt: Without his insistence on you joining Madame de Treville, we wouldn't have met." He started to pace, then paused halfway, face morphed in thought. "Up until this winter, I hated him. In some ways, I still do—he was too smart for his own good. He nearly exposed everything we'd worked for. He was so close to uncovering the truth; he intercepted a message I'd sent to my uncle in Paris.

"But your father made the mistake of thinking he was in the clear. He had no way of knowing we had procedures in place to discover if messages were tampered with. Special ways of arranging letters, folding envelopes, placing seals . . . he never even stopped to consider that the invitation to my father's house was a trap. He thought he could sneak into the office, steal secrets, and close the case himself, as if he were still a real Musketeer! The gall, the absolute gall, of that man. He had plans, you know, to take you and your mother to Paris. Find you better doctors, find a way to restore your mother's title. Another tidbit from his letters. But he didn't want to return unless he knew his family wouldn't be cast aside again. I think he thought if he proved himself, if he solved it all himself, the King and Mazarin would have no choice but to welcome you." He laughed, and I couldn't take it anymore.

"My father was a great man!" I shouted.

"He's also a dead one!" he spat back. A second later he was tenderly cupping my face, even as I pushed him away. His guilty expression was so familiar it was like being thrust into a memory. "I shouldn't have said that. I am so sorry; ma tourterelle, say you'll forgive me."

My mind flashed to Papa, and a cry forced through my teeth. I couldn't tell whether it was a sob or a curse. "That's why your father killed him. Madame de Treville was right all along. Your father killed Papa so he wouldn't expose the plot."

In that moment, with his warm and insistent attention, under the shadow of the city, any ignorant observer might've thought us completely and totally infatuated with each other. Completely and totally in love.

In that moment, I'd never loathed him more.

"What does my father have to do with this?" Étienne appeared genuinely confused.

"Everything," I said. "He's the leader. He's the one who made you like this."

"You think I just followed orders like a dutiful son? You think I'd stoop to be someone's lackey?"

Dread seeped through every inch of my body. "What are you saying?"

"I've told you again and again: My father and I have never seen eye to eye. He's always been weaker than me. Too wrapped up in our duty to our household, our family, rather than reaching for greater and better things. It was easy to recruit the Comte de Monluc and the other nobles, what with their righteous anger for the inept King. There wasn't anything for Father to do but sit back and watch his son orchestrate the greatest plot in our country's history. He tried to sway me, even came to the Sorbonne to attempt to change my mind . . . but he'd never risk the end of our family line by turning me over to the Musketeers. I'm his heir, after all. Although if he had it his way, all I'd have when he passed was land and money. And what are those without a title?"

"I don't know why you're lying but you are, I know you are!" My voice reached a pitch as sharp as my sword. "You're lying. All you do is lie."

"I've never told you anything but the truth." His mouth continued to move, but all I heard was a rushing roar so loud I could only read his lips, Papa's last laugh echoing in my ears. *"I did what had to be done."*

CHAPTER THIRTY-THREE

"DRAW YOUR SWORD."

"You can hardly expect me to—"

"Draw. It." My words were serpent's fangs.

Even as he did so, Étienne let the sword hang by his side. He didn't ready himself. "Let's talk about this," he said. "Let's take a step back, look at this logically."

"Before we left tonight, Madame de Treville told me something. Would you like to know what it was?" I whispered, my voice all silk, all steel.

"I—"

"She told me," I proceeded, "not to kill Verdon. And I agreed. It was my duty, and I wasn't going to give up the first place I've truly been accepted for the chance of slitting a murderer's throat. I'd already disappointed her, almost lost my position. I didn't want to risk that again." I bent my knees and held my arm just like Papa taught me. "But duty isn't everything."

"Tania, I don't want to hurt you."

"I promised to follow orders," I said, brimming with ice even colder than the air around us, "but I'll make an exception for the man who dared to think he loved me after he killed my father." It didn't matter how many times I'd pushed my anger aside, or how I'd tried to ignore it when I told Madame de Treville I wouldn't kill him. I had never wanted blood before. But I wanted his blood now.

I lunged. For a moment, both my feet were off the uneven stone. When they landed, the familiar blistering burn of my soles was accompanied by a crash of blades. Étienne's face morphed in shock.

Attaque composée. Redoublement. Prise de fer. Balestra. Lunge. Papa's voice echoed in my ears with each movement. A rhythm built as my feet slapped against the ground, as my heart rang in my ears, as Étienne continued to avoid anything but the simplest parries. He only ever blocked, never riposted.

"Fight me!" I shouted. "I am not the fragile, breakable thing you'd have me be. I am a Musketeer." Beating his blade to the side, I renewed my attack, watched the emotions war on his face until he countered.

And then, then we were fencing. Moonlight glancing off our swords, cold air slicing our skin, sweat dotting my cheeks like tears. No—there was no more holding back.

Another lunge. Attaque au fer. I nicked his face. A trickle of blood dripped down his jaw.

Our blades came together, crackling. Sparks erupted from the metal like glimmering, blistering stars.

Look how powerful you are, ma fille. Look at what you've created with your own hand and sword.

For a split second, Étienne's disbelieving face was lit in the glow. He hadn't expected me to actually be a true fencer. A real Musketeer, in every sense of the word. All he'd seen was a girl in a pretty dress.

I brought down my blade. But he was quicker, darted away to block my attack. Spinning, I thrusted, only to scream in frustration as my blade connected with the silver guard of his sword. I wanted to feel my blade sink into his flesh. Wanted to rip through his skin and watch his blood rain down onto the stone.

As my chest heaved, as sweat pooled above my collarbones, the outline of his body began to shadow and blur. Had the clouds shifted? Colors distorted in an awful, familiar darkness.

It wasn't the clouds. Wasn't the first snowfall. It was my dizziness.

I fought harder. Faster. Tried to focus on the rhythm of the bout even as the dizziness came stronger and stronger. I couldn't let it overtake me, not now. It wasn't about me anymore. This was for the fate of the King. For the fate of France.

This was for Papa and my sisters in arms.

My entire body was one painful, flickering flame. It screamed as I parried his lunge, as I made to redouble my attack. But I faltered. Even though the footwork was as familiar as breathing, the ground shifted and crumbled. My legs soft as smoke.

Pain, exhaustion, it all coursed through me; I gasped, struggled to pull myself back up, my hands scrambling at the side of the bridge.

"Maybe I was wrong. Despite it all, you're weak. Just like your father," Étienne said as he advanced, as my world shimmered. "But I'm willing to forgive you all of this. I'll see past it, for you. For you, Tania."

My vision was no longer gray. It was the white center of a flame. It was the gray-streaked brown of Papa's hair, the blue and red of the flowers in Maman's garden. The incandescent steel achieved when my sisters and I lifted our blades together, as one.

With a pain-filled cry, I used my arms to hoist myself up the ledge of the bridge. I raised my sword as my entire body shook. With my left hand, I grabbed the wall for balance. With my right hand, I thrust my sword forward. With my right foot, I sailed into a lunge.

He barely parried my attack before he was forced to block another, and another, and another. I didn't let him rest. My fingers bit so hard into the bridge that they throbbed scarlet, warm liquid trickling down my nails and slicking my palm.

"I knew you trained, but I never thought it actually possible . . . a female fencer." He panted, taking a deep breath as I brought my blade down on his with all my strength. It went tumbling to the ground, clattered on the stone as I raised my sword and brought it directly in line with his heart. He retreated, only to meet the wall and slumped down it.

"I don't need your validation. I never did," I said.

Étienne's stunned eyes darted to his weapon. My sword point was inches away from his heaving chest. He stared up at me: Fear. Anger. Love. "Ma tourterelle . . ."

I took another step; my blade grazed his jacket. I pressed hard enough that it punctured the fabric. The only thing that separated his chest from my sword was a thin white shirt.

I knew that bones separated his heart from his skin. I knew that muscles separated his stomach from his ribs, his ribs from his collarbones. Muscles that would fight back, would prevent me from running him through. Madame de Treville had taught us well, but she hadn't taught us how to make it to a target's heart. But I would find a way. "Damn you." All I had to do was thrust forward. One final lunge and it would all be over.

He was desperate now: "I'm sorry for what I said about your father, my darling . . . I wouldn't have killed him if I'd felt about you then the way I do now. He was smart; maybe if I'd known what was to come, I could've persuaded him to see the true nature of France's current leadership."

"You cut off his beard." My heartbeat rushed and scrambled and fought as I held the tip of my blade to his chest. "You cut off his hair. You left him unrecognizable."

"Come now, Tania—being a leader means getting your hands dirty. How else could I ensure de Batz's death would be enough of a warning to anyone who'd consider sabotaging us?"

"Get his name out of your mouth. I could kill you quicker than you could blink." I grew angrier by the second. I knew what I had to do. For Papa. For my sisters.

Tania. Tania. Tania.

This time, when I saw the flash of a reflection in my blade, I didn't mistake it for Papa's face. It was my face. All mine.

Arms, legs, everything shaking, I slowly lowered my sword. "I'm not you. I'm not a murderer." He visibly exhaled. "Do not mistake this as you winning, as you using my feelings against me." I threw the words at him with all the grief and pain and fury I'd kindled for months. "You will never hold anything over me ever again. You know nothing about who I am. You don't get to decide who I am." Tearing my gaze away, I glanced at the end of the bridge. This time it was my turn to exhale.

Two sets of arms grabbed him. The Musketeers who'd approached silently from behind were soon joined by more of the King's Guard. They'd hidden themselves in the shadows, the winter air, as Madame de Treville said they would. But now they fanned out on the opposite end of the bridge to prevent any last means of escape. Starlight danced off their swords, their spangled coats, their gleaming leather boots.

"Tania, wait!" Étienne struggled against the onslaught. "You know a traitor's death is no way to die. You can't let them do this to me!" When I didn't respond, his face calmed and he spoke, placating, in a voice I knew all too well. "If you ever cared for me, kill me now. Spare me. Ma tourterelle, please." His eyes seared through the freezing night.

"I am no one's dove."

Étienne's expression darkened as he thrashed against his captors, shouting. One of the Musketeers clapped a gloved hand over his mouth before dragging him away. Seconds later, I realized it was Monsieur Brandon, after the man nodded to me over his shoulder.

This was the moment I'd waited months for. But I did not move. I could not move.

When Portia, Aria, and Théa arrived, I was rooted to the bridge. Words, thoughts, prayers frozen in my throat as I stared at something so very far away. I heard them approaching, slowly, softly. I knew their footsteps like I knew my own.

They didn't try to move me. Didn't try to touch me. Didn't tell me that we'd won, that everything was all right, that things were finally, blessedly over.

They stood with me, close enough that I could feel the heat radiating from them. Close enough that I knew they were there. Even as the clouds opened for the first snowfall, light and shimmering gossamer.

This was how Madame de Treville and Henri found us: the four of us side by side in our battered gowns. Heads held high. Shoulders back. Arms whispering against one another and wind whistling across the bridge.

CHAPTER THIRTY-FOUR

"TANIA?" THÉA ASKED from the hallway, through the study door—but I couldn't answer her, not yet.

Madame de Treville said if I really wanted to write my mother a letter, if I really wanted to stop agonizing over my words and covering my bed in ruined pages, I'd need access to a proper desk—so here I was, in her office.

Perhaps that was true. Perhaps the reason why I'd had so much difficulty writing Maman before was that I needed a change in place and perspective. But I knew there was something else in the undercurrents of Madame's offer; it'd rung in her words for the past two weeks. Ever since the night when everything changed.

Our mentor had stuffed us into warm clothes and passed so many cups of tea our way that we probably consumed a potful each. "Ridiculous," she kept on repeating. "Standing out there in the cold. A miracle you didn't freeze." But she never stopped examining us when she thought we weren't looking, as if to check we were still there.

Aria hurt her ankle at The Gryphon dueling two nobles at

once. She told me it wasn't my fault. That I had to go after Étienne, that the injury would've happened regardless—and she continued to tell me this as the uninjured Théa wrapped bandages tight around Aria's purpling skin, swollen like an overripe fruit. It was even worse when Théa moved on to cleaning and closing Portia's wound. Portia had yelled at me to follow after Verdon, but I hadn't realized how deep the gash in her arm was. Portia had said, gritting her teeth, that was the point. If I'd known, I wouldn't have left.

That night, Monsieur Brandon called on Madame de Treville in her study. When she returned, her face was all pinched. The remaining four men at The Gryphon were in custody. One look at the prison cells and guards awaiting them and they divulged their dark secrets. Within an hour, Musketeers raided the palace kitchens. The bags of salt bought for the noble dinner celebrating the Winter Festival had been traded out with enough strychnine to poison the entire court.

"Makes sense," Aria had said, grimacing as she hoisted her bandaged ankle onto a tufted pillow. "It doesn't act quickly. Even with a royal taster no one would've known. Not until it was too late. And the leftovers would've gone to Parisians. A sign of goodwill for the holiday."

"There shouldn't be too much trouble confirming the coconspirators, given they can interrogate . . ." Madame de Treville's voice faltered.

All eyes flickered to me. But then Portia made some comment about how absurd she found the Musketeers' boots, and then Théa was arguing with her, and if I scrunched my eyes tight and dulled the pain radiating from my sternum, I could pretend things were almost normal.

Later, when I asked Aria and Portia about the man who'd stumbled away from Théa in terror, they went silent. The next day, Monsieur Brandon sent word that a prisoner died from his wounds. A chevalier from somewhere in Provence. Next to me, Théa's entire frame relaxed. I didn't need to ask her who this man was. No, I remembered the halting memory she'd mentioned. The one from before Paris. The one that haunted Théa down to her very skin.

I remembered all of this. Which was why, when Théa found me later that night, scrubbing my face raw, I didn't shy away. I used an entire water jug trying to wash away the imprint of Étienne's fingers. Clean the cheeks he cupped with his hands. Eviscerate all flesh memories.

Now, Théa waited in the threshold, tight curls limp against her cheeks.

"Madame de Treville asked me to find you," Théa said. I took one last, lingering glance at the letter. *Je t'embrasse* felt wrong. When was the last time I'd hugged Maman? I scratched it out. Replaced it with: *À bientôt. See you soon.* "I can come back later," Théa said.

"No, I'm finished." After folding the parchment, I withdrew my chain and removed a second ring.

"I think it's good of you," she continued.

"Hmm?"

"To tell your mother about . . . well, all of this, what you can of this . . . even though she wasn't very nice to you."

Maman's second letter had arrived yesterday. Months in the making. Ten pages full of script. I could tell where her hand cramped and she wrote through the pain. She detailed how the villagers found Beau wandering the path to Lupiac, flea-bitten and gaunt and hollow-eyed. My uncle would retrieve him, would bring him back to my mother so he could be cared for. So he could finally rest.

I couldn't tell her about my involvement in the mission, the duels, the truth of L'Académie des Mariées.

But what I could tell her was that Papa's murderer was brought to justice. That she'd been right all along—I learned later, after Étienne was interrogated, that it took more than five of his men to bring Papa down, men with orders to silence my father in the most brutal fashion. I didn't know how they extracted that information from Étienne. I didn't want to.

No, I did not tell Maman of the nightmares, of the bloody bodies and the hazel eyes. What did I tell her about? The map of Lupiac. How I hung my cloak on my wardrobe door so I could see it as I fell asleep. How my dreams, the good ones, tumbled with sunflowers and fleurs-de-lis and Papa's laughter. How I hoped she would visit me in Paris so she could see, even if only a partial image, who her daughter had become. An unbroken, unfragile girl. A girl of petticoats and straight shoulders and steel hidden at her hips and in her heart.

After dripping molten wax onto the back of the envelope, it was time for the seal I'd commissioned. The same as Papa's signet ring, with one exception: a moon in place of the fleur-de-lis. "What was it that Madame de Treville wanted?" I asked Théa.

"Everyone's waiting in the fencing room. I can tell them you're not ready," she added when I hesitated. I hadn't been there since the Winter Festival. I could only make it a few steps down the hallway before that night came back to me. Before he came back to me.

"No." I squared my shoulders. "No, I'm ready."

Out of the study, through the small door, hoisting myself into the pulley's seat and rising through the air. I was a few feet off the ground when Théa spoke again. "You know, Aria said the funniest thing the other day!"

"Oui?"

"About me and Henri." I almost fell from the seat. "Oh, Tania, I nearly cried from laughing—I mean, we're practically cousins! I know some people think that's fine, but the very idea makes me want to hurl. Our family relations are distant, but we spent our childhoods together—besides, I know Henri, and he's not one to throw his feelings around all willy-nilly."

"So he's interested in someone else, then?"

"Well, of course," she laughed when I reached the landing.

"Oh?"

She examined me curiously as I finished untangling myself. "He's interested in you! You can't even begin to imagine how embarrassed I was when I interrupted your rendezvous amoureux!"

The seat plummeted off the landing, rope whistling through my hands as the whole contraption crashed to the ground. Théa frowned. "Henri will have to fix that," she said as she peered over the landing, then straightened up. "Are you feeling sick? You've gone completely red. Should I go grab a chair? No? Well, then, come on!"

The murmur of voices, ones I'd heard when we entered the hallway, cut off as Portia's head popped through the wide open archway. "She's here!" she crowed, rushing to grab hold of my hands. "Close your eyes."

"Is all this ceremony really necessary?" Aria called from some-where inside.

"Yes!" Portia retorted. Every time I tried to close my eyes an invisible force pried them open. "Don't worry," she told me. "I won't let you fall."

I relaxed into the darkness. But it wasn't darkness. Not really. Not with the soft glow of light behind my eyelids.

Portia took her time. She told me when to turn, when the carpet would change to plaster . . . Finally, we stopped. "Now open!"

The sudden wash of brightness left me squinting, then blinking as shimmering forms concretized in my vision: Aria and Madame de Treville a few feet away. Portia on my right, Théa on my left. And then, Henri. So astonishingly bright the light could have come from him and not the high windows, which were unshuttered for the first time.

"What do you think?" he asked. His voice was raspy, and he was looking at me.

"About what?" My words faded.

Ever since I'd arrived in Paris, I'd known the room as one large mass of gray and white. Rack of swords in the corner, mirror for drills by its side. Théa's sewing materials and changing screen. Benches to watch bouts from, extra scabbards, and the large, turning whetstone used to sharpen swords.

But now the far wall was covered with the largest mural I'd ever seen. Off in the corner was a propped ladder surrounded by empty paint containers. There was something about the stark black brushstrokes against the off-white wall that made our likenesses look even stronger. The four of us in an arc, swords' points down, arms extended so our blades met in the middle. Steel intersecting steel intersecting steel intersecting steel.

Henri rushed to speak as my eyes watered. "I'll go to the

market and see if I can't find some colored paint that'll work. It's expensive, but—"

"No." I held up my hand "Don't change it. It's perfect."

"Well, it wasn't difficult. I just sketched you—I mean all of you! And then went over the outline with paint. And then filled in the sketch with charcoal. And then painted over that. And then did some more shading with charcoal. It wasn't that much trouble at all!"

"And you"—I turned to Madame de Treville—"you had to agree to this."

"It's not as if I had a more efficient use for the wall space," she declared, nose upturned as she examined her nephew's work. "I *suppose* I can see the likeness." By the joy on Henri's face, you would've thought she'd called him the next Simon Vouet.

"Did all of you know?" I asked the others.

"Found out today. Good thing, too, as I had a chance to point out some of the flaws in his shadowing. Now, *this* one saw Henri coming through the hall a few nights ago. Nearly scared the poor boy to death." Portia looked pointedly at Aria beside her.

"How was I supposed to know what he was doing?" Aria said. "It was my duty to question him."

Madame de Treville shook her head at Henri's mortified expression. "Mon neveu, it seems you don't have a future as a spy, a fact I'm sure will leave you utterly heartbroken. But as for your future adjacent to the Order . . . well, the last line of defense for France will always have good use for a code breaker."

Portia rushed Aria over to me and Théa, positioned us so we mirrored our larger-than-life images. "Look—the Four Muske-teers!" Portia said. Then she hesitated, as if the title might be too painful—might remind me of Papa. But I smiled. Seeing myself how others saw me, this glorious, powerful creature—knowing that *we* were seen as these glorious, powerful creatures . . . I was finally able to firmly tether myself to the ground. Before I'd been drifting, unsure, some cloud-like thing.

But not anymore. We found one another. We were together.

"The Four Musketeers," I murmured. "Un pour tous, tous pour un."

I'd been wrong about so many things. And as I stared up at Henri's mural, I discovered another: I'd believed that one dance, one kiss, was as close as I'd ever get to flying.

But standing here, surrounded by les Mousquetaires de la Lune—*this* was how it felt to fly.

I could feel Henri's gaze on me like the sun. Could see the pride in Madame de Treville's eyes. Could hear Papa's voice lingering in my ears.

Tania. Tania. Tania.

I breathed out, long and slow.

And I smiled.

AUTHOR'S NOTE

One for All is a work of fiction, but Tania's chronic illness is very real.

Postural Orthostatic Tachycardia Syndrome (POTS) was first diagnosed in 1993, but there were patients with POTS symptoms much earlier. From early examples like "Soldier's Heart Syndrome" diagnosed after the American Civil War, POTS and POTS-like cases certainly predate the early '90s. It's impossible to know how many patients suffered from POTS in the past centuries . . . *especially* when you think about the long history of society dismissing women's health complaints as hysteria, since POTS is most often diagnosed in young women. Girls like Tania were everywhere, are everywhere, even if they aren't in textbook pages. Tania having POTS, as a girl in a fictionalized version of seventeenth-century France, is the least fantastical element of *One for All*.

POTS is different for every individual. Tania's experience is just one of hundreds of thousands of unique experiences. She does not, and cannot, represent every person with POTS—or for that matter, every person with a chronic illness. But she does represent my experience as a chronically ill young woman. I was never a teen in seventeenth-century France, dueling in ball gowns . . . but I was the girl in high school who hid in the bathroom between classes in order to take medication without anyone seeing. I was the girl who was pulled off the school's elevator because she didn't look sick enough to "belong" there, who sat on the sidelines during fencing practice because she was too dizzy to stand, who promised herself the night before she left for college that she would tell absolutely no one about her condition because nothing good could come of people knowing the truth—who would want to be friends with or date a sick girl?

When I was at my most sick as a teenager, I lost myself in books, despite never seeing myself in their pages. I thought that meant stories like mine, about people like me, weren't worthy of being told. That chronically ill, disabled girls couldn't be main characters. That because I was sick, I'd never be the hero of my own story.

I can't go back in time. I can't reach out to that girl and tell her that she is worthy and good and that it is okay to trust others. That there is nothing, absolutely nothing, to be ashamed of. But what I can do is use what I am good at—turning words into stories—to prevent disabled readers from feeling that way now.

I am not Tania, but Tania is a part of me.

A sick girl, a brave girl, a girl who learns to love herself. The hero of her own story.

And now, here she is. She belongs to all of you.

About Postural Orthostatic Tachycardia Syndrome

POTS is most often characterized by a drop in blood pressure, accompanied by an increase in heart rate, upon standing—to a heart rate increase of at least thirty beats per minute in adults and forty beats per minute in adolescents. The jump in heart rate is the body's response to the blood pressure drop; the heart is trying to pump blood faster to get it through the body. Common symptoms of POTS include dizziness, brain fog, fatigue, headaches, nausea, heart palpitations, and many others. Doctors say POTS symptoms are most similar to congestive heart failure symptoms.

Today, most POTS patients are forced to see multiple doctors to finally receive a diagnosis (the average diagnosis time is five years and eleven months). More than half of people diagnosed with POTS will be told by doctors that their symptoms are "all in their head." Over a quarter of patients will be forced to see over ten doctors before they finally know the truth.

For more statistics, information, materials, and/or to donate to POTS and dysautonomia research, readers can visit:

-Dysautonomia International

-National Institutes of Health

-Hopkins Medicine (Johns Hopkins)

-Mayo Clinic

Acknowledgments

I have looked forward to and dreaded writing *One for All*'s acknowledgments in equal measure: I could fill another book with gratitude for everyone who has helped me reach this point. But I also know I will inevitably forget someone, because such is the way of things, and for that I apologize in advance.

Thank you to my agent, Jennifer Wills, who got me to believe in myself by sheer force of will: We did it. We finally did it. To Nicole Resciniti, for pulling me out of the query trenches.

As always, to my editor, Melissa Warten: It was worth three years on submission, all those near misses, to end up with you and FSG. I can't believe how lucky I am to work with you.

Thank you to everyone at FSG and MCPG, including but not limited to Rich Deas and Kevin Tong for bringing back the girls in fancy dresses on YA covers trend so disabled girls could finally have their moment. Jamie and Isabelle, interns extraordinaire. Special thanks to Ilana Worrell and John Nora for making sure *OFA* was the very best book it could be, and to Cynthia Lliguichuzhca, Angela Jun, Kathleen Breitenfeld, and Molly Ellis.

To Estelle Paranque, for her expert eye and attention to detail.

In addition to encyclopedias and textbooks, I am in debt to This is Versailles blog series, World4.eu for costume and fashion history knowledge, Dancetime Publications (and many sleepless nights of watching minuet reenactments), Party Like 1660 (bless you, Aurora von Goeth and Jules Harper), and JStor, you shining star of a database. To thirteen years of French teachers, merci beaucoup. Especially my Yale professors, who taught me how to love the language that had been the source of so much frustration since age six. And Alexandre Dumas for providing the foundation for it all.

Enormous thanks to the writers who read an early version of *OFA* and/or cheered me on, including Tana Mills, Jessica James, Brittney Arena, Miranda Asebedo, Tochi Onyebuchi, Kati Gardner, Leigh Bardugo, Melissa See, Cara Liebowitz, Gabe Moses, Rae Castor, Bethany Mangle, Laura Genn, Kess Costales, Alaina Leary, and K L Pennington. My fellow 22 Debuts: I'm so happy to be on this journey with you.

Kerri Maniscalco, who made me think "wait, hold on, people might actually like this book?" To Kami Garcia, Chloe Gong, Joy McCollough, Emily Lloyd-Jones, June Hur, Tamora Pierce, Jennieke Cohen, Carly Heath, and Marieke Nijkamp, for your generosity of time and kind words for *OFA*.

Sabina Nordqvist and Lara Ameen: What would I do without you? Thank you for never letting me give up hope. I can't wait until our books are on shelves together.

Tracy Deonn, I am eternally grateful for your friendship, guidance, and wisdom. Somewhere, in an AU crossover, Tania and Bree are dueling side-by-side. Alice Wong, you didn't have to help a random unknown disabled writer all those years ago, and yet you have supported me and inspired me (in a badass disabled activist way) ever since.

To Disabled Kidlit Writers: I've said it before, and I'll say it again. Today it's me. Tomorrow it's you.

My endless gratitude to every blogger, bookseller, librarian, and reviewer who's championed *One for All*.

To the NY State Writers Institute, Iowa Writers' Workshop Summer Program, Yale Writers' Workshop, Sackett Street Writers' Workshop, and all the faculty I studied with, especially T. Geronimo Johnson, Rick Moody, Terra Elan McVoy, and Ted Thompson.

Thank you to my Yale professors who inspired me, challenged me, taught me: Liz Miles, Anthony Reed, Lynda Paul, Jill Campbell, James Berger,

Camille Lizarribar, Rebecca Tannenbaum, Brian Scholl, Katie Trumpener, Joanne Freeman, and Jill Richards, who handed me my first book of disability theory.

One for All wouldn't exist without my creative writing professors at Yale whose generous advice and guidance shaped (and continue to shape) me as a writer and a person: Richard Deming, Michael Cunningham, Caryl Phillips, Leslie Jamison, Adam Sexton, and John Crowley (it was an honor to be your last advisee).

To Yale University and Jonathan Edwards College for putting me on the paths of other students who changed my life. To the dean's office, the admin staff, and all the dining hall workers, especially Connie, Tim, and Theresa. (Theresa, I hope this makes up for the whole "graduating and leaving JE" thing.)

To the teachers and administrators who got me there: Anna Wilder, Jonathan Shea, Paulette James, Patrice Maites, Kathy Richardson, Rachel Gayer, Eser Ozdeger, Sesame Frasier, Carole Hurwitz, Grace Katabaruki, and Kajal Guha. To Sandy Wright: I wish you were here to see this.

To the doctors who took thirteen-year-old Lillie seriously, and to Mayo Clinic.

All my love to my real-life Order, my sisters in arms: Kristy, Sai, Sarah, Claire W., Claire C., Leigh, Michaela, Steph, Julia, Taylor, and Liz.

Thank you to my UEA Creative Writing Prose Fiction cohort, and to my UEA professors. To Twishaa and Becky, the newest additions to my Musketeers, and all the other wonderful women at UEA who supported me and my writing through a difficult year.

To my fencing coaches Janusz Smolenski and Coach Harutunian, and especially Dariusz Gilman: You didn't give up on me when I was at my most sick. There is so much of you in this book.

To Hockley, Eleanor, and Henry. To Sarah, the very best big sister.

To my family. To Grandpa and Grams, who never got to read this book:

Grandpa, who taught me to love stories, and Grams, who told me she just wanted to live long enough to see what I accomplished. Getting an offer from an agent a couple weeks after you passed? I refuse to not let that mean something. And to Grandma, who I already miss very much. You were so excited for me. I wish you could've held *OFA* in your hands.

To Dad, who asked me once why I write so many stories with absent or dead fathers. I didn't answer then. (Come on, Dad. It's a YA novel.) But I've thought about it, long and hard, and my conclusion is this: It is my way of making a story as fictional as possible. Because I could never imagine my world without you. To Charles—no, I'm sorry. You will always be Charlie hugging Pooh Bear at Disney World to me. It isn't easy to have a big sister like me. And yet you still love me, and I love you. Mama, this book is dedicated to you, and is for you. Everything I ever write will be for you.

And finally, to my brave disabled girls, the ones in doctors' offices and hospital waiting rooms, the ones fighting to be taken seriously, to get a diagnosis. The ones learning to navigate the world in chronically ill bodies. You are worthy of so many books and so many stories. *One for All* is only the beginning.